THE
SECRET
LOCKET

BOOKS BY CATHERINE HOKIN

The Fortunate Ones
What Only We Know
The Lost Mother
The Secretary
The German Child
The Secret Hotel in Berlin
The Train That Took You Away

HANNI WINTER SERIES
The Commandant's Daughter
The Pilot's Girl
The Girl in the Photo
Her Last Promise

THE
SECRET LOCKET

CATHERINE HOKIN

bookouture

Published by Bookouture in 2025

An imprint of Storyfire Ltd.
Carmelite House
50 Victoria Embankment
London EC4Y 0DZ

www.bookouture.com

The authorised representative in the EEA is Hachette Ireland
8 Castlecourt Centre
Dublin 15 D15 XTP3
Ireland
(email: info@hbgi.ie)

Copyright © Catherine Hokin, 2025

Catherine Hokin has asserted her right to be identified as the author of this work.

All rights reserved. No part of this publication may be reproduced, stored in any retrieval system, or transmitted, in any form or by any means, electronic, mechanical, photocopying, recording or otherwise, without the prior written permission of the publishers.

ISBN: 978-1-83525-092-1
eBook ISBN: 978-1-83525-091-4

This book is a work of fiction. Names, characters, businesses, organizations, places and events other than those clearly in the public domain, are either the product of the author's imagination or are used fictitiously. Any resemblance to actual persons, living or dead, events or locales is entirely coincidental.

*For Jools, for all the world-righting sessions and the laughs.
Thank you.*

PROLOGUE
JUNE 1941

'I'll do it. I'll come. I choose you.'

His words were everything she'd longed to hear, but they weren't real. They were a trick of the wind. They were her heart making a fool of her head. And even if he had changed his mind and shouted them to her at the last minute, even if he was still shouting them now, what did it matter? Unterwald had disappeared, lost to the twists and turns of the railway track, and Pascal had disappeared with it.

Noemi slumped onto the wagon's grime-covered slats as the train rumbled away down the line, her hand leaping instinctively to her throat. But the locket he'd given her was too dangerous to wear, and she'd left that piece of him behind too.

I can't think about what might have been; it won't help me.

It was all she wanted to think about, but she closed her eyes instead and forced herself to remember the last time she'd let herself fall into his arms, and the misery that moment had led to. To remember the reason why she'd leapt onto a moving goods train to escape her home town.

Because my parents have been taken and my life is in danger. And his father is at the root of it all.

That helped her to breathe easier. It allowed her to shift the focus to the father not the son, to picture his cruelty instead. Viktor Lindiger. The man who'd unleashed hatred across their sleepy Bavarian village and destroyed her family. The man who'd brought the swastika into their lives and turned her Jewish family into prey.

Noemi opened her eyes, but she was blind to the trees and the fields. Instead, images of her and Pascal as they'd once been flashed past as the train ate up the miles. Crawling and toddling and running together; making the flower-filled meadows above the village their own. Turning their eyes to the mountains and announcing, *We're going up there,* in the same breath, and then doing it. Learning the language of the peaks until they could scale them as quickly as goats. Until they could ski the steepest runs without blinking and traverse scree-covered slopes as if their hands could read the jagged rocks. Learning to read each other's thoughts too. Becoming fearless together. Doing everything together.

Until Hitler took over our world and rewrote my place in it.

The film she'd been watching stopped racing towards its happy ending. The screen filled instead with jackboots and uniforms and a Führer who hated Jewish girls like Noemi. Who'd ordered his faithful disciples to round up Jewish families and confine them to camps so that the plague they supposedly carried wouldn't spill over and pollute good German blood.

Which is where I would be if Pascal hadn't saved me.

Noemi wrapped her arms round her knees as the train picked up speed and the memories grew muddled. He'd helped her escape without hesitation, without any thought for himself. There'd been love in his eyes when he'd done it; there'd been love in her heart when she'd agreed. There'd been a moment, as they'd waited for the goods train to appear, when she'd almost weakened and begged him to leave Germany with her for a second time. But that moment had been lost in the frantic scramble into the moving carriage, and to the wind which had whipped their promises away.

The air had swapped pine forests and cut hay for the smell of coal and engine oil while she was dreaming; the train had begun to slow down. Noemi flexed her knees and her shoulders, belatedly checked her body for any bruising from the leap into the wagon that could hamper her on the leap out. Any moment now, the train would pull into the goods yard and her chance of discovery would escalate.

She got up and moved as close as she dared to the open door. She'd been a climber from the moment she first set foot on a slope; now she had to behave like one. She knew how to take fear and danger and turn them into adrenaline. She knew better than to look down and imagine the worst.

I'm going to survive this. One day I'm going to come home.

She refused to dwell on *home* and how cruel that had already become. She refused to think about the years it could take before the war ended and the Nazis were beaten. Because they had to be beaten. Light had to come back to the world.

Home.

Everything had to live in that word. Whether she or her family would be welcome in Unterwald once the war was done was out of her hands. Whatever Pascal became was also out of her hands, no matter whether she loved him or hated him or was lost somewhere between the two. Dreams of a life lived with him were surely nothing but dreams now.

I might never see him again.

That thought wouldn't help her. One day, she would come home and gather up the scattered pieces of her life, no matter how far away the road led her. But first she had to keep that life safe.

So she took a deep breath and she jumped.

PART ONE

CHAPTER ONE
SEPTEMBER 1934

'Noemi, will you please hurry up. Herr Lindiger is here; he's parking the car. If you want to go with them, you have to come down right away. Unless you've changed your mind about going.'

Noemi hovered in her bedroom doorway, pulling at the blue ribbons wrapped round the ends of her tightly bound plaits. She'd taken such care over those, but getting the style right wasn't the problem. It didn't matter what she did with her hair and her clothes to fit in, her chocolate-coloured braids and hazel eyes would always be the wrong colour.

Tell me to stay home and I will. I'll listen to you this time.

She knew he wouldn't do it. He wasn't the kind of father who laid down the law; besides, she'd argued her case for attending the National Socialist rally with Pascal far too forcefully for her father to attempt to talk her out of it at this late stage. And her mother – who hadn't been so easy to convince and wasn't as tightly wound round Noemi's little finger as Hauke was – had already left for work and taken her arguments with her.

'Why on earth do you want to go to Nuremberg and mix

with thousands of Hitler's adoring fans? Talk about walking into the lion's den. Their world doesn't seem to have room for us, Noemi. I don't know what that means yet, but none of us can afford to ignore the way the tide's turning, including you and Pascal. There's heartache coming, I can sense it. One of you needs to open your eyes.'

Frieda's frustration had bounced unheard off her daughter. Noemi hadn't wanted another lecture about *their world* or to be reminded that Jewish girls like her didn't belong in it. She didn't care about politics or Germany's new leader. She was thirteen years old: all she wanted was to be part of the crowd. And to do whatever Pascal did. He was her best friend and she was his; they'd been inseparable since before they could toddle. As far as Noemi was concerned, a world in which there was *him* and *me* and not *us* didn't exist, and she had no interest in any so-called facts that said it did. When she'd pointed that out to her mother, it hadn't helped.

'Nothing's changed, really? So, if that's true, why aren't you allowed to join the same clubs as Pascal and the rest of your "properly German" schoolfriends?'

Noemi's lip had wobbled at that; she hadn't been able to help herself. And Frieda – who was far more worried about her daughter than angry – had instantly softened.

'I know it hurts to be excluded, sweetheart. But following Pascal to the rally in Nuremberg isn't the answer. The city is a very different place to Unterwald and, trust me, if you're starting to feel left out here, you'll feel ten times worse there.'

They'd hit a stalemate then which they hadn't resolved. Pascal wanted her to go with him, and that was enough for Noemi. His mother wanted her there too, and Carina's 'She'll be company for me and I'll keep an eye her, don't worry,' had to be enough for Frieda.

And maybe nobody will care that I don't have the right

clothes or blue eyes or flowing blond hair. Nobody except Viktor cares here.

'Are you coming then or what?'

Herr Lindiger leaned on the car horn; her father called to her again. Noemi picked up her suitcase, but she only made it as far as the top stair. Although she would rather have died than admit it, she was nervous about the trip, and her head was bursting with reasons why it would be easier to stay.

Autumn had arrived, which meant trees heavy with fruit and ready for harvest. If she went, she would miss the first jam-making of the year. Her mother had already gone to the workshop behind the café which was one strand of her parents' string of businesses to get that started. While Noemi dithered on the stairs, Frieda would be sorting out the last haul from the cherry trees and the first from the plums. Laying out the jars and the *Produce of Café Drachmann* labels ready for the cooks to use; preparing the pans that would make the air sweet and sticky. And next Saturday was the day when the cattle would be brought down for the winter from their summer pastures, wreathed in flowers and mirrors and bells. Every season in Bavarian villages like hers had its own rhythms and celebrations, and Noemi's life had been shaped by them since she was a baby. She wasn't sure who she would be if she let the rituals slip by without marking them. And she'd also never been to Nuremberg; she'd never been to a city at all.

'Which is why you have to come with me. I've never been there either – or to such a huge rally. It will be an adventure, and we always do those together, don't we?'

Pascal's voice chimed through her head, louder than Frieda's or her own. Louder than the increasingly irritated car horn. Herr Lindiger wouldn't wait long – he'd been very definite with her about that. Unlike his son and his wife, he'd be perfectly happy if Noemi stayed behind. His, 'I'm not comfortable with her coming, it's not as if she can pass for one of us,' had not been a nice thing to overhear.

But Pascal doesn't think like that about me, and he never will, whatever my mother says. And I'm not going to disappoint him or miss out on an adventure because some people have stupid ideas about Jews.

'Noemi, will you please hurry up and decide what you're doing. He'll have the entire street cursing me if he carries on.'

'I'm on my way.'

She needed to do, not to think, or she'd never get anywhere. She clattered down the stairs as her father began walking up them, planted a kiss on his cheek and ran out of the door while he was still throwing out advice.

'You'll be careful, won't you? I know we keep—'

Hauke stopped abruptly in the doorway behind her and didn't finish the sentence. Noemi instantly understood why. Pascal had opened the car door ready for her to climb in; his father Viktor had wound down his window. Both of them were visible from the house. And both of them were dressed in the brown uniforms Hauke hated and she'd been trying her best for a year to ignore...

'What on earth are you both wearing?'

The instant she asked Pascal the question, Noemi wondered why she hadn't suspected that this would be the next step. National Socialism had come slowly to Unterwald, but nobody was surprised that Viktor Lindiger was its first champion or that Pascal was his father's first protégé. Especially not Hauke Drachmann.

'That man lives half his life in the past, moaning about how Germany should have won the war and how unfair the Treaty of Versailles was. And just because he met Adolf Hitler once in

1923 – and fought with him, by the way, in what was a glorified Munich bar brawl, not some crusading attempt to found a new Germany, whatever he says about the so-called putsch – he thinks he's part of the Nazis' inner circle. God help us all if that's the kind of fool they attract. And God help poor Pascal.'

Noemi normally took very little notice when her father started another of his rants about Viktor. Hauke hadn't fought in the war because of a hearing problem; Viktor had won two medals and carried himself as if he'd single-handedly won every battle he'd fought in. Noemi didn't believe her father was jealous – he was far too decent to stoop to such a petty emotion – but it was the wives, not the husbands who were friends.

She didn't take a lot of notice either of the stories about the Great War, or the revolutions and attempted coups which had followed it, which the men who came to her father's bar always fell back on when the schnapps took hold. But *God help poor Pascal* was a strange thing to say, so that registered, and so did the broken-cross lapel pin Viktor wore at the unveiling of the town's war memorial in November 1931 because it upset Hauke. And nobody could miss the way those pins began to spread like a rash across the chests of the postmaster and the local policemen in the weeks afterwards. Or the red armbands – with what she'd soon learned was called a swastika inside their white circles – which appeared next and bloomed like summer roses all over the town. So the Lindigers wearing uniforms shouldn't have come as a surprise.

By the summer of 1932, Unterwald's colours and allegiances had shifted, due in no little part to Viktor's determination to make the town, as he put it to anyone who would – or wouldn't – listen, 'a shining example of National Socialism's glorious new future'. Bavaria's blue-and-white flag vanished from the public buildings. Posters proclaiming Adolf Hitler to be 'Germany's Great Hope' covered the lampposts and the market square's noticeboard. People's arms started springing up in the air by way of a greeting as if half the town had turned into traffic policemen.

It was all very odd in a place that hadn't changed for centuries, but the mountains Noemi loved stayed the same, and so did the flower-filled meadows where elections and armbands seemed a million miles away, and that was far more important. Her life carried on as it always had, which meant – or so she assumed, given that they'd been born barely twenty-four hours apart and they'd always shared everything, including their thoughts – so did Pascal's.

The pair of them continued to roam the way they'd roamed since they were big enough to scamper away from their mothers. Climbing higher than they were supposed to, skiing faster than they were supposed to. Daring each other on. Living a life full of secrets and as far away as possible from adults. Learning to fish and to hunt rabbits with slingshots, and, on one memorable occasion when they were eleven – because Pascal found his father's army pistol and managed to liberate it for a day without Viktor catching him – to shoot at old bottles. They didn't worry about getting caught or getting into trouble. And they didn't worry about National Socialism or about communism – which was more politics and apparently belonged to the devil – or who believed what. Noemi wasn't particularly interested in who Hitler was or what he was doing, and she assumed Pascal felt the same. Until she arrived at school on a snow-covered day in early February 1933 to find him standing with his father at the gates and seemingly dressed for a war.

'It's my new uniform. I've joined the Hitler Youth and Dad's joined the SA.' Pascal had rattled on at top speed as Noemi looked blank. 'The SA. The Sturmabteilung, Hitler's special soldiers; you must have heard of them. The youth brigade is sort of part of that, and I'm meant to be in a different group till I'm fourteen – one for little kids – but Dad pulled strings because I'm so good at climbing and swimming and everything, and he's been keeping this as a surprise for when Hitler became Chancellor, which he has now. Isn't it brilliant?'

Noemi hadn't been sure how to answer that. The new clothes had turned Pascal into someone she didn't recognise, and that made her nervous. And neither he nor the father he worshipped looked as glorious as he seemed to think.

Viktor was too fat for the brown shirt and jodhpurs he'd poured himself into; Pascal's shorts were too big on the waist and flapped at his knees. She also didn't like the way they were both standing, as if they were expecting to wade into a fight. Arms squared to show off their swastika bands, thumbs tucked behind heavy belt buckles embossed with a swastika and an eagle, and the words *Blood and Honour*. She wanted to say, 'You look as if you're in a play, as if you're pretending,' but she knew that would upset him, something she hated to do.

Luckily, she was saved from saying anything by the group of boys, and girls, who swarmed around Pascal like overexcited monkeys and swept him into the playground where the headmaster instantly started clapping. Noemi didn't follow them, although no one had told her she couldn't. She didn't know why his new outfit felt like a barrier between them, but it did. And the barrier had kept on building as more and more of the boys in the school joined the brown-shirted ranks of the Hitler Youth, and more and more of the girls joined an equally loyal league that had been set up separately for them.

Unterwald's landscape transformed again once the uniforms spread. Sundays stopped being about church bells and quiet family dinners. Instead, the streets and the market square rang to the sound of trumpets and drums and the thump of marching feet as the youth groups and the SA led the crusade to spread National Socialism and root out unbelievers. On Wednesdays, the League of German Girls gave out leaflets after school, encouraging the right kind of girls to join them. On Friday evenings, the meadow above the town was filled with the strident blare of marching songs and the charcoal scent of a campfire as the Party's younger members celebrated together. And Noemi, who apparently wasn't the right kind of anything and wasn't included, stayed at home.

She's not one of us – look at her eyes and her stupid brown plaits.

'Wake up, sleepy head; we're almost there. You've been out like a light the whole way. You can tell you're not used to travelling by car.'

It took Noemi a few moments to pull herself out of the deep sleep the journey had lulled her into. Her dreams had been filled with high walls she couldn't climb over, and girls dressed in black skirts and white blouses, laughing at her colouring and pulling at her braids. Pascal, who was almost jumping out of his seat with excitement, tugged at her arm until he had her attention.

'Hitler's coming tomorrow – we're going to watch the procession. He's going to fly over the city in a special Junkers D-2600, which is his own personal plane. Can you imagine owning something as amazing as that?'

Pascal began quoting aeronautical statistics at her and didn't listen to Noemi's reply. Viktor did, and he clearly found her sleepy, 'Not really,' lacking in enthusiasm or reverence, or both. She had to force herself not to flinch when she glanced up and caught sight of his curled lip in the mirror. She wasn't used to anyone looking at her so unkindly.

The car slowed down. Noemi stared out of the window as the traffic thickened around her. As half-timbered buildings five and six stories high, topped with turrets and gables and tiny windows embedded into the roofs, replaced the rugged mountain skyline she was used to.

'Nuremberg isn't Unterwald, which I know sounds obvious, but you need to be on your guard there. We're part of the community here, for the moment at least. Being Jewish might stop you joining in with your friends, but that's all. But there?' Frieda had bitten her lip then, as if she had far more to say than she wanted Noemi to know, and settled on, 'That city's never been kind to Jews. And if you're surrounded by people who'll look at your colouring and hear your name and think they know who and what you are... Well, attitudes may not be so welcoming.'

Noemi hadn't really understood what Frieda had meant by *who and what you are*, and she'd been too busy trying to wriggle out of the conversation to ask. She'd assumed her mother meant Jewish. Everything kept coming back to that in a way it hadn't done before Hitler came to power, but nobody would tell her why a faith she rarely practised and rarely thought about had turned overnight into the most important thing about her.

Her parents wore their Judaism lightly. The town was largely Catholic and there was no synagogue there, but they never went to the nearest one in Munich. They only kept the holidays for the sake of Hauke's elderly and ailing parents, who had moved to Unterwald from the city long ago in search of healthier air and brought their traditions with them. Noemi had no memory of ever discussing what being Jewish meant – it was simply one part of her heritage. Then Hitler had become chancellor of Germany and started saying unpleasant things about Jewish people, and one part had suddenly become all of her.

Her grandparents had both died by the time she was ten, and they'd only ever been shadowy – and rather forbidding – figures in her life. Noemi couldn't remember being allowed to talk to them about anything except their health. Her parents were very different people – they liked her curiosity. But when she'd asked them why Hitler didn't like Jews, they'd been reluctant to answer the question, and they'd grown even more close-lipped when she'd gone looking for answers herself.

The *Völkischer Beobachter* – the newspaper Hauke hated for being a Nazi mouthpiece but couldn't ban from the bar or the café without losing trade – was full of strange stories neither her mother or father would discuss. Reports of Jews being paraded through the streets of Munich for 'daring to behave like their betters'. Promises to the paper's readers that Jews would learn their lesson when 'the fist finally came down'. All Hauke had offered her by way of an explanation was, that 'Some people like a target to blame their troubles on,' which he wouldn't expand on. Frieda had simply ordered her to stop reading it.

Noemi hadn't. But when no one she knew was taught a lesson about their behaviour, and the nationwide boycott of Jewish businesses which the Nazis ordered never materialised in the town, she'd stopped worrying. She'd couldn't, and wouldn't, get used to the fact that she wasn't allowed to go everywhere Pascal went anymore, but she'd never felt unsafe. Or at least not in Unterwald.

Their world doesn't seem to have room for us.

Frieda's words suddenly felt more serious in Nuremberg than they had at home. Nuremberg felt more serious. Everything in the city was so different, so big and so busy. The thronged pavements. The houses and shops blooming with flagpoles, bristling with giant swastikas. The uniforms, brown ones and black ones, which stretched out as far as she could see.

What if they can tell I'm Jewish from one look? What if that matters more here?

There was no one in the car she could ask. She didn't want to risk another scowl from Herr Lindiger or spoil Pascal's excitement. And Carina was sweet and kind-hearted, but, unlike Frieda, she always deferred to her husband and never answered a question without looking at him first.

I shouldn't have come here. I should have listened to my parents when they said I wouldn't fit in.

Noemi shrank back from the window as the car lumbered its way through streets that suddenly felt as if they very definitely belonged to the uniformed men striding down them but not to her. Wishing she'd brought a hat to hide her dark hair.

CHAPTER TWO
SEPTEMBER 1934

'We're going to have the best time, I promise. You're going to be so happy you came.'

Except it's been almost a week since we arrived and he said that, and I've not been happy at all.

Noemi didn't have the words to admit her true feelings to Pascal – she was having enough trouble sorting them out for herself – but she knew she had to say something before he dragged her off to yet another 'entertainment'. She couldn't sit through one more parade or exhibition or speech as if nothing was the matter. And she didn't like feeling so awkward around him; they'd never had to explain themselves to each other before.

I should have told him I was miserable from day one. And that his mother felt the same way. He would have listened; he hates it if I'm upset.

Not so long ago, before Pascal joined the Hitler Youth, telling him what she felt about anything and everything had come as naturally to Noemi as breathing. Most of the time he already knew. In Nuremberg – where the speechmakers used words as if they were blacksmiths wielding a hammer and the crowds seemed to be permanently hypnotised – her tongue had tied. She didn't know how to say, 'I don't like this,' in a way Pascal would understand. And it didn't help that he was so wrapped up in the rally's ceremonies, he hadn't noticed her discomfort for himself. He'd been having the time of his life from the start.

The first day had played itself out at full volume from early morning until midnight, and that pattern had set the tone for the rest. They'd been trapped in the crowds thronging Nuremberg's central streets for hours waiting to see Hitler's motorcade drive past, despite the frightening crush. Pascal swore when it was finally over that he'd seen the Führer as clearly as he could see his father.

Noemi hadn't been able to catch even the tiniest glimpse of his car. She'd been buried in a forest of arms which sprang up and down like maddened puppets, deafened by the shouts and the screams and the loudspeakers which blared out from every street corner, encouraging the crowd to cheer. Not that anyone had needed the encouragement – nobody around her could stay silent or still; they shivered and shook as if they'd been plugged into a giant electric current.

Carina had been as overwhelmed as Noemi and had tried to dig them both out. But Viktor had noticed his wife was trying to leave before she'd managed more than a handful of steps. He'd dragged the two of them back and fastened Carina to his side with a grip that made her wince. Noemi had been so scared of his temper after that, she'd pretended to cheer as loudly as everyone else.

The noise had been as bad as the crowds. By the time they left the cavalcade's route, the fanfares and the drums and the never-ending tramp of marching feet had taken up residence inside Noemi's body. And the chants and the songs had drilled into her head.

Millions full of hope, look towards the swastika.

Germany, Germany, mightier than every land.

One people, one Führer, one Reich.

Every line was a roar; every beat was an invitation to march. And the crowds had obeyed the call to do that in their thousands, tramping out of the city to the Zeppelin Field parade ground, waving their banners and singing as they went.

Noemi was swept along with the procession and into the arena in a daze, clinging on to Carina's hand. Her feet ached by the time they reached it; her head was a pounding muddle. The field rippled with as many flagpoles as the city; she could barely see the tops of some of them, they were so high. Two giant stone eagles stood guard over the gates; more eagles topped the swastika banners which surrounded the huge field. Noemi felt as if she'd been transported to one of the Roman arenas she'd seen in her history books. She half expected Hitler – who was fully visible now, perched on a towering platform, alternately waving and haranguing the crowds – to raise or lower his thumb like an emperor as the soldiers marched past.

And from that moment on, every cavalry parade and mock war game and every torchlight procession magnified by giant spotlights was staged on a scale that was so vast and so loud, she couldn't think clearly. She got up each morning with her ears ringing, dreading the onslaught to come. But there was no possibility of slipping away and spending a quieter day in the city's shops and cafés as Carina had hoped. Viktor wouldn't let either of them out of his, or Pascal's, sight. Noemi was exhausted; she wanted her mother. But Pascal had been having so much fun, he was convinced she was loving every moment too.

'Forget about the stuff you've seen so far. That's been amazing, but tonight's going to be epic. The wreaths they use are so big they take two men to carry them, and the light from the fire pits will be high enough to see from a plane. They'll consecrate the new flags first, then...'

On and on he went – he'd become a walking encyclopaedia of National Socialism. Noemi tried to pay attention as he described yet another elaborate ritual whose purpose she didn't understand. It was hard to focus when she'd not only had enough of the rally, but she also had other things on her mind and no idea how to talk to him about any of that either. She wasn't sure whether Pascal had seen how roughly Viktor had grabbed Carina on the first day. If he had, he clearly didn't suspect – like Noemi did – that it wasn't the first time. She could hardly blurt out, 'Never mind flags and wreaths, have you seen the bruises on your mother's arms? Do you think maybe your father hurts her?' That would be impossible.

Pascal adored both his father and his mother; he would never suspect anything was wrong between them. And he wasn't a boy who paid any attention to clothes – he wouldn't think there was anything odd in Carina wearing cardigans and jackets even when the sun was at its height. Noemi had thought that was strange, but she'd only spotted the purple marks running from Carina's wrist to her elbow because the wince and the grip – and Carina's constant jumpiness around Viktor – had unsettled her. Unfortunately, when she'd gone into the Lindigers' hotel room to borrow a hairbrush and actually seen the bruises, Carina had instantly covered them up, and she'd looked so horrified, Noemi had had no idea what to do.

She'd never tell Pascal, and she wouldn't thank me for telling him either. But I'll speak to Mother when I get home – I have to do that. Maybe she'll be able to help.

'Noemi, are you listening?'

'Yes, of course I am. Go on.'

He didn't believe she'd heard a word, but he was too excited to get cross with her.

'I'm trying to tell you about the ceremony at the Hall of Honour tonight, the one to remember the martyrs of the 1923 putsch. Father's going to be carrying the Blood Flag, the one the fighters carried with them through the streets of Munich. It's a huge honour. And Hitler's coming in person to give a speech of thanks. It's the highlight of the rally – you have to see it.'

She really didn't. Noemi had heard enough about blood and sacrifice and heroic deaths in battle to last her a lifetime. All the glorifying of war didn't make sense to her. She couldn't match up the speeches about honour and the joy of dying for the good of a greater Germany with the sad-faced women who haunted Unterwald. The ones who wore black for their dead husbands and sons even though the war had ended sixteen years ago. Who Frieda said lived a half life. And she wasn't sure if Pascal, who thought soldiers were the same as gods, would understand her confusion. She'd never noticed before they came to the rally how accepting of everything he was.

I've never wished he was different. That he asked more questions.

The thought that her best friend wasn't perfect was a startling one. She doubted she would ever have felt that way at home. Concentrating only on what was in front of him and not worrying about the next step until he reached it had made Pascal into a very good climber, one she would trust on the trickiest slope.

But it's not so helpful here, in this place where I can't always tell what's real, and he doesn't seem to care.

The longer Noemi had spent at the rally, the more she'd started to feel like the little boy pointing out the flaw in the emperor's new clothes. But every time she'd pointed out something that looked fake – the part of the Zeppelin Field which was still a muddy construction site, the spectator stands made from cheap splintery wood painted to look like stone, the spectacular entrance to the great hall which was actually painted cloth – Pascal had frowned and asked, 'Why does it matter?' And when she'd got muddled by the myth-laden rituals and questioned what they were based on – because it wasn't the German history they'd learned in school, no matter how many postcards Pascal bought which featured Hitler's face frowning over a parade of medieval knights – he'd dismissed her with a 'You don't understand', which hadn't convinced her that he did either. She'd got stuck at *he loves it all and I don't,* and that had become a rather lonely place to be. So she didn't have the energy to sit through any more ceremonies, especially if Viktor was fully occupied and wouldn't be standing guard to make sure she did.

'I'm sorry, Pascal, but I'm too tired. All I want to do is to go back to the hotel and read a book. You go have fun and I'll see you in the morning.'

Leaving and spending a little time on her own sounded like heaven as soon as she said it. If she slipped away now, the trains wouldn't be as horribly overcrowded as they were in the late evenings and early mornings, and the city would be quieter. Nuremberg was bursting at the seams, and finding any kind of space to breathe was a challenge, but there was a lake between the Zeppelin Field and the Glockenhof area of the city where Viktor's connections had managed to secure them a hotel. She could be out in the open air listening to the birds in less than half an hour. Except Pascal wasn't ready to give up.

'Oh, Noemi, come on. It's our last night – you can't spend that with your nose in a book. What about if we did something fun first? We could go to the youth camp – there's going to be campfires and races, one of the older boys told me. I'd go on my own, but I'd rather you came too. I don't really know anyone there, and I bet you'd win everything if you tried. You're the fastest runner I know.'

Noemi sighed as her silent lake and her book disappeared. She knew how disappointed Pascal had been that he wasn't old enough to stay in a tent with the other Hitler Youth boys. And he was right: she was fast, and she did like to win. But she wasn't sure that was a good-enough – or a sensible-enough – reason to stay. None of the songs or the speeches had specifically mentioned Jews, but they'd all talked about the 'right blood' and the 'right heritage' and the importance of something called the 'Aryan ideal', and – whether she had reason to be or not – that made Noemi nervous.

'Do you think they'll let me join in? You know, given that—'

'You don't have a uniform? It's getting dark – no one will notice or care.'

He'd deliberately misunderstood her; he'd deliberately ignored the real issue. It wasn't the first time he'd done that, moving the conversation onto safer ground when Noemi tried to talk to him about how it felt to be Jewish and excluded. It was odd and uncomfortable, and one day she would have to tackle him about it, but maybe not now. Not when she could smell the smoke from the campfires drifting across in the wind, and the charcoal promise of roasting sausages.

'Fine, you win. I'll race you there.'

His cheer quickly turned into an outraged roar when she turned round quicker than he could and streaked away at top speed.

The youth camp was a sea of tents and energy and teenage boys trying to turn every activity into a competition.

Pascal was soon enveloped by a group who were intrigued by the fact he was wearing the same insignia as them but wasn't in their camp, and were impressed when they discovered his age. He blended in the moment he produced his collection of postcards and souvenir badges and offered to trade some. Soon, he was regaling his new audience with stories of his climbing exploits in the Alps, which Noemi was too kind to point out were somewhat exaggerated. Pascal was perfectly at home, but it was clear that the boys had no interest in her – they laughed when he mentioned how good she was at running and told her to go and play with the girls.

Noemi had no intention of doing that, although she said she would. Unlike Pascal – whose shyness around new people rarely lasted more than a moment and who had no doubts about his right to a place at the centre – she was all too aware that she might not be made welcome. She started to slip away instead, but the girls in question had been watching her, and they had other plans.

'How old are you?'

The question seemed innocent enough, but after all the warlike songs she'd heard and ceremonies she'd watched, Noemi wasn't convinced that anything in Nuremberg was innocent. She kept her answer to a very straightforward, 'Thirteen.'

The girl who'd asked – who was indistinguishable from her equally blond friends in their identical black skirts and white blouses – nodded. 'So old enough then to be in our junior league. But you're not dressed correctly, and everyone else is.' She ran a critical gaze over Noemi's loden green dirndl skirt and cropped jacket with its pewter buttons and red scroll stitching. Then she raised her voice so her audience could hear her. 'Or perhaps you've come in fancy dress, is that it?'

Noemi's fingers instantly started to curl, although she kept them hidden. Her outfit wasn't one she would have chosen – she was happier in a pair of lederhosen or trousers, something she could climb and run around in – but the skirt suit was what Bavarian country girls wore on smart occasions, and that made her proud of it. And deeply resentful of the older girls' sneers and giggles.

'I'm not a member of the League of German Girls. It's not compulsory.'

Her aggressor took a step closer. Noemi didn't take a step back.

'That's true. But membership is important, as every decent girl who does join it knows. I mean, who wouldn't want to pledge their life and their loyalty to the Führer?' She paused and glanced round at her entourage before she turned back to Noemi. 'Unless, of course, there's something stopping you?'

The wind had changed. They were both standing in the flickering light cast out by the campfire. Noemi forced herself not to react as the girl leaned closer and started slowly scrutinising her hair and her face. Suddenly, the cartoons she'd seen in a copy of the violently antisemitic newspaper *Der Stürmer*, which a customer had left in the café and her father had burned, leapt into her head.

What's she looking for? Horns? A bend in my nose? A forked tongue?

Noemi wasn't foolish enough to ask. Or to show any trace of the fear pricking her neck when the girl grinned as if she'd discovered it.

'You're a Jew, aren't you? You're one of the ones they warned us about. The really dangerous ones who look all nice and respectable but are actually filled with poison. Is that it, Jew? Am I right? Have you sneaked in here with your nasty dark eyes and your ugly brown hair to infect us?'

Noemi felt the air snap as the word *Jew* hit it. She'd never felt so vulnerable, not even the first time she dangled from a rope on a rock climb. And there was nothing she could do if she wanted to stay safe but lie and deny it.

'Don't be ridiculous. What a stupid idea.'

She would have sounded far more convincing if her voice hadn't immediately started to shake.

The older girl whooped and turned to her friends, her voice loud enough to catch the attention of some of the now arm-wrestling boys. 'She's a Jew – I knew it! We've caught ourselves a live one!'

Noemi twisted round, looking for Pascal, as the other girls began to move into a circle around her. He wasn't looking her way; he was too busy cheering on a boy who appeared to be intent on breaking his opponent's wrist. She doubted he'd hear her even if she shouted, and she'd never reach him if she tried to run – the circle she was now trapped inside was too tight.

While she was trying to work out what to do, the group's leader began goading her again. 'What was the plan, little Jew? Were you going to rob us? Were you going to throw stones? Or are you here to cause a worse kind of trouble and throw a bomb at the Führer?'

The lead girl's eyes were wild; her companions were breathing as heavily as horses readying themselves to stampede.

You have to show it who's master. Don't run or cower; snarl back. Maintain eye contact, and strike first and fast if you have to.

Once Hauke realised that his only child was going to explore the forests and mountains surrounding Unterwald with or without his permission, he'd taught her what to do if she was ever faced with danger, particularly from the grey wolves who came sniffing when the snow started to fall and hunting was harder. She and Pascal had taken Hauke's lessons and practised being hunter and prey until nothing could scare them. Now her father's words came flooding back to her and triggered the instincts buried deep in her bones.

The girl who'd started the bullying was quick, but she wasn't quick enough. Her hand shot out towards Noemi's braids. Noemi snatched it with a twisting grip that made her tormentor squeal. The others immediately began moving even closer towards her, their bodies elongated by the campfire's flames. Noemi didn't look at them. All she had to do to break the pack was cripple its leader.

She swung her other fist back and struck hard, with a punch that turned the girl's nose into a gushing red waterfall. There was a moment of silence, then the screams flew like tortured cats. But the circle fell back exactly as Noemi hoped it would, and their leader fell screeching to the ground.

'She hit me. The Jew hit me!'

The shout went up like a battle cry, but Noemi was already hurling herself through the space her punch had created, horribly aware that one stumble would set the wolves on her.

Unless he gets to me first and stops them.

She could see Pascal clearly now, and he could see her. His mouth and his eyes were saucer-like, but he didn't get up. He didn't make one move towards her.

'Help me, please!'

Perhaps he hadn't heard her. Perhaps he was too shocked to think. Whichever it was, she didn't have the breath or the time to call him again. Or to worry about the shouts building into a tidal wave behind her. This wasn't one of the fairy stories she'd grown out of long ago; there wasn't a prince about to ride to her rescue. There was no one to trust to get her out safely except herself and her instincts, so Noemi gave herself up to those. And she gave up on Pascal.

She bit down on her panic before it snatched away any chance of escape, plunged into the darkness and ran.

CHAPTER THREE
SEPTEMBER 1935

'I messed up and I'm really, really sorry. But when you hit that girl and sent her flying... It was such a shock. Honestly, I didn't know what to do. Which is a rubbish excuse, but it's true.'

It was, but it took Pascal three attempts to make Noemi listen. She'd forgiven him in the end, and they'd stuck enough patches over their friendship in the year since he'd literally left her to fight her own battles to hold it together. But she'd made him think about his behaviour first, and that wasn't something he liked to do.

'Friends are supposed to have each other's backs; they're meant to be loyal. And you weren't – you didn't stand up for me. That really hurt.'

He'd hated seeing her upset, and he'd hated what she'd said to him. Loyalty was the basis of every honour code Pascal and his Hitler Youth squadron held dear. It was the ideal Viktor had told him he should live his life by. And Noemi was his best friend, so failing her when she'd needed him was the absolute worst.

No, it's not. The worst bit is I can't tell her why I hung back.

He hadn't seen the danger she was in until the girls started screaming, and he had been shocked when he'd realised what Noemi had done. But that wasn't what had pinned him to the spot. He'd heard the word, *Jew*. He'd known the other boys had heard it too, and that they would ostracise him at once if he'd gone to her aid. So he'd chosen the coward's path and deliberately stayed out of the fight. He wasn't going to tell Noemi that: he wasn't sure she'd forgive him; he wasn't sure he could forgive himself. Fortunately, no one but the two of them knew what had happened in Nuremberg, so nobody else could judge him. Noemi had been too afraid of the consequences to tell her parents, and Pascal couldn't tell his. Carina would be ashamed of him, but he had a horrible feeling Viktor would cheer, and he didn't want to have to face that.

'Why do you bother with her so much? Never mind she's a girl, she's a—'

The boy who'd started that question knew better than to finish it. Everyone looked up to Pascal; he was a natural leader, but – if they wanted to be his friend – they soon learned he wouldn't discuss Noemi. Pascal couldn't put the importance of his relationship with her into words to himself never mind to anyone else, and especially not to people who didn't think their friendship should exist. After the unpleasantness at Nuremberg, he'd decided not to try. She was Noemi. She'd been by his side since his first memory, thinking the same thoughts, loving the same things. She was his best friend in the world. Who or what she was beyond that was of no interest to him.

'They're peas in the pod the pair of them – always have been, always will be.'

He'd heard both Carina and Frieda say that. And that their closeness was a blessing given they were both only children, which was a rare state of affairs in Unterwald. That wasn't a subject either woman lingered on – or that Pascal wanted to hear about – because it invariably made Carina cry. There had been another baby once, a sister, but she'd died before Pascal could really remember her and only existed now in photographs. Besides, although he knew better than to say it, he didn't mind not having siblings: he liked being Viktor's only son, the focus of all his attention. His father was an important man, and Pascal liked that too.

Viktor had become Unterwald's mayor in 1933, and the Lindiger farm was the biggest for miles. Along with the Drachmann café, bar and shop – and the bakery and bottling and distilling workshops behind those, which Hauke's parents had founded and he and Frieda had expanded – it was one of the town's most valuable sources of employment, and the town was grateful for it. People sometimes laughed when they saw him and Noemi together and teased them about founding a dynasty one day. It had become a running joke to say their name in one breath and to make endless jokes about when they were going to get married. That was confusing and embarrassing, but Pascal didn't mind once he looked up what *dynasty* meant: the thought of following in his father's footsteps and becoming as respected as Viktor made him walk taller. Even if Viktor wouldn't stop making Noemi's Judaism an issue. Which was another thing Pascal kept having to apologise for.

'I know it's not just those girls who say mean things, and my father can be as bad. That's why I'd rather meet at your house than mine. But I don't think nasty things about… people like you, and I don't think many others really do either.'

He wasn't actually sure he believed that about his father's friends and his Hitler Youth leader, who were more than capable of saying nasty things, and he was almost certain Noemi didn't. It was hard to know. He didn't like talking about her being Jewish, so he avoided all the problems that seemed to come with her religion and didn't. Besides – although she frowned at him sometimes when he sidestepped the issue – she never made a fuss about it either.

She never acted like some of the growing awkwardness

around her family being different upset her. She raised her arm in the Hitler salute every morning in school once she'd been sent home a couple of times for refusing to do it. After they came back from Nuremberg, she'd stopped being cross that she couldn't join in with the same clubs he went to. And yes, he was aware she missed out on a lot of fun, but he'd tried to make up for that by spending as much time with her as he could, doing the things they'd always done, and having more adventures.

They'd done their first ice climb together in the winter after the rally and skied at break-neck speed down a steep tree-lined slope nobody else in the town had dared to attempt. They'd driven the Lindigers' goats to pasture together in the spring, the way they'd done since they were seven. They'd completed a rock climb in the summer which had taken them across ledges so narrow they'd been left clinging to the rock face like lizards. That had been amazing. They'd been so full of adrenaline when they finally returned to solid ground, they'd run round the meadow howling like wolves. It had been a good year; he hoped the fun they'd had had wiped away that last night in Nuremberg. But – for all the patching up they'd done – he knew better than to ask her to go to the rally there with him again. Not that she would have done, or that Viktor would have allowed it.

'This year's gathering could be the making of you. You're fourteen – you're old enough to stay in the youth camp, and the focus of events this year is going to be on the army. There could be officers there scouting young talent. So there'll be no talk about taking that girl with us a second time. I won't hear of it.'

His father always referred to Noemi as *that girl* nowadays, as if she was something clinging to the bottom of his shoe. Pascal hated that, but he hated arguing with his father more. The times when Viktor was angry and cold with him might be few and far between, but they were unbearable. So instead of speaking up, he stopped mentioning Noemi at all, and he let his father think their friendship had drifted apart.

Which might actually be a possibility.

Pascal tried to focus on properly packing his brown shirts so they wouldn't crease and make him look sloppy, rather than worrying about the cracks between the two of them that he didn't know how to fix. Unfortunately, it wasn't as easy to switch his thoughts off as he wanted. He knew what the problem was, even if he acted like he didn't. He'd had to stop talking to Noemi about quite a lot of things lately, and that made him feel uncomfortable. She seemed to have forgiven him for Nuremberg, but she didn't want to hear about his Hitler Youth activities or the upcoming rally. She'd cut him off in midsentence when he'd told her how badly he wanted to enlist in the army and how excited he was that it might now be possible. Her, 'I don't want to know about that,' had hurt him. He hadn't told her that either. It had been a shock to realise he couldn't always share his dreams with his best friend.

He really wished she'd stop saying, 'I don't want to know.' It had become her chorus to everything good that happened – in his world anyway. In the spring, Hitler had announced he was overturning the restrictions the Treaty of Versailles had imposed on Germany's defeated armed forces at the end of the Great War, and was reforming the Luftwaffe and reintroducing conscription. Viktor had clapped at that radio bulletin and laughed not shouted when Pascal leaped round the room like a firecracker. Pascal had longed to be a soldier since he'd listened wide-eyed to his father's war stories as a small boy and dreamed of being as brave, but – given that Germany had only been allowed to maintain a skeleton army since before he was born – he'd never imagined it would happen. Now Hitler was promising him the future he'd imagined while he'd spent hours lining up his toy regiments.

But Noemi's response to the news had been a curt, 'Why? What's so glorious about war, which is the point about joining the army isn't it? Why is that better than the life you could have here? And don't tell me about honour and dying a hero's death – I had my fill of that in Nuremberg.' The strength of that rebuttal had hurt too. He adored her, he always would, but he was getting tired of her bad temper spoiling things. So he wasn't going to let it keep happening.

She'll come round. Mother always does when she's confused or worried by some of the things Father does. It's being reminded of the rally that's upset her. Once that's done with for another year, we can stop getting all mixed up with each other and go back to being PascalandNoemi again, the way we've always been.

Pascal finished packing his case. He straightened his neck scarf and gave his belt buckle a final polish. And set off for Nuremberg sitting next to his father in the front of the car, feeling very much in charge of his life and very grown-up.

'Why have you put them up there, instead of down here with the rest of us?'

Pascal hadn't wanted to attend the town meeting. They were incredibly dull and taken up with issues he had absolutely no interest in. Disputes over a boundary wall. Changes in licence regulations. They were utterly boring. Besides, he was still spinning with excitement from the rally.

'You're exactly the kind of youngster we're looking for.'

He couldn't get General Kübler's words out of his head; he didn't want to. The man was a legend in Bavaria. He'd become a soldier at nineteen and fought with distinction in the Great War. Now he was in command of the newly created *Gebirgsjäger*, the elite alpine mountain troops based in Garmisch-Partenkirchen, only an hour's drive away from Unterwald. Pascal had never met anyone more impressive, and – to his shock and delight – the general had been impressed by him.

'Winning first place in your own climbing category was highly commendable, young man, but the way you helped your team to victory? That's what I want to see. That's what makes a true soldier.'

His father had nearly burst with pride. He'd actually been speechless when Kübler invited Pascal to the Garmisch barracks to learn more about the brigade. Pascal had been floating in a bubble ever since, so the last thing he wanted to do was waste his time in a meeting, but Viktor had insisted that he put on his uniform and come. There was, apparently, going to be an announcement he needed to hear.

Whatever it is, this is weird.

Normally the only person allowed on the stage was Viktor. He liked the audience, and the lectern, to himself. This time, however, there was a small group of people already seated on the platform, and none of them looked happy to be there. Pascal scanned their faces, trying to work out the connection between them.

Herr Schuster the tailor was in the middle with his wife and two children, looking very uncomfortable. On one side of them were Herr and Frau Fleck, an elderly couple who lived on the edge of town and were devoted to their garden. They'd chased him and Noemi more than once as children when they'd tried to steal apples from the couple's small orchard. He couldn't imagine why any of them needed to be on the stage, but when he asked Viktor for the second time why they were there, and who the empty seats were for, his father carried on ignoring the question. He turned as the door opened instead and rubbed his hands together.

'Excellent. The whole cast is here.'

He was off before Pascal could try and interrogate him again. It took a moment for the penny to drop. For Pascal to realise the new arrivals Viktor was ushering towards the stage were Noemi and her parents. To understand that Viktor had singled out all the town's Jewish residents and separated them from the main audience. He could finally see what was happening. But what Pascal couldn't fathom out was why.

These new laws are going to change everything – you mark my words. This is the step into the future we've been waiting for.

Viktor's words on the journey home from Nuremberg suddenly swirled through his head and chased out the general. They made no more sense now than they'd done then. Pascal racked his brains, trying to remember exactly what his father had been talking about, but he couldn't. He'd barely been listening. He'd been too busy daydreaming about scaling impossibly high peaks in his alpine soldier's regalia to pay much attention to Viktor. Now the words sent a shiver round his neck. What laws? And – if those were what the meeting was about – why did Noemi need to be on the stage in full view to be told about them?

'What's going on? What's Father up to?'

Carina wouldn't answer him either. Her lips were drawn into a tight line, and she kept rubbing at her wrist under her jacket. He turned away from her and tried to catch Noemi's attention, but her head was down. She huddled closer to Hauke as Viktor walked to the podium.

Why is he grinning? Why does he look as if he's got some hold over them they don't know about?

Viktor's expression mirrored the one he wore when the two of them were out hunting, and he had to stand over a wounded animal and deliver the killing shot. He'd always told Pascal that was an act of mercy, and Pascal had chosen to believe him...

But he always looked as if he was enjoying it.

He looked as if he was enjoying himself now. By the time Pascal finally caught Noemi's eye, his skin was crawling, but he couldn't do anything except shake his head when she mouthed, 'What's going on?' at him. Then Viktor unhooked the dagger from his belt, clapped his hands for silence and tipped the world on its side.

'Most of you will have seen the motto engraved on this dagger. And on the belt buckles worn by your sons. *Blood and Honour*. We could also add *soil* to that. Blood, honour and soil. Simple enough words, but what do they mean?'

Viktor waited, his stare jumping from face to face. A couple of people shuffled and coughed as if they thought they were expected to answer.

Viktor smiled at them. 'I am sure many of you can tell me, but let me remind you anyway. What these words stand for is us.' He paused to let the word *us* sink in and spread his arms out as if to pull them all into it. 'Us. A pure German people. United by our blood which runs back through the centuries, and our love of the land which sustains us, determined to always uphold its honour.'

He paused again, put the dagger down and folded his hands together. It took a moment for the audience to take the hint and burst into the loud applause he was waiting for. The families on the stage behind him looked at each other and didn't join in. Viktor drew himself up, puffed out his chest and started addressing the room in a voice that belonged to a far more important man.

'Thank you. But those aren't my words; they are the principles our Führer has pledged himself to protect. And now – at the recent party congress in Nuremberg, which I and my son were privileged to attend – he has set out the pathway for us all to follow. The future he wants for *us*, his people, is coming. We know how he will defend our honour: by rebuilding our once proud army and by training the next generation of heroes. Now we – or at least I – know how he will defend our blood.'

He paused again and turned to look at the confused faces behind him. Hauke had reached for Noemi and Frieda's hands at *defend our blood*. Noemi's eyes were fixed on Pascal's. It was like Nuremberg all over again. She looked helpless, and she clearly needed him, but Viktor had started talking, and there wasn't time for Pascal to work out what, if anything, he could do.

'As many of you are aware, we have a problem which goes to the heart of our country. A contagion which lost us the war and threatens to weaken our great nation again if it's not isolated. When I met him twelve years ago in Munich, and fought at his side, our Führer already knew the source of the vermin, and he was determined to banish the disease. And now he has made the laws that will do it.'

Pascal had stopped looking at Noemi. He couldn't take his eyes off his father. It was as if he'd transformed himself into Hitler himself. His hands gripped the sides of the lectern, except when he was hammering a point home. His voice was louder than the hall needed. His tone was hectoring, belligerent. His cadence ran up and down, swelling and breaking in waves that transfixed his audience. It was an impressive performance, clearly modelled on the speeches Viktor had attended in Nuremberg, but it was also deeply unsettling in a way Pascal didn't understand.

'Oh dear God, poor Frieda. And the rest. I begged him not to humiliate them like this, but he wouldn't listen – he didn't care.'

The sob in Carina's voice whipped Pascal's attention onto her. He'd never heard his mother criticise Viktor before, and that was unsettling too. He reached for her hand and held on tight to it as he turned back to the stage.

Noemi's face was colourless. As Viktor pulled a clip of papers out of his pocket, her hand dropped from Hauke's and her body froze.

I could stop this. I could stand up and tell him this isn't the right way to do things. I could go onto the stage and lead them all down, tell him to finish whatever he has to say when they're gone. He'd listen to me – I'm sure of it.

Pascal got to his feet before the thought was finished, his courage sparked by the sight of Noemi's bitten lip. 'I'm sorry to interrupt, but...'

His father's face mottled with fury; his eyes turned molten. Pascal had never felt the force of Viktor's fury targeted so brutally at him before, and it paralysed him. It took all Carina's strength to drag him back down.

'Stop it. It won't help her; it will make matters worse. She'll need you later, and you have to go to her then, which you won't be able to do if you rile him.'

If you rile him woke him up to the danger he'd put himself in. Pascal sank into his seat as his father switched his focus back to the rest of his audience as if the disturbance hadn't happened.

'Tomorrow every household will receive a copy of these. They will also be posted in the market square and announced through the town's loudspeakers so nobody is in any doubt about what is coming.' He laid the papers on the lectern, smoothed them out and began to read their contents, striking the key words so they rang out.

'From the first of January 1936, the following statutes will become legally binding and subject to punishment if broken. Firstly, the *Law for the Protection of German Blood and Honour*. This forbids marriage and physical relationships between Germans and Jews. Secondly, the *Reich Citizenship Law*. This removes all citizenship rights from Jews, who are now to be classed at the lower level of state subjects. In the following weeks, definitions will be published determining who is Jewish and to what degree.' He looked up. 'There will no longer be any doubt about who is a true German. There will be no doubt who is the enemy.' He paused for a second or two while the room digested *enemy*. Then he turned to the families behind him. 'Not that anyone in our town needs to question that.'

'You bastard. So that's why your invitation was so insistent we came.'

Hauke's voice rang around the silent hall. Frieda had her head in her hands. She made no attempt to stop him as he launched himself to his feet.

'Did you have to do this with so much pleasure? Did you have to humiliate honest people who've lived their entire lives here and never done you or the town any harm?' He looked Viktor up and down and shook his head. 'I always knew you were no good, and now you've proved it. What's your plan after this? Are you going to march us round the market square wearing placards? Are you going to chase us from our homes?'

The two men stared at each other while the hall coughed and looked away. Nobody stood up; nobody protested. Carina's hand was a vice on Pascal's arm. But there were one or two mutters of, 'Shame,' and, 'Let them alone, for pity's sake,' which Pascal wished had come from him.

Viktor clearly hadn't expected a challenge. Hauke laughed as the muttering, and the lack of applause, reached the stage.

'It's not so easy, is it, when you stick an evil label on your neighbours? Look out there – look at them. They know us. They can't look at us and see *vermin* or *disease*. But they can look at you and see a bully and a fool because that's what you are. A show-off in a sad uniform.'

It was a brave speech. From the tears on Frieda's face, she clearly thought it was a reckless one.

And it's not entirely true. There's more people on my father's side than Hauke thinks.

Pascal gazed round the familiar faces who were staring at the two men squaring up to each other on the stage. Some of them were shrugging as if the new laws weren't entirely unwelcome. Some were smiling to themselves. Everyone was silent now; everyone was keeping their own counsel.

But why is he doing it? Surely he doesn't want people here to behave like those girls did in Nuremberg?

Whatever Viktor intended, Pascal knew that's what Noemi was thinking. He knew she was afraid – she looked as if she was about to be sick. And when Viktor's temper snapped and he grabbed Hauke by the collar and snarled, 'You'll regret this, if it's the last thing I do,' she finally burst into tears.

* * *

'Noemi, wait. Please. I need to talk to you.'

The last thing Noemi wanted to do was to wait – or to talk. Especially not to Pascal. She ignored him and flung herself out of the hall after her parents, flinching away from the towns-people who flinched away from her. Nobody spoke to her. Nobody had spoken to Frieda or Hauke as they stumbled off the stage. Or to the Schusters or the Flecks, even though Frau Fleck had wept and clung to her husband as if she was about to collapse.

Vermin. Disease. Contagion.

The words stormed through the air until she thought they would blind her. When Pascal grabbed her arm, she whirled round ready to strike him. It was a good thing he ducked.

'Did you know about the new laws? Did you know what your father was going to do?'

'Don't talk to him, Noemi, do you hear me? He's not your friend, not after this.'

Frieda's voice tore through the night's frost before Pascal could answer. Noemi half turned away from him, but Pascal's, 'Please give me a chance to say sorry for how you were treated in there,' pulled her back. She could feel her mother's fury spilling through the, 'You're a fool if you listen to him,' she shouted next at her daughter, but Noemi had no choice. She could easily hate his father; she couldn't switch so quickly to hating Pascal. But she definitely couldn't bear to be watched anymore.

'Down here. I don't need more eyes on me.'

She pulled him round the corner into a deserted back lane as the hall started to empty.

'I didn't know about any of it, I swear.' He started talking before she could tell him he only had a minute. 'You've been to Nuremberg – you know how many speeches there are. I didn't go to half of them. I didn't go to any in the Congress Hall where all the politics gets done. The only thing I was interested in was the army stuff and the competitions.'

Noemi dropped his arm, although she couldn't uncurl her fist. Her body felt as if it would never relax again. But she believed Pascal: she knew he would have spent every second he could in the youth camp, proving how fast and strong and brave he was. She tried to push away the fear and the anger Viktor's performance had filled her with and focus as he carried on.

'I don't know why my father chose to humiliate you like that; if I'd known what was coming, I'd never have let you sit up there, I swear it. That's why I tried to stand up, to stop that part. You have to believe me.'

She did, although she wished he'd tried harder.

'Nobody spoke up for us. Not one single person.'

The weight of that tore at her shoulders; it took her knees away. She sank onto a wall and stared at the ground.

'I thought we were welcome here. Everyone comes to the café and the shop and the bar, and nobody gets married without my mother's wedding cake. She always says she gets to hear about engagements first. That she can tell from a girl's smile that it's time to get out the special cherry compote and the best vanilla. I thought that meant we were part of the fabric, like the seasons. But now we're a *disease*? What does that even mean?'

She looked up, but Pascal was shuffling his feet, and he looked as if he was about to cry. She waited while his silence stretched out and the rest of his words came back.

'What did you mean by *that part*?'

He shuffled and coughed. She hadn't been properly listening to his stumbled apology, but she was listening now.

'Oh dear God. You would have tried to get us off the stage, but you wouldn't have stopped the announcement. That's what you meant, isn't it?'

It was dark in the lane, but she could see the blush creep across his cheeks. His reply was a patch of black ice on a pathway, its jolt sharp enough to take her breath.

'How could I? It's not my father's doing. They're new laws; it's his job to tell people about them. I didn't like the way he did it, but I can't change what he has to do.'

How can he separate one thing from the other? Does he not understand what happened to me and my family in there?

Pascal was a head taller than her now and broader than he'd been a year ago. He had a shadow on his top lip by the evening. But Noemi felt twice his age as she pulled his answer apart.

'You understand what these laws do, don't you? You understand they make me – and everyone else your father paraded up there tonight – worthless? That they make us not citizens, not German. Not part of the *us* the country apparently belongs to now?'

The silence that followed was so complete, she could hear him breathing; she thought she could hear his heart. The confusion clouding his face made him look like the little boy she'd raided orchards and licked stolen icing spoons with. It made her hope he'd seen the cliff she was dangling over. Until his frown cleared, and she realised this was Pascal, who had his own way of making everything well with the world, and he hadn't understood a thing.

'No, no. That's all wrong.' He dropped down onto the wall

beside her, his voice growing stronger as he explained how she'd been the one who didn't understand. 'When Hitler talks about the Jews being a problem, he means the crooks and the swindlers. The ones who turned traitor in the war or made money out of it. That's who these laws are intended for. My father used you and the other Jewish families as examples to make a point, which was a stupid and mean thing to do, and I'll tell him that, I promise. But the laws themselves are nothing for you to worry about.'

He sounded so sure of himself. It would have been the easiest thing in the world to drop her head onto his shoulder and believe him. She longed to do that. She'd never craved comfort more, and nothing could have been more normal than physical contact between them. As children, they'd collapsed and slept curled round each other wherever they ran out of energy. They could lose a summer afternoon now lying in a meadow, listening to the bees buzz and watching the clouds with her head on his stomach, planning their next climb.

You can no more separate those two out than you can extract the eggs from a cake.

Frieda's long-ago words floated back into Noemi's head. She'd loved that description of them when she'd heard it, although she'd laughed off her father's, 'Don't I know it, I should probably start saving for the wedding.'

Frieda wouldn't celebrate that closeness now. Noemi would be surprised if she ever let Pascal back into the Drachmann house.

And our wedding would be illegal.

Whether she'd ever thought about marrying Pascal, or wanted it, or dismissed the idea as the adults talking nonsense, no longer mattered. The possibility no longer existed.

All of a sudden, his body was too close; it was alien. She stood up, her head full of Viktor's contempt. Wondering how long it would be before Pascal gave in to the beliefs he spent so much of his time immersed in and started displaying that same contempt too. The thought was unbearable. Which meant she had to make him listen to the truth.

'I know you're trying to make me feel better, but please think for a moment. How can what you said be right? How are they not about me? They're about Jews, and I'm Jewish. There's no changing that.'

Everybody who'd ever smiled at her simply for being young had talked about *innocence* as if it was a state they longed to return to. *They were more innocent times* was a line she'd heard repeated countlessly by old men and women reminiscing about the days before the war had taken their loved ones or the country's subsequent economic collapse had wiped out their savings. She imagined they would describe Pascal – with his bright eyes and his bright smile – as the picture of innocence now. He looked delirious to Noemi – or deluded. His answer confirmed it.

'But you're not... that sort of a Jew, are you? You're not a crook; you're not a traitor. You and your family – and the Schusters and the Flecks – are good Jews, not bad ones. So trust me, you've got nothing to worry about. Good people don't get punished – everyone knows that.'

Good Jews and bad Jews.

It was such a simplistic view of the world. She didn't have the heart to explain to him how naive and insulting and wrong it was. And she couldn't find the words to ask him how the National Socialists intended to tell the two kinds apart if they ever decided it was time for the *vermin* to be gone.

CHAPTER FOUR
JANUARY 1937

'What's going on? What's happened to your grades? Why are these two essays marked as a fail, and why aren't there any others in your book? I've never known you to skip homework or get less than a *good* for anything.'

Frieda had barely waited for Noemi to get through the door, or unwrap herself from the layers of damp wool that had collected ice crystals deep in their folds, before she went on the attack. It took Noemi a moment to warm up and focus. To realise that her exercise book must have fallen out of her bag. Now Frieda was brandishing it like a mislabelled bottle of poison and gearing herself up to explode. Noemi stared from the notebook to her mother, wishing she'd been more careful. She hadn't been hiding her problems at school to spare herself – as Frieda clearly believed was the case – but to spare her parents. She should have known from the start that wasn't possible.

The Drachmanns had spent the months after their humiliation in the town hall waiting for the new laws to bite and take away their businesses. Hauke's hair began to turn grey with the worry; Frieda lost her curves. It had taken them most of the first half of 1936 to accept that – after a few difficult weeks immediately following the meeting, when the café was filled with empty tables and there was no morning queue for bread – Unterwald had decided to carry on as normal. Once the loudspeakers stopped booming and the notices in the marketplace faded, the customers began to drift back. Nobody came knocking on the door insisting their property had to be surrendered to more suitable owners. The 1936 Winter Olympics, which were held close by in Garmisch-Partenkirchen, brought trade to the whole area, and business doubled. The summer games which followed had turned the holidays endless and put everyone in a mood as sunny as the sky, increasing their appetite for the Drachmanns' famous cakes and schnapps and preserves. Frieda and Hauke's world had eventually righted itself, but Noemi's hadn't.

The new year had swept new teachers into Unterwald's high school along with the chill winds. The men and women standing at the blackboards now wore their swastika lapel pins with pride and had turned their classrooms into shrines to Hitler, where the chart explaining who was German and who was Jewish took centre stage. Pascal went to the Olympics in February to cheer on Germany's medal-winning skiers and figure skaters. Noemi was moved to a desk at the back of the classroom and had to watch as a group of girls as blond as the ones who'd tormented her at Nuremberg drew a ring round it with soapy water 'to keep the bugs at bay'. The curriculum shifted and shoved her out of place. Lessons began to focus themselves around the Nazi's pet 'Theory of Racial and Hereditary Science', which went to great pains to describe how far from the Aryan ideal she was.

Noemi, who'd always been a curious and diligent pupil, started to skip lessons rather than listen to all the ways she was a failure. She began to hide in the corridors or in a far corner of the playground until the worst teachers were done. None of the subjects she'd previously achieved high marks in had room for her contributions anymore. She gave up trying to write history essays when the class were asked to explain 'the treacherous role played by Germany's Jews in the Great War'. Or stories when they were asked to respond to the title *The Jew: a Master of Crime*. She knew when a battle was one she couldn't win. But although Noemi stopped expecting good grades, she'd deliberately avoided telling her finally smiling parents that poor grades were her new reality. Except now, in the face of Frieda's fury and the start of a lecture beginning, 'If you spent less time daydreaming about climbing and...' she could no longer keep up the pretence.

'I don't get good marks anymore, no matter how hard I try. It's impossible. I'm Jewish, and Jews are stupid and have to be kept in their place at the bottom of the class.' She back-pedalled a little as Frieda gasped. Not worrying her mother had been the point of hiding her exercise books in the first place; spilling her frustration without thinking would completely negate the point of that. 'I don't believe that obviously, but most of the teachers do. And yes, I know I should have told you before, but you'd finally stopped worrying about the business, and I thought I could manage the situation myself.'

She stopped. She'd been so busy trying to do that, she hadn't let herself accept that she couldn't. It was a relief to finally admit the truth.

'I could stay and stick it out if you want me to, until the summer when I'll be sixteen. But I don't see the point. They don't care if I'm there or not, and they're not going to make life any easier for me. And as for sitting exams and going to university...' She tailed off. Like marrying Pascal, whether university was the right pathway for her or not wasn't what mattered. The possibility had slipped away without her involvement. 'Well, it might be easier to start working in the business sooner rather than later.'

Frieda sat down with a soft thump. She stared from the essays which had been scored through with red back to her daughter's pinched face as her fight drained away.

'Is everyone unkind to you?'

There was nothing to be gained now by keeping her problems hidden. Noemi shrugged, trying for one last moment to act as if being so cruelly isolated for so long hadn't deeply upset her. It was clear from her mother's white face she wasn't fooling anyone.

'To different degrees, yes, I suppose they are. Except Pascal, although I've been trying to keep my distance from him. I don't want his father accusing me of ruining his prospects or accusing Dad of putting me up to that.'

Frieda closed her eyes for a moment. Viktor had been keeping his distance from the Drachmanns too, but none of them had forgotten his furious, *You'll regret this*. Which was why, Noemi assumed, her mother latched so quickly onto *trying*.

'Trying but not succeeding. You haven't broken with him entirely, have you?'

Frieda fixed Noemi with the stare she hated. The one that said, *I might give you a long rope, young lady, but I'm reining you in now*. Noemi had never had any defences against that particular look.

'No.' Her mother's flare was instant, but Noemi wasn't a child anymore, and she was determined to be heard. 'I understand you're angry – I understand why. And I did try, I really did. But Carina was struggling, and Pascal asked me to go and see her. How was I supposed to say no to that?'

Frieda bit back whatever retort she'd been planning. 'Is it

Viktor again? Is he hurting her, like you told me you thought he'd been doing?'

Noemi started to say, *No, I don't think so,* because she hadn't seen any more evidence, but that was too easy an answer.

'I don't know, although he's a brute so I'd be surprised if he'd stopped. She's clever at hiding things, and I'm certain Pascal hasn't a clue – you know how he hero-worships his father. But he was right about her being lonely. She told me Viktor said she gets in his way. That "men with dowdy wives and one child don't rise through the ranks the way they're supposed to." It was so sad. I didn't really know what to do, except to keep visiting her.'

Frieda's sigh was strong enough to blow out a candle, but she knew when she was beaten. 'Poor Carina. I've not been a good friend to her. I didn't ask her about the bruises you saw; I didn't know how to. And I've avoided her since the town hall meeting. So it's partly my fault if she's lonely, and she's so fond of you. I suppose you're the daughter she always…'

This time it was Frieda who didn't finish the sentence, although they both heard the *wanted* which should have filled the gap. Which Noemi now could never be.

Frieda rubbed her eyes and went on. 'I hope you've at least been going to the farm only when Viktor's not there. How often? Please don't say every week.'

When Noemi answered, 'For the last six months or so, pretty much, yes,' Frieda's shoulders slumped.

'So not trying at all then. Visiting Pascal as much as his mother.'

Denying it would have been a lie, and while Noemi had always told herself that hiding parts of her life – especially the riskier exploits she and Pascal got up to on the mountains – made things easier for everyone, she drew the line at actually lying. But her mother did not need the details. Frieda certainly didn't need to know that staying angry or disappointed with Pascal had made Noemi miss him too much, so she'd licked her wounds for a little bit again, given in to his apologies again, blamed the father not the son, and let her anger go. Or that she and Pascal had drifted back into spending whole days in each other's company when they could snatch the time, hiking through the alpine meadows and forests and practising their climbing skills on the peaks behind those. Or that Carina encouraged their wanderings and smiled when they went off together.

And she definitely doesn't need to know that those days with him are the one time I feel like my old self.

As she couldn't say any of that, she simply nodded and waited for another explosion.

It didn't come. Frieda reached out for her daughter's hands instead.

'I wish I could order you to stop seeing him, but that's pointless so I won't. But I do want you to listen to me, Noemi, even if you ignore everything I say. This friendship you two have – I know how deep it runs. I know you both think nobody will ever understand you in the same way. But it can't continue. You're both clinging to a bond the world we live in now is determined to break.' She held tighter as Noemi – who couldn't bear the pain in Frieda's eyes or the fear she might one day have to share it – tried to wriggle away. 'And I know that hurts, sweetheart, but it will hurt far more when he rejects you. When he's forced to make a public stand by his father or by his Hitler Youth leader. Or because spending so much time in rotten company spreads its own sickness and he starts to believe what they say about us.'

'He won't do that.' Noemi twisted hard enough to pull herself away and refused to give in to the tears pricking at her eyes. 'He would never reject me like that, whatever his father does. He's promised he won't.'

She could escape her mother's hold on her hands, but she

couldn't make her mother stop loving her or spelling out what they both knew was the truth, no matter how painful that truth was to hear.

'Then you'll have to be the brave one, Noemi, and break away from him. Because there's nothing but misery coming for you if you don't.'

CHAPTER FIVE
NOVEMBER 1937

'Why didn't you tell me you're going to Innsbruck? We've been talking about doing that climb for years. Surely you're not going to attempt it without me?'

Noemi stared at the maps spread over the table as Pascal – who clearly hadn't heard her come into the farmhouse – stopped trying to tidy them away and sighed.

'Well yes, that was the plan. I'm sorry, but it's meant to be a solo challenge.' He took one look at Noemi's frown and gave up. 'Which I'm assuming it's not going to be now you've seen these.'

Noemi started to explain to him how right he was, but she was too excited to stay angry, and she didn't want to waste time having a row when they could be sorting out their kit and making a route plan she was certain she could improve on. The crossing from Bavaria into Austria over the Karwendel Pass was an expedition Hauke always talked about as being his favourite climb, but he'd never attempted it during the winter. Repeating his journey along trails covered in snow and ice would be the biggest challenge either of them had ever attempted, and Noemi wasn't about to miss out on it because of some silly show of male pride.

'You need me there – you know you do. That pass is a two-person job, whatever your youth leader says. Besides, my new ropes are far stronger than yours, and they only go if I can.'

Pascal gave in in the end. He said it was the promise of the silk climbing ropes Noemi had received for her sixteenth birthday which swayed him, but they both knew he wanted her skills and her company, whatever he'd said about rules. Now all they had to do was swear Carina – who'd walked in halfway through the conversation – to secrecy.

'It will take at least a week to get there and back, Noemi, and I doubt your parents would agree to it. Herr Lindiger certainly wouldn't, and I'm not sure I should either, not with these new rules. I worry about the trouble you two could get into.'

Carina's concerns were real, but they were no defence against Noemi's smile or her own sentimental heart.

'You're right, they wouldn't. And I wouldn't ask you to lie for me – I'd never do that. But you don't really want him doing this on his own, do you, whatever the rules say?'

Noemi's smile widened as Carina reluctantly shook her head. 'I'll leave a note explaining where I've gone. All you have to do is pretend you knew nothing about it if my parents come here and ask.'

Noemi didn't need to add, *Which they won't*. She wasn't about to argue with Carina's, 'You've always been able to get round me, young lady, and you know it.' And Carina – who, like her son, didn't want to face the truth and accept that the anti-semitic laws had anything to do with the girl she'd always hoped would one day marry her son – was too much of a romantic to say no.

The sun was barely touching the sky when Noemi slipped out of the house and into the frost-tipped garden, dressed in her walking boots and the thin layers that would hold in the warmth without adding unwieldy bulk. The crisp morning air had never tasted so sweet. Frieda had a wedding order to prepare, including one of her famous pink-iced cakes, and had left for the bakery before dawn to get it ready, calling to Noemi to come later. Hauke was travelling to Garmisch to meet a prospective supplier and had left early too. She'd left a note under her comforter which she hoped would stop them worrying, she had a rucksack full of food. All she had to do was collect her climbing equipment and her skis from the garden shed and the adventure could begin.

The first stage of their journey was through familiar territory: the broad plains of the Isar Valley. Winter had already established its hold there. The snow was smooth and flat, untouched except for faint animal tracks. The river had vanished under a thick layer of white. The trees had turned black under their crystalline coating. To anyone who didn't know the landscape, it could appear as if it held no colour in it apart from the sky's violet-edged blue. But Noemi and Pascal were Bavarian born and bred, and they viewed its winters through country-trained eyes. The ice crystals and snowflakes twinkled like a treasure chest for them – flashing gold under the sun's morning rays, turning to rose quartz as the day lengthened towards sunset, swapping silver for bright opal blue as the temperatures cooled.

Whatever colour the land took, their skis flew across it, and they completed the relatively flat run to Wallgau in record time. The town, with its mural-covered houses, was a delight; they could have happily stayed there, except their adrenaline was soaring too high for them to slow down. They decided to push on instead to Scharnitz and an overnight stay which would let them make the far more complex climb across the north-west ridge of the Breitgrieskarspitze with fresh legs the following day. That seemed like a good idea to them both, but it was almost a step too far. The terrain around Wallgau wasn't flat – it rose and fell as if it had been caught up in soft gathers. Skiing across it was like riding over tumbling waves. They arrived in the little town exhausted and exhilarated, their cheeks red with cold, their bodies aching.

As tired as she was, Noemi was instantly entranced by the white church and the wood-framed houses clustered at the foot of the towering Karwendel Mountains. But it was a few moments before she realised why she felt so at ease.

There aren't any red banners dangling from the buildings here. There aren't any swastikas; no one is dressed up as a soldier.

'Welcome to Austria. We crossed the border about forty minutes ago.'

Noemi grinned at Pascal as the pieces fell into place, although she didn't want to spoil the mood by explaining why she was so pleased to be out of Germany. She'd been telling herself, *They won't know you're Jewish, so don't worry*, as they'd got nearer to the town, forgetting Scharnitz was in Austria where nobody would care.

'We should look for somewhere to stay.'

She began scanning the street for a welcome sign, but Pascal was already ahead of her, waving her towards a small hotel. To her relief – because she was desperately in need of a hot bath and a bed – the inn he'd spotted with its cheerful gingham curtains proved to be a good choice. Even though it was no longer climbing season and the walkers who flocked to the town in the summer months were long gone, the owner welcomed them in with a broad smile. Two rooms were aired and heaped with extra pillows and comforters, there was no lack of hot water. The restaurant was closed for the winter, but the owner's wife was more than happy to provide her unexpected guests with schnitzels the size of a serving platter and a thick pile of *Kaiserschmarrn* – a local speciality of torn-up fluffy pancakes smothered in plum compote and powdered sugar which Noemi devoured until she was too full to move. She would have crawled straight into bed after that – her eyelids were blinking as she scooped up the last pancake – but the star-filled night sky had attracted Pascal's attention, and he persuaded her to go outside onto the veranda and admire it too.

'It's so perfect, I'd have said it was like looking at a photograph, except it's more like standing inside a negative.'

The view was a black-and-white vision. The sky and the mountain had looked flattened out by the lack of colour at first sight, but it only took a moment for Noemi to spot its textures. The moon hung full and pitted, balancing on the top of the ridge's jagged outline. The stars danced across the inky black carpet like shimmering shards of glass. The snow was as fluffy as the pancakes she'd filled herself with.

'It's so...' Noemi stopped and laughed. 'I wanted to say beautiful, but that's not a big-enough word.' She turned, hoping Pascal could fill in the blank. But he was staring at her as if he'd never seen her before. 'What?'

He shook his head. Moved a step closer. Noemi was suddenly aware of the ice in the air, of the breeze whispering against her cheek, of the faint brush of a snowflake falling onto her hand. She didn't know her skin could feel so alive. Now she was the one shaking her head. Hearing the new words forming like ice crystals between them; reading their meaning in his darkened eyes. Wanting them, and the kiss she knew was coming, and dreading them at the same time.

We can't; we mustn't. We'll start an avalanche we won't be able to stop.

'Noemi, I...'

If only he hadn't spoken. If only he'd carried on reaching out for her in silence, the spell would have stayed. But her name woke her up and snapped her back to reality. She stepped away;

broke their gaze. And slipped back into the hotel before the night could cast its dangerous magic across them again.

Noemi slept, although she didn't expect to. She came down for breakfast not knowing where to look. Pascal apparently felt the same. They ate quickly. Neither of them mentioned the full moon or the veranda. They set off discussing the intricacies of the climb and nothing else. The potential for low cloud and sudden fog which could be a hazard in the area. How to spot and test for the snow bridges which looked solid but could crumble to air beneath them with one misplaced step. How best to traverse rock faces on limestone mountains like the Karwendel, where seemingly secure handholds could dissolve into gravel at a touch. They didn't look at each other; they kept an arm's length apart. Noemi had never felt so separate from him – or so uncomfortably close. Until the climb across the peak began, and they were PascalandNoemi again.

They'd been climbing together for so long, they worked as one body. Pascal took the lead, scraping away the ice from the rock, fitting the pitons into place for the rope which would be their lifeline. Noemi ran that round her shoulders and under her arms, watching where his hands and feet found the crevasses as he began the ascent, calculating how much further than him she would need to stretch. Trusting him to keep them both safe. Once he was clear and she'd hoisted their packs up, it was her turn to set out. She pressed her body close to the stone, feeling its solidity and its strength, letting that certainty soak through her. She slowed her breathing against the inevitable adrenaline rush; checked her ice axe was securely fixed in her belt. Banished *I can't reach it* from her head and began.

Her muscles began to burn within minutes; her lungs started shivering as the oxygen levels dropped. None of that was unexpected; none of that frightened her. *Move your left foot up.*

Extend your right arm. There's the hold, well done. The running commentary in her head was deliberate, designed to squash any lurking self-doubt. Because that was the real danger, not the narrow ledges or the almost invisible handholds. If self-doubt crept in, she might stop trusting her instincts, and no climber could afford to do that. Hauke had drilled that message into her – and Pascal – from the moment they'd first pointed at a mountain and said, 'We want to go up to the top.'

'If it feels wrong, stop. It doesn't matter what the reason is – a change in the weather, an unsteady rock face, a partner who's lost their nerve. Trust your instincts and stop. A mountain's no place for heroics.'

They'd both followed that advice rigidly and learned their craft carefully because the prize for doing it properly was…

Breathtaking. As Noemi pulled herself over the ridge, the view exploded around her. The sky was a cloudless cornflower blue, so vivid and close she could have wrapped herself up in it. The snow stretched out untouched as far as she could see, rising and falling in sharp silver crests. This wasn't simply beautiful either. This was…

A magic I want to be part of.

She couldn't take her eyes from Pascal's; she didn't try. They watched each other as she unknotted the silk rope and released herself from him. As she peeled off her wet gloves and he gathered her white fingers inside his before she could cover them again. When he reached for her cheek this time, she didn't back away. She stopped worrying about consequences that had no place in the pure wonder of a mountaintop. They moved into each other's arms as if they'd known the way there for years. His body was so familiar to her and yet suddenly so new.

There was a second when their eyes met, when they caught their breath and the world shrank to the two of them. And then their lips met too, and the world slipped away. His mouth was sweet; his kiss was as perfect and pure as the snow and the sky.

If the light hadn't dipped and opened her eyelids, she would have stayed buried in its warmth forever.

'There's fog coming – I can feel it.'

He said that like a caress, although they both knew the clouds were a warning.

They broke away from each other more slowly than was sensible, as if they'd forgotten how to be separate. They gathered their packs; stuffed fingers that wanted to stay in contact with bare skin back into their gloves. There was no tension between them this time, no awkwardness. This wasn't the veranda's misstep. They turned back into the careful climbers the mountain's changing moods demanded, but they didn't turn away from each other. They made their way off the ridge and towards their next stopping point as if they were still locked inside the kiss.

Whatever's coming next, I won't stop it.

Noemi caught Pascal's eye and smiled at him, her heart swelling as he smiled back.

I love him, and he loves me. What else matters?

She didn't care what the rest of the world would have to say about them being too young – or too wrong. The rest of the world with its laws and its judgements and its hatreds wasn't watching. So she smiled at him again and let her heart bloom. And she stopped worrying about avalanches.

'You said it was a climbing hut. It's gigantic.'

When Pascal had told her they would be able to stay overnight in the Karwendelhaus climbers' lodge before they continued to Innsbruck, she'd been expecting the kind of small wooden structure which was a feature of Bavarian and Austrian mountain trails. Instead, the building in front of them was three stories high and appeared to have grown out of the rock face. It was also – if the shuttered windows were anything to go by – completely deserted.

'Don't worry about that. The door's never locked, and there's always a store of food and bedding. Or so my youth leader promised.'

Pascal sounded confident, but Noemi breathed a sigh of relief when the door opened on the first push, and the lodge proved to be as well stocked as he'd hoped. A check of the kitchen revealed stacks of tinned and bottled food; there was also wood for the fire and coal for the stove. They dumped their packs and began making the space their own, both falling without thinking into the patterns their parents had set. Pascal began laying a fire; Noemi worked her way round the stove, opening cans of stewed chicken and waxy potatoes. They were hungry and cold, so they dealt with those needs first. But the kiss was there in every movement and sideways glance, waiting while they warmed themselves up and ate their simple supper. Rippling out, spreading into, *What comes next?*

Noemi kept telling herself she didn't know the answer to that. It wasn't true; she wasn't a child. They were alone, there were countless bedrooms above them; she was with the person she trusted more than anyone in the world. She knew what was possible, although she'd made no decisions. Her mother had only discussed the subject with her in the broadest terms, and the movie cameras always cut away once the hero had kissed the heroine, but Noemi knew what happened between men and women. The girls who ignored her at school, and didn't care if she overheard their gossip, were obsessed with boyfriends and husbands and babies – it was all their heads were filled with. The ones who'd been kissed, who'd done more, were objects of endless fascination – to their faces anyway. Noemi had listened to the talk, and to the judgements that came hand in hand with an upbringing overseen by a priest. She was also aware how many of her classmates had giggling crushes on Pascal. As for her?

I've thought about it. About him.

Noemi glanced over at Pascal, who was staring into the fire. She'd never admitted that to anyone; she'd barely admitted it to herself. At first, the idea that there might be more to their friendship had been little more than an echo of the town's assumption they would marry one day. An assumption that had fallen away with the introduction of the blood and citizenship laws, and his move into his beloved Hitler Youth uniform and away from her. Or it should have done. Until they'd slipped back into their old ways with Carina's blessing, and Noemi had realised that fifteen was very different to twelve, and sixteen had brought a whole new wave of emotions.

Which don't matter.

She shook herself. The fire was playing the same tricks on her that the moon and the snow had tried.

The laws are the laws – the world won't allow this. He shouldn't have kissed me; I shouldn't have kissed him. It wasn't magic; it was madness.

She scrambled to her feet, excuses springing to her lips. But he was there, beside her, before she could find the words.

'Don't run away from this. Don't pretend it means nothing.'

His arms found her in the same moment hers reached for him. Their mouths merged. Her body took over. Her fingers found his face, found his hair. When he tipped her head back and kissed the base of her throat, he wiped the world and its nonsense away. Noemi stopped thinking; she let herself melt. If the fire hadn't suddenly burst into a last loud crackle, she wouldn't have surfaced at all. The pop opened her eyes. The flames had burned down to embers, and the temperature outside their arms was mountaintop cold.

'Give me a moment to relight it – it's my turn.' She slipped out of his embrace and smiled at him. 'There's no hurry. There's no sense in us freezing to death.'

'We'd best not use all the hut's matches up. There should be some in my pack.'

Pascal sounded as dazed as she felt. Although he woke up with a speed that stunned her when she began to rifle through his bag.

'Stop! Wait. There's something in there you're not meant to see. A surprise I've been waiting to give you.'

It was too late. Somewhere inside her, she'd always known it was too late, but that did nothing to staunch the pain.

'What are these?'

It wasn't the surprise he'd intended – his groan told her that. Noemi pulled out the bundles her digging had unearthed and laid them on the floor. They were leaflets, three kinds, each bearing different pictures. One showed an eagle with its wings wrapped round a smiling blond family. Another depicted a giant standing under a broken bridge, fitting the word *Anschluss* into the gap. The third was dominated by a smiling soldier and a worker marching arm in arm. They all had a swastika in the top-right-hand corner. They all carried the same message, which she read out loud.

'National Socialism protects the people: Austrians, join your German comrades and let us build our future together.'

She stared up at Pascal. She stared back at the bundles, feeling ancient. Knowing there was nothing he could say to bring back the magic; trying not to break apart with the pain.

'You're right, it's certainly a surprise. I don't suppose I was meant to see these, was I?' She brushed away his clumsy attempt to explain himself before he was half a dozen words in. 'This is why you're going to Innsbruck. It wasn't a solo challenge. You're delivering recruitment messages. You're spreading the poison. No wonder you didn't want me coming along.'

He flinched on *poison*, but he didn't deny it. He didn't say anything, but Noemi couldn't stop.

'Given that I did come, what was your plan? What was I meant to do while you were off playing postman? Sip hot chocolate, stare at the Alps and turn a blind eye?'

His flush told her he hadn't made any plan at all. She pushed the leaflets away. She would have thrown them on the smouldering fire if he hadn't scooped them up first.

'You don't understand. The Tyrol, and the rest of Austria, is German by rights. We speak the same language; we share years of history. We're supposed to be joined together.'

'You sound like your father, which isn't a compliment.' She couldn't look at him. 'Is that the big idea then? Germany's going to become the great power you're always going on about by widening its borders and sucking everyone else in?'

She could sense him bristling before he spoke.

'No one's being sucked in. Most Austrians want us here. The rest can be persuaded.'

It was *persuaded* that gave him away. That explained the warmth of the hotel owner's welcome and how confident Pascal had been about the provisioning of the Karwendelhaus. That was nothing to do with youth leaders.

She got to her feet and moved to the table. She needed a barrier between them.

'You've done this before, haven't you?'

He couldn't help himself. There was a pride in his voice as he answered her that spilled like salt over Noemi's cracked heart.

'I've been acting as a courier for the *Gebirgsjäger* for a while now, yes. They recruited me after the 1935 rally in Nuremberg. I'll join them as a soldier when I'm old enough, but for now I deliver leaflets to the hotel in Scharnitz and to here, for National Socialist cells in Austria to collect and distribute. And they asked me to go on to Innsbruck this time, which was an incredible—' He stopped as Noemi shook her head, and he finally remembered who he was talking to and that *honour* was not the right word to win her back. 'I'm sorry. I should have told you what I was doing from the start.'

'Why didn't you?'

His answer was a schoolboy's fumbling. 'Because you would have told me not to do it, and I'm proud I was chosen. So's my father.'

He was one step away from asking her not to be angry with him. He should have asked her not to despair. Noemi sank into a chair as the fire fell to ashes and her dreams crumbled.

'I'm a fool, and so are you. You can't see Hitler for what he really is. You're too lost in the badges and the marching and the promises of glory.' She looked up at him, willing him to look at the world through her eyes. 'We're not children anymore, Pascal – we can't keep pretending it will all be all right. Hitler is full of hatred – you have to see that. He's selling you a Germany with no place in it for me, never mind for us.'

He was so eager to make things right between them, he fell back on the last thing Noemi wanted to hear.

'You're wrong – I've already told you that. He doesn't hate you, or—'

'Stop, Pascal. Please, stop.'

She rubbed her eyes. She was suddenly desperate for sleep. If he couldn't hear her after the connection which had just formed between them, where was the hope?

'Don't tell me about good Jews and bad Jews again. Tell yourself that nonsense to salve your conscience if you must, but don't say it to me. Nobody at school calls me *good*. They prefer *dirty*. They use *Jew* like a weapon, and your beloved Führer does the same.' She waved her hand at him as he started to argue. 'Fine. If I'm wrong, then tell me what kind of plan is in place to separate the "deserving Jews" from the less valuable ones if such a thing exists. If you can do that, maybe I'll listen.'

He stared at her with his mouth open and empty. She could see pain dawning in his eyes, but she couldn't help him with that. Not until he accepted that he was the one in the wrong, not her. Perhaps not even then. She stared away from him into the cold grate and tried again.

'Do you know why he hates us? Do you think about that? You've swallowed the rhetoric, but have you really considered what every last bit of it means? Because you have to. If you want to be part of Hitler's glorious new world, you have to accept all the cruelty that goes with it. You can't pick and choose. And you have to ask yourself where this ends.'

'What do you mean, *where this ends?*'

Noemi took a deep breath. She didn't know if Pascal couldn't or simply wouldn't understand, and she didn't have an answer for him, but he couldn't be allowed to escape the question. Not when she increasingly lived her days in fear of it.

'For me and my family, and the rest of Germany's Jews, Pascal. If we really are vermin, a contagion Germany needs to be rid of, where does all this hatred end?'

'Don't say those words. Don't use them about yourself.'

He'd slumped into the chair opposite her, all the colour drained from his face. For a wonderful moment, she thought she was starting to get through to him.

'I have to. It's what the teachers and your Hitler Youth leader, and your friends and your father, would say about me. And if they knew what had happened between us, they'd think I'd infected you with my poison.'

He looked up at her then. She wished that he hadn't. He couldn't hide the panic that flashed over his face. Her body turned into a bruise.

'Thank God then that it didn't go any further. I wouldn't want your life to be ruined because you'd broken the law with me.'

Her despair spilled over and shocked him to his feet. He ran to her side, pulled her up and into his arms, swearing that he didn't regret anything. But Noemi's body no longer fitted his, and she pushed him hard away.

'I'm going home. I'm not going one step further with you.'

Now the panic was in his voice as well as his face. 'You can't do that – it's too dangerous on your own.'

She gave him a moment to add, 'So I'll not go on either. I'll take you back to Unterwald and make this right.' He didn't. Instead, he started to explain how she didn't understand the importance of what he'd been asked to do and how it was only a job and didn't have to affect them, and her heart was too heavy to bear it. She stepped back out of his reach and wrapped her arms round her aching chest.

'Then you've made your choice. You don't have to worry about me. There's a different path marked on the map, a longer way that skirts the ridge and the pass. I'll take that one. Go do what you need to do. But don't pretend that things can ever come right between us. And don't come looking for me when you get back.'

She walked away from him then and went up the stairs alone.

When morning came, she crossed her fingers as she got up and sent prayers to anyone she thought might listen that he'd changed his mind. They didn't work. He wasn't there. But there was an envelope on the table.

She picked it up, presuming it was an apology, not certain she wanted to read it. She tore it open, expecting a letter, but instead there was a birthday card which someone – she assumed Pascal – had amended to say *Happy Late Birthday Wishes* on the front, and a locket inside whose beauty took her breath away.

> *I know you've already had your present from us, but this is something special. My mother called it her little piece*

of the sky, and she wanted you to have it; so do I. I hope you like it and will wear it for me.

Love, your Pascal

She turned the card over. He must have written it before the trip, before the events of last night, but he hadn't added an apology or anything else to it.

This must be the surprise he intended.

She held the necklace up. It was the locket with the bright blue stone surrounded by a wreath of enamelled white flowers that Carina used to wear to parties, the one everyone envied.

A family heirloom filled with hope that she's passing through him to me. As if I still have a right to it.

The tears she'd been holding at bay all night splashed onto the card, blurring Pascal's untidy handwriting. She didn't know what to do. She couldn't imagine wearing the locket, not after all his lies. Part of her wanted to fling it off the balcony down into the valley and never see it again. The rest of her knew she'd never forgive herself if she did and Carina found out. So she stuffed it deep into her pocket instead and trudged out alone into the cold.

Noemi walked the long way back to Scharnitz in a daze. She avoided the town, spent a second sleepless night in a cold and tiny hut and set out again for Unterwald as soon as there was enough light for her skis to safely navigate the snow-covered paths.

Where does this end?

She couldn't silence the question. She had no hope of an answer. Every path from it led into a darkness she couldn't fathom. And she couldn't think about Pascal either, or the feel of his lips on hers, or the fact of his leaving, or she would give herself up to the snow and the ice and howl.

'I'm home.'

She entered the kitchen worn thin from hunger and fatigue and what felt like the loss of a limb, braced for a furious onslaught. Instead, Frieda leapt out of her chair and threw her arms round her daughter.

'I'm sorry. I'm so sorry. I shouldn't have gone off like that. I shouldn't have frightened you.'

Her mother's face was ravaged. Her clothes were mussed as if she'd spent more than one night in the chair. But she accepted Noemi's apology so quickly, it was clear her disappearance wasn't the sole cause of her mother's distress.

'What's happened? What's the matter?'

She caught her mother as she crumpled, but it took more than one attempt to make sense of Frieda's words.

'It's your father – he's been arrested. He's gone.'

CHAPTER SIX
FEBRUARY–OCTOBER 1938

Hauke had been charged with non-payment of his suppliers and non-payment of his taxes, neither of which was true, and taken to Munich's notorious Wittelsbacher prison.

And Pascal's father put him there – I know it. And I'll never forgive him for that.

Noemi slipped her arm through Frieda's as they made their way from the railway station to the prison, trying to separate the father from the son, which was becoming increasingly impossible. It had taken days to discover Hauke's whereabouts and weeks for a visiting order to arrive; Noemi suspected Viktor had had a hand in both delays. As for the charges, they were false, but they hadn't come entirely out of the blue. It seemed that she hadn't been the only one in the family keeping secrets. After almost two years of letting them feel safe, Viktor – because his fingerprints were all over the accusations, even if his name wasn't – had used his Party connections and snatched the rug away from under her parents.

It has come to our attention that the Drachmann Café and its supporting businesses are in the ownership of a Jewish state subject, not a recognised German citizen. Please inform this office at once as to when this situation will be rectified.

'The memo came about six weeks ago. It wasn't an order to sell, so your father ignored it. But then Viktor came round, asking to see the books, asking what the business is worth. Hauke refused to tell him; he told him to get out. We hoped that might be an end to things – which I know was foolish, but we'd been left alone for so long, we convinced ourselves this was just another bit of grandstanding. Except then the police came for him while you were away, and I've had no word from him since.'

Frieda had shown Noemi the letter from the Gauleiter's office in Munich the day she'd come back from the mountains. Whatever her parents had told each other to keep their spirits going – and why Viktor had suddenly felt empowered to tighten the noose he'd waved over their heads in 1935 – it was clear to Noemi that the world as they knew it had finally broken. It was also clear that Viktor had orchestrated the whole thing, including informing the authorities about the extent of Hauke's holdings. His pudgy fingers were everywhere in Unterwald, pulling his friends up, pushing his enemies down. It was impossible not to read the letter and hear, *You'll regret this.*

He must have got so much pleasure watching my parents convince themselves they were safe. I bet he's had this takeover planned since that night.

'Goodness, this wind – it really does barrel down the streets here.'

Noemi pulled her attention back from imagining the extent of Viktor's thirst for revenge – and what Pascal knew – as Frieda spoke and her teeth chattered.

'You're shivering. Here – take my scarf as well.'

Frieda stopped and let Noemi wind the soft wool round her neck. She increasingly let Noemi take the lead in everything;

she'd aged rapidly with Hauke's arrest. The brisk February day was cold enough to turn their coats to paper, and Frieda was frail. Noemi knew her mother needed to sit down and rest and prepare herself for the ordeal of the prison, but Munich wasn't Unterwald. Every restaurant and café they passed had a sign in the window saying, *No Jews*. Noemi would have taken her chances, but Frieda had trembled at the suggestion, so the two women put their heads down and pressed on through the wind, trying to pretend they weren't out of place.

'This can't be it – it's far too grand.'

Frieda was right. The Wittelsbacher Palace was much too elegant to be a prison. It was easier to imagine the princes and kings who'd once owned it sweeping past the two stone lions guarding the entrance, or gazing down from behind the perfumed splendour of its arched windows, than the Gestapo dragging frightened prisoners inside. It wasn't until Noemi asked a guard where to go that she was brusquely redirected.

'The bit we need is round the back, behind the main building. Hopefully it will be as nice.'

It wasn't. Noemi hadn't expected it to be, but she wanted one more kind moment for her mother. The prison's high walls were made from granite, not soft-hued red brick; its windows were barred. The room they were left to wait in was grey and cheerless and smelled of stale cigarettes and clothes badly in need of dry cleaning.

'But it's not as bad as you'd think, I promise. My cell is warm and there's no shortage of blankets. The food's not bad – cheese and sausage and stew at mealtimes and plenty of bread. I've been well treated, and they've assured me that this is for my own good. That I'm safer in here while things are being ironed out than I would be on the outside, where my creditors might come looking for me.'

Noemi had to fight hard not to lose her temper at the ridiculous idea of creditors. Or that Hauke's imprisonment was for his own protection. She only said nothing because she knew he was desperate for her to play along. Hauke's sideways glances at the guard and his dreadful appearance made a lie of his relentlessly cheerful manner. His eyes were dull and had sunk inside bags that suggested regular sleep was a luxury. His face was gaunt and patched in fading purple and yellow. When he put his hand out to touch Frieda's – before the guard barked at him not to – it shook.

'That's all good to hear, but do you have a trial date yet? We need to instruct a lawyer.'

His mask slipped when Noemi asked that. Noemi had to blink hard when she realised how carefully he'd been holding himself together. His body sagged. The tremor in his hand spread to his knees. He stumbled as he tried to find a positive-sounding answer.

'Well, there's the question. I don't think there'll be a trial; I'm not sure that's their way of doing things.'

'What do you mean, no trial?' Noemi couldn't stay quiet this time – she couldn't follow what he meant. She hadn't yet learned that the systems she'd been brought up to believe in had been dismantled for non-citizens. 'Where's the justice in that? How are you meant to prove your innocence without a proper hearing?'

Hauke glanced at the guard again before he replied. The tremor in his hand grew worse. 'I don't know. I'm not sure how the system works anymore, if I'm honest. Apparently, they can keep me here without a hearing for as long as they like. Or they can send me to one of their other facilities if I cause problems, which naturally I've no intention of doing.'

'What *other facilities*? What are you talking about?'

Noemi reached for her mother's hand as Frieda's voice rose. The guard who was monitoring their conversation had already looked at his watch. There wasn't time for anything but practicalities.

'How do we get you out if there isn't a trial?'

Hauke's mouth twisted in what could perhaps have been described as a smile. His eyes were begging Noemi not to correct him.

'That's more straightforward. We can pay the suppliers I owe money to and the taxes I've defaulted on. That will obviously take a lot of money which we don't have, but the authorities have suggested a way round the problem. It seems Viktor Lindiger has offered to buy the shop and bar and the manufacturing businesses that go with them. And he's set a value on them, which I've been instructed to accept.'

And there it was, the price Viktor had been waiting patiently to extract for Hauke's attack on him in the town hall.

Noemi gripped Frieda's hand tight and hoped her mother would understand the need not to react. She forced herself to stay calm too.

'And the café?'

'We keep it for now, and the house, although not the bakery.' Hauke stopped looking at the guard; he focused entirely on his family. 'But I imagine we won't keep them for long, that this is simply another part of the game. You need to steel yourself for that coming.'

Where will this end?

Noemi left the prison with more understanding of the answer to that than when she'd gone in. Ruin. Humiliation. Being made to feel powerless – because that's what they were.

Hauke had already been forced to write a letter to Viktor accepting his offer; the guard gave it to Frieda as she was trying to say goodbye to her husband. Noemi took charge of it. She delivered it to Viktor's office the next morning and made sure to hand it to him herself, although she did that in silence. Then she and her mother waited for the rest of the charade to play out.

Viktor took the shop and the bar, the bakery and the

bottling and distilling workshops a week later, for a sum so small it was an insult to her parents' and grandparents' hard work. Noemi held her tongue; all that mattered was getting Hauke safely released. That took another two months of delays and no explanations. In the end, Hauke arrived home without warning, thinner and greyer, but determined to keep the café and the family afloat. Or to act as if keeping them afloat was possible until he had the strength to contemplate the impossibility of a new start somewhere else.

A month went by and stretched into two. The days warmed and the customers trickled back. Hauke regained a little of the weight prison had taken from him; Noemi and Frieda forced themselves to fuss over him slightly less. Summer came and brought the tourists, the café ticked steadily on. The Drachmanns started to look out at the world again, and to hope that the worst was done. Which was the moment Viktor pounced.

Hauke was charged with more financial irregularities nobody was interested in explaining and hit with a fine three times the size of the last one, although he wasn't taken to prison. Instead, Viktor graciously offered to act as a go-between and find a buyer for the family's last assets.

'It's the only way to clear your debts, I'm afraid. But I'm not an unreasonable man – I don't want to see you out on the streets.'

Noemi hadn't truly understood what despair felt like until Viktor sat down in her father's chair and smiled his oily smile. He dropped his gifts into their laps like a malevolent Santa Claus.

'I've arranged for you to live in the flat above the café again, for a reasonable rent. You lived there before your parents left you this delightful house, so I'm sure you'll enjoy the return. And obviously we don't want to lose your skills, Frieda, so there'll be a job for you in the bakery. Not running it of course, but I've no doubt you'll adjust. As for you, Hauke, the new owner of the Unterwald Hotel – who will be taking over the café – has very generously offered you a position as a porter and will take on Noemi as a waitress too. It's a very good solution all round to your troubles, don't you think?'

There were so many things Noemi wanted to say, and *good* wasn't one of them. But she caught Hauke's eye and caught hold of her tongue and let Viktor leave as if they were thankful to him.

'We'll be all right. We have each other. Nobody can change that.'

Her father needed her to be brave and steady so he could keep his head up, so Noemi stayed brave and steady. Until she saw him a week later, watching the *Café Drachmann* sign come down and the *Café Edelweiss* sign go up, with tears pouring unchecked down his face. She cried like a baby then.

* * *

'I know you don't want to see me, and I don't blame you after everything that has happened between our families. But I'm leaving in the morning, and I need to talk to you before I go.'

Pascal had learned a little from their disastrous trip to the mountains, so he didn't explain that he was leaving Unterwald to take up a place at Sonthofen, an elite officer training school, and what an honour that was. He was painfully aware that even a few minutes alone with her was more than he deserved; he didn't want to stack the deck further against himself. Noemi's world had fallen apart and, while he didn't know if his father had instigated the attack on Hauke – and didn't want to – Viktor had certainly profited handsomely from the Drachmanns' fall. Pascal was deeply ashamed by that, but he doubted Noemi wanted to hear his second-hand apologies.

'Please, Noemi. Give me a chance.'

She didn't answer, but she at least put down the tray of

empty glasses she'd cleared a moment before from a table filled with the town's new great and good, and followed him into a quiet corridor. He was feeling almost hopeful, until she rounded on him with a, 'Why should I?' that was so curt, his heart curled up.

'Because I'm going to be away for a long time.'

He paused. He'd been going to say that he might also be called on to fight in a war. There were rumblings in Europe, even though nobody had actively opposed Hitler's recent annexation of Austria or the Sudetenland. Conflict wasn't impossible.

And all that will do is remind her that I'm going to be a soldier, fighting for a leader she hates. She'll walk away the second I say it.

So he spoke to her from his heart instead. 'And I'm ashamed at what my father has taken from yours, and I need you to know that.'

She didn't soften, but she didn't leave. He took that as a good sign.

'Did you get my letter? I know you said not to come and find you when I got back from Innsbruck, but I had to say sorry somehow. I should never have let you come back home by yourself.'

'And that's all you're sorry for, is it?'

He'd misstepped again. Noemi brushed his floundering, 'Well no, but...' away.

'What do you want me to say, Pascal? Yes, I got your letter. My mother found it, and she was furious when she read it. She's got no forgiveness for you or your family. She wouldn't let me reply, or see you, not that I wanted to. She'd never forgive me if I slipped back into our... friendship again.'

He kept on grasping at straws; he couldn't help himself. He heard *she's got no forgiveness* and decided that, because Noemi hadn't said *I've got no* there was hope.

'Is that possible? For us to be friends again?'

The scorn on her face stripped at his skin. He'd never understand how they could be the same age and yet she was so often years ahead of him.

'How, Pascal? Never mind what you were doing in Innsbruck. Never mind that your father has destroyed mine. Never mind I don't think I'll ever trust you again. Don't you see what else Viktor has done to the town? There's curtains twitching everywhere; there's noses in everyone's business. Just because you won't accept what I am doesn't mean the rest of Unterwald's pretending I'm someone different. It's not safe for you to talk to me, to even look at me. Don't you get that? What will happen to your precious military school place if this conversation gets reported? What will happen to me if Viktor finds out you still want to be my friend?'

Pascal flinched at the sarcasm in *friend*. And at the thought of what his father would do if he gambled so recklessly with the future Viktor's connections had carved out for him. She knew where he was heading; she'd always known everything about him. She was also right. The way Viktor had profited from Hauke's downfall had opened Pandora's box. Old scores had boiled up all over the town, and the police were happily stirring the pot. Hauke wasn't the only person who'd been dragged in for questioning on baseless charges, motivated by greed and a hope that their assets would be redistributed. Unterwald had become a powder keg, as Noemi clearly knew all too well and was apparently determined he should face up to.

'There's nothing neighbourly about this place anymore – we've moved miles away from that. There isn't a day goes by here when I don't hear gossip about somebody. Most of it is so trivial – Herr Mansell at the newsagent's reporting Herr Seger for cancelling his subscription to the *Völkischer Beobachter* and calling it trash. Frau Berkel failing to display a portrait of Hitler in her hall. It's so petty, although it all ends up with an arrest.'

She glanced back at the dining room. 'But some of it seems far more sinister. Doctor Brodmann's in there now, talking about some "special arrangements" he's made for a sick child, and the way he said it...'

She shuddered. When she looked back at him, Pascal could see she wasn't making any distinction between him and the rest of the town's Party faithful at all, and he hated it.

'This is the world we live in, Pascal, whether you choose to see it or not. Nobody outside the Party is safe in it, including me. And as to the possibility of the friendship between the "dirty Jewish girl" and the trainee Nazi hero carrying on without anybody caring? Forgive me, but I really can't see it somehow.'

She's deliberately trying to hurt me so that I'll leave her alone.

The first part had worked; the second couldn't. It was his last chance to prove he wasn't like the rest of them before she slipped completely through his fingers.

'Don't make us into those people, Noemi, please. I won't accept it. I've hated not seeing you, I hate that my father's actions have hurt you.' He stopped; took a breath. Hoped he sounded like the man he was trying to be. 'And I love you. I should have told you that in the Karwendelhaus, not run away.'

It was said. He couldn't believe how light he felt. And she loved him too – he knew it. If she didn't, she would have said so, not, 'You can't love me; it's forbidden.' That was the next chink his hopes needed. He reached for her and tried not to panic when she shrank away.

'I don't care about that. Nothing can change how I feel, not even a law.'

It was her eyes – it was always her eyes. He could fall into those and stay there forever. Especially now, when the light creeping back into them had to mean that she felt the same. And when she looked at him and told him that was true.

'Then don't go to Sonthofen, Pascal. If you truly mean what you say, don't join the army. Let's leave here together instead. Let's go somewhere where nobody cares whether we're Catholics or Jews or nothing at all. Somewhere we can be together and be in love without fear.'

It sounded so simple the way she said it; it sounded perfect. In that moment, it was all Pascal wanted to do. But his life wasn't only about one perfect moment. It was about family and making his father proud of him. And about honour and service too.

If she can just understand that, we can have everything.

'I want to, but I can't.'

He hated the way her face fell. All he wanted was to make her happy and to make the world better. There had to be a way to do both.

'Giving up my place at Sonthofen would break my father's heart. I don't want to hurt him like that, any more than I want to hurt you. But what if I went and used my time there to help us?' The second the idea jumped into his head, he knew it was right. All he had to do was convince Noemi. 'I'll work hard and prove my loyalty, and I'll rise through the ranks. I'll get to a place where the people who make the laws listen to me, and I'll make them see that there are Jews who've earned their place in the Reich. Decent ones like you and your family. I'll help build a future that includes both of us.'

He was so certain he could do it, he could see the Führer shaking his hand. He grinned and waited for her to grin back at him. But he hadn't heard the arrogance or the cracked record stuck in its groove the way Noemi had. She didn't smile; she didn't tell him how clever he was. Instead, her face looked so bleak, it terrified him.

'Dear God, can you hear yourself? You sound as if you think you can be the next Führer. *I'll make them see*? Your father really has built you up in his twisted image, hasn't he?' She shook her head before Pascal could answer. 'Good Jews, bad Jews; Jews who've earned their place. It's always the same with you; it's always wrong. And it all leads the same way as the version where we're a plague. To ruined lives, to disaster. Until you can see that, and walk away from playing any part in it, there's no more to be said. There's no more chances for us.'

He stared at her open-mouthed, unable to understand where he'd gone wrong.

'No, Noemi. You've misheard me; you've misunderstood. This can't be our ending.'

But she'd already turned on her heel and walked away, and it was.

CHAPTER SEVEN
JUNE 1941

'Thank the Lord for this day; we've been waiting for it long enough. No more pretending Stalin and his filthy communists are our friends – now we're going to teach the Russians the lesson they've long needed instead. Get a bottle of schnapps from the cellar, girl, and call the farmhands in. This news needs celebrating.'

Noemi hated the cobweb-ridden cellar, but anything was better than being within reach of Herr Distel and his vicious views or his vicious walking stick. She inched her way down the rickety staircase and into a gloomy basement which was stocked with more food than her parents' meagre wages from the hotel and the bakery would buy them in a year. The first time she'd ventured down there, the sight of all the bottles and jars with their old *Café Drachmann* labels had frozen her to the spot. Now she hardly noticed them. She picked up a bottle of the cherry-flavour schnapps her boss hoarded, dusted it to save herself from another barrage of insults about dirty Jews and returned to the kitchen. She didn't stay once the men came in – not that they'd have let her. She slipped away to the stables instead, where there was plenty of work to be done, and plenty of punishments waiting if she didn't clear the muck out to Distel's liking. Not that anything was ever to his liking. She was certain he'd only employed her because no one cared if he paid her next to no wages or worked her to death.

He'd probably get a medal for doing his duty if he managed to do that.

The war Hitler had been courting for most of 1939, and before, had arrived on a hot September day, when the summer wasn't yet ready to change seasons. Its coming had altered the town's landscape again and pushed the Drachmanns even closer to the cliff edge. Unterwald no longer turned a blind eye to old neighbours: Jews were Jews, and nothing else counted.

Noemi had heard the announcement shortly after Germany had invaded Poland and forced Europe into action. It came crackling through the town's loudspeakers as she walked back from the farm which had employed her once the hotel decided she wasn't fit to be seen in its public rooms. Unlike the rest of Unterwald, she hadn't stopped to listen to the belligerent announcer. She had no intention of joining in with the cheers and the show of excitement which had quickly followed the initial stunned silence. How could she, when she wasn't part of the glorious new Germany the loudspeakers were promising the war would lead to? When that war could – if Hitler had his way – spell the end of her?

'If Europe plunges us into a conflict, which Germany will win, the annihilation of Europe's Jews will follow.'

Hitler had made that pledge in the deadlocked weeks after the first shots were fired at the quickly conquered Poles. Nobody had taken issue with it then; its promise was common currency now. He hadn't yet explained how he was going to do it; Noemi wasn't sure if that was better or worse. Whatever the final move would be, her world was shrinking. No Jews were allowed to own businesses anymore; no Jewish children were allowed to attend school. Every pathway to every kind of a future was closed.

She stopped in the middle of the yard, ignoring the depleted woodpile and the hay spilling in messy clumps across the front of the stables. She'd made the mistake of looking up towards the horizon, and now the longing to be in a flower-fragrant meadow or, better still, high up on a ridge with no space in her head for anything except finding the next foothold was overwhelming. She couldn't focus on her tasks, not yet, whatever the consequences. She needed a moment to breathe. She made her way to the edge of an uncut field instead of the stables and sank down out of sight in the long grass.

Let's leave here together... Let's go...

She'd desperately hoped Pascal would say yes when she'd blurted that out in the hotel and told him she loved him without actually saying the words. She should have known that he wouldn't, that his ties to his father and the Party were too strong. That had upset but not surprised her. But the depth of his blindness, his certainty that he could persuade men who wore hatred like a medal to look kindly on 'good Jews', had been a shock. She'd fallen back on blaming Viktor's influence then, to soften the blow, but Pascal wasn't a child; he'd made his own choices.

I should have gone away without him.

That wasn't a thought that brought any comfort. Leaving Germany with her parents could have been a solution, but only in a different life. They'd waited too long in the hope that things might improve and missed the moment to make it happen. Emigration demanded resources they didn't have: the family's cumulative earnings barely totalled one non-Jewish salary and certainly wouldn't pay for a passage or cover the fees the Nazis extorted from its fleeing Jewish population. Besides, even if they'd had the money, they didn't have the contacts – there was no one in America or England to vouch for them. There was nowhere for them to go abroad; they couldn't even travel inside Germany. Freedom of movement for Jews had been restricted since the end of 1938, and the local police chief wouldn't have signed a travel pass if her family had asked for one. He was firmly under Viktor's thumb, and Viktor was firmly the king of Unterwald. The Drachmanns were trapped in a town, and a country, that didn't want them. Which was why Noemi rarely looked up at the mountains anymore; she couldn't bear their promise of freedom.

'Girl! Girl! Where are you?'

Noemi was about to jump up and respond to Herr Distel's call, but some sixth sense stopped her. She shuffled to the edge of the grass instead and peered out, making sure she couldn't be seen. Distel was standing on the porch, his gun in his hand. And Viktor Lindiger was standing beside him.

He's coming for me. He's coming for us all.

Oddly, the first emotion which struck her wasn't fear. She'd been waiting for this day on some level since the war began. Or since the night in November 1938 when a band of thugs in Hitler Youth uniforms had roamed through the town, singing songs about spilling Jewish blood, and wreaking havoc. Most of them had been bussed in from Munich, or so the gossip went, although where they'd come from seemed the least-important thing about them to Noemi. The boys had certainly been well briefed; they knew who they were looking for. They'd smashed and looted Herr Schuster's tailor shop and thrown stones through the Drachmanns' windows. They'd set fire to the trees bordering Herr and Frau Fleck's home, causing Herr Fleck to have a fatal heart attack the next morning. Frau Fleck had left the town a week later. The Schusters were living in circumstances as reduced as the Drachmanns. Neither family had felt safe since that night, and their nerves kept being tested. Soldiers returning home on leave brought stories about Polish Jews being forced into ghettoes and being made to wear armbands embroidered with the Star of David. 'So they're easier to catch,' according to one of the farmhands who'd stared pointedly at Noemi as he'd said it. So not fear then, but a strange sense of relief that the danger had stopped lurking and revealed itself.

If it's out in the open, at least I can see what I'm fighting.

Viktor was scanning the farmyard; Herr Distel had shouldered his gun. Noemi instinctively twisted onto her stomach and scanned her options. She'd hunted enough prey herself to know what animals under threat did. They froze. They lay low and blended in with their surroundings. And, when they moved, it was rarely in a straight line.

And they still get caught far too easily.

Noemi refused to listen to that. She took a moment to calm her pulse and survey her surroundings. The hay field beside her hadn't been harvested yet and the stalks were high. If she could cross it without being detected, she could reach the road which circled the back of the town and was too rough for Viktor to risk driving his precious car across. She began to crawl in that direction, keeping to the tracks the farmhands had made, only rising to a crouch when she was well inside the thickest cover. Luckily, the wind was blowing the stems in the direction she needed to go, which would camouflage her movements.

She forced herself to stay as focused as she would on a mountaintop and to push away the dangers, including the possibility that Viktor had gone for her parents or the Schusters first. That wouldn't have been a logical move. She was the quickest. She was the one who could get to everybody else and warn them to hide…

Where?

She stumbled as she hit the path, twisted her ankle, lost her breath. Where could any of them go? Who, if anyone, would shelter them? She ploughed on, trying to imagine each step as a foothold, telling herself she could reach it. Anything not to panic at the thought of what might be happening in the town and freeze.

'Noemi. Noemi. Wait.'

The voice wasn't Viktor's, and it wasn't a shout. It didn't sound like someone trying to raise the alarm. That didn't mean she could trust it. She scanned the path for a rock or a stick, anything she could use as a weapon.

'It's all right. It's me. It's Carina.'

Noemi didn't have time to decide if that was all right or not. Carina was at her side, a hand on her elbow, her eyes nervously scanning the path behind them.

'Listen to me. You can't go home; you can't go to Unterwald at all. Your parents have already been taken.' She grabbed Noemi as she started to sway and held her close. 'There was a phone call for Viktor, to tell him that the round-up had gone ahead but you were missing. I didn't dare go to Distel's and warn you – that could have been disastrous for us both. But I prayed you'd take this route, not the main road, if you managed to get away. I've been waiting here for you.'

'I don't know what to do.'

Noemi's mind had gone blank at *your parents have been taken.* The fear she'd been running from finally crashed in. Her head was filled with the impossibility of *what if I never see them again?* and wouldn't hold another thought. Luckily, Carina, for once, had found enough strength for the two of them.

'You come to the farm.' She tightened her hold as Noemi tried to spring away. 'You have to trust me. I don't know exactly what part Viktor's played in this, but I do know he'd never suspect me of helping you or of hiding you under his nose. There's an unused barn where you'll be safe, at least until we work out how to get you away from here.'

It wasn't until they were inside the barn on the furthest edge of the Lindiger property that Noemi thought to ask Carina the obvious question.

'Why are you helping me? I know Viktor's hurt you before. God knows what he'd be capable of if he catches you doing this. Why would you put yourself in such danger?'

Carina glanced down at her wrist and automatically tugged at her sleeve. But her new-found courage didn't falter.

'Because I don't believe Jews are any different to anyone else, whatever Hitler or my husband says. Because my son loves you, even if he doesn't have the sense to see that matters more than his dreams of glory. And because I always hoped you'd be my daughter one day. I still do, despite all these horrible new rules.'

She shook her head at Noemi's exhausted, 'How can that ever be possible?'

'I don't know. But I have to hope that these men will be beaten one day; anyone with an ounce of humanity has to want that. And whatever his flaws – and I'm not blind to those, especially the way he only sees what he chooses – Pascal is not his father. So I'm deciding to put my trust in that, and praying he eventually comes to his senses and stops believing the Führer is some kind of messiah.'

Noemi sank down on a straw bale, wishing she had even a fraction of Carina's faith. 'I want to believe that too, but I don't: he's in far too deep. The last time I saw him, he told me he planned to become one of the inner circle and make the Party understand that some Jews were "good" and deserved to be treated better than the "bad" ones. I couldn't get him to realise how wrong and deluded that was.'

Carina sighed. 'That hurts me to hear it. I've no idea how he can be that short-sighted, or naive, or why he can't admit that all this dreadful separating is wrong. But I can't hate him for being a fool or for going to fight; he's my son. I hope you can find it in your heart not to hate him too, although I've no right to ask it.'

But I don't hate him, despite everything, and that's the worst of it. I want to, but I can't.

It would have been a kindness to admit that to Carina – it was what the woman's bravery deserved. But Noemi could barely admit it to herself, so the only thing she had to offer was her silence.

* * *

'Noemi, are you awake? It's me. It's safe to come down.'

The voice pulled her out of a deep sleep and plunged her into confusion. She had no idea who *me* was. But it wasn't Carina calling her, so how could it be safe? There was no point, however, in hiding if she'd been uncovered; that could make things worse for Carina, never mind her. She shuffled out of the sacks she'd been using for the last three nights as bedding and carefully approached the hay loft's edge. It was dark outside – her wristwatch said it was not quite three o'clock. The only brightness came from a circle of pale yellow lamplight below her. And the voice belonged to Pascal.

She couldn't stop staring at him, although she couldn't speak. It was the first time she'd seen him in almost three years. The jump from seventeen to twenty suited him. He'd grown taller; the rest of his body had filled out to match his broad shoulders. There was a strength to his jaw which had turned his face from attractive to handsome. He looked different but somehow the same.

Except he can't be, not if everything Carina's told me about his war is true.

She had to hold on to the truth of that, to stop her heart racing. She had to see the man he'd become. The Pascal who had left Sonthofen as soon as the war started and joined the First Mountain Division. The one who'd fought in Poland and was an officer now; who'd been on dangerous training missions in France. Pascal had become the soldier he'd always wanted to be, which had to make him a danger to her.

Or it would, if he was wearing a uniform.

Noemi's head began whirling as fast as her heart. He'd gone to be a soldier, but he hadn't come looking for her dressed as one. All the longing she'd refused to let herself acknowledge since she'd walked out of the hotel came instantly flooding back.

He's left the army like I wanted him to; he's come home for me. He's going to stand up to his father and help mine, and make everything right.

The hope Carina hung on to that Pascal would one day see sense surged through Noemi too, and she gasped from the joy of it. But then he lifted the lantern a little higher and she saw the edelweiss *Gebirgsjäger* pin on his lapel next to his Party badge, and that hope and that joy rushed away just as fast.

'What do you want? Have you come to arrest me? Are you going to hand over your mother to the Gestapo as my accomplice?'

Pascal sucked in a long breath, but he didn't rise to her goading. 'No, I'm not going to do any of that. I'm here to help you, to take you to the station. There's a goods train due in two hours which will get you as far as Munich.'

Her too-willing heart told her to believe him, but her head wasn't ready to let her come down from the loft. 'What are you doing here? Your mother said she thought you were in France; she never said you were coming home.'

'She didn't know.' He hesitated for a moment, as if he wasn't sure how much he should tell her. 'I was in France for a while, that's true, but now I'm being deployed to the Russian front. They need mountain fighters there. I've been given a few days' leave first.'

He hadn't stopped being a soldier then. But he hadn't said anything about honour or glory, or how being an officer felt, and that was a welcome change.

Noemi moved a little closer to the ladder. 'Why would Carina tell you I was here? Hasn't that put you in a difficult position? What if your father finds out? Whose side will you take then?'

She expected him to hesitate before answering and then fall back on old ties. Her heart skipped a beat when he didn't.

'I don't care about anything except helping you. My mother understands that, and as for my father – he doesn't suspect a thing, and he's left for a conference in Berlin, so this is the perfect time to move you. I can't blame you if you don't trust me, but please let's not waste a chance that could be your last one.'

Noemi knew he was telling the truth. She was also aware how quickly time was ticking and that she needed to act if she was going to catch the train, but she had one question left that Pascal needed to answer the right way before she could move.

'Never mind about me; can you do anything to help my parents?'

Pascal looked down for a moment, and that movement – that break in their eye contact which had been drawing her in – told her the response she wanted wasn't coming. It was all she could do not to burst into tears.

'No, I can't. I'm sorry. There's been an allegation that they were using an old key to access the café and steal food.' He spread his hands as Noemi started to argue. 'I know that's not true, but it's in the law's hands now. Hopefully there will be a resolution soon, but you can't wait for it.'

He hasn't changed. You have to ignore your heart. You have to hold on to that and forget everything that was and everything that might have been. You have to be as strong as you were when you walked away from him the last time.

She clung on to that certainty for dear life.

'Why will there be a resolution? Because they're *good* Jews?' She was glad he flinched – she wanted him to. 'You say you're here to help me, but then you pretend justice exists for Jewish people. That hasn't been true for years. If you really want me to trust you, tell me one honest thing. Let's see if you can do that – or go and I'll take my chances without you.'

The silence stretched as Pascal struggled, leaving Noemi to wonder how deeply his year at Sonthofen and his years of combat had marked him, and how deeply his already blind faith now ran. She didn't interrupt when he finally began talking.

'Fine. You're right, justice has... changed. Whatever the reason that was given for the Unterwald round-up, it's part of a wider sweep. Jews are being interned, or moved out of their homes and relocated, across the entire country, for their own protection. Given where we are, it's most likely that your parents have been sent to the prison camp at Dachau.' He stopped and sucked in a breath that told Noemi more than she wanted. 'I don't know much about that place either, except that it's... well, challenging might be a good way to describe it from what I've heard. And I can't help them, although I wish I could, but whatever else happens, I don't want you put in there too. So let me help you instead, please. That's all I want to do – I swear it.'

For their own protection.

He could believe that old lie. Noemi didn't. But she came down the ladder anyway, chilled by the look in his eyes when he'd said *Dachau*. She wasn't sure how much she could trust him or anyone, but at least now there was a reason for going to Munich. From the little she knew of the camp, it was close to the city. If Hauke and Frieda were there, she might be able to find a way to get them out.

They edged around each other, avoiding eye contact, staying out of each other's reach. Pascal had brought her a bag with food and money, some hot water for washing and clean clothes he told her to change into.

'They're my mother's, but she's altered them so they'll fit you. It's important you look... It's important you don't attract the wrong kind of attention.'

He didn't say, *clean and tidy and not like a Jew,* but Noemi heard that anyway. She knew the stereotypes. But she was too embarrassed at what he said next to take issue with him.

'If we meet anyone on the way to the station, which we shouldn't given how early it is, I'll have to pretend we're a couple to protect you. Do you understand what I mean?'

He'll have to pull me into his arms. He'll have to kiss me so my face is hidden.

What had once been the best thing she could imagine was suddenly the worst. She couldn't let herself be that vulnerable to him again. She also couldn't argue and put them both in danger. She nodded and turned away, waiting for him to go outside so she could change into the summer skirt and jacket Carina had sent. That done, she bundled her old clothes under a pile of sacks for Pascal or Carina to collect later and – mindful of not drawing attention in Munich – she added her identity papers, which were stamped with a letter *J* and the middle name *Sarah* which all Jewish women were legally obliged to use. It felt as if she was shedding one skin with no idea what the next would look like or even if it would fit. And she didn't have time to fret about it. But she did have one last thing to leave behind, so she called him back in.

'You should take this.'

She held out the blue enamelled locket. Pascal stared at it as if he didn't know what it was.

'It's your mother's, the one you left for me in the hut after...' She couldn't finish the sentence, and she didn't understand why Pascal's eyes had suddenly reddened.

'I thought you must have thrown it away. I wouldn't have blamed you if you had. You didn't give it back, and my mother's never mentioned you wearing it.'

'That's because I didn't wear it.'

That wasn't strictly true, but it was all Noemi would give him. She'd never been able to explain why she'd kept the locket

– or worn it in her room or tucked into her dress on the days and nights when loneliness overwhelmed her – to herself. She wasn't about to let him think it mattered now.

'And I can't take it with me. No Jew would still have a piece of jewellery like this – wearing it would get me picked up in a heartbeat. You need to return it to your mother.'

He took it; he didn't argue. There was too much truth in her words. He stowed it away in his pocket and followed her out of the barn.

They met no one on the way to the station, to her relief; there was no need for him to hold her and test her resolve. When they reached the empty platform, the line was already starting to hum.

'What do I do when I get there?'

She was finally leaving Unterwald after years of thinking that was the only sensible thing to do. But the circumstances were all wrong, and she wasn't ready. She was alone. She didn't know Munich; the visit to the prison had been her first and last time in the city. She didn't know its rhythms or its rules, or who she was supposed to be when she got there. And for all she'd tried to keep the panic from her voice, Pascal heard it.

'Don't be Jewish. Get new papers however you can. Be you – watchful and careful and braver than anybody I know. And be safe, Noemi. For my sake, be safe.'

His eyes added so much to his words, Noemi felt herself faltering. She took a sudden, unplanned step towards him, but the train was approaching and there was no time to waver. Pascal had already explained that it would slow to a crawl as it passed through the station, so the guard could throw the town's mail bags onto the platform. That she would only have a moment or two when it did so to jump into one of the open wagons at the back. They hadn't discussed what would happen if all the freight cars were sealed up, or if she missed her footing, or if the train didn't slow down. There was no time to discuss it now. The front carriages were already alongside the platform. She didn't have a moment; she had seconds.

The doors on the last carriage were open. Noemi sprinted out from the hedgerow where they'd been hiding. She jumped with all her force, swung herself over the wagon's edge and landed on the hard wooden floor as the train began to pick up speed. She was winded, but she was in one piece. She'd done it.

But I didn't say a proper goodbye.

She scrambled up off her knees and turned back to the open door, not caring if anyone saw her. Pascal was heading to the Russian front, into a battle Herr Distel had predicted would be the biggest bloodbath to come.

Never mind not saying goodbye, I've let him go without telling him the truth.

She told him then. She flung the 'I love you' she'd sworn never to say out into the dawn. But the train was roaring at top speed down the tracks and twisting away from Unterwald. She shouted the words again, telling herself that the wind was strong and the wind would carry them. It was too late. The station was no bigger than a speck in the dust. Pascal was gone. And the love which she'd carried and fought against for so long could never be more than a memory.

PART TWO

CHAPTER EIGHT
JUNE 1941

'What are you doing here? Are you trying to get yourself arrested?'

Don't let him see that you're scared. Take the upper hand.

Noemi turned round, pretending her heart was beating at the right rhythm, furious at being so easily caught out. She'd been focused on trying to make sense of the camp, which was far bigger than she'd expected it to be, and hadn't heard the man approaching. That wasn't a mistake she'd make twice.

'Why do you want to know? You're dressed as a civilian and you're sneaking about, so I could ask you the same question. All I have to do is start screaming and those guards will be here in a flash.'

It was bravado. Nothing would have induced Noemi to attract the attention of the soldiers patrolling back and forth outside the camp gates. But it was also a good test. The flicker of admiration in his eyes and the step he took away from her suggested she wasn't in immediate danger.

'No one needs to scream – I'm not here to hurt you. But I would like to know what you're doing. Especially given you were here yesterday as well, standing in the same spot.' He shook his head as she clenched her fists. 'I don't work for them, I promise. I'm watching the camp, same as you.'

That was a risky admission for one stranger to make to another, a stone's throw from Dachau. Noemi let her hands fall and took a moment to properly look at her interrogator. He was closer to her age than his tired face had suggested at first glance, somewhere in his early twenties. His dark-blue shirt and black trousers were respectable-looking, but they were also showing signs of wear and tear. There was a small rip in his rolled-up sleeve, and one of his belt loops was missing.

He's in hiding from the Nazis like me. He could be Jewish. Whatever he is, I can trust him.

She had nothing to base that on except *watching*, and a worn shirt and a hunch, but – from his next question – he'd apparently come to a similar conclusion about her.

'Do you have people in there – is that it? Were you hoping to see them?'

She could have said no. But that would have required her to make up a story to explain why she was hiding in the trees for the second day in a row. Noemi had become very adept at making up stories in the brief time she'd already spent in Munich, but – even though she'd proved to be good at it – the process of collecting and selecting the right details to use wasn't an easy one.

My bag was stolen. My papers were lost. I've come from the countryside to take a job in a factory.

She'd told anything but the truth since she'd jumped out of the train as it eased to a stop in a vast goods yard somewhere on the edge of the city. She'd crossed that by hopping from behind one set of parked wagons to the next, before slipping through an unlocked side gate into a street with no landmarks. That had been a long and lonely moment. She'd arrived with no papers and no map. She had the kind of colouring that marked her out as Jewish, not Aryan. She'd half expected to be spotted and caught the second she left the wagon. She certainly couldn't ask anyone for help. And whatever she did to stay safe, as Pascal had begged her to do, she might not survive. It had been a long moment, but she'd had to pull herself out of it. She'd taken one step and then another; she'd forced herself to trust that she was heading towards the city, not away. The relief when she'd begun spotting signs to the Hauptbahnhof and Königsplatz – the places she remembered from her one visit to Munich – was as good as successfully tackling a difficult summit.

As more early risers had joined her and the pavements started to fill, Noemi had begun to feel a little less vulnerable and more confident about trying to ferret out information. She'd attached herself to the edges of a group of women standing on a street corner who were dressed in matching blue overalls and smoking multiple cigarettes. They'd smiled when she took out one of her own and accepted a light, completely unaware she was listening with a bat's ear to their chatter.

The girls were on their way to the Ritter factory in a suburb called Pasing, two pieces of local knowledge which gave Noemi a place of work she could refer to when she looked for a place to stay. Unfortunately, that had proved to be a more difficult challenge than eavesdropping. In the first boarding house she went into, ready to trot out her new story, the desk clerk's response to her smiling, 'Good morning,' was to glance at her dark hair and dark eyes and demand her papers. When she couldn't instantly produce those, he'd reached for the telephone. Noemi had fled, convinced sirens would come after her within minutes.

At the second establishment, she was quicker to explain that her papers had been lost on her way to the city. The clerk there didn't pick up the phone, but he wouldn't check her in either. Noemi had finally turned into a side street where the boarding houses were a long way from respectable and the only thing of interest was her money. The room she'd moved into had peeling paint and sagging nets and a view onto a brick wall. But it was a roof and a bed, and she'd told herself it would do until she could get a better sense of the city and a feel for how she might live in it.

She'd attempted that the next morning after a fitful night's sleep punctuated by loud curses from the alley outside. She'd walked its streets and squares for hours, feeling even further from home – and further from safety – with every step. Munich was Nuremberg on a more intense scale: it was a city forged from uniforms and temples to National Socialism. The pavements were choked with men bearing air force wings on their chests, or silver lightning flashes on their shoulders, or – in the case of the ones spilling out of the taverns by early afternoon – the dazed look of soldiers on leave. The buildings were a lofty procession of columns and banners, an echo of the homage to ancient Rome Noemi had seen years ago at the Nuremberg rally. And – as they had in 1938 when she couldn't find a place to get her exhausted mother a cup of tea – every shop and café and bar bore the same sign: *Jews Forbidden*.

Don't be Jewish.

Pascal had understood the kind of world she was running towards and its scale.

But he wouldn't have thrown me into it unless he'd thought I could manage.

That wasn't much comfort, but it forced her to do what he'd told her to do and be someone else. She'd cast off the previous day's nerves, squared her shoulders and put her head up, staring down anyone who looked twice at her. She'd sat in the corner of a busy nondescript café as if she belonged there and eaten a plate of *spaetzle* and sausages without anybody challenging her, although every mouthful tasted of sawdust. The next morning, she'd successfully bought a train ticket from a distracted clerk without being asked for her papers and set out to find the camp at Dachau, determined to make contact with her parents. They were little victories, but they were victories. And they'd lulled her into a false sense of security.

Were you hoping to see them?

All at once she couldn't speak. The obvious answer to the man's question was yes, except Noemi now knew how hopeless that was. Nothing had prepared her for what she'd found once she'd stepped into the woods. Certainly not the pretty town she'd walked through from Dachau station, with its comfortable cream houses and wide tree-lined streets. Or the *challenging* that Pascal had used to describe the place. She didn't know this man well enough to admit that she'd thought a camp might involve tents, not high walls and watchtowers and barbed wire. Or machine guns and dogs. She didn't want him to think she was a fool or know how terrified she was for her parents. So she settled instead for a shrug and a qualified, 'Yes, but I underestimated how hard it would be.' She wasn't prepared for his compassion.

'I'm so sorry. You must have arrived here with hope – everyone does until they see what they're dealing with. I assume you came back today because at least standing here keeps you close to them.'

She'd been right about him. He understood. He looked away and didn't judge her despair while she got herself back under control. When Matthias offered her his name, Noemi – who'd been viewing everyone new she'd encountered for years as a threat – instinctively knew she'd found a friend. It wasn't easy to surrender to that impulse – without Hauke's voice ringing in her ears and reminding her that her instincts were exactly what she should trust, she might not have managed it. The moment she did so, the tight band that had settled round her chest slipped away, and her tongue loosened.

'I'm Jewish. I come from a small town, not from here.'

She waited for the moment of betrayal. She waited for Matthias to tell her his kindness had been a trick, for him to call the guards to arrest her. She waited to be wrong. And could have cried with relief when he nodded at her to go on and she wasn't.

'There was only us and one other Jewish family left there after the Kristallnacht attacks, and it's been getting steadily harder since then. My parents lost their business; they lost everything. They went from being respected to being hounded. Now they're in here – or that's what I was led to believe – on some trumped-up charge based on hatred and jealousy.' She swallowed hard as the fury she'd kept in check for so long came bubbling to the surface. 'I escaped the round-up that caught them, but I can't get to them, or help them, can I?' She watched him looking her over and wondering. 'Tell me the truth – don't sugar-coat it. The only thing I can't cope with is not knowing.'

The admiration was back in his eyes as he answered. 'All right – if that's what you want. You can't help them if they're in there, no. And Dachau is brutal; I won't pretend it's not. They recruit eighteen-year-olds from the Hitler Youth who are all fired up with love of the Party and turn them into' – he glanced down at the gates – 'guards who don't know the meaning of mercy. People who've survived it – and some do, but rarely Jews – describe the violence inside as chaotic, without any connection between punishment and crime. And being spared that, or released, as a lottery.'

His words were too close to the lack of justice Hauke had experienced in Wittelsbacher for her to doubt him. She forced herself not to react to *brutal* or *chaotic* or *rarely*. She could see he had more to say.

'The other thing you should know is that there are no women in there. We monitor the camp and, as far as we can make out, women who are arrested and brought to Munich – particularly Jewish women – are sent on to another place somewhere outside Berlin. So your father could well be inside Dachau like you were told, but your mother won't be.'

The thought of them being separated was impossible. Frieda hadn't done well when Hauke was in prison the first time; he never did well without her. Noemi blinked hard; drew a deep breath. She couldn't afford to waste time on tears or self-pity – she needed to be strong enough for them all.

'You said, *as far as we can make out*. Do you have people in there too?'

He shook his head, but he didn't elaborate, leaving Noemi with no choice but to find the questions that he would answer.

'Okay. But I'm assuming you're operating outside the law in some way, that maybe you're Jewish too. And that there's a wider community here than just you.' Her breath came a little easier as he nodded. 'I've told you a lot, which I don't normally do, but that doesn't mean we know each other. I'm not asking you to trust me or tell me your secrets, any more than I'll volunteer mine. But I need help – I know that much. This place is full of more traps than I can see. So I need papers that aren't marked with a J, and a job to keep me afloat, until I work out what to do next. Is any of that possible?'

Matthias nodded. 'All of it. As long as you understand the danger you're putting yourself in if you go underground and pass yourself off as an Aryan. And the danger you'll put others in if you make a mistake or get captured, which many do. If that sounds too frightening, I understand and I'll walk away, if that's what you want.'

Be safe. For my sake, be safe.

Pascal had used *safe* as if it would save her, but it wasn't a word she understood anymore; it wasn't a state she believed in. Her parents weren't safe in the Nazis' brutal camps. If Pascal was right and Jews were being swept up all over Germany, and perhaps beyond, how could any form of safety exist?

If Hitler meant what he said about war leading to the annihilation of Europe's Jews, why would it?

Noemi looked down at the watchtowers and the barbed

wire. Dachau wasn't a place where people were sent for their own protection, which was also the lie that had been peddled to Hauke about Wittelsbacher. Dachau was a place where people, where Jews, went to disappear. No doubt the camp Frieda had been sent to was the same, and all the other camps and ghettos Noemi was certain existed even if she didn't yet know their names. Someone had to tell the world the truth about that. Someone had to stop the evil. Because if they didn't, if Germany went on and won the war and spread their prisons and their notions of vermin across Europe or further, nobody would ever be safe again. Noemi had no idea how to fight against a regime as well honed and powerful as the Nazis. She didn't know if any kind of resistance was possible – she'd only discovered a moment ago that resistance was what she was burning to do.

But I think I might have found the first step on the way there.

She stuck out her hand for Matthias to shake. 'It sounds frightening because it is, but that doesn't worry me. And if you're trying to find a way to work against them, which I think you might be, I want to be part of it. I want to derail the Nazis the way they've derailed me and my family, whatever that means, whatever the consequences.'

He took her hand, and this time he didn't just nod at her. He grinned.

CHAPTER NINE
SEPTEMBER–NOVEMBER 1941

Matthias – who was Jewish and Polish and, at twenty-two, only two years older than Noemi – proved to be a man of his word. He couldn't get her any information about Frieda or Hauke, but within a week of their first meeting, he'd found her the tools she needed to survive in the city, and he'd softened its dangers a little.

'You escaped the round-up, which means you'll be on a list somewhere, so we need to make a couple of small changes to your identity. Noemi's common enough, so you can keep that, but I've switched your last name to Denker, and I've moved your birthplace from Unterwald to Lenggries, which is only a couple of dozen miles away. It's best to keep things as simple as possible, so you don't make mistakes if you're challenged.'

Not making mistakes was Matthias's first rule. He coached Noemi through keeping her head up and maintaining eye contact whenever she was asked to hand over her papers. He told her to choose the most ordinary family she could think of from home and make their life her backstory. And he warned her not to make the most common mistake and change her brown hair for blond because even purchasing the dye to do it could set a nosey chemist on her trail. Under his guidance, Munich became a lot more manageable.

His advice and his contacts, and the veneer of confidence they gave her, allowed Noemi to move undetected around the city. The landlady he pointed her towards in the working-class Au district glanced over her papers and asked only the most basic questions about her life in Bavaria. Her new boss in the small brewery two blocks away had been happy to take her on when it was clear she understood the basics of brewing, something he apparently thought all country people knew. Nobody found a reason to question her, in the same way nobody questioned the pronounced limp and weak right arm Matthias adopted in public to avoid being asked why he wasn't at the front. The district was a hard-working and relatively poor one, its people more focused on the pressures the war was causing for their families and their livelihoods than the possibility Jews might be hiding in plain sight among them. Or so the Jews hiding among them thought.

'That should make for some good entertainment – they'll certainly be easier to spot.'

'You hear talk all the time that there's hundreds of them hiding in Munich, using fake papers and working alongside us. What do they call it? Going underground? Well they'd better watch out now there's rewards for catching them, or we'll properly put them down there.'

Everyone in Noemi's new circle had a similar snatch of gossip to pass on. All of it was damning; nobody was able to report any signs of concern or protest about the latest Nazi decree. All Jews over the age of six being forced to wear a yellow Star of David badge on their chests was apparently a popular move.

The group of young Jewish men and women who – like Noemi and Matthias – had found themselves alone in the city and had taken refuge in each other to stave off the loneliness and fear normally only met in groups of two or three. They weren't a resistance group in the way Noemi had imagined they might be, engaged in acts of sabotage and spying, although Matthias wished that they were. A few of them, like him, had chosen to monitor the Dachau camp and collect information about who was kept there, but most simply craved the reassurance that they weren't alone. And a wider meeting was a rare thing. It only happened when the Nazis shifted the ground, like they'd done with the stars, and forced one, because the risks involved were considerable.

Any large gathering that didn't include uniforms or drinking attracted attention. A group of slightly shabby, slightly nervous and predominantly dark-haired young people congregating together might as well have set up an advertising board. They couldn't use a public place or anyone's lodgings. Instead, they relied on a rabbi who no longer had a synagogue but had at least acquired a key to the factory where he was now forced to work and could offer them a brief place of sanctuary. It was Rabbi Mendel who'd organised that night's meeting – he was the only one who knew everybody's names. Now he sat twisting his hands in the darkened room as one after the other offered up the gossip they'd collected in Au's increasingly outspoken cafés and pubs.

'We've seen this pattern of enforced identity badges and imprisonment before, in Poland and parts of occupied Russia. It wouldn't surprise me if the next step is to build a ghetto the way they've done there. And – as some of the talk you've collected has mentioned – there's always a very generous system of rewards for bringing in anyone who's evaded the net. Which encourages the thugs. The whole process is intended to be—'

'Barbaric and terrifying?'

The Rabbi nodded as Noemi butted in. He tried to resume speaking, but she wasn't done yet.

'But we can't let it paralyse us. These badges cut Jews out of

German life, far more clearly than any of the Nazis' previous laws. You said it yourself, Rabbi: they mark us out, they make us into targets, and then they dump us into ghettoes. And God knows what happens after that. So surely we have to hit back this time, before they get a chance to really get started? I don't see that we have a choice.'

The room had tightened on *ghettoes*. It broke apart on *hit back*.

'What do you mean, we've no choice? What on earth d'you think we can do? We're ex-students living in hiding, not masters of guerilla warfare.'

'Are you trying to get us arrested – or killed? Don't you understand we're just trying to survive?'

The voices flew from all corners, but not from everyone. Half the room was shouting at her, but half – including Matthias – was silent and waiting to hear what she was about to say next, and that gave Noemi hope, if not a clear plan.

'I do understand that; I'm trying to do the same. I can't help my parents, which is why I came here in the first place, but I have to do something. And I know the idea of fighting in any way is a tough one, especially as most people here have never handled a weapon. But the thing is, some of us have.'

She nodded to Matthias, who had spent his early teenage years in the forests round Warsaw, learning to hunt with his grandfather. And Vitta, whose father had been an Olympic marksman when Jewish athletes were permitted to take part in sports and had passed his passion for shooting onto his daughter.

'And none of us are killers, which is what you seem to be suggesting should be our next step. That's quite a leap for anyone.'

Everyone turned to the rabbi. Noemi knew how much influence he had, including over Matthias. Matthias's German father had studied medicine in Munich before he'd met and fallen in love with a Jewish girl from Poland and made Warsaw his home. Matthias had come to the city to follow in his father's footsteps. He'd told Noemi that it was Mendel who'd helped him manage his first days as a medical student in the city, when he was lonely and unsure why he'd agreed to come to a country which was increasingly hostile to Jews. And it was Mendel who had taken him in when Germany had invaded his country and the German cousins who'd reluctantly offered him a home had finally decided he was too Polish and too Jewish to stay. The rabbi did everything he could to bring more Jewish escapees into the fold and had a wide network of contacts to help with that, but he was a pacifist. He wasn't a supporter of active resistance in any form. If he told the group there was nothing to do but dig themselves deeper shelters, that's what they would do. And that wasn't enough anymore for Noemi.

She turned to Mendel and began to choose her words as carefully and honestly as she could. 'I know it is. I've never shot anything bigger than a rabbit. I've certainly never imagined killing a person, and – although I want to find a way to strike back against the Nazis – I didn't come here tonight intending to advocate for violence. I need you to know that before I say anything else.' She gave him a moment to appraise her and to nod. 'But the things that are being said, the hatred and the threats... They're getting worse; they're going to go on getting worse, and I can't sit and wait for someone to turn me in to the Gestapo. So I want to make some kind of a stand against them, or I want to try. And if that involves taking up weapons, so be it.'

'Why, Noemi? Do you think using their methods against them will change their minds about us? Do you think an assassination, or a bomb, or whatever's in your head, will save Germany's Jews?'

There was nothing unkind or accusatory in the rabbi's question – his voice was as gentle as his face. Noemi focused on that, not the tension crackling around her.

'No, I don't. It could lead to worse; it could lead to reprisals. And none of us have ever planned or carried out any kind of an attack before, so perhaps it's a crazy idea. But what if we did try to hurt them and it worked? What if we could prove the Nazis aren't the supermen they claim to be? What if we could show that they're vulnerable, that maybe they could be beaten? Couldn't that help make the tide turn one day?'

Mendel didn't have an answer to that any more than she did, although he offered her a muted, 'Perhaps.' Noemi pulled her attention back from him and looked round their silent audience, trying to gauge the wider reaction. It was mostly shock and shaking heads. Nobody was behaving as if they were on her side.

'I know I'm not speaking for everyone. I wouldn't try to. I don't even have a plan yet. And I don't expect anyone to follow me if I make one. We all have to follow our own hearts.'

'I can get guns. At least two, possibly three.'

The room swivelled from Noemi to Vitta.

'I have a friend who... Well he isn't Jewish if that matters to you, but he was a communist, and that's given him as many reasons to hate the Nazis as us. He'd go after them himself, except they broke his legs in Dachau and left him crippled, but he knows people. If I ask him, he'll get what we need, for the right price. And I'm with you, so I'll ask him.'

'I'm with you too.'

The room started to argue again as Matthias added his name to the mix, although they stopped when he called for quiet.

'And I also agree with Noemi: how any of us choose to resist is a personal matter. Even staying free and out of their clutches is powerful. So there's no pressure on anyone here, and we understand if you don't want to meet with us again after tonight. That probably would be the safest choice.' He looked across at Rabbi Mendel. 'And I won't ask for your blessing – that wouldn't be fair. But I hope you won't condemn us.'

Mendel looked at Matthias, then at Vitta and Noemi before he answered. 'I can't bless you if you choose violence, that's true, and I certainly won't carry a gun. But I'd never condemn you, and I won't abandon you either. Whatever you decide to do, if you need my help when it's done, you must ask for it.'

Vitta moved to sit next to Matthias and Noemi and added her thanks to the rabbi. The rest of the room fell into an uncomfortable silence after that; no one else volunteered to get involved.

Mendel gave Matthias the key to the room as he said his goodbyes in case they needed a safe haven at short notice, although he warned them not to use it more than once. Soon people began slipping away after him into the night until there were only the three of them left. Watching each other, aware they'd crossed a line which had led them away from the companionship they'd come to rely on and could lead them into terrible danger. Each of them wondering, *What now?*

'I keep going round and round in circles. Hitler or Himmler would be the ideal choice and they visit the city a lot, but they're both impossible targets. They're out of their cars and into their offices in minutes, and surrounded by the SS and the Gestapo at public events. We'd never get close to either of them.'

Noemi pulled her coat tight against the autumn wind blowing across the empty sweep of Munich's English Garden and watched the leaves dance in golden coils round her feet. It had taken three weeks of scraping every available penny together and trusting in Vitta's mysterious contact to get to this point. The price had risen twice during the negotiations, and that had turned the deal into two guns not three, but now the weapons had finally appeared. Luger P08 semi-automatic pistols, with a magazine and eight cartridges each and an accuracy of up to fifty metres. Noemi, who'd been expecting something far less sophisticated, had weighed her gun in her hand and watched Matthias doing the same, as Vitta outlined how much damage the pistols could do even from further away. They'd gone through all the mechanics of firing them that day, but they hadn't – then or since – discussed how it might feel to shoot a bullet into a body.

Because we don't know. Any more than the soldiers who marched into Poland knew what to expect. And, by the time we do, it will be too late. We'll be changed whatever the outcome.

She shivered, but she let Matthias think that was the ice nipping through the stiff breeze. She'd started to study him, which felt a little odd: she'd never had to work hard to understand Pascal. Matthias was brave, she didn't doubt that: he'd insisted Vitta had done enough and it should be him not her wielding the second weapon. He was also guarded, and she didn't know a lot about him yet. She was as sure as she could be that Matthias was no more cavalier about the act of killing than she was, but all their conversations had focused on possible targets and the problems of planning and logistics and – now that Noemi had a potentially workable idea, and time was ticking – she needed more surety.

'You're right about mounting anything in central Munich being impossible. The last time Hitler was here, every inch of the route from Karolinenplatz to Königsplatz was a forest of SS guards. But we don't need to carry out an attack there or on him. As long as we hit at their heart, and do it in the most public way possible, that's a win, isn't it?'

His, 'Yes, of course,' was as instant and trusting as she needed it to be, and so was his response to her newly formed plan. He didn't interrupt while she outlined it. He asked carefully considered questions. He was as methodical as Pascal had been when they were planning a new climb, not that a comparison between the two men was something Noemi wanted to consider or to dwell on, even if it kept happening. Matthias would hardly thank her for judging him against a Nazi.

'It will be incredibly dangerous wherever we do it, and there's no guarantee we'll succeed. But the targets are good ones and the risks are less than the other options we've considered. So...'

If it feels wrong, stop. It doesn't matter what the reason is – a change in the weather, an unsteady rock face, a partner who's lost their nerve.

Hauke's words were suddenly there in her head, and Noemi realised that she couldn't carry on pretending that the precipice wasn't dancing in front of them, or only having half the conversation they needed to have. She wasn't working in tandem with a man she knew inside out this time, and that was a risk to them both.

'So the only thing left to think about is us and whether we can actually do this. Take a life, I mean. I know we've not talked about it, but it's not a thing I take lightly, and I don't imagine you do either.'

Matthias didn't respond straight away, which was a relief. She needed to know he was a man who carefully assessed not only the plan's risks but also its wider impact.

'I don't. I trained as a doctor; my intention was to save lives, not end them. If this works and I kill someone, I don't want that to be an act I'm proud of, whoever it is. I want to feel it; I want to be changed by it because that's the whole point, isn't it? To feel and to take charge, not to wait and shut down and accept? For as long as we're able to do it.'

He was a good man. She'd known that since they'd first met, but now Noemi could see it in the time he took to acknowledge the weight in *kill*. And the bravery in *I want to feel it*. No matter how much she agreed with him, that remained a daunting thought.

So picture it. Imagine the gun and the magazine heavy with bullets in your hand and your finger squeezing the trigger. Imagine the impact and the blood and the scream.

'Stop, Noemi. Leave it there. Trying to guess how hard it will be won't help you to do it.'

She looked up. Matthias was watching her as if he was trying to read her thoughts. She nodded, but she didn't reply. Finding herself even partly in tune with someone else again was reassuring, but it stirred up old memories she'd rather not revisit. And implied a new closeness with Matthias she wasn't ready to consider. Despite that, she followed him back through the darkening park with a lighter step. The connection might be uncomfortable, and unlooked for and unexpected, but if it led to a plan they could execute together, she wouldn't shy from it.

The ninth of November. It was one of the most sacred days in the National Socialist calendar. The day on which the Party commemorated its dead comrades from the 1923 Beer Hall Putsch with even more reverence in Munich, where the battle had happened, than anywhere else in Germany. It was, as Matthias had agreed, the perfect day to mount an attack that would tear at the heart of them. But there were hours of watching in the cold to get through first.

Noemi and Matthias mingled with the well-padded crowds gathered in front of the sixteen black sarcophagi laid inside the Honour Temples which dominated Königsplatz, waiting for Hitler to arrive and lay his wreath. The silence which had to be observed by anyone crossing or standing close to the memorials was in sharp contrast to the hysteria which normally greeted the Führer, or the booming fanfares Noemi would forever associate with Nuremberg. But, reined in or not, the fervour was there.

Soaked through the faces straining for a glimpse of their leader, quivering through the tightly packed bodies. Neither of them wanted to be part of that; it was all Noemi could do not to shrink away from the sighs and the shivers. Unfortunately, they had no choice: they had to be at the memorial, monitoring every minute of the day, alert for even the tiniest change.

Noemi watched the arms shoot up as the Führer's cavalcade approached, noting the fact that it was exactly on time. Once they'd decided where the attack was going to take place – during the celebration of youth rally to be held later in the day at the Dachau Palace, which was a short train ride outside the city – she and Matthias had fretted for days over the best way to pin down the Nazis' plans. They'd presumed that security would be watertight given how many dignitaries were expected to be in attendance. All they'd actually had to do in the end was to spend their evenings sitting in the corners of the pubs frequented by the hordes of overexcited Hitler Youth boys who couldn't hold their drink. Munich, as it turned out, was a very leaky vessel.

The celebrations, which would continue to run like clockwork, began with the Führer and the wreath-laying ceremony. That completed, he would retire to the sanctuary of his mountain retreat in Berchtesgaden, handing over the reins for the rest of the day to Baldur von Schirach, the head of the Hitler Youth, and Ludwig Siebert, Ministerpräsident of Bavaria. The targets.

'So far so good. Once the bulk of the spectators have moved off, we'll go to the station along with the last bunch. If we're right, the hill should be crowded by the time we get there and it'll be easier to blend in.'

Noemi nodded as Matthias whispered a final check in her ear. They'd blended in perfectly well so far. They hadn't been able to source Hitler Youth or League of Girls uniforms – no one they knew had safe contacts for those – but they'd dressed carefully. Matthias wore a brown coat over a brown shirt and trousers, Noemi had found a black one to put over her dark skirt and white blouse; both of them were swaddled in thick scarves to hide their lack of Party badges. It would be packed tight on the train and dark by the time the main ceremony started – nobody would notice their clothes were a little loose and a little threadbare. Or suspect that a couple of illegal Jews with illegal pistols would be lurking among the revellers, on the hunt for two of the most important Nazis in Bavaria. As Noemi had pointed out when she'd explained her plan to Matthias, they at least had the element of surprise.

The next stage advanced perfectly too. Nobody gave them a second glance on the train from Munich to Dachau. The boisterous groups of young men and women crammed into it were too busy singing at the tops of their voices and flirting with each other to care about anyone but themselves. Noemi still kept her hat low and kept her distance from the uniformed girls. It might have been seven years since Nuremberg, and she was twenty not thirteen, but she had a feeling a punch like the one she'd delivered wouldn't have been easily forgotten, and she had no desire to spot – or be spotted by – a familiar face.

'Here we go.'

She could hear the adrenaline in Matthias's voice as they got off the train and began making their way towards the gently sloping hill which led to the palace. The torchlit procession – which had been allowed because Reichsminister Göring, the head of the Luftwaffe, had personally guaranteed there wouldn't be any air raids that night – was already halfway up, its flames flickering across the dark hill like a spill of orange ribbon. They followed behind the singing crowds, reaching the summit and the huge cauldrons of fire set up in the grounds as the band began playing, the drums rising and falling in a hypnotic beat. The light from the torches and the firepits sent a gold-and-crimson arc into the sky which cast its rays down onto the blacked-out town below. And across the camp Noemi turned quickly away from.

'Inside there, hurry.'

They slipped into the shadow of the treeline as the crowds surged towards the stage where the dignitaries were waiting to start the speeches which would lead into the medal ceremony.

'There's younger children out there than I expected; they must have involved the junior leagues too. So it's even more important that we strike before the winners get called onto the stage. I don't want to kill a ten-year-old.'

Matthias looked as worried as she felt. It was a detail neither of them had planned for, but she knew he wouldn't turn back unless she asked him to, and they'd come too close to stop now. They separated at once as they'd agreed and edged carefully round the crowd to take up their positions on opposite sides of the stage. Her target was von Schirach; his was Siebert. So far, so good again. Except the plan had already started to shift out of shape.

Noemi swore under her breath as she located her sight line. The torches planted at the side of the stage had heated the cold air, distorting distances and blurring bodies. She took a deep breath and waited for her pulse to slow, trusting that Matthias – who must have encountered the same issue – was doing the same.

Everything is going to schedule; everything will be fine. A couple of glitches are nothing to worry about. And if my nerve starts to fail, I'll imagine the target is Viktor.

Her racing pulse eased as Dachau's mayor completed the introductions. According to the timetable of events everyone in Munich knew off by heart, Siebert would address the audience first, then von Schirach would speak. But both men would stand up together when the compère finished, to shake his hand and acknowledge the crowd's applause.

And that's when we shoot them, both at the same time. One burst and they're gone.

Noemi stopped thinking about *gone* or what was needed to get the men there. She let herself do what she'd been training to do for the past fortnight. She checked no one was nearby, she took the pistol carefully out of her pocket. She inserted the magazine, took another steadying breath, pulled the toggle back and raised her right arm, cupping her right hand with her left to ready the angle.

The official waved to his guests; the two men stood up. Noemi pictured Matthias's body mirroring hers. She pictured the moment of their success. Then she emptied her mind of everything but her target and fired. But the heat haze had blurred her angle, and Siebert and von Schirach didn't know the parts they needed to play for the plan to work. In the same second as the bullets burst from the barrels, one man stepped back and turned round; the other leaned to the side. The shots missed their targets. They ploughed into the rows behind.

Someone screamed, someone fell; a ripple of panic ran through the crowd. Noemi fired again and again until her magazine was empty and her hand was numb. It was too late. The two men who were supposed to be dead were very much alive and surrounded by a ring of armed guards whose guns were already blazing. The ripple of fear ran wider. The crowd began to push and shove, before breaking apart into hundreds of terrified boys and girls desperately trying to get away from the stage and the bullets flying in both directions. Noemi dropped her gun and kicked it away into the undergrowth. Her body wanted to run towards Matthias to check he was safe, but her brain wouldn't let it.

'Whether it goes right or wrong, we can't meet up anywhere near Dachau. We have to make our own way back to Munich, and wait a day before we contact each other.'

They'd both said it; they'd both agreed. But Noemi had

been as overconfident that day as her partner. She hadn't allowed for failure, or for the terror which had taken hold of the hill, and the very real possibility of injury or capture.

Crowds were already streaming past her as the gunfire continued, crying about bodies and murders and madmen. Every instinct told her that the chaos wouldn't be allowed to continue, that a cordon would appear in a minute or two and cut off the escape routes. She couldn't take her chances with that. She could only hope that Matthias would recognise the danger and save himself as quickly.

'Are you hurt? Did you see what happened?'

She flung herself into the nearest group of girls, no longer caring about familiar faces. She clutched on to the one who was crying the most, adding her own – not entirely fictitious – panic to the rising tide. Together they stumbled down the hill, Noemi sobbing as loudly as the rest, and scrambled onto a train, minutes before the Gestapo appeared, took control of the station and closed the line down.

CHAPTER TEN
JANUARY 1942

'The post's arrived. God knows where it's been – there's half a steppe's worth of mud in the bag, and the snow's made most of the names unreadable. But you got lucky, so maybe this'll cheer you up a bit and give us all a break.'

Pascal caught the envelope flying his way before it landed on the tent's dirt-packed floor and gathered another layer of grime; he let the insult go. He knew his men were unhappy with him, which wasn't an ideal state of affairs, but that wasn't his fault. Their behaviour had been... Pascal couldn't find the right word, although he'd been searching for it since dawn. Shocking? Cruel? Certainly not *a bit of fun*, which was how his junior officer had painted the scene. And if it really was *all the old Jew deserved*, as the soldiers involved had muttered, what did that say about them?

That they're doing exactly what Hitler would expect them to do. Treating Jews as if they're not human. He'd have been proud of them.

The thought had arrived in his head in Noemi's voice, and it had clung hard when he tried to shake himself free of it. Not that Pascal would accept it carried any merit. Yes, his second-in-command had stood in the village and grinned as the troops cut the beard off a terrified old Jewish man. And yes, the man had laughed when the soldiers had forced their bleeding trophy to clean a pair of dirty boots with his tongue. But the Führer wouldn't have been proud or amused, Pascal was certain of that, whatever laws he'd enacted. Hitler would have been as disgusted by the bullying as any decent German. He would have delivered the same furious lecture about dishonouring their uniforms as Pascal had done, and disciplined the poorly behaved officer.

It was a one-off, no more, an isolated incident. I've a bunch of bad apples under my command I need to straighten out.

He'd hit on that explanation as the morning's first light crept into his tent and decided it was a far better fit than Noemi's. Which was why he hadn't bit back at *cheer you up*, and wouldn't punish all the men involved, although that had been his first inclination. A calm approach was what was needed, a restating of what it meant to be a good German soldier. And he'd get started on that as soon as he'd read the letter he'd been waiting too long to receive.

The absence of any word from home since the battalion had arrived in Russia six months earlier had worn them all down. The official line was that the post couldn't keep up with the vast distances the Russian campaign had already forced the German troops to cover. Whatever the reason, the waiting had been drawn-out and dreadful. The letters were a lifeline for the soldiers, a connection to home; a reminder of who and what they were fighting for. The letters they wrote in return were a promise to their loved ones that they would survive. Pascal felt that as deeply as any of his men. Despite the delays, he'd written to his mother as regularly as he could, although he had no idea if the field service to Germany was any better than the one from it. His mother – who made almost no demands on him – had insisted on knowing he was safe and well as often as he could put pen to paper. Which was almost all he could tell her.

Russia wasn't Poland – Pascal had learned that very quickly. The Poles had been desperate to resist the German onslaught, but they'd lacked the manpower to do it, or the time to prepare a counter-attack, and the invasion there had been sharp and short-lived. The Russians were unbreakable. Even when they were in retreat, they fought with a ferocity that was terrifying. He couldn't tell Carina that. Even if a word of his feelings got through the censors, which was highly unlikely even for an officer, it would frighten her too much. And – unlike France, where he'd carried out a number of clifftop training missions after Poland – there was nothing interesting he could tell her about Russia. All he'd seen of the country was endless, exhausting flat plains which turned to yellow dust clouds when the troops marched through them and wore their legs out far faster than a mountain range could have done. And the weather was no better than the landscape.

Summer's oppressive heat and thick humid mists had given way to autumn's torrential rain and oozing mud. As for the winter... The mountain men were used to snow and ice, but not the depths of the relentless cold which had gripped Russia at the start of December and turned the wind into sheet ice. In the end, he'd fallen back on the kind of bland anecdotes about his comrades she told him about their neighbours in Unterwald, and hoped the sense of connection the letters brought her made her as happy as the sight of a long-overdue letter had made him.

He opened the envelope carefully – supplies were low and he might have to reuse it – and told himself it didn't matter that there was only one sheet of paper inside. That perhaps this letter had been written at a busy time on the farm and there were more to follow. Or, like his, it was short because there were things she couldn't or didn't want to say. Her letters had gaps in them too. She never mentioned his father beyond, *He is well.*

She never mentioned Noemi, not that Pascal expected her to. Noemi was a gap everywhere.

He shook his head and focused on the page in front of him, forcing his thoughts away from her. He couldn't lose himself in the empty space that was Noemi – or at least not today; not when home was finally with him.

Dear Pascal,

I hope this letter finds you well.

He stared at the writing in confusion. It wasn't his mother's rounded hand but his father's spikier style. And it was short, little more than a paragraph. Viktor had never written to him before, and there shouldn't have been a reason for him to start. Pascal read on, although every instinct told him he didn't want to.

I'm writing with unfortunate news. Your mother has passed away after a short illness. Please remember her in your prayers.

Your father,

Viktor Lindiger

He stared at the date and forgot all about his men's questionable behaviour. September the fifteenth 1941. She'd been dead for five months. He'd been writing to a ghost.

He turned the letter over, looking for some personal outpouring that would wipe away the coldness wrapped round *unfortunate* and the business-like signature.

There was nothing.

His hands began shaking as if the ice had crept in and coated them. Pascal rarely allowed himself to think badly of his father, but now the slam of *he never loved her* tore through his head. How could he have done, if he could despatch her so easily? *He never knew her; none of us did* followed so quickly, the ground lurched. His mother had lived in his father's shadow for as long as Pascal could remember. He'd become so used to it, he'd never questioned why she didn't seem to have a life or dreams of her own.

But she was different on my last leave. She was strong.

The pain took his breath away. Of losing her, of not knowing her. Of not thanking her properly for saving Noemi and putting herself into danger.

Which she did because she loved me and I loved Noemi, and nothing else ever mattered to her but the things that mattered to me.

The pain was a physical weight, pressing on his heart, squeezing his throat. He closed his eyes and let the tent and the frightened Russian villagers and the battle he was meant to be preparing for disappear. He wanted his mother, the way she'd been the last time he'd seen her. Bursting with love and refusing to be afraid. He wanted the memories, no matter how much they hurt...

'There was a round-up of the town's Jews and Noemi's family were taken. She escaped and she's hiding in the back barn.'

Of all the ways Pascal had imagined Carina greeting him when he appeared out of the blue on a short leave, that wasn't it. He dropped his bag, wondering why – given the insanity of what she'd said – she looked so proud of herself.

'How long has she been there?'

'Three days.' Carina poured him a cup of coffee he struggled to hold as he sank into a chair. 'Which is obviously too long, but I had to wait until your father left for his conference before I could move her. I was planning to do that tonight.'

'Where to?'

It seemed easier to ask simple questions than to grapple with the bigger picture that his mother was hiding a fugitive from his father. Or that Noemi, and her family, were in danger.

Carina sat down on the opposite side of the table, her face creasing into a frown. 'That's a good question. I don't know, to be honest. I didn't really think any of this through. The only thing that mattered was that she needed my help, so I gave it to her. And I know I've broken every command you and your beloved Nazis live by, but don't you dare tell me I did the wrong thing.'

Your Nazis.

Pascal didn't know how to respond to that; he wasn't sure who he was looking at. He'd always assumed his mother was as devoted to the Party as he and Viktor were. She'd never criticised either of them for their beliefs or said anything negative about Hitler's rise to power. Yet now here she was, saying *your* and putting herself firmly on the other side of the fence, a side Pascal thought belonged only to criminals and traitors. He didn't know what to make of her. He didn't recognise her at all.

He sat back, trying to hold on to the mother he knew while all the pieces of her jumbled themselves up. She didn't even look like the same person. Pascal had never thought of his mother as anything except old, although he knew she was younger than his father, which had to put her somewhere in her early forties. Her grey hair and worn face had added years to her age for as long as he could remember. But not now. Now there was a fire in her eyes which told him a very different woman had once lived in her body. It was on the tip of his tongue to ask where that woman had gone. But that would lead to a conversation about his father he didn't want to have. Either about the nature of his marriage to her or the part he might have played in the Drachmanns' downfall. Or to a conversation about how his mother really felt about Hitler that he felt honour-bound not to listen to. So Pascal avoided all the questions he should have asked and shook his head instead.

'I won't do that. And I don't want to know why you did it, but I will help. I'll take care of it. I'll get her to the station – there's always an early goods train. I'll get her to Munich and then...'

Pascal stopped. He was an officer in the German army about to help a fugitive Jew. They both knew there wasn't a *then*.

He sat alone in the kitchen while Carina gathered the clothes and money Noemi would need, and filled a pail with hot water. He was halfway out of the door before she stopped him.

'Are you going to tell her the truth? If you get this wrong, you might never see her again after tonight. Are you going to tell her that you love her?'

He could barely meet Carina's eyes as he explained that he already had but that loving Noemi wasn't enough. He'd never heard her swear before; he didn't know that she could.

'Then make it enough, you silly boy. Go with her. Forget the army and your ridiculous loyalty to the Führer. Stop bending yourself to fit hatreds you don't share and make a life for yourself that's worth living.'

He didn't answer. He didn't know what to say. And when he came back hours later and saw the disappointment in her eyes because he hadn't left with Noemi, there was nothing more to be said.

I broke her heart. I broke my own. I've no idea if Noemi even made it to safety, and now I've lost my mother too.

Pascal dragged himself back into the present with a shudder

and crumpled the letter up. It was too short, too cold, too unworthy. Both the women he'd loved were gone, and that knowledge punched holes through his heart.

And both of them thought I was blind.

He snatched at a breath as his head swam. *You and your beloved Nazis.* What if his mother was right? What if the scene he'd witnessed in the village wasn't an isolated event and there was more hatred than he'd admitted? What if he'd pledged his loyalty too freely?

Pascal stared at the gun propped against the tent's opening. He stared at the plans littering the table. *What if there's more than I've let myself see?* was too dark an idea to spend time with. In an hour or two, he'd have to lead his battalion back out into the chaos and persuade them to keep going in another blood-soaked battle too many of them wouldn't survive. He had to do that – his honour demanded it. He couldn't give way to doubts. He couldn't let echoes of Noemi or his mother's fears cloud his judgement. He was a German soldier; he was an officer. He believed in his country and the cause they were fighting for, so he'd do what he was charged to do and spur his men on with every ounce of his being.

Pascal left the tent with his head up. He began his rounds, clapping shoulders and promising victory. He swaggered with the best of them and acted as if a frightened and violated old man meant nothing to him. And he smiled when his men finally remembered he was a good soldier, not a thorn in their sides, but he'd never felt less like a hero.

CHAPTER ELEVEN
APRIL 1942

'There's a resistance movement in Czechoslovakia which might be a good fit for you. It's fragmented. It operates through loose circles for safety's sake, but if we can get you there... I was going to say you'd be safer, but I don't think that's something either of you want to be, so I'll settle for useful instead.'

It was Matthias who had called on Rabbi Mendel's help after the disaster of their first mission. He'd scrambled down the hillside moments after Noemi and he – although neither was aware of the other – had managed to catch the same train back to Munich.

It had not been an easy return for either of them. They'd survived the massacre at the palace, but plenty of others hadn't. Their targets had lived, but two of the other dignitaries on the platform had been killed, as well as three teenagers in the crowd. Countless more than that had been injured in the crush. Instead of striking at the heart of the Nazis, Noemi and Matthias had struck at the heart of the city by hurting its children, and the authorities had seized on that as a victory. They'd whipped every neighbourhood into a hunting frenzy and wiped away any association with bravery from the attack. Neither of them knew whether their bullets or the ones fired by the bodyguards had caused the deaths, but that didn't help: they'd started the gun battle; they carried the guilt. That hadn't got any lighter on the long journey which came after, although the rabbi had stuck to his word and not judged them.

'You can't stay in Munich, that's a given, but I won't pretend there's an easy way out. It's a miracle both of you got through the station cordons on the first night, and we can't take that risk again, especially now every soldier and policeman in the city's involved in the manhunt. Your best, and probably your only, option is to go across the Šumava mountains and into Czechoslovakia. And you have to leave at once. Vitta's strong, but nobody could blame her if she breaks.'

That was the other burden Mendel had given them to carry. Vitta's ex-communist friend had been under surveillance for months, not that she could have known. He'd been dragged into the Wittelsbacher prison on the first morning after the shootings, while Noemi and Matthias were still hiding from the world and forcing themselves to stay apart from each other. The papers had called him a key suspect, the head of an organised gang. And two days after he was arrested, Vitta had disappeared. Mendel hadn't downplayed the danger in that.

'The papers are calling the assassination attempt a communist conspiracy, the last gasp of a broken opposition, because that's what they've been told to call it. The authorities will know different. Now they've got Vitta, they'll know Jews are involved. Not that a word about that will reach the public – no Nazi will ever admit Jews have got that kind of fight in them; it doesn't fit with the narrative of cowardice and disease they prefer. But they'll flush out every factory and boarding house in the search, and nobody whose background and papers aren't watertight will be safe.'

He'd sent them off the next morning with a tattered old map of the mountain passes and a list of contacts along the route they'd been told to memorise. And no time for Noemi to plan a route or study the terrain, or worry if Matthias was up to the crossing.

The journey wasn't one Noemi wanted to be on – it took her away from her last link with her parents with no timescale for when she'd be back. It was also, as she knew it would be, long and exhausting and unpleasant, with sleep snatched in poorly provisioned mountain huts and sheep pens open to the elements.

Luckily, the mountains themselves were rounded not rocky and the snowfall they encountered was light. But the route was waterlogged, and the ground was a mess of black peat bogs. Noemi's skin was permanently slick with rainwater and a damp that seeped in icy flurries through their coats and their boots. The detours round the waterfalls which seemed to flow across every inch of the mountainside ate up their food stocks. Too many of the paths marked on the maps were blocked by boulders, and landslides were a constant threat. She'd worried for the first few days that the climb and the conditions would be too much for Matthias, who didn't possess a quarter of her mountaineering skills. But nothing defeated him. Whatever the obstacle, he kept moving. And when his spirits flagged, he talked, and then he asked Noemi to talk while he listened.

They'd traded their life stories over the miles and strengthened the foundations of their friendship. Matthias had told Noemi how much he'd loved Warsaw, where his parents had settled once his mother inherited her family's jewellery business, and how beautiful the city was. He'd told her how frightening it had been in 1939 to be stuck in Germany as a Pole, classified as a Jew in the second degree, living with a distant cousin who wanted to be rid of him, and with no possible way back home. In return, Noemi had told Matthias about the café and the bakery and Bavaria's beautiful mountains, and how happy her life had been until Hitler came to power and gradually ruined it. She'd told him about the way her family had been destroyed by people they'd once trusted and what good people her parents were. But she hadn't told him about Pascal. She couldn't find a way to work who her best friend had become into her narrative. She hadn't wanted to explain the tangled mix of emotions that arose with his name.

When the stories ran out or became too complicated, Matthias had taught Noemi the basics of Polish and the few words he knew of Czech. They'd talked themselves into keeping going. They'd talked their way over the border and into the small town of Domazlice, where they'd arrived starving and filthy on a spring day that was far fresher than they were, convinced that Mendel's contact would be gone. Or the townspeople would know them for Jews and fugitives and hand them over to the German authorities.

We worried about every catastrophe that could befall us and wondered if they'd be our punishment for the palace debacle, but none of the things we feared came to pass. If there's any luck left in the world, we've had a good share of it.

Noemi sat back against the rough, unplastered wall and scanned the faces listening intently to Lüdek – a man she knew nothing about beyond his first name – as he relayed the contents of the latest bulletin which had been broadcast on the BBC from the Czech government in exile in London to the Czech resistance fighters in Prague who were gathered around her.

About us, without us.

The phrase the Czechs used to describe the disposal of their country in the 1938 Munich Agreement ran like a pulse through every room with a partisan heartbeat.

'It was a betrayal – there's no other word for it. Britain and France sold Czechoslovakia into slavery for a few months of peace. They fed the demon and then they were shocked when it turned round to consume them. There's no pity or forgiveness here for that.'

The anger at the way the Allies had allowed Hitler to annex Czechoslovakia without that country's involvement was still as raw as it had been four years earlier. There wasn't a meeting where it wasn't raked over. Lüdek spoke for everyone Noemi and Matthias had encountered in the underground chain which had led them from Munich to Prague. There was no forgiveness for the countries who'd turned their backs, and there was nothing but hatred for the Germans.

'I remember it happening.'

Lüdek frowned as Noemi turned to him, but he let her speak. The testimonial she'd come with courtesy of Rabbi Mendel's contacts far outweighed her German upbringing.

'The mayor of the town I was living in then was a Nazi and rotten to the core. He was in Munich when the agreement was signed, and he carried on as if he'd acted as Hitler's personal advisor. He organised a special meeting to "celebrate the Allies' generosity" and laughed when he announced what had happened.'

'Somebody should engrave his name on a bullet.'

She didn't know which of the men and women assembled in the cramped attic had said that, but who voiced it wasn't important: the entire room applauded the sentiment. Viktor wouldn't have lasted a minute if he'd walked in. Nobody shied from talking about revenge and how best to deliver it in Prague, which was why Rabbi Mendel had sent her and Matthias there. Now the exiled government had asked for intelligence about the latest round-up of Czech workers – who were to be used as forced labour across the Reich – which had been ordered by Reichsprotektor Reinhard Heydrich, and everybody wanted to help. She didn't know anything about the people surrounding her except their first names, but she knew she trusted them. And they trusted her and Matthias because the chain worked. A nameless man had taken them in and fed them in Domazlice at Rabbi Mendel's request, and he'd passed the message up the links that led to Prague that everyone else could trust them too.

And without the rabbi and the nameless men, not one door would have opened to us.

Prague was not a safe place. There was a resistance movement as Mendel had promised, but the Nazi machinery was so well oiled that every time it reared its head to carry out even the smallest act of sabotage, it was crushed. Matthias and Noemi had learned very quickly that life under the occupation was brutal, and not only for the Jews who'd been gathered up in their thousands and despatched to a ghetto in Moravia called Theresienstadt, which everyone spoke of as a hellhole. Student protest leaders had been a target from the start; hundreds had been arrested in 1939 when the Germans rolled in. They had disappeared into the Gestapo-controlled prison system, along with thousands of ordinary Czech citizens. The gaps those young men and women left behind were intended to serve as a warning, and to plunge the country into a state of fear and anxiety it couldn't pull itself out of. That anyone would meet and share the contents of banned broadcasts or act as intelligence gatherers for the exiled regime was an act of bravery Noemi remained in awe of. Particularly given the nature of the Nazi who now ruled over them.

Everyone in occupied Czechoslovakia knew Reichsprotektor Heydrich's name and so did Noemi: he'd been one of Viktor's heroes, which was all she needed to know about the nature of the man. Hitler called him the 'man with the iron heart' and sang his praises. He was known as 'the Butcher' in Prague. Heydrich hated the Poles and he hated the Czechs and he hated the Jews with equal ferocity. He branded them all as vermin.

Lüdek had told them what to expect from him on their first night in the city; he didn't want them to be under any illusions. He'd described the Protektor's first days in power in September

1941 as a blood-soaked purge. Heydrich had immediately declared martial law and unleashed a reign of terror. One hundred and forty-two people had been executed in the first five days; five thousand had been arrested and not yet released. Everyone in the group could recite those numbers, although they could only guess at the scale of the murders which followed. Everyone in the group hated the man with a passion that ran deeper than even Noemi – who'd witnessed her country's passion for the Führer at first hand – had ever seen.

'Where've you gone? Did you hear what he said?'

Matthias's nudge forced her to concentrate again. Luckily, Lüdek – who wasn't usually a man given to repeating himself – had heard the gasp of disbelief in the room.

'You didn't mishear me. We've had confirmation that the plans London's been working on are finally in place. Nobody, it goes without saying, breathes a word about that outside these walls. Anyone who doesn't want to be involved should leave now – there'll be no judgement. Anyone who stays needs to be clear that, when it happens, however it happens – and that won't be ours to dictate – the reprisals will be swift and furious and no Czech man or woman will be safe.'

He paused: no one moved to leave, including Matthias and Noemi. He nodded. 'Then let me say it again. From this moment, everyone who loves Czechoslovakia and hates what's been done to it by the Nazis should have hope; in fact, everyone who hates the Nazis should have hope. We're going after them this time, not them after us. And Reinhard Heydrich has a target we won't miss stuck firmly on his back.'

CHAPTER TWELVE

MAY 1942

'If you can get out of Prague, you need to make your plans to do it now, not when the mission's been completed and the city's locked down. And whether you can leave or you can't, you need to think and act at all times as if you're going to get caught.'

Which we didn't do in Munich, and that could have been the flaw that finished us.

Lüdek's advice made perfect sense. But what he said next was a shock.

'There are cyanide capsules in the basket by the door if anyone wants them. Taking them – or using them – is not a sign of cowardice. I don't know anything about the assassins except they will certainly carry them. If you are acting as a safe house, before or after the event, I'd advise you to do the same. Please God we'll all make it through this, but let's not pretend that one capture ends with one capture. Consider that if your time comes.'

Nobody looked at the basket. Noemi knew Lüdek wouldn't ask who wanted the tablets or check how many were gone once the meeting ended. It was hard in that moment not to think about Vitta, and Mendel's, *Please God she's not,* when Noemi had asked him if he thought the arrested girl might still be alive. It was hard not to imagine a cell and a torturer forcing her to spill names. But she didn't take the poison with her when she left. The climber's part of her brain, which had taught her never to look down or doubt that the rope would hold her, wouldn't let her take that leap.

That was the last meeting Lüdek called, and they learned as little at it as they had at the rest. The operation was a tightly controlled one. Each person had their individual tasks, but that was all they had. Roles had been assigned in private, and no one was supposed to share the details, although Noemi and Matthias had broken that rule with each other. And they'd also shared their frustration at how small their roles were. No one else would listen, and no one was interested when they said, 'But we could do so much more.'

'We have German papers. That gives us a level of freedom to move round the city Czechs can't rely on. We can shoot, and we've proved we're as good as anyone else when it comes to intelligence-gathering – being able to speak German has helped there too. You could make better use of us.'

That may well have been true, but Lüdek had his orders and Lüdek wouldn't budge. They continued to be bit players. Noemi had couriered food stamps to a changing roster of addresses twice a week. Matthias had sourced and supplied bicycles and items of clothing which were left at unmanned drop zones. They were trusted, but they were under no illusions that Czechs were trusted more. Despite the credentials they'd brought with them, being German, and being Jewish – which most of the resistance members weren't and some only pretended to tolerate – pushed them down the ranks.

Being part of a key resistance operation was what they'd both wanted, and they were learning valuable skills. But it was frustrating to be on the outer rim.

Matthias – who pumped anyone he could for news of the

Warsaw Ghetto but rarely got any answers beyond the fact that it was a crowded and disease-ridden place – had said more than once that he wanted to fight for his own people. Noemi had come to agree with him, even if he defined his people as Polish as well as Jews, and she couldn't put a country to hers. Any role, however, was better than none; even the smallest act of defiance was part of the wider struggle they both wanted to believe was possible. Besides, nobody knew the bigger picture, not even Lüdek. The control centre for the Heydrich operation was in London, not Prague. And London had made it clear that anyone asking for information regarding the identity of the assassins or their planned route which they weren't cleared to receive – including Lüdek himself – would be treated as spies and eliminated. He'd only revealed the twenty-seventh of May as the planned date of the assassination to give anyone who could take it time to organise their escape from the city before martial law was imposed. And he'd warned them that date might not be true, that they could be needed for weeks to come. True or not, Noemi and Matthias weren't prepared to wait a day past it.

'What's going on? Why have you stopped? We haven't reached the stand yet.'

Noemi craned round the man cursing at the delay. There was a policeman standing on the tram line a little way ahead of them, waving a red flag and shouting. Matthias started to get to his feet the second she whispered what she could see, but Noemi held him back.

'Wait a minute. If we immediately start pushing towards the front, we'll draw attention. Which is the last thing we need if...'

She didn't need to finish the sentence. They both knew it ended in *if it really is happening today*. They were on a tram which had been brought to a forced stop. It was the twenty-seventh, the day the assassination was due to be carried out; that did not feel like a coincidence. It was also the day they'd planned their escape for, although they hadn't known what time the operation would start or where it would take place.

Noemi checked her watch, not that any of the guessing games they'd played actually mattered: there was only one train a day they could catch, and that left in two hours' time at one o'clock. It was now a little after eleven; the rest of the tram journey should have taken less than twenty minutes. In theory, they'd left plenty of time to make the journey. Now she remembered the speed with which the Nazis had reacted in Munich and closed down the city and wished they'd taken the first train to anywhere they could and worried about the connections later.

'He's coming over. Whatever happens next, we can't look as if we're worried or in a hurry.'

Matthias slipped his hand around Noemi's and smiled at her as if they had all the time in the world. She knew it was an act for public consumption, but his touch – which he'd never offered before apart from to help her over a rocky path in the mountains – was a welcome moment of reassurance. Especially as the policeman had reached the tram while they were slipping into their roles. A ripple spread through the carriage as he barked orders at the driver through the window.

'Did you hear what he said? Someone's thrown a bomb under Protektor Heydrich's car.'

'What was that? Someone's tried to shoot the Butcher?'

'Didn't you hear him? There was a whole gang of them throwing missiles and shooting, but apparently they've all got away.'

The further the rumours spread through the tram, the bigger they grew, each voice amplifying the details and the speaker's importance. Until the reality of what an attack like that could actually mean for the city began to sink in and the voices fell as quickly away. Heads went down as fear pushed in.

Noemi reached for her bag, ready for the inspection she was certain was coming. It was over a year since she'd carried papers marked with a J, but she couldn't shake the feeling the red letter would have bloomed across her picture again.

'Everyone off. Wherever you're going, you'll have to get there on foot.'

Her breath came back in a rush. She didn't realise she'd been holding Matthias's hand in a vice until he shook it out when she set him free. Being seen to hurry stopped being a black mark as soon as they got off the tram. The rest of the passengers dispersed with lightning speed – nobody wanted to be seen gathering or gossiping. Noemi looked around her, squinting against the bright sunshine, trying, and failing, to get their bearings. The last thing she wanted to do was approach the policeman for directions.

'It's okay, I know where we are. That's the Invalidovna.' Matthias nodded at the huge coral-and-cream building running along the entire block behind them. 'I'd guess it's about a forty-five minute walk to the train station from here, providing there's no cordons or police checks.'

Forty-five minutes. That was no time at all in terms of the distances they'd already walked together.

It was the longest walk of their lives. It was a warm, sunny day, but the city was curiously silent, the air holding its breath. None of the buses or trams were running. The few knots of people accidentally coming together at newsstands turned away again the instant they noticed each other. Noemi and Matthias kept up a steady pace and avoided everyone who was avoiding them. They didn't speak – there was nothing to be said except, *I don't hear any sirens yet*, and that felt like tempting fate. But when they finally arrived in front of the long row of columns which stretched across the front of Prague's central station, they caught hold of each other's hands again.

'I honestly thought it would be surrounded. I thought there'd be SS or Gestapo everywhere.'

Noemi was grateful when Matthias didn't respond by pointing out that they weren't clear yet. That they were too early for the train, which could easily be cancelled. That the station could easily close. That the fact they were travelling out of the city at all could turn them into suspects. Or tell her to act normally when she couldn't remember what normal was.

'He's badly hurt, but he's not dead. Thank God.'

'There were two of them firing apparently; one got away on a tram and one on a bike. There were so many witnesses, please God they'll be caught right away.'

'It can't only be two; there must have been dozens involved in a set-up like that. An attack on a car and a shooting? The Germans will have the city locked down by nightfall, you'll see. Please God they pick the right ones up quickly and don't stick us all in the frame.'

Only the last *Please God* sounded genuine. The other prayers were added as an afterthought when the speakers heading towards their platforms looked hastily round.

You need to think and act as if you're going to get caught.

Now she was the one thinking, *Please God.* Hoping that Lüdek and the rest of the cell had followed his advice, no matter how tiny their involvement had been. Knowing she would probably never find out how their stories ended. Even with Matthias's hand on her elbow, that was the loneliest feeling in the world. Her life was full of empty spaces. Her head was full of people she loved or admired and might never find a trace of again. Every footstep she took towards their platform echoed with a name. Vitta, Rabbi Mendel and Lüdek, and – loudest of all – Carina, Hauke and Frieda. But not Pascal; she wouldn't let his name in.

'This is our platform. And the train's here.'

Noemi faltered as she looked up at the sign suspended high

above them in the cavernous station. Warsaw. Another city, another country; another huge leap far away. *I want to go home and find my parents. And I want to fight for my own people.* She'd understood that impulse when Matthias had said it, in the same way she'd known she would go with him before he asked. Her parents were beyond her immediate help, and too many people had disappeared for her to want to lose her only real friend.

And, besides, where else would I go?

She reached instinctively for her throat, forgetting for a moment that the locket was gone and she had no links left to home.

I can't go back to Germany whether I want to or not. I can't stay in Prague.

Those roads were closed to her for as long as war raged. She was as sure of that as she was sure that, despite every setback and frustration and danger, she wanted to fight. She'd stepped across a line she couldn't retreat from when she'd fired her first bullet into the crowds at the Dachau Palace. She knew what guilt felt like now. She knew how long the nights could be, and how hard it was to shake off the sound of the screams that had filled the dark hillside. But she also knew far more about the realities of the Nazi machine than she had when she'd run away from Unterwald. Concentration camps, round-ups, deportations and ghettos. A web of hateful words that had trapped her parents and were part of her normal vocabulary now.

Where does this end?

The question kept getting bigger; the answer kept getting darker. Heydrich might be badly hurt, he might be dying, but even if he did, he was only one man. There were too many more who shared his bloodlust. Who wanted every Jew in Europe wiped out.

But every one of them we manage to get rid of could leave one of us alive.

Home was behind her, if home even existed. There was no way to find that out until the Nazis were beaten. That fight might not be possible; it might not be winnable. Taking part could lead to her death.

But I have to try, for myself, and for all the people who've been taken or broken and can't.

Noemi walked along the platform wondering if this was the point where she disappeared, where her story was lost. If the loved ones who survived and might one day come looking for her would find only gaps and empty spaces too. She let herself hold that thought for a moment, and feel the pain and the fear inside it, and then she let it go. She was moving forward; she wasn't waiting. She wasn't anyone's prisoner yet.

She climbed onto the train behind Matthias and closed her eyes as it finally pulled out of the station without the SS or the Gestapo anywhere in sight. Another city, another country; another chance to stay a step ahead, to make a mark. To say, *Not me, not us, not now*.

It wasn't a lot to hold on to, but it was hope.

PART THREE

CHAPTER THIRTEEN
AUGUST 1942

'Listen up, you lot – it's time to move out. The advance troops have finally managed to clear the route into the Caucasus Mountains, and now it's over to us to secure them. This is it. This is the moment we've been training for.'

Pascal barely had time to finish the sentence before his men began cheering. Their relief at the news – which he shared – rattled through the flimsy mosquito-plagued barracks. Mountain fighting was what they had trained for, it was what many of them believed they'd been born for, but – other than the assault on the Tatra Mountains which had taken them into Poland in 1939 – most of the battalion had seen very little of the high-altitude action they craved. And although they were grateful for the leave they'd been granted in Yugoslavia to recuperate from their role in the Russian campaign, now they'd been redeployed, they were itching to be useful again.

Pascal shared his men's frustration. The first eighteen months of his war had not been what he'd imagined they'd be when he'd sat in the classroom at Sonthofen studying military tactics. After the initial burst of almost entirely uncontested action in Poland, he'd been sent to France to train in cliff-climbing techniques in preparation for the invasion of Britain and Gibraltar. Neither of those campaigns – which he'd been desperate to lead – had come to fruition. Instead, he'd been sent into Russia, which was at least back to the war, but the battlefields he'd encountered there hadn't been a birthplace for heroes and giants. And the doubts he'd encountered still plagued him.

The Russian campaign had dissolved into an endless slog of grinding marches which had left his men swaying and sleepwalking. It had led them along roads lined with burning trucks and burning bodies and a smell that haunted his dreams. Into a world of chaos and carnage, where soldiers didn't advance in orderly rows but ran and crawled to stay alive while bullets ricocheted around them and grenades blew the earth into craters. Into a cold so intense, men could lose fingers and toes they hadn't even noticed were frozen. And into days which – when they weren't filled with brutality – were filled with boredom. That was the other thing Pascal hadn't understood about war. How much time was spent sitting and waiting. This latest campaign had been no different. He'd stopped counting how long they'd been stuck in the damp and heavily fortified hinterland of the Mius River, waiting for the advance troops to secure their forward path when the number of the days grew too high. He'd almost forgotten how terrible fighting could be, he was so desperate to get back out into it and put his real skills to the test.

Especially in these mountains and on this mission, where we can finally be the best we can be.

Pascal let the men quieten down before he shared that nugget with them. He rarely raised his voice off the battlefield; he rarely had to. His troops were not, as he'd once imagined they would be, his closest friends. This wasn't the Hitler Youth anymore, and the incident in the Russian village – which had been pushed aside by the battle that followed – had forced him to accept that high ideals weren't always the glue between soldiers he'd believed them to be. But the men respected his track record, and they listened to him. Once the nudges and shouts of, 'Shush, he's got more,' finally stopped, he smiled and began again.

'The part we've been given to play is a huge honour; I want you to understand that. If this offensive succeeds – which it will – Germany will take control of the vast deposits of silver and lead and oil and timber in these regions that Russia has been helping itself to. When we do that, when we secure those resources for the German war effort, victory will be ours all the sooner.' He laughed as the cheers shook the roof again. 'And if that isn't honour enough, there could be more to follow. During the ascent, there will be an opportunity to conquer the summit of Mount Elbrus, the highest peak in the range, and claim that glory for Germany too. But that mission is only open to the strongest and the fittest men across both mountain battalions, so I don't imagine many of you will be interested.'

This time the cheers were cut through with catcalls from one mountaineer to another as they competed for Pascal's attention. He left them to their drinking after that, promising to put all their names into the wider ballot. There was no other way to select the final team: every man in the room could scale Elbrus with the confidence of a mountain goat. But he knew how much being chosen mattered because he'd already been selected, and he'd been walking a head taller for days.

Pascal had used the word *honour* twice in his speech. It was a word he used a lot, despite what the Russian campaign had shown him was the real face of war. It had been a daily struggle to hold fast to the ideals he wished more of his men shared when he couldn't keep his own troops fed and warm, never mind the prisoners they'd initially taken. And after he'd let the incident in the village go unreported and unexamined, it was easier for others to go the same way. Pascal had had to subdue his conscience more than once in the interests of winning the war, although he'd refused to countenance cruelty. He'd told himself that the firing squads he'd finally been ordered to deploy were more humane than leaving their Russian captives to starve or freeze to death. But he'd court-martialled the field officer he'd caught spraying his victims with bullets and laughing, even though that punishment almost turned his men mutinous. He'd struggled, but he'd kept his doubts at bay and his men in line, and he'd kept honour and comradeship – the two principles he'd associated with life in the military for as long as he could remember – to the fore of every action he took. Unfortunately, the first was a challenge and the last seemed to be failing him.

His men trusted his orders, but his determination not to ignore or condone what he called acts of barbarism, and his troops called 'teaching Ivan a lesson' had set up barriers between them. He refused to accept that the women they encountered in the overrun villages and towns were the collateral of war and fair game. He refused to permit discussion of some of the brutal behaviour towards suspected partisans that was apparently commonplace among the other mountain units. In return, his men called him 'The Monk' and rolled their eyes when he began one of his honour-filled lectures.

But not today. They remembered what German soldiers stand for today. And I'll make sure they don't lose sight of it, whoever we encounter.

He began to check over his kit. Laying out his white camouflage jacket and trousers. Running his fingers through his thick woollen socks, searching for the holes that could let in the frost which would cripple him. Enjoying the sense of preparing for a mission that was worthy of his men. And refusing to listen to the voice nipping like a draught at his ear, reminding him that the one person who would truly understand the beauty in scaling Mount Elbrus would never know he'd done it – and wouldn't care if she did.

. . .

The journey took them through fields thick with sunflowers and orchards bursting with sweet honey-scented apples and plums, and villages where Pascal ensured nobody was mistreated. The troops followed his lead and kept their focus on the horizon and their energies for the mountains whose beauty reduced them to silence. Pascal stared up at the green foothills dotted with sheep, and the pine forests which ringed them, and imagined himself back in Bavaria. It was an idyllic moment, almost a homecoming. Until he began the climb.

The ridges towering above them were jagged enough to tear holes in the sky. These weren't mountains which welcomed summer tourists and guides. They were wild and untamed and had no patience with the men trying to conquer them. Tree trunks served for bridges; animal tracks stood in for paths. The wind blew great drifts of snow across the rock faces the moment the troops climbed out of the valley and whipped their sense of direction away. Fog fell without warning; ice turned their bodies numb. The Caucasus Mountains were as dangerous as the Russian armies they'd faced, but the men were finally in their natural element, and every challenge they faced – in the early days at least, before the peaks swallowed their strength and the partisans found them – was met with bright, willing eyes.

'This is where we leave the porters and the rest of the army behind. From there we go on alone and carry everything we need ourselves.'

From there was the mountain hut perched above them which would act as the Elbrus ascent team's base for the climb. It was the strangest building Pascal had ever seen. It had the elongated and rounded shape of a Zeppelin airship on the outside and looked as if it was perched to slide off the slope. It was even more extraordinary inside. The men were greeted with polished parquet flooring and hot showers, a stock of mountaineering equipment that was in far better shape than the supplies they'd hauled with them, and more food than a battalion ten times their size would need. The building, which they later discovered had once been the world's highest weather station, would have been better designated as a luxury hotel. And being in it brought the Karwendelhaus and Noemi back to Pascal with a speed that almost jack-knifed him.

It's like standing inside a negative. It's so...

She hadn't said *beautiful* when they'd stood together on the veranda that day, but there'd been no other word in his head. Pascal at sixteen hadn't been a novice around girls – he attracted them like a magnet, and he'd had his share of exploratory fumbles in the dark. And Noemi had always been Noemi, his right arm, his extra limb, his best friend; he hadn't looked at her in that way. But that had begun to change in the stolen summer they'd spent together before the Innsbruck climb.

Carina had noticed it first, which was why she'd given him the locket that he was too awkward to give to Noemi face to face. His mother had known before he did what his heart wanted. But he'd known it that night. He'd looked at her framed by the moon and with snowflakes scattering her hair, and he'd never wanted to kiss anyone more.

When she'd stepped away from his tentative approach, he'd been afraid she had no interest in him beyond friendship, although he'd finally written his stilted message in the belated birthday card when they'd gone back to their rooms, in the hope of trying again. So nothing had prepared him for the next morning's mountaintop – or for a kiss which had turned all the others to dust. Her lips had tingled with the snow and the ice that surrounded them, but they'd been as warm as a soft blanket when they'd touched his. She'd run through his body like fire. All he'd been thinking about as they made their way off the summit was when he could kiss her again. When he had, he'd known the meaning of magic.

And that vanished in, 'What are these?'

He'd watched her take him apart and rebuild him in a version he didn't want to face and she'd never want to fall in love with. He could still feel the pain of that if he let himself, the heat of it bursting like blisters over his skin. But the choice she'd offered him wasn't a choice. He hadn't wanted to leave Germany or the army. He'd wanted it all: the medals and the glory, and Noemi. That would never change, whatever the law said. Just because she didn't believe it was possible didn't make it true. And it had to be true because a world without her in it was...

Empty and cold, and unthinkable. And most likely my future now she's gone.

'What's up with you? If you've gone off the idea of climbing, there's a dozen men down the line desperate to step into your boots.'

Pascal hadn't realised anyone had seen him sink into the chair and drift off into his memories, or gasp at the shock of them, and he answered without thinking.

'No, it's not the climb. There was a girl, before the war, and we once had a place like this to ourselves. I messed everything up that night, but she's impossible to forget.'

The whooping that greeted this admission, and the speed with which it travelled round the base, turned The Monk instantly back into one of the men.

It didn't matter how much the ascent team wanted to conquer Elbrus, or believed they had a right to her, the mountain was no easy prize.

A blinding snowstorm followed by freezing fog ended the first attempt at the summit and forced the men back over the glacier which coated the base of the ridge. Arguments raged all night when they returned. Some of the other division commanders didn't want to risk their men's lives on what they now viewed as a dangerous propaganda exercise. But Captain Groth – the man in overall charge of the mission – beat their views down, much to Pascal and his fellow climbers' delight. And he had the team back on the mountainside at first light, and in equally bad weather, before anyone more senior could stop him.

Every step they took to the top was a fight. Pascal expected more than one of them to be his last. The wind blew him onto his knees over and over again and battled to hold him there. The fog wrapped them in shrouds, dropping visibility to a hand's span. By the time the ground began to level off and reaching the summit became a possibility not a suicide attempt, most of the men were flat on their stomachs and almost too exhausted to crawl. But Pascal couldn't stop, and he couldn't give up. What they were doing was a struggle, but it was a million miles away from the horrors of a battlefield. And it held all the purity he'd been looking for in the cause he longed to believe held a better world at its heart.

'Get up, all of you. We've done it. We're here.'

Pascal could hardly catch a breath, the air was so thin. He could hardly make his voice heard in the wind. But the men could see him waving and pointing at the summit he was only minutes away from, and Groth was soon staggering around them too, clapping their exhausted shoulders, cheering them onto their feet.

Pascal's hands moved like shovels as he unpacked the swastika-crested flag from its bindings. His fingers struggled to bend as the team worked together to secure that and the division's regimental pennant into the packed ice and powdery snow. But they did it. And no one cared that the flags lasted for less than a moment before the wind shredded them into streamers or that the camera whirled away and was smashed before anyone could take a picture. They'd done it. They'd fixed Hitler's emblem on Europe's highest point. Besides, Pascal didn't need a photograph. He'd moved outside his body. He could see himself standing there on the topmost point of the ridge, the flag he loved waving above him, his men flanked beside him like the true giants they were.

'We are heroes, exactly as the Führer promised us we'd be.'

Nobody could hear him; he didn't care about that either. He'd heard the words; he felt the pride. He'd heard the echo of another mountaintop when he spoke and felt Noemi's lips pressed against his in the same moment.

She's with me; I can feel her. And whatever else has gone wrong between us, she's a climber – she would understand what this means.

He was as lost to the men as they were to him as the snow continued to swirl, but – for the first time since he'd led her to a deserted train station and watched her disappear – he could feel Noemi properly beside him. He closed his eyes. He conjured her face up. And there on a mountaintop in the middle of nowhere, he forgot about medals and glory and flags, and he finally understood where his whole heart lay.

This is nothing without her. There has to be a way back; there has to be a way to have it all, like I promised her.

He was a true hero now. He could change things. If there really was a darkness at the Party's heart – in its leaders or in its followers – he could help root it out.

'What are you laughing at? You look like a madman.'

Groth was at the flagpole with him, pulling at Pascal's hand before he froze to the spot. He didn't wait for an answer. There was a rumbling like thunder coming along the ridge and no time to waste before what sounded like a storm hit them. Pascal stumbled after him; he barely registered the descent. But he drank along with the men that night and he carried on laughing, and he'd never felt more alive in his life.

CHAPTER FOURTEEN
MARCH 1943

'You have to blend in from the first moment; that's the most important – and the most difficult – thing. No matter how shocked or frightened or lost you feel – and you will feel all of those things – you can't show it. There are informers inside the ghetto as well as outside, people who will do anything and sell anyone to stay alive. And if this is the only trip you make in there – if you don't want to go back or stay – no one will think the worse of you for it.'

Their guide – another in a long line of men whose name they didn't know – shook his head as Noemi and Matthias both tried to answer him at the same time.

'I don't need declarations – your bravery isn't in question. I'll see you, hopefully, back here tomorrow night and we can revisit your roles in this then.'

He stepped back into the shadows, leaving the two of them to carefully slide the heavy manhole cover clear and drop down into the sewer system which ran like a web underneath the Warsaw ghetto. The stench was atrocious. Once Matthias pulled the metal disc back into place, the darkness was complete.

This is a mistake. I can't be down here; I can't do this. I have to get out and go back.

Adrenaline surged through Noemi's body, priming her for flight. It was all she could do to stand still, to hold her stomach down and stop herself scrambling back up the ladder to the surface. Her courage had been forged on mountaintops, not in dark, stinking drains. She was a creature who needed the light.

Reach for the next foothold; take the next step. Don't worry about the ones which come after. Breathe and move forward and you'll get there.

Pascal was in her head – she could almost feel his hand reaching for hers. Guiding her the way he'd done the first time he'd taught her to climb up inside the vertical gaps in a rock face that mountaineers called chimneys. She'd hated that first attempt: she'd hated how narrow it was, and the sense of confinement and the unexpectedly grimy conditions. She'd put her hand into a spider's nest halfway up and felt their bodies scattering over her skin. Muck and gravel had fallen from a ledge above her and down onto her face, blocking her nose and temporarily blinding her. But she'd kept going, and she'd beaten the spiders and the dirt.

I hated it, but I did it. And the next time we went up, I wasn't scared at all.

Matthias was beside her, breathing deeply, gathering himself up, getting ready to move. She almost yelled, *It's not your voice I need*, when he asked her if she was ready, and his words pushed Pascal's away. She reined that impulse in too; she let her anger with Pascal bury it. He might have helped her to escape, but he'd hadn't chosen her. His guidance was no use to her now; Matthias had to be the man she trusted.

'Yes, I'm ready. Let's go.'

She shifted her body, feeling the weight of the guns and grenades and the bullet-loaded magazines tied round her waist and filling her pockets. *This is why we've come* pounded through her head, driving her on through the filthy water as they counted the steps which the crudely drawn map had promised would lead to a second ladder and an exit. Warsaw had been Matthias's choice as their destination once they had to leave Prague, but it had also been their only logical option. The city was part of the network which had linked Rabbi Mendel to Lüdek and moved them safely out of Munich. Now Lüdek had given them the name of the Warsaw link in the chain. The Jews there were living under terrible danger; they desperately needed help. So Noemi understood why Matthias had chosen Warsaw as the next place where they could make a stand for their people and fight, and she shared his convictions. But a sense of purpose was one thing and reality was another, and they'd completely underestimated the nightmare they walked into.

'It's so beautiful. My mother always said it was as lovely as Paris. And I know the Nazis have been in charge there for years, and there's a ghetto in the city now, but – even with the damage the initial occupation must have caused – I doubt it's changed all that much.'

The closer their long journey took them towards Warsaw, the more animated Matthias became. And the more lyrical he grew about the delights of the city he'd been born in. The only time he stumbled was when he mentioned his mother, and he only did that once.

'Wait till you see Łazienki Park. Forget the temple and the tower in Munich's English Garden, there's half a dozen palaces there, including one on a lake that will take your breath away. And the Bristol Hotel, oh what a place. I went there for dinner on my sixteenth birthday and the chandeliers nearly blinded me, the crystals were so bright. And Ujazdów Avenue on a

Sunday, that's a treat too, with everyone dressed in their finery and parading about.'

He conjured up such a wonder-filled place, Noemi wanted to believe it existed unchanged almost as much as he did. Unfortunately, that bubble burst the moment they exited the train station.

'They've decimated it.'

Their instructions had been clear and no different to the ones they'd followed in Prague or Munich. *Don't loiter. Go straight to the safe address you've been given. Don't draw any kind of attention.* But Matthias was rooted to the spot, trying to make sense of a cityscape which had shifted beyond every reference he knew, and Noemi couldn't move him. When she finally shook him hard enough to get a response, he stumbled through the streets as if he was in a trance. Nothing was as he remembered. Every building he tried to find in the centre was gone or reduced to a broken shell; every square had been renamed. As for the ghetto, the scale of it defeated them both.

The red brick wall surrounding the enclosure was easily ten metres high. Fierce shards of glass and coils of barbed wire covered the top. The sign on the heavily guarded main gate read, *Entry Forbidden: Plague Zone*. It would have been easier to walk into Dachau.

Matthias tried to trace his way round it, but the circuit was endless. The perimeter had turned once busy thoroughfares into dead ends; it had cut houses in two. In the end, Matthias stopped saying, 'But I should be able to reach Saxony or Sienna Street this way.' And stopped asking how anyone could carry on living a normal life in the midst of the rubble and in the shadow of the hostile, towering walls which had effectively smashed up the city.

When Noemi asked him if he wanted to break the rules and go to his parents' house first to try to find some news of them – although she had no hope they'd be there now she'd seen the ghetto for herself – he shut down. He didn't speak again until they finally located Lüdek's contact, then he couldn't stop.

'I knew about the ghetto, although I've been trying not to think about it, or the very real possibility my parents and grandparents are somewhere inside it. I certainly didn't expect it to be so huge. And I don't understand why the city is still in such a terrible mess so many years after the occupation. Why hasn't anyone cleaned it up?'

'Because the Nazis won't let us. They don't want us to forget that they won and they're in charge, as if their constant presence and their flags aren't enough. The rubble and the ruins and the headless statues are there to remind us we lost. Everything in this city is a warning of what they can and will do to break any attempt at resistance. Including the ghetto.'

Szymon was a lean and wiry and exhausted-looking man. Unlike the others they'd been handed over to since Rabbi Mendel sent them on their path out of Germany, he was also Jewish. And like them, he was utterly committed to resisting the Nazis and didn't care where that led.

'I grew up in this city, like you did. Or perhaps not quite like you.' He glanced at Matthias and nodded to himself. 'You've a German father, haven't you, and you said your mother inherited the family jewellery business? So I'm guessing you grew up in Stary Żoliborz?' He nodded again as Matthias agreed, and turned to Noemi. 'That's a pretty neighbourhood, a little oasis full of elegant villas and wealthy Jews. Or it was. I, on the other hand, grew up in Powiśle, which, as he will tell you, was crime-ridden and poor and full of thugs with knuckle-dusters for brains. I learned to fight hard there; I've been fighting ever since.'

It was clear he was trying to establish his credentials, even if the comparison was a clumsy one. But their different backgrounds wasn't what Matthias was focused on.

'You said, *or it was*. What's happened in Żoliborz, Szymon?

You're right that I was brought up there, but I left it in 1935, and I've had no word from my parents or my grandparents since the war started, which has been...' He fumbled for the word but couldn't find it. His body shrank. 'I've been trying to convince myself they'd have escaped the round-up and the ghetto. I've been holding on to a picture of them quietly getting on with their lives. But now I'm here and I've seen it...'

He stopped; turned in on himself. Noemi reached for his hand, but he didn't notice and didn't take it.

I don't know him half as well as I think I do. He keeps so much of himself hidden.

Matthias had talked about his parents so frequently, Noemi had started to feel as if she knew them, as if she was involved in his life. But everything he'd told her had stopped at 1935; he hadn't let any darkness in.

And everything I've told him has been cast in the same rosy light. We don't talk about our fears for our families or our guilt for surviving. We never admit they could be suffering – or lost. We live in the moment or in a safe version of the past.

It wasn't a realisation she wanted. But it explained why part of her hung back and let the looks he'd started giving her – the ones that hinted at deepening feelings – go unseen. She hung back now too and let Szymon step in. He lit another cigarette before he answered – he was rarely without one clamped between his nicotine-stained fingers – but his voice lost its belligerent edge.

'I'm sorry, but there's no point in lying to you. Nobody from your area would have escaped. German officials and their families live in Żoliborz now – it was one of the first areas to be "swept", as they called it, when they got here. They began herding Jewish families from there into houses in the city centre where the ghetto now stands long before the wall was built. And freezing our bank accounts and forcing us into armbands and into factories where they work us like slaves.'

'But you're not in there – you got away. So it's possible they did too.'

Noemi couldn't bear to look at Matthias as he leaned forward; the hope in his eyes was too bright for the news that was surely coming. Szymon must have seen it flare too, but he was clearly a man who dealt only in the truth, and he didn't allow it to last.

'It's possible, yes, but it's not likely. I wish I could tell you a different story, but I can't. I got away and went underground in 1940 because I've always lived on the fringes of what most people would consider to be a respectable life. I was tough enough to do it, and so were the other escapees I've met since. But that wasn't an option for most Jews – certainly not for the older ones or for the wealthier classes who'd lived more sheltered lives. They went where they were told because they had no other choice, and they thought it was the law-abiding thing to do. Nobody could have guessed at the start how bad things would become. For the first few months, renegades like me were able to get in and out of the ghetto with food supplies and medicines. That's also how we mapped out the tunnels and sewers. But the Nazis got wind of what we were doing and closed it off, and now it's a sealed world.'

Matthias sat back, his face a closed mask. It was left to Noemi to ask the question he couldn't.

'How many people are in there?'

They'd seen the walls; they knew how far the perimeter extended. The ghetto was huge, but it wasn't huge enough to contain Szymon's answer.

'It's hard to be certain. We estimated over four hundred thousand at the start, but the boundaries keep shifting.' He carried on talking over their strangled gasps. 'And it's not just the overcrowding that's the problem. The conditions inside are horrific. The houses are filthy and riddled with rats and disease. The Nazis cut the power off at night and increasingly during the day. The daily food ration wouldn't keep a cat alive. We try to smuggle food in, and we're inventive as we can be – the hearses that go in to collect the dead are currently our main form of transport for bread – but it's a risky business, and the Nazis are brutal with anyone they catch smuggling. They kill the entire family, not just the culprit.'

Matthias had turned grey. Noemi could see him trying to calculate the odds of his ageing family trying to survive under such frightening conditions and reaching an impossible conclusion. She was doing the same exercise with hers. And she felt as if she was about to explode.

'How can this be happening? The ghetto isn't a secret; it's not hidden away. How can human beings be penned up like this in the middle of a city while people on the outside go about their business as if the walls and the broken glass and the guards have somehow become invisible? Do we really matter so little?'

Szymon's face turned old. His eyes dimmed and wouldn't meet hers. It was obvious he'd been wrestling hopelessly with the same questions for far too long.

'I wish I had an answer for you, but better men than me have tried to find it and failed. The one thing the ghetto certainly isn't is invisible.' He shook his head as if he couldn't believe what he was about to say. 'Chlodna Street, which is one of the city's main thoroughfares, runs through the centre of it. Closing that completely would have caused chaos, so the Nazis built a bridge over it instead to allow the good citizens of Warsaw to carry on about their business undisturbed. I've watched them go across it on their way to their offices and shops and schools. There are starving, terrified people no distance below them; there are dead children lying uncovered in the street. But nobody crossing the bridge sees them because nobody looks down. That's a choice they make every day, but as to how they do it and how they live with themselves?' He shook his head again. 'I've no explanation for that. Like I've no explanation for why we are hated or why we're described as vermin. Or for why one group can only rise up by standing on the bodies of another.'

The room fell silent. When Matthias eventually recovered his voice, it had taken on Szymon's harder edge.

'They're not going to keep the ghetto going forever though, are they?' He didn't wait for an answer. They all knew it was *no*, even if they hadn't voiced that aloud before. 'There were rumours doing the rounds in Prague that tens of thousands of Jews had been taken out of the ghetto in Vilna and murdered in the nearby forests. There's the same whispers circulating about Riga. I imagine you've heard them too.' He exhaled hard as Szymon nodded. 'Is that what you're expecting will happen next here?'

Szymon drew in another lungful of nicotine. 'It's possible. They're certainly doing something to reduce the numbers, although we've not heard anything about actual massacres yet. There's a train line that runs through the ghetto, and they've started moving packed trains out in the early mornings. The wagons are sealed when they come through, but we've heard cries for help and screaming from inside.'

Noemi had to close her eyes for a moment. Every time Szymon spoke, he delivered another blow. And he wasn't done yet.

'Where are the trains going, do you know?'

It was yet another question she had to but didn't want to ask, and another answer they couldn't avoid. For the first time since they'd entered his tiny flat, Szymon looked less sure of himself.

'Our information – which is patchy – says they're sent to a camp called Treblinka, which is about a hundred kilometres from here. Unfortunately, we don't know much about it yet: we've no idea if it's a work camp or a death camp, or what happens to the ghetto's residents if and when they get there.

We've no idea if that's where the whole ghetto is ultimately headed. So we want to send someone there to gather more information, but it's not an easy mission – or a priority for the Polish Home Army, who are the main resistance organisers here and mostly not Jewish. And we haven't found anyone ourselves yet with the right set of skills to get there and back, or spy on the camp, without being caught.'

'You have now.'

Noemi wasn't sure if she said it first or Matthias, but they were both equally determined to volunteer and to prove themselves. And they didn't give Szymon a chance to argue.

Treblinka. The ghetto's last stop. Nobody else is going to get sent there, not if we can rescue them first. Which is why we have to hold on, trust to the map and keep going.

The camp's name flashed like a torch through Noemi's head as the darkness pressed round her. From the moment she and Matthias had seen the truth of it, they'd both known that saving the trapped residents of the Warsaw ghetto before their bodies were fed into Treblinka's flames had to be their next fight.

In a repeat of their flight from Munich, they'd gone to the camp on their reconnaissance mission dressed as hikers, carrying their German papers which Szymon said carried the same weight in Poland as they had in Czechoslovakia, although it was a relief when that assumption wasn't tested. Spring had arrived dry and mild so they were able to walk most of the way and keep their bus journeys short. They stuck to back roads and paths which led them to the forest where the camp was believed to be sited and avoided anything except the most isolated farms when they needed supplies. They found the forest itself easily enough, and the barracks and gravel pits which lined up with the features drawn on their map. But the scale of it was too small for the trainloads Szymon had described leaving the ghetto, so they kept walking deeper into the trees.

The faint sound of dogs barking was the first clue that there was another site, and it wasn't long before that noise altered its pitch and turned into what sounded like human cries. They forced themselves not to weaken at that and followed the sounds in a silence that deepened as the cries grew.

Treblinka wasn't as easy to find as Dachau – the barbed wire cresting its walls had been camouflaged by a layer of interlaced branches which confused the sight lines. But there were other clues. The heat haze shimmering from what looked like a long series of fire pits at its furthest side. The crackle of flames and the thick scent of smoke in the air. The screams which were definitely human and definitely afraid. Noemi had heard her parents' voices in those; she knew from his white face that Matthias had heard his. They'd sat in the woods with their arms round each other and tears patterning their cheeks, watching and listening until early morning. They'd heard the whistle of an engine approaching; they'd seen its white plume. They'd heard the dogs and the shouting, the gunshots and the screams. They'd understood they were witnesses to cruelty, and murder, on a scale they couldn't begin to imagine. And they'd brought that grim knowledge back to Szymon, who'd fed it to his contacts in the ghetto.

And now we have a chance to stop the machinery. To stop thousands more from disappearing into those woods. Even one life and one voice left to tell the tale has to be worth it.

Noemi's eyes had finally grown accustomed to the dark. There was a battle coming – that's why they were pushing each other on through the blackness and the filth. That's why they were carrying weapons and messages of hope for the fighters already gathered inside the ghetto. That was why, if this run succeeded, there would be another tomorrow, and the next day.

And when there's nothing left to bring in, we'll stand with them and fight too.

Matthias had stopped. He began running his hands over the dirty wet wall. She heard his sigh of relief when he hit metal.

'The ladder's here, which should mean there's a manhole above it, exactly as the map said there would be. So far, so good.'

She almost laughed, it was such an incongruous choice of words. She doubted many people would see anything good in their situation. But it was right, and right would do. She held on as tightly to that as she did to the ladder's rickety frame as they climbed up it and into the unknown.

CHAPTER FIFTEEN
APRIL 1943

'This is a battle to the death. Everyone who chooses to stay and fight must understand that. The Nazis have pledged to murder every Jew in here; we've pledged not to surrender. But it is also essential that some of us survive. To tell our stories, to keep our faith and our culture alive. There might be a moment when the commander of your section orders you to get out. There might be a moment when you decide leaving is the right thing for you to do. There are maps of the sewers and tunnels for anyone who wants to consult them and try. Whichever choice you eventually make – to stay or to leave – it's a brave one.'

Noemi counted and recounted the Molotov cocktails hidden in the dark cellar which passed for a munitions dump and wished she could conjure up more supplies. Five days had passed since Mordechai Anielewicz – the commander-in-chief of the Jewish Fighting Organisation and a key co-ordinator in the ghetto uprising – had delivered his message and his absolution. Five days since the ghetto's hastily convened army had exploded onto the streets in a flaming cauldron of homemade bombs and grenades and smuggled-in bullets that had left a trail of Nazi not Jewish corpses slumped across the ghetto, and a thick pall of smoke clinging to the glass shards and the barbed wire. The fighters who'd gathered to hear him that morning – in one of the many hidden bunkers they'd carved out of the hovels they'd been forced for too long to call homes – had expected to die en masse on that first day. Most of them were still standing.

She finished checking the gasoline-filled bottles and switched her attention to the stack of guns and ammunition which had been stored in a drier corner. Some of the weapons were Polish, supplied by the Home Army. Some were British and had come via Allied airdrops. Some had been stolen from the holsters of newly dead German soldiers. Whatever way they'd been sourced – whether by smuggling or stealing – every gun brought into the ghetto had risked a life and claimed far more. Noemi and Matthias had made three runs through the tunnels which linked the labyrinth-like cellars to the surrounding city before they'd decided to stay and fight.

Each trip had aged them. Each one had become more frightening, not less. But – unlike some of the equally brave fighters from other resistance cells – they'd managed to evade the Polish blackmailer gangs who lurked near the entrance manholes, waiting to catch smugglers on their way in and sell them to the Gestapo. Or the Jewish policemen inside the ghetto, who mistakenly thought that working with the Nazis would protect them and their families, and were waiting by the exit holes to catch them on the way out. And unlike the bodies they blundered past in the dark sewers, they hadn't lost their footing or their way. Noemi and Matthias and their unknown companions had brought in every weapon and weapon-making device they could carry with them. But that hadn't stopped the supplies running out.

'Find me more lightbulbs that we can fill with gasoline for when there's no bottles left. And more nails to pack into the pipes you've collected – pull those out of anything you can. Be careful, okay? Use the attics and the cellars to move around, not the streets.'

She said the last part mostly for herself: the children waiting to begin their next scavenger hunt didn't need a warning. They knew the ghetto's warrens and its ways far better than she did. They understood that it was a place where the rules changed daily and punishments were arbitrary and unconnected. They'd adjusted to its dirt and its shortages and the disease and hunger which was never in short supply. It was heartbreaking how well adapted they were to an inhuman life, not that Noemi would have told them that. The boys and girls in her supply chain were proud of the fact that they had so many routes at their fingertips – they could switch in a second when the Nazis chose a new set of buildings to spray bullets into. They wore their ability to dodge the ongoing round-ups like a medal. The truth was that everybody in the ghetto – from the fighters engaged in the increasingly heavy battles, to the hundreds of civilians hiding in the maze of underground bunkers and praying for those battles to end – had the same slim chance of survival as the next. Nobody, whatever their age, wanted to be reminded of that.

'This is it. The SS have thrown a huge cordon round the perimeter, and they're increasing the number of deportation trains. They're planning our last days, whether that means dragging us out to the forests and shooting us there, or blowing this place up. So we've arrived. We're at the moment when we fight.'

It was Mordechai's call to action which had kept Naomi and Matthias in the ghetto, although they could – in theory – have left. If the danger hadn't been so imminent, if he hadn't been so inspiring. Most of the bonds of trust and decency people had lived their lives by in the outside world had been smashed apart by the degradation the Nazis had cast them into. But everyone trusted Mordechai. Everyone – including Noemi and Matthias – believed that if anyone could save the ghetto's

Jews, he could. His fighters called him 'The Angel'. His kindness and his determination not to shy away from the truth reminded Noemi of Hauke refusing to be cowed when Viktor singled them out on the stage. Mordechai was as clever and compassionate as he was fearless. He didn't hector; he didn't bully. He didn't expect or demand that everyone should take up arms just because he was determined to. Which meant that when Mordechai spoke, the ghetto listened, fighters and civilians the same. He'd helped the terrified families clinging on to each other to keep their nerve on the day before the uprising began, when he'd ordered everyone into hiding and an eerie silence fell. He'd helped them keep their nerve when the fighting began too, and the screams and the bullets and the terror tore at the skies and their ears.

Because they are invisible and forgotten and lost, and he's their last hope. And there's nothing left but madness if they lose that.

Noemi sent the children away to hunt for more bomb-making equipment, gathered up the weapons the fighters in her section would need to get through the day, and made her way back to headquarters, a gigantic bunker which ran the length of three buildings on Miła Street. Like her scavenger squad, she clung to the tunnels they referred to as rat runs and didn't take a single step outside. She hadn't done that in daylight since the first shot was fired.

Day one of the ghetto uprising had already turned into the stuff of myths, a David and Goliath story no one could stop retelling. 'We blew up a tank!' The opening would never grow dull. The fighters had swarmed out of their hiding places, clutching their precious weapons and expecting to meet death. Instead, they'd destroyed a tank and two armoured cars, mown down a platoon of German soldiers and delivered a shock which had caught the German authorities unawares and sent them reeling.

THE SECRET LOCKET 169

The Nazis had regrouped and retaliated quickly – there'd been buildings on fire and machine guns blazing within an hour. But then darkness fell, and the Nazis – afraid of the narrow streets and the ambushes waiting for them there, or so the story continued – fell back from their guns and pulled out. Everybody had run into the open that night to celebrate. They'd danced and laughed and toasted each other as if freedom was only one more ruined tank away. On the second day, a successfully detonated mine had killed at least eighty German soldiers, and the ghetto's new army had celebrated with more homemade vodka and increasingly elaborate stories. Since then, despite the vicious reprisals and the mounting number of Jewish casualties, the ghetto had never felt more alive. Every day the uprising continued was another day the Germans hadn't destroyed them. It was another day filled with hope.

And another day when that hope's tested, while we wait in vain for the rest of the city to rise up in support and join us.

Noemi forced that thought out of her head as she re-entered the bunker. It wasn't easy. Five days of fighting had spilled black smoke and red sparks and the charred stink of burning wood and burning bodies into the heavens and over the walls. Nobody could pretend it was business as usual in Warsaw; nobody was that deaf and blind.

And yet five days of gunfire and screams from inside the ghetto has produced nothing but silence from outside.

She breathed deeply, closed her eyes for a moment, tried to shake the blackness away. She pulled a smile onto her face as she roused the rest of her troop from a much-needed sleep and they conjured up breakfast from their dwindling rations. She spoke as if success was a certainty while they discussed their next fighting position and how best to deploy their overstretched weapons. What mattered now was no different to what mattered halfway across a challenging cliff face when there was no going back: confidence and self-belief, whatever the odds. Her doubts were for herself and for the brief moments she tried to share them with Matthias. Their first day in the ghetto had been an assault wave of sights and smells they'd struggled not to sicken at, but it had been a far worse experience for him. He'd been forced to accept that his entire family was lost, dead within the first months of their imprisonment. She'd held him that night as he'd questioned his reason for fighting and become temporarily lost in his grief, and some of the barriers between them had fallen. But he wouldn't talk about his parents again.

Which is his right and his choice. And being private about his feelings doesn't make him any less open to mine.

That wasn't strictly true. Matthias wasn't always comfortable around situations he couldn't control or define. He sometimes struggled to understand what was worrying her, or closed down if he didn't have an instant solution. But he never rejected her, so she sought him out as she always did, in the minutes before she had to pick up her gun and go out again. Whatever Matthias's shortcomings, there was no one in the ghetto she trusted like she trusted him.

'I'm uneasy – I can't help it. The people outside must know what's happening in here. They must know the Germans haven't beaten us yet, which is a miracle by anyone's telling, and surely a sign that beating them is possible. So how can they act as if there isn't a battle raging in the middle of their city? How can they keep on ignoring us and not get involved?'

She'd kept her voice low and looked round before she spoke. Mordechai wouldn't tolerate what he called *compromising morale*. Matthias did the same as he replied.

'You know the answer, Noemi; we both do. And – while I share your anger and frustration – it's pointless worrying at it now. Focus your energies on staying safe; you getting hurt worries me more than what's going on over the wall.'

His care over her was comfort of a sort, but it wasn't the

insight she wanted. His use of the word *pointless* had closed the conversation down.

Why doesn't he understand that I need to talk through what I'm afraid of? Why do I need to ask him to listen to me?

She didn't want those thoughts. They were unfair. Nothing Matthias had said was wrong; given their situation, it was practical advice. But the thoughts were there, and they'd let others in. *Focus your energies on staying safe* had conjured up Pascal's plea at the train station. They'd conjured up, *He always understood that I had to talk my worries out to get them under control; he always understood what I was thinking*, which wasn't strictly true either. She hated these moments – and there were too many of them – when she judged Matthias unfairly and by the wrong man. The question of why nobody would fight with them was impossible – no wonder Matthias didn't want to answer it. She didn't push him again; she let him go back to his men with the smile he deserved. What could he possibly say that would help when they both knew the truth?

How can they keep ignoring us? Because we're Jews and the citizens of Warsaw don't care when or how or if we die. Our fate is of no importance to them. Viktor would be very at home here.

Accepting that meant accepting that no support or rescue was coming. And accepting too that, even if the impossible happened and they won, breaking out of the ghetto would not guarantee their safety. That there was, in fact, no guarantee of safety at all while even one Nazi was left alive and determined to kill them.

So there can't be even one Nazi left standing, can there?

The question came to her in her father's voice, in an echo of the bravery he'd shown when he'd stood up to Viktor on the night the Nuremberg Laws were announced.

Noemi closed her eyes. She could sense both men hovering close by her. Hauke filled with pride; Viktor, please God, filled with fear at the thought of a Jew with a gun.

This is our fight. And the world outside will stop ignoring us when we win it.

She stopped worrying about the people of Warsaw and why they did or didn't care. She sent a kiss to her father wherever he was. Then she went back to her unit and she picked up her gun.

CHAPTER SIXTEEN
MAY 1943

'Are you all right?'

Noemi gulped down the water Matthias ladled out from yet another barrel that was emptying too quickly. The streets outside were baking in an unseasonal heatwave. Her mouth was dry with brick dust. Her clothes were sticky with the tar that coated the attics, a gluey residue of melted glass and sodden wood no amount of scraping could remove. Her limbs were screaming for a bed, for an hour's unbroken sleep; for silence. She was a long way from all right, but she nodded anyway.

'How bad is it? Have they brought more troops in?'

She let him check her hands for splinters and burns while she struggled to recapture her voice. She didn't think she was hurt, but it was a while since she'd stopped and taken any notice of her body.

'Yes, and it's escalating fast. They've brought in another flamethrower which is a real problem – there's not enough water left to tackle the fires as it is, and those are causing issues we didn't foresee. The heat from the buildings that are already burning has started to boil the air in the bunkers underneath, which means they're not safe anymore. Anyone caught in them will suffocate. And every time the soldiers find an exit hole, they block it up, or drop gas or grenades down. People are...'

She let him think a sudden and deliberate coughing fit was what stopped her. The truth was she didn't have a word for what the civilians still hiding a dozen days into the uprising were suffering. *Terrified* wasn't wide enough, neither was *desperate*, although both were true. *Going mad* was probably more accurate. The few hundred who'd survived this far had been through more trips to hell than the Bible would wish on the worst sinner, and they'd committed no sins at all.

From what Noemi and Matthias had gleaned since their first exposure to the cruelty that was life in the ghetto, most of its inhabitants had tried, to varying degrees, to co-operate at the start and make themselves useful to the Germans. They'd taken on roles as policemen or on the Jewish council, which was there to carry out German orders and administer daily life, because they'd thought that would make conditions more bearable and themselves indispensable. They'd registered for work in the factories, which were delighted to have a source of forced labour, because they believed nobody would harm or get rid of a key workforce. They'd carried on believing in justice long after that disappeared and had tried to behave inside the ghetto as if they were the respectable members of society they'd considered themselves to be on the outside, whatever the Nazis said to the contrary.

None of that had worked. Instead of being valued, they'd been dealt blow after blow and suffered humiliation after humiliation and lost themselves in the process. No one was whole anymore. By the time Noemi and Matthias entered the ghetto, the people shuffling through its filthy streets were little more than a collection of broken pieces loosely held together by skin.

Everyone Noemi encountered had watched a family member suffer and die because they couldn't provide the most basic medicine or food to save them. Or had been forced to watch as their loved ones were executed for 'infringements' no one explained and which changed on a whim. The men and women they'd helped find hiding places for when the uprising began had learned to survive by becoming as blind to the dead and the dying they walked past every day as the rest of the city was blind to them. They'd learned to be grateful when somebody else was summoned for deportation rather than them. To survive one day at a time and not to think forward or back, until the morning the ghetto had exploded with cries of revenge and filled them with hope. There was precious little of that left now. The enraged Germans might have been caught by surprise on day one, but this was almost day thirteen. The Germans had recovered the upper hand. They'd roared back with every weapon they had, from an arsenal that – unlike the beleaguered and isolated fighters forced to make bombs out of scrap – they could easily replenish. The struggle went on, but – while the struggle sustained the fighters – for the civilians, there was no hope anymore. There was precious little of anything beyond the near certainty of a pain-filled death.

'Did you hear about the announcement they broadcast this morning?' Noemi wiped her mouth and passed the empty ladle back to Matthias. She didn't bother asking if there was any food. 'The Germans have offered one last day of free movement. Anyone who comes out of hiding and voluntarily reports for transfer to a 'labour camp' will be spared. Anyone who doesn't will be burned along with the buildings. They've basically offered people the choice of facing the flames here or in Treblinka.'

Matthias produced a small square of black bread from his pocket and answered while Noemi fell on it.

'Yes, I heard. Mordechai's been going round trying to explain what the offer actually means, that it's a trap, but all most of them can hear is *spared*. Which is why he wants to get things moving. He's asking for volunteers to lead the civilians who are fit enough out through the tunnels and sewers and into the relative safety of the Kampinos Forest.'

Noemi shuddered as an extra choice that wasn't a choice was added to the toll. She'd spent the morning leading dazed and empty-eyed men and women through the connecting holes into a slightly less dangerous attic than the bullet-ridden one they'd been hiding in. She couldn't imagine any of them having the strength to wade through filthy waist-high water in the dark. They would panic; the soldiers would hear them and throw grenades down. It would be a suicide mission. And if they made it through, surely none of them had the stamina to cope with life in the open; that would be a challenge enough for the fighters. She was about to say that – until she caught the pinched look on Matthias's face.

'You're going to lead one, aren't you?'

Her heart plummeted when he nodded.

'Yes, I'm taking the first group out tomorrow. I know the risks, but we have to give them a chance, and they won't get one stuck in this death trap. And he wants you to lead a group of fighters out too, in a couple of days' time when the civilians are clear. He knows the battle here is as good as over. He wants to keep our best people alive for the next one.'

Noemi's first instinct was to refuse. She didn't want to be without Matthias, but she also didn't want to leave. She'd stopped thinking about her own survival; she'd stopped thinking about anything except standing with the ghetto to its end. She'd taken her cue in that from The Angel.

'Is Mordechai going too?'

Matthias shook his head. 'No. He was never going to leave – he made that clear from the start. But he was also very clear this morning about what he expected from us, and it wasn't taking part in a last stand. And he told me to tell you that leaving is an order.'

The speed with which he dropped to his knees beside her as she started to argue took Noemi completely by surprise.

'I can't make you do it, and neither can he, but listen to him, I'm begging you. I'm twenty-four years old; Noemi, you're twenty-two. I want to beat these bastards one day, and we will – we have to. But I also don't want to die in here. I want to live and fight again; I want to have stories to tell my grandchildren. And I want the same future for you.'

Grandchildren. She rolled the word round her tongue, but it didn't make sense to her. Neither did the word *future*; she couldn't remember the last time she'd considered it.

I always hoped you'd be my daughter one day.

Noemi had to bite her lip as Carina's words came unbidden into her head. And Pascal's face instantly followed them in a memory that filled her with fury and she didn't want.

This has to stop. That life out there was never going to be mine. Besides, he wouldn't rescue me if he was in here. He wouldn't care. He's a Nazi now. He'd be leading a charge on a bunker, he'd be wielding a flame-thrower.

There was a corner of her heart which hoped that – whatever Pascal might have become in the last two years – he'd never take part in such a callous act against civilians, especially if it involved her. She wouldn't let herself listen to it.

'What's wrong? What's the matter?'

Noemi couldn't meet Matthias's eyes. How could she admit what kind of a man had sprung into her head when a good man like him had mentioned the future and hinted that it might be a shared one? Or how her heart had leapt at the thought of Pascal before she'd crushed it back down when they were fighting for their people's survival? He would never trust or respect her again.

'It's nothing – a memory, that's all. It's not worth—'

'Don't listen to it. Whatever it is, it won't help you.'

When she finally looked up, there was more love in his eyes

than she'd remembered could exist in the world. She stared at him, pushing out the thought of grenades and panic and the flames gobbling up the buildings less than a block away. Pushing out the thought of Pascal. Desperate to feel what Matthias was feeling, desperate to feel anything at all.

This is the man I should love. This is the man who fits with my life, who my parents would want for me.

She reached for his hands, needing some way to ground herself, to make his feelings for her real. She let him pull her into his arms. She let him kiss her and felt her body stir when she kissed him back. And she told herself his embrace was exactly what she'd been craving, at the same time as she prayed it would wipe away her ghosts.

'You made it. Oh God, Noemi, you made it. I told myself you would, but these last few days waiting for you to arrive have been endless.'

Matthias's eyes turned red as he stumbled into the partisan camp in the centre of the Kampinos Forest and saw her sitting by the fire. It was a relief to see him too. Her life had been so full of goodbyes that seemed destined to be final, she only realised how much she'd been afraid to miss him when he reappeared. Noemi tried to stand up and tell him that, but the adrenaline which had powered her out of the ghetto had completely drained away, and all she could do was pat the space on the log beside her and smile.

'How was it? Did you all make it through?'

How was it.

Noemi stared into the campfire's dancing flames and willed her body not to start shaking again. Fire would feature in her nightmares for a long time to come. She didn't want to relive the details of her escape – her dreams were so vivid, she'd woken up twice convinced that she was wading through water. But she didn't want to hold back from him.

'It was... difficult. I don't know which tunnel you took and how damaged it was, but the one we had to use – from Muranowska 7 – was partially blocked with collapsed masonry and bricks, and trying to clear it quietly was a struggle. Not that we had much time to prepare it – we were barely in place in the cellar before the tanks started coming up Nalewki Street. The noise they made was terrifying.' She swallowed hard and tried to shake the grinding tracks from her ears. 'But it was worse when they stopped. Then we could hear the grenades rumbling through the bunkers to the left of us and the crash as those bunkers caved in. We had to stop trying to clear the tunnel then. We had to run.'

Run made the crossing sound simple. It had been anything but. The tunnel wasn't only half filled with broken bricks that could easily snap an ankle; it was also pitch-black and waterlogged and coated with mud. They'd stumbled through it, running their hands along the slime-coated walls, trying to hold on to their balance and their sense of direction. Without any way of knowing if the exit hole in the cellar on the other side of the perimeter wall would be clear, or fringed with guns, or if they'd even find it. The minutes they'd spent underground were imprinted like burns through Noemi's body. But, yes, they'd made it; all twelve of them. She and her troop had survived.

'Luckily Mordechai's message that we were coming and would need help also made it through. We came out inside the right basement; there was a guide waiting with water and food. And there were two hearses ready for us outside in the street. We lay on those under piles of empty coffins with no idea where we were going, and then...' She paused, although her pulse was racing as she tried to condense the fear that had flooded her when she realised what the coffins were for into a handful of words she could speak. 'Then we were buried in them, in the ground. Under branches in a corner of what I now know was the Jewish cemetery.'

Matthias's body, which was leaning against hers, turned as rigid as Noemi's had done when she'd been lowered into her roughly dug grave.

'It was all right. Actually, no, it wasn't. It was horrible. I've been frightened before, but that – waiting for the partisans to come and dig us up and knowing how easily they could be caught before they got to us, and what that would mean – was an experience I never want to repeat.'

She let her limbs tremble this time – she wasn't sure she could have stopped them – and let her breath go as Matthias swore.

'I'm alive, that's the main thing. And at least it made my first night in one of those things a little less strange, since I'd had a chance to get used to the smell of wet soil.'

She nodded to a group of *zemlyankas* – underground bunkers built almost entirely out of and under the earth – whose entrances sat a short distance from the campfire. Noemi had been allocated to one of the women's dugouts when she'd first arrived. The structure had been bigger below the surface than she'd expected, almost six metres long and two metres high, and there'd been more light than they'd managed to create in the ghetto's cellars. But the smell of damp soil and rotting leaf mould had seeped through them so strongly, it wouldn't leave her nose.

Matthias shifted on the log until they were facing each other. 'I'm using one of the smaller two-person spaces. I wasn't sure if you knew.'

Noemi knew. She also knew why he was telling her and why he'd elected to take one of the more cramped dugouts in the hope that she would eventually arrive. The system of women taking forest husbands had already been explained to her before Matthias returned from dealing with a food problem in the separate civilian camp.

'Most of the men treat us like fellow fighters and equals. A few think we're fair game. If there's someone you like, it doesn't hurt to throw in your lot with them and get yourself some extra protection.'

She'd known then that Matthias would offer himself to her. It wasn't a surprise when he took hold of her hand.

'I love you. You know that, don't you?'

Noemi did. She'd felt it in his kiss during their brief moment of peace in the ghetto before they'd been called into battle again. She could see it wiping the strain from his face when he nodded. And again, when he asked if she'd live in the forest with him as his wife and she'd nodded a second time. It had only dimmed a little when she didn't say the words back.

But I will. I care for him deeply; I know I do. So one day, I'll say them to him too.

She let her head drop onto his shoulder and hoped that, for now, the bond they'd forged since they'd first slotted their paths together would be enough to build a life. Because she wanted to do that; she wanted to snatch a chance of happiness in the midst of so much loss. And she wanted to love him the way he loved her, she really did. As much as she needed to finally bury the memories of her past love for good.

CHAPTER SEVENTEEN
MAY-JUNE 1943

This could be deliberate. If the rumours are true, this really could be what happens everywhere.

Pascal had hit that possibility more than once since he'd understood what was about to take place, but he couldn't accept it. The beard cutting and boot licking he'd witnessed in Russia had been unkind; it had been designed to humiliate. But this? It was a mistake – it had to be. If it wasn't...

No. I won't allow that to be true. Teyber's a decent man; he's a good soldier. He can't have realised there's nobody left in the village except women and children and old men. He'll be glad I intervened and stopped this.

Pascal was exhausted; they all were, including the divisional commander, General Teyber. The brief magic of conquering Mount Elbrus felt like a lifetime away. In the ten months since then, the mountain brigade had been redeployed to the Balkans – a place most of them could barely find on a map – and another battlefront which had drained their strength and their spirits.

And produced levels of savagery I never thought we were capable of.

Pascal took a deep breath. He was a captain now with

greater responsibilities. He couldn't afford to be clouded by what men who were less loyal than him might say was evidence that inhumanity could indeed be a deliberate act. The Balkans was a complex place. They'd all been fooled and misled. The local Yugoslavian partisans weren't the disorganised rabble the Germans had been told to expect. They were a ferocious opponent, highly disciplined and possessed of a knowledge of guerilla warfare the mountain men had struggled to match. It had taken weeks and terrible casualties on both sides to make a breakthrough against them. They'd all had to take the kind of snap decisions in the field no classroom could prepare an officer to make.

Which is why Teyber must have miscalculated the village's importance, and why it's more essential than ever that I keep a clear head.

Pascal pulled himself up straight, even though every inch of his body was desperate to curl up and sleep. He screened out the other officers gathered in the spartan house which the division had commandeered as its headquarters, without realising how misguided that decision was. That what he should have done instead was gauge the mood before he'd jumped in with his request for a hearing. Then he might have noticed how sour that mood was. Even when he paused for a moment and sensed it, he wasn't surprised at the frowns. He imagined the others were all as surprised as he was by how easily the situation could have run out of control. Their reaction simply underlined the need for his intervention.

'I do appreciate how a mistake could have happened, sir, and I don't mean any offence. On paper, the fighting should be all but over, but these partisans don't know when to stop, and they're getting reinforcements from somewhere. They're pinned down in that canyon by the Sutjeska River and hemmed in by the high mountains like sheep in a pen. They're being bombarded on a daily basis by German planes screaming across their camp at frighteningly low levels. Everyone but them can see it's hopeless. Anyone but them would surrender. And that stubbornness has forced us into reprisals that have been... Well, fierce I suppose you would say.'

Pascal had found them horrific, although he wasn't naive enough to admit that. The order to take no prisoners had been followed to the letter. Dogs had been sent after the fighters who escaped the German raiding parties, and the dogs weren't called off once their quarry was caught. Two compounds, including one with a hospital inside it, had been burned to the ground. Any concept of glory and honour had dissolved into kill or be killed. And Pascal had fought in the hand-to-hand battles alongside the best – and the worst – of them. He covered his momentary hesitation with a cough and continued.

'Obviously, we're soldiers and we signed up for that, and the same could be said for the partisans. But surely not for the villagers. So that's why I wonder if, with respect, there might have been a mistake?'

He stopped. Nobody spoke. Teyber hadn't looked happy when Pascal had asked for permission to speak and pulled his attention away from the maps spread out across the top of the rough wooden table. He didn't look any happier when Pascal finished. He didn't react; he didn't rescind the order. But his face grew more not less thunderous in the silence which followed Pascal's speech. And then he spoke, and Pascal's stomach somersaulted.

'You keep saying that word, Captain Lindiger, but who's made this mistake, you or me? I thought my order was perfectly clear, and yet you're not happy with it? What am I missing here?'

Pascal wanted to say, *All of it*. The words were on the tip of his tongue. He wanted to say, *What is it you don't understand?* That surely the state of the village spoke for itself. All the hamlets and small towns they'd passed through on the approach to the canyon had been shockingly impoverished by German standards, and Doli Pivski was no exception. The house they were currently using had barely a stick of furniture in it and only the lowest-grade lamp oil for lighting, and it was judged as the village's best home. But that was too blunt. And perhaps the general had been too busy with his battle plans to properly notice his surroundings, so Pascal resolved to try again and gestured to its emptiness as he answered.

'Forgive me, sir, but this place and these people, they have nothing, and there's no fighting men here. A quarter of the population appears to be children. As I said, I don't see that we have any quarrel with them. And so – and I say this again with respect – I wondered if, perhaps, the order to destroy the whole village was based on the wrong information.'

If you want to be part of Hitler's glorious new world, you have to accept all the cruelty that goes with it. You can't pick and choose.

Noemi's words – the warning he'd so easily ignored – suddenly roared through his head.

The general's face darkened again, but Pascal had come too far to stop. He'd forgotten his rank in the heat of the moment; he'd forgotten he wasn't Teyber's equal, and he hadn't noticed himself doing it. *I've got this all wrong* was written all over the general's face, but Pascal misread that too and jumped onto *I've misjudged this* instead. He cleared his throat as it gradually dawned on him that he should perhaps have requested a private meeting and not spoken so candidly in front of the other officers gathered round the map table. As he finally realised that what had sounded perfectly respectful and reasonable in his head had landed like a slur, and that needed correcting.

'Forgive me, sir, I'm sorry. I haven't handled this well.'

'That's true. But it's not what you should be apologising for.' The general's voice had dropped below his usual bark and became twice as menacing. 'Tell me, you did read the conduct guidelines that were issued before this campaign started, didn't you, Captain?'

The question wrong-footed him. The only answer Pascal could give and not face punishment or derision was, 'Of course.' He certainly couldn't admit that, once he'd read the first few paragraphs, he'd skimmed through the rest. The sentences packed with references to Bolsheviks and Jews as *the embodiment of the infernal* and *the revolt of the subhuman* had struck him as yet more rabble-rousing rhetoric that wasn't worth his time. Teyber nodded, although Pascal had an uncomfortable feeling that he'd seen right through him.

'So you do understand the war we're fighting. That's good. And you understand then that these people, in this village you're suddenly so keen to protect, aren't like us. That they are probably communists and Jews, and certainly contaminated and a long way beneath our contempt.'

Contaminated. Pascal knew with that word his battle was lost. That *deliberate* had been the right word all along. His stomach flipped again; his throat ran dry. He couldn't give up, but he couldn't control his fear of what was coming, and that wiped all considerations of rank and protocol – the pillars Pascal had built his career on – away. His words fell over each other. He was so desperate to make Teyber understand, he almost fell to his knees.

'Yes, I mean in theory, I do. I understand we'd say that, or about the partisans anyway, to give the men a sense of purpose, to stir them up and make the... whole business of battle easier on them. But, sir, I beg you – we're not talking about fighting men here. The people we've rounded up outside are innocent women and children. And doesn't their innocence matter more than any of the other labels we stick on them?'

The look of contempt on the general's face was the same one Noemi had worn when he'd talked about good and bad

Jews. When she'd asked him how anyone would be able to tell the difference.

Where does all this hatred end?

Pascal rubbed his hands over his face as if he could wipe her away. He didn't want her or her questions in his head. Not now, when he finally knew the answer. When he finally knew how badly he'd failed.

I was sure my view of the world was the right one – that's why I ignored her. And because acknowledging the truth of what she could see would have led me here, to this darkness I refused to look into.

He couldn't ignore it anymore – neither his conscience nor Teyber would let him. The general was watching him like a boy about to pull off a fly's wings.

'It gives the men a sense of purpose, does it? Well that's an interesting view, and one that leaves you so beautifully untouched. And as for innocent women? Does such a thing exist?' He smiled round at the officers, who obligingly laughed along with him. 'Have you seen the females fighting with the partisans and with the Russian army? They're as bloodthirsty as the men. And as for the brats they breed...' He shook his head slowly as if Pascal was the child. 'Think for a moment. Why would we let Jewish, or Bolshevik, children live? They're the next generation of the plague – they have to be stamped out. If you really had read the guidance notes, or listened in your racial science classes, you'd know that, wouldn't you? And yet apparently you don't. In fact, you question it. Do you have some suspect blood of your own – is that it? Should we be throwing you into a pit too?'

Teyber started to laugh as Pascal's knees buckled and he crumpled to the floor.

'For God's sake, pick him up before he says yes.' He nodded to two men who dragged Pascal back onto his feet. 'Go and see that my order is carried out. Spare nobody. And take the captain with you – if he tries to interfere and stop it, tie him to a post where he can watch the place burn.'

They had to tie him up at the first flames and the first shots or he would have thrown himself to his death. But he watched it all after that. He forced himself to. He had to finally see.

Five hundred and twenty-two civilians were murdered that day. Five-hundred and twenty-two innocents were thrown into pits and shot as they tried to climb out, or locked inside burning buildings and reduced to ashes. One hundred and nine children, including a baby just moments old, were shot in front of their hysterical mothers before they were killed too. Entire families were annihilated. Pascal knew the numbers because Teyber made sure to tell him the final total when the massacre was done.

'You chose this cause, Captain Lindiger. You chose this fight. Nobody lied to you about what would happen to our enemies. No one lied to you about the fate waiting for the Jews or the communists. Everyone who marches under the swastika understands what pure blood means, and no one gets to choose who lives or who dies because they have a moment of weakness. That's been set in stone from the start.'

Good Jews and bad Jews. His ignorant words haunted him harder than ever because Doli Pivski had given the 'vermin' faces he would never not see. The disgust in the general's voice was an echo of Noemi's when she'd asked him if he understood how many lives would be ruined.

He did now. There would never be any turning away from the truth again. There would never be any more pretending that hatred came with distinctions and without cruelty. Pascal had stood at the post they'd tied him to and saw the man he'd been through the flames' flickering light: a fool who'd filled his head with medals and glory and stopped up his eyes and his ears to the rest. His only consolation on the night of the massacre was the thought of the firing squad that would greet him in the morning. But Teyber had seen through him as clearly as Noemi, and he refused to deliver such a simple way out.

'You thought you could pick and choose which bits to believe in, didn't you? You thought all the talk of plague and preserving the blood was a sop to the thugs and not intended for brave heroes like you. Well your eyes are open now, although I'm sure you wish they weren't. So I'm not going to give your newly awakened conscience a coward's exit or waste bullets on you. You can take all your self-loathing back into battle and take your chances there. Perhaps one of our side will shoot you faster than the enemy. I don't care. But if you survive this fight or the next? Don't think you'll escape. I'll be keeping my eye on you.'

The bullet which took Pascal away from the battlefield with a badly damaged shoulder hit him three days later. He didn't fire it himself – he was watched too closely for that. It wasn't the fatal one that he wanted. Because he wanted death like he'd never wanted anything before. Which was why he prayed for the searing pain or the field hospital's rough treatment or the bone-shaking journey back to Germany to kill him. And was sorrier than he could express when nothing did.

Unterwald wanted a hero to cheer back into its midst; so did his father. Pascal wanted... Punishment was one possibility, oblivion was another. The only reason he didn't take that path was because he couldn't put his father through the scandal of a suicide. He retreated instead and bitterly missed his mother. He became a recluse under the excuse of convalescing. He refused to talk to anyone about his war, not even his father. He begged Viktor to take his copy of the Mount Elbrus photograph off the wall, but – when he tried to explain what a lie that had become, which was another truth he'd been loath to accept – Viktor told him to be quiet.

Viktor had hardened even more in the years since Pascal

had left. He ran the town on military lines, and his best friend was the bottle. He told Pascal to be quiet on an almost daily basis, particularly when he tried to ask about his mother's illness and death, or uncover what he called the truth about the war and Viktor called vicious lies. Pascal became obsessed with finding out how many other villages had suffered the same fate as Doli Pivski. He became obsessed with finding out what exactly went on in camps like Chełmno and Treblinka and Auschwitz, names he'd kept on the edge of his thinking for years. He pored over the newspapers, scanning the war reports looking for clues, looking for any reference to a specific policy designed to bring about the end of the Jews. Desperately hoping he'd never find it. His constant, 'But that's a lie,' when he found a spun story nearly drove Viktor to violence more than once.

Nothing in the newspapers Pascal scoured tallied with the truth he was now so painfully aware of. The brave partisans taking up arms across Poland and Yugoslavia were dismissed as 'an easy-to-defeat irritant'. The ferocious Russian fighters who Pascal knew would battle on to their last drop of blood were mentioned only in passing as 'not worth our concern'. Even the scale of the German defeat at the Battle of Stalingrad and the terrible death toll sustained there had been buried. Nobody mentioned the Jews, except to promise that Germany would soon be free of them. And nobody questioned anything. Life had continued in Unterwald as if war was still a sport played by heroes.

Pascal watched the young boys lining up across the street for the regular Sunday morning marches and wanted to weep and warn them what war really meant. He wanted to call a town meeting and tell the townspeople whose losses were already mounting to start pushing for an end to a war no one would ultimately win. But when he tried to explain his misery and confusion and guilt to his father, the man who'd taught him about honour and glory, Viktor threatened to have him committed rather than live with a coward in the family.

'What is wrong with you? Did the bullet hit your brain, not your shoulder? Do you want Germany to lose?'

The argument ran round in circles, never changing its course no matter how many times it flared.

'No, I don't think so. I certainly never wanted Germans to suffer. But given the things we've done, given the terrible atrocities we've committed, and the worse ones I'm almost afraid to imagine, maybe losing is what we deserve.'

Viktor's fists clenched. Pascal braced himself for a blow he'd promised himself as a good son he wouldn't return. But some remnant of paternal feeling always stopped Viktor's hand, if not his tongue.

'Atrocities? What kind of a soldier uses a word like that? Surely you've learned by now that war isn't a Sunday picnic? That bad things get done by both sides in battle, and then it's over and both sides move on.'

Bad things. Pascal shook his head, wishing he hadn't spent so many years treating his father like an oracle.

'I'm not talking about what's done on a battlefield. I'm—'

But Viktor was always a step ahead of him. 'You're talking about things that aren't your concern.' He shook his head as Pascal tried to argue back. 'I've seen you combing through the papers, muttering about death camps as if you don't quite believe in them. They exist – of course they do. What did you expect? The Führer said himself that a war in Europe would spell the end of the Jews. How did you think that would happen without some way to get rid of them?'

He could have been General Teyber, except Viktor had a more personal sting in his tail.

'You were always soft. I used to watch you tying yourself in knots over the Drachmann girl. Trying to persuade yourself that she was a different kind of Jew, a *good* one, as if such an idiotic idea existed. Acting as if you could bend the rules – and Hitler's plans – to fit around her. She turned you into a fool; she could have been the end of you. Well, hopefully she's at least got what she deserved by now and a bullet or the gas has done for her.'

Pascal wasn't back to full strength. Viktor had him in a stranglehold that sent a sheet of pain knifing through his left shoulder the second he stopped trying to hold on to his temper and leapt to his feet. And his father's tongue was as brutal as his grip.

'Don't get clever with me. I know far more about what's gone on than you think. And I'm the one who's in charge here, I'm the one who's respected in this town, not you, especially after this apology for a homecoming. If you threaten my position with your talk of *atrocities* and who deserves what, I'll deny you as a son and hand you over to the Gestapo as a traitor myself. And I'll get a medal for doing it.'

I'll deny you as a son broke the last tie between them. Pascal looked at Viktor and finally saw the bully he'd always been. He knew Viktor looked at him and saw failure. That would have destroyed him once; now, he no longer cared.

The two men avoided each other after that bout, although *I know far more* added itself to the dark clouds of suspicion whirling round Pascal's head. They didn't speak again until the envelope with its embossed swastika arrived.

'Here.' Viktor flung the letter onto the newspaper Pascal was painstakingly combing through. 'It's about time they called you back in and let me be done with you.'

Pascal waited for Viktor to leave before he opened it. He'd been expecting the summons – his shoulder was stiff and painful and his arm tired easily, but the bullet hadn't done enough damage to keep him permanently out of a war that needed every man it could get. He didn't know what he was hoping for. He couldn't bear the thought of putting on a uniform again, not now he hated what it stood for. He couldn't go back to the Balkans and watch babies die. For all Viktor's faults, he didn't want to shame him and desert. The best solution would be a training position at the Garmisch barracks, but he doubted that would come his way – soldiers gossiped worse than old women at the market; he assumed the entire mountain brigade would have heard about his stand-off with Teyber by now and labelled him as a coward.

Maybe it's a discharge; maybe they won't want a man like me back.

He brushed away that hope in the same second it came to him. Whatever the papers said about Germany's successes, he knew how stretched the battlefronts where. Any soldier still breathing would be found a post.

In light of your injuries, we have been advised by your previous commander that a return to active service is not the best use of your abilities. You have therefore been reassigned.

Pascal almost admired his *previous commander* as he read through the rest of the letter. Teyber had kept his promise and kept an eye on him, and he'd had the last twisted laugh. The captain who'd refused to massacre a village full of people who definitely weren't a threat, and probably weren't communists or Jews but were simply 'other', was being redeployed to a command post at Dachau.

CHAPTER EIGHTEEN

JANUARY 1944

The Warsaw ghetto was gone. The Nazis had destroyed the last remnants of it in the middle of May 1943, after twenty-eight days of relentless fighting. The explosion which blew it apart had trembled the earth sixty-five kilometres away in the heart of the Kampinos Forest. The flames which roared into the twilight that night turned the sunset from a gentle peach glow into an angry scarlet storm. The partisans had watched the ghetto's shell burn in silence, mourning the men and women who'd defended it till the end. Whose bodies had been turned by hatred to dust, whose names would live on as legends.

'Whose memory we will avenge when the city finally wakes up and rises.'

That promise had become the forest's refrain, although nobody knew how long they would have to hide and train and hope before the Poles decided they were sick of existing under a Nazi yoke and fought back.

If they ever do. It's been four years since the occupation began, and the noose round the city is as tight now as it was in 1939.

Now that she was outside the ghetto and back in some level

of touch with the world, Noemi knew that *if they ever* was unfair. The Nazi war machine had continued to hurtle at full speed across great swathes of Europe, and – despite the terrible losses inflicted on the German army in Russia – nobody had managed to put a conclusive stop to it yet. She could hardly expect a country which had been so brutally and swiftly occupied as Poland had been to do what the combined weight of the Allies couldn't. But Noemi had fought inside the ghetto's smashed walls, and she'd heard the silence outside them. It was hard to shake off the sense of betrayal. It was harder still to accept that the years she'd already spent fighting might only be a drop in the ocean, that there was no end to the conflict in sight. That their time in the forest was merely a pause between battles, not a chance to plan or rebuild, whatever she and Matthias told themselves to keep going through the long winter nights.

Noemi had gradually adjusted to life in the Kampinos, although she hadn't been certain at the start that she would. The first headlong dash from the cemetery into the densely packed trees – which had soon slowed to a clumsy half-run, half-walk as the miles tore at their starving and exhausted bodies – had been far more frightening than she'd initially admitted. The fighters had come at the forest blind, forced to put their trust in men none of them knew, praying they were being led to a place of safety and not into a blackmailer's den.

Everything had been a threat in the first few days on the run. The mosquitos which never stopped biting. The German patrols constantly sweeping the forest, determined to flush out the rebels who'd not only dared fight back against Hitler's soldiers in the ghetto but had escaped with their lives as it burned. The Jew-hunters who came carrying clubs and pitchforks and collecting fugitives to trade with the Nazis – dead or alive – for money or sugar or salt. Nothing had been familiar.

The Kampinos was so riddled with marshlands and

swamps, it was as if the entire landscape had been fashioned from black and bitterly cold water even in summer. Wet mist clung round the trees, ready to wrap itself in curtains around the survivors; thick mud sucked at their ankles at every step. As for the sky... there was barely a trace of it to be seen, beyond the odd pinch of deep blue caught like a scrap of torn silk on a treetop. This deep into the forest's heart, there was no hope of the sun either: its rays had been conquered centuries ago. This was a subterranean world, heavy with shadows; creeping with damp and the fungal scent of decay. The forest had felt like a nightmare she couldn't wake up from. But now... *I'm learning to tame it.*

That had felt like an impossibility at first. Noemi's first hours in the camp had been spent learning survival skills that were a foreign language to a girl brought up in Bavaria's mountains and meadows. *Look for the bright patch of green which marks a swamp before the water swallows you. Listen for the twig's snap before the enemy's boot fully lands. Understand which swooping bird call is actually a comrade calling a warning.* But then one – *learn how to make yourself one with the trees and use them for cover* – had made sense, and she'd realised staying safe was simply about learning to read a landscape, something she'd been born to do. Now she moved when the leaves moved, and she could hear the sound of a patrol coming as clearly as a swooping owl picks out a mouse. And she knew not only which plants could kill her but also which ones could keep them alive.

Noemi sealed the pot of paste she'd made out of steeped yarrow buds with a circle of wax and added it to the growing medicine shelf. The remedy wasn't as powerful as an antibiotic, but it would help stop a wound bleeding and could fight an infection that hadn't bitten too deep.

She stood back and admired her work, imagining Frieda picking up each jar and praising her talents while offering advice on how to do a better job next time. It was a warming thought for a cold day, even if the few tears she allowed herself to shed fell like frost on her cheeks. She dashed them away and rubbed her hands as clean as she could with snowmelt and dried them on a scrap of cloth which might have frozen slightly but at least wasn't blooming with the mildew that had eaten everything in the summer months.

She had one preparation left to make – an infusion of pennyroyal and mugwort – but that could wait. None of the malnourished forest wives were likely to need it: their bodies were struggling to support their own needs, never mind sustaining a pregnancy which would likely mean death for both mother and baby in such an unforgiving forest if it went to term. Besides, someone was singing outside by the campfire, somebody was laughing and that was the medicine she needed right now. She pushed a few loose strands of hair back into her braid – there wasn't a mirror to check it in, even if she'd had the desire to do so – and went outside.

The heavy snowfall had turned the *zemlyanka* she shared with Matthias into an ice palace inside and out, but at least the cold snap meant that the Germans wouldn't risk sending a search party into the woods and the partisans could stay in one place for a while. Summer – and the spring she hadn't yet experienced – demanded constant movement and constant vigilance. Nothing could be left visible. Tracks had to be swept clean with branches. Ashes from the campfires had to be thrown into the swamps. Anything that had been buried had to be covered with stones and leaves so the ground looked untouched but not suspiciously tidy. Sunny days and wet ones were as much of a threat to the partisans as the Germans, but snow was a godsend. Snow meant the campfires could burn at night as well as in the day. It meant they could stop and sit together, sing and tell stories. It gave them the chance to be more than survivors eking out a dangerous existence. It allowed them – however briefly – to be a family.

And – although we don't tempt fate and talk too often about the future – it's given the two of us the time to learn more about each other, for good and for ill.

Matthias was already at the campfire, surrounded by the bustle he always attracted. Noemi loved how popular he was and how easily he gave his time to others, whether they wanted a listening ear or advice. Nothing was too much for him. He was one of the few fighters who regularly visited the civilian forest camps, to see what help was needed there. Most of the other partisans, including her, avoided those – even the toughest of them stumbled when faced with starving, frightened children they could do little to help. She loved a great deal about Matthias; she cared very deeply for him. But she hadn't been able to fall in love with him in the wholehearted way he'd fallen in love with her. And he knew it.

'It wasn't meant to be me, was it? You'd been imagining someone else.'

Noemi tried to wipe the memory of those words away as she walked towards his welcoming smile. It always took an effort. They'd lurked in her head since they'd spent their first night together, when she'd woken up to find herself alone in the fur-covered bed.

'What do you mean?'

She'd found Matthias outside the dugout as the sky was slipping gently towards dawn. He was leaning against a tree, his arms wrapped round his body. It had felt kinder to wait until she knew what he'd sensed than to go straight to him.

'There was a moment, afterwards, when you weren't there. When your eyes were looking away from me as if you were searching for a different face. You seemed so...' He shook his head. 'Sad, Noemi. You seemed so very sad. And I was so stupidly happy. Does that make me a fool?'

She'd gone to him then and wrapped her arms round his. All the things she'd done with a gun or a grenade in her hand and yet she'd never felt so cruel.

'Not a fool, never that. I wanted it to happen; I wanted to be yours. You're the best, the kindest of men – you know that.'

His quiet smile had cut through her. 'But I'm not him, am I? Tell me who he was or who he still is to you, Noemi. Don't leave me wondering where I stand.'

She'd led him back inside the dugout before she explained, away from early-morning risers and prying eyes. She told him about the locket she'd once worn and the kind woman who'd been a second mother to her. She'd told him about the boy she'd grown up with who'd given it to her, and the hopes the town, and eventually they, had shared for a future together, despite the impossibility of their situation. She'd tried to explain the connection they'd shared, although that had always run too deep for words. She'd stumbled horribly when Matthias had asked, 'Why was it impossible?' And then reacted in horror when she completed the story.

'You're in love with a Nazi?'

He'd sprung away from her touch as if her skin carried hot coals in it.

'No! I was then, but that was a long time ago. I'm not now. How could I be, given what he is?'

The denial had been instant and heartfelt. In the end, they'd both decided to believe it.

But Matthias was right. I was thinking about Pascal while I was lying in his arms that first time, and about the bed we could have shared. And I hate myself for it.

Noemi had tried as hard as Matthias to wipe that memory away. She'd forced herself to remember the leaflets she'd found in Pascal's rucksack, not the kisses which came before that crushing moment. Or the slow walk upstairs with him she'd been ready to take. She forced herself to stop hearing Pascal's voice saying, *I love you*. She told herself those were words he'd never had a right to say. She told herself, in the same way she'd done time and time again, that he was the enemy, that the flag he'd chosen to follow had written him out of her life, whatever the ties that had once bound them. Because those things were true and what she was determined to believe. And they were what Matthias's goodness deserved.

She crossed to the firepit and sat down on the log beside him. His arm found her waist; her head found his shoulder.

We are together. We come from the same people; we share the same purpose. This is how the world is meant to be.

That was also true, and it was right, by every standard she lived by. So it was time she made her treacherous heart listen.

'I love you.'

It was true in so many ways, and it wasn't so hard to say it in the end, not to him. The look on his face as she finally handed him what he'd been waiting to hear was so pure, it stopped mattering that the words were, at their heart, a lie. There was, after all, still time to grow into the *I'm in love with you* that he'd heard.

CHAPTER NINETEEN
FEBRUARY 1944

Pascal was Bavaria-born; he was used to impossibly picturesque towns, and Dachau certainly fitted that description. Red roofs, onion domes, gabled houses painted in pretty pastels. An elegant palace sitting on the top of a hillside which burst into flowers in the spring. Dachau was so picture-postcard perfect that – according to the guidebook someone had left in the officers' mess – it had once been a haven for artists who had flocked to the town to paint its buildings and stunning landscapes. Pascal doubted any artists would want to paint it now. Pretty houses or not, Dachau was no longer simply a picturesque Bavarian town. The camp on its edges had stolen its name and become a byword for the kind of terror no visitor would come to see – and no inhabitant wanted to know about.

Challenging might be a good way to describe it.

Pascal winced every time the words he'd used to Noemi about the camp came into his head, which happened on an almost daily basis now that he knew its real face. He didn't know if he'd been arrogant or naive or – and he hoped this was the truth – he'd been trying to stop her worrying about her parents when he'd skated over Dachau's miseries, but he loathed that he could so easily have done it. He loathed a lot about the man he'd been then.

'The site's an old munitions factory, although it's expanded a lot since the first camp was opened here in thirty-three. There were less than a thousand prisoners in the first year; now there's a base level that's twenty times that. There's a lot of Poles here, but not so many Russians as there were – we had a whole army of them a couple of years ago, but the SS despatched them quick enough. There's Jews, obviously, although we're working our way through those too. Scum basically. The ones who are fit enough are put to work in the factories on site here, or at the sub-camps. If they're too weak to be of any use, and taking too long to check out, there's a handy shooting range a couple of kilometres away. Or we can use the euthanasia centre at Hartheim if we're getting backlogged. You'll get the hang of the rest of it. Just make sure you remember discipline is kept deliberately tight – they jump when we say jump. Not that many of them could actually manage to do that.'

Pascal had spent his first windswept day in the camp in October 1943 being taken through an induction programme by a brute of a man which had almost eaten through his stomach. And wearing the SS uniform which went with his new post, a uniform that – in an irony he couldn't share with anyone – no longer felt like an honour to put on but a casing his skin did not want to touch. That day, and all of them since, had required him to act a part he'd never have guessed at fourteen – when his heart was full of love for the Führer, and his head had blindly followed it – he'd ever be called on to play. Not that anybody watching him would have guessed he was struggling; he played his part far too well.

He'd admired the camp commandant's whitewashed villa and the neatly kept SS residential compound that day as if it was perfectly normal for elegant homes to occupy the same space as stinking and overcrowded barracks. He'd nodded at the guard towers and the electric fence – which was, according to his guide, 'a great source of sport on a dull afternoon' – with the same blank expression he'd used to note down the processes by which the inmates were stripped of their dignity. He'd done everything very well indeed. Until he'd come face to face with a squad of rain-soaked and skeletal prisoners shovelling ash from the crematorium into the long fire pits which edged the far side of the camp, imagined Noemi among their number and wondered at what point he'd go mad.

Which would have been easy to do and would have been one way out of this. That, or the alternative.

Pascal shifted the weight of the gun at his hip, remembering how often he'd sat staring at it in his first few weeks, considering the alternative to the post he'd been assigned. Trying to summon up the courage to turn himself into a target. *Challenging*. There were so many regrets he had about Noemi, so many things he wanted to apologise and atone for, and that word was high on the list. He should have said *cruel* or *inhuman*. He should have said it was one of the worst places on earth, whatever the Nazis pretended about the camp's importance as a place of correction.

There is only one path to freedom.

The slogan painted on the roof of the building which housed the camp's kitchen and laundry was impossible to miss, which was the point of it. So were the nine milestones that the prisoners needed to follow to attain that enviable state, which were also painted there, including hard work and obedience and love of the Fatherland. Except the truth, as Pascal and every inmate knew, was that the only pathway to freedom in Dachau was death, and there was no shortage of ways to find that.

The prisoners – who he'd managed to confirm from the files had included Hauke but not Frieda – succumbed to starvation or typhus in their thousands. They were shot, or overworked, or beaten until there wasn't an unbroken bone left in their bodies.

Or, if the numbers were small, sent to Hartheim to be despatched by lethal injection. Or Auschwitz if the numbers were big. And once they were gone? They were replaced by the trainload, and the cycle of cruelty and ill-treatment and murder went on.

Where does this end?

That question had hit Pascal like a second bullet when he'd discovered *Auschwitz* written next to Hauke's name. He'd been as sick in his office bathroom that day as if he'd swallowed poison. And now he could no longer turn away from the answer – not that he wanted to. He'd seen it in the pits at Doli Pivski. He'd seen it a thousand times bigger in Dachau. It ended with mass murder on an industrial scale.

But it cannot end with cowardice or self-pity.

For the first few weeks, Pascal had stared at his gun in despair and thought that the cycle couldn't be broken. He'd thought he couldn't continue as a witness to the regime's horrors and certainly not as an overseer of one of its brutal camps. But then he'd caught his breath and looked up. He deserved to feel shame, and he deserved to feel guilt. But the people whose lives he'd pretended were nothing to do with his deserved more.

'Do you have a moment?'

Pascal slid the pile of work permits he'd been up since dawn signing under a folder on his desk as his office door opened and Captain Rohmer – one of his fellow compound leaders and a man who thought closed doors didn't apply to him – walked in. Pascal hated him. Rohmer's favourite pastime was extending a roll call until a prisoner collapsed, so he could punish an entire barracks' worth of inmates for hiding a sick one. He found the man a smile anyway because a smile and a ready ear served his purpose.

Like the mountain brigade, the SS officers who formed Dachau's command staff and oversaw the camp's daily life were a tight unit, bound by comradeship and shared beliefs. Most of the younger ones had come from other work camps or had been recruited from the guard unit's lower ranks. The oldest had been part of the SS in its earliest days and had been rewarded with an office job and a healthy salary for staking their loyalty so quickly. They all viewed tolerance as a weakness and ruthlessness as their duty. Prisoners were there to be degraded; their lives held no value. Weapons were always kept loaded. Although Pascal held the same rank, his background meant he wasn't one of them, but it soon became clear that wasn't the black mark it could have been. Instead, his past, or the edited parts of it which were common knowledge, became a story he'd turned to his advantage.

Despite his fears, his actions at the Doli Pivski massacre hadn't followed him to Dachau, although his fellow officers had investigated his background as far as they were able. They'd ferreted out that he was an alpine brigade man, that he'd trained at the fabled Garmisch barracks and fought in Russia and the Balkans. And that he'd been wounded at the Battle of Sutjeska, a conflict which had already taken on mythic proportions. That had impressed them. Once one of them unearthed the Mount Elbrus photograph with his name printed underneath it, Pascal stopped being an oddity and became a living legend.

Every attribute that had raised eyebrows on his arrival suddenly strengthened the hero's narrative Pascal didn't want, but had gradually learned was both a blessing and a workable disguise. He was taciturn and aloof because that was the way of the mountain men, not because he was overwhelmed by the horror of his new surroundings and how he was meant to act there. He kept to himself because he was a lone wolf, not because the other officers' brutality sickened him. In another irony Pascal couldn't escape, he'd never hated the regime more, and he'd never been such a trusted part of it. Or more determined to use that to his advantage.

'What can I do for you, Rohmer? What's giving you grey hairs so early today?'

Rohmer didn't waste time on pleasantries – he never did.

'We need a complete sweep of the camp. I've been reliably informed someone's been smuggling medicine in – presumably via a work placement. We need to catch whoever's responsible and make examples out of them.'

Making an example of inmates was Rohmer's other favourite pastime, next to holding punishing roll calls. The man was endlessly inventive when it came to devising new ways of torture. Making a group of prisoners dance beside the electric fence until they overbalanced and fell into it was his latest foray into camp entertainment. Pascal loathed him with a passion none of the other officers knew he possessed. But he wasn't about to reveal any trace of that now, not when a sweep of the camp was shorthand for a mass execution that – with a little care and a little time – he could at least partially prevent. He nodded to Rohmer as if nothing could be easier.

'Of course. I'll get my block leaders on the case and make sure the word is passed round to the other commanders. Although the sweep itself will obviously have to wait until later – we can't do anything that will impact on today's workforce, as I'm sure you agree. Reliable information or not, none of us, especially the commandant, have time to deal with aggrieved factory owners who've been left without workers. Let's hold off until evening roll call, so we can make alternative arrangements for tomorrow if, as you say, widespread punishments are required.'

Rohmer wasn't particularly happy with the response, but there was nothing he could do about it. The commandant wasn't a patient man at the best of times, and he wouldn't thank any of his staff who caused him to be accused of hampering production lines.

Pascal picked up a folder as Rohmer reluctantly agreed and

managed to hold himself calm till the man left, although his heart was racing. Rohmer was a notoriously lazy man who was fond of his home comforts and the shortest hours he could work; he'd go off the idea of a night-time sweep within an hour.

But he won't delay forever. Which means I have today to prepare as many more work permits and transfers as I can, and warn everybody who needs warning.

He pulled himself together and took another sheaf of blank forms from his desk drawer. The Mühldorf sub-camp needed more men to hollow out the tunnels where the next generation of Messerschmitt fighter planes were going to be built. The bunkers under excavation at Kaufering also required more labour. He'd had those requests on his desk for a few days, which meant he could move prisoners from his compound to both those places and no one would question him doing it.

Pascal reached for his pen and his embossing stamp and began writing. Neither solution was ideal. The men he transferred would be safe from a sweep, but safe was a relative term. The work he was sending them to do was dangerous, the likelihood of an injury was high and there were no medical facilities at either sub-camp. Given the high mortality rates and the expendability of the workforce, the rations and living conditions were likely to be worse than at Dachau. But both places offered a better short-term chance of survival than staying put, and sometimes one chance was enough.

It was late by the time he finally completed the task – hiding away all day and devoting himself to it wasn't an option. The camp was quiet; there'd been no word of an air raid. Once evening roll call was done – and that passed, as Pascal had expected, without any interference from Rohmer – all that was left to do was to carry out an unscheduled barracks' inspection. No one would question that either: he'd be commended for his diligence if anyone noticed. Which made it the perfect cover for Pascal to meet with some of the prisoners he'd already persuaded to trust him. The meeting would be quick and limited to a small core. Then it would be up to them to spread the message for people to stay on their guard until they could be moved, without alerting the inmates who were in the Gestapo's pockets, not his.

And to make sure that the medical supplies Pascal had been smuggling into his compound – to save lives and win trust – since the previous December were very carefully hidden.

CHAPTER TWENTY
OCTOBER 1944

'Get down, Noemi! There's a Goliath coming straight towards you. If you can get to a vantage point, try and take it out.'

Noemi flung herself onto the blood-sodden ground and began half scuttling, half crawling out of the miniature tank's range. She couldn't see who'd shouted at her, and she hadn't heard the remote-controlled mine clattering towards the pile of bricks where she'd stopped in a hopeless attempt to hide and draw breath. She could hardly hear anything above the whirlwind of noise that roared relentlessly round the city. The last remnants of mercy had been stripped from Warsaw. The misery and chaos which had once been confined to the ghetto had spilled out over the whole city. Its streets rang day and night to the thump of pounding shells and collapsing buildings, to the bellow of rocket launchers and the wail of agonised screams. Peace no longer existed in any form. The Germans only paused the flames and the bullets so they could switch on their loudspeakers.

'Surrender now – your allies have deserted you. Surrender now and no one will be harmed.'

Explosions and lies followed by more ear-shattering explosions, which left a silence behind them that sucked in the whole world. The cycle of destruction and threats was endless and nerve-shredding, and the Germans had long held the upper hand. The orders from the resistance commanders to keep striking back flew as thick as the grenades, but it was almost impossible to carry them out. There was nowhere left standing that could safely act as a vantage point. Noemi had nothing left to use which could take out a Goliath. And – unlike some of the more fervent Polish fighters who were prepared to die for their city – she wasn't going to use her body to throw the miniature tank off course. Despite everything she'd lived through, and everything she'd lost, she wanted to stay alive too much to make that kind of sacrifice.

'It's seconds away from you – move!'

Noemi stopped waiting for a brief break in the bullets and threw herself through a hole in the nearest wall as the Goliath swivelled and homed in on its target.

'In here, quickly.'

She plunged after the voice, hurling herself through another ragged opening and down a cracked flight of stairs, praying she wasn't about to swap fire for fire and find herself trapped in an overcrowded cellar. Thankfully her luck held. Her invisible saviour had led her into one of the few underground hospitals the Germans hadn't yet destroyed. Noemi stopped and tried to take stock of herself. Her hands were cut and bleeding; one of her knees was torn. Her throat was so parched every breath spluttered out on a cough, and her legs had no more substance than water. She sank down onto the damp floor and dropped her head into her arms. Warsaw needed her, it needed them all, but it had almost broken her too.

The partisans had spent over a year hiding out in the forest, waiting for Warsaw to finally decide to fight. It took until summer 1944 for the war's tide to turn strongly enough for the citizens to believe they could do it. Germany's armies were no longer the sole rulers of Europe by then. That stranglehold was broken in June, when the Allies had invaded Normandy and started to take the continent slowly back. And if that hadn't been cause for celebration enough, the Russian army was also on the march and had reached the Bug River, the border between Poland and the Soviet Union. The partisans had celebrated deep into the night when that news filtered through the forest.

'Once the Russians cross that, they'll be unstoppable. It's a straight path from the Bug to Warsaw, and on to Berlin.'

'The German garrisons won't stay around for this – they'll retreat rather than face the Soviets after what happened at Stalingrad. And the city will finally rise up.'

'Warsaw can be taken; it can be won back for Poland. This is the end for the Nazis.'

The battle cries had rung like church bells round the trees, and the partisans had put all the frustrations and betrayals of the failed ghetto uprising behind them. They'd formed themselves up for battle and marched back into the city, expecting a vast people's army to come running to greet them. Expecting the Soviets to swarm over the Vistula River and the Germans to take to their heels.

Acting as if the stars were aligned and fixed on their course. Acting as if the Nazis would simply accept the fate we'd assigned them. Except it's been three months and they haven't accepted that yet.

Noemi opened her eyes and blinked until they adjusted to the gloom. Once her legs felt a little less shaky, she got up and went in search of anything clean she could use to bandage the mess the broken glass and brick fragments had made of her hands and her knee. She knew better than to disturb the nurses moving from one hopeless case to another.

The makeshift hospital was dark, lit only by candles and paraffin lamps which flickered and jumped with every explosion. Noemi was glad of the shadows: she had no desire to see the twisted and crying bodies crowded onto the floors and planks of wood that stood in for stretchers any more clearly than she already could. The partisans had marched into Warsaw confident of victory, but the Germans hadn't given up and retreated the way they were supposed to do. They'd brought their ghetto tactics onto the city's streets instead, driving Warsaw's citizens into shelters they'd already laid with mines or into cellars they immediately stuffed with grenades. They'd employed flamethrowers too, wielding them like tamed dragons through the closely packed streets. The charred smell of their violence hung everywhere.

Noemi cleaned and repaired her hands as best as she could – the wounds were superficial, which was one good thing because there was no medicine left to fight an infection – and made her way back out into the ash-darkened streets. She was so weary every step was a punishment, but there was no time to rest. They'd lost far too many fighters for anyone who could function to stand idle.

'The dawn of freedom is burning.'

The partisans had sung that on their first night in the city, weeks ago at the start of August when the Home Army resistance fighters, if not Warsaw's frightened people, had clapped their arrival out of the woods. They'd been confident the battle's outcome would be quick and decisive.

And now?

Noemi picked her way round landmarks that were so shattered, she could no longer remember what they'd once been. The city was long past the point where street maps had any value – it redrew itself every day.

And now we're fighting over broken walls and brick dust and Warsaw is barely an idea.

She'd lost sight of how or when the battle for the city would end. She wanted to live, but she couldn't picture that actually happening. She measured her life in seconds, by the distance from a corner to a doorway, from one tiny patch of shelter to the next. She'd lost count of the number of bullets she'd fired, or the number of bodies that had fallen dead as a result. She threw grenades and Molotov cocktails at soldiers and snipers she no longer gave any thought to. The days of worrying about taking a life and wondering how that act would make her feel were long gone. She'd lost sight of everything except the need to kill or be killed. She'd become... *Part of the war machine.*

The tears came out of nowhere then, flooding her face, pouring over her bandaged hands. It wasn't supposed to be this way. The fight for the city wasn't supposed to be a repeat of the uprising in the ghetto, but that's exactly what it was.

On the first day, the combined resistance forces had achieved success after success: they'd captured a key German arsenal, a train station, the main post office, a power plant and a great swathe of the city. The celebrations had continued until dawn. But then the second day had come, and the next, and the Russian troops hadn't. The two to three days the Home Army had expected to have to hold Warsaw on their own had stretched into weeks and stretched their numbers and nerves and resources. Tens of thousands of civilians had been caught in the crossfire and killed. And the Germans hadn't run. They'd decided to punish the city for its arrogance instead, and they'd unleashed hell across it.

And they won't stop until they've wiped every trace of it from the planet. And we won't stop either. There'll be nothing left to say Warsaw was ever here. There'll be nobody left but the dead and the dying.

The atrocities had escalated on both sides. A group of young boys had thrown petrol bombs at a German tank and set it on fire, burning the crew alive. The next day the Germans had left a second tank in Kilinski Square, but this one was packed with explosives. More pointlessly brave boys and girls had died that day than the Home Army could count. They had retaliated by blowing up the German barracks on Listopada Street; the Germans had burned down a hospital packed with civilians in the beleaguered Praga district in revenge for that. On and on it went, blow for blow, savagery matching savagery, until Noemi could no longer remember why she was fighting.

Because our dreams of freedom and a future have vanished in the smoke and the rubble and the ruins. And the fighting has become an end in itself.

All the hope of a better tomorrow that she'd been clinging to since the first time a blond girl in a black skirt had thrown insults at her drained away. She slid onto the rubble-strewn ground, curled up against the shell of a house and cried until she was as empty as it was. Then she got up, because there was nothing else to do but get up, shouldered her rifle and walked on.

'Every time I find you, it feels like a miracle.'

Noemi had no idea how Matthias had laid his hands on candles or a clean pile of bedding in the broken city, but she was very grateful that he had. He'd turned a small corner of an abandoned brickworks into an oasis. For an hour or two anyway. He'd barely rolled out of her arms before his body tightened up.

'What is it? What's happened?'

Noemi pulled herself up and reached for her shirt. She'd seen him look bleak and despairing before as the battle for the city dragged on, but this was something far darker. She could see death standing at his shoulder. She could see its shadow in his eyes.

'Whatever the news is, you have to tell me.'

The candles had tricked her into thinking the room was warm. Now she could feel the ice cutting through the wind snaking between the bricks that loosely made up the walls, and the damp that heralded rain settling onto her skin. Matthias was already on his feet and in his clothes, but he came back to her when she reached for him.

'The Germans have found our dugouts. They swept through the Kampinos two days ago with tanks, burning the villages that edge it, shooting the villagers who didn't run fast enough. And they hunted our fighters down until...' He paused, sobs clogging up his throat. 'They're all dead, Noemi. The group's been completely wiped out. They used dogs to make sure they found everyone.'

Noemi had thought she was finished with crying; she'd thought she'd spent all her tears in the street. She hadn't. The Kampinos had been her home and her shelter. The men and women who'd risked their lives to travel back to the camp from the city in order to collect the last of their supplies were her friends and her family. She couldn't speak as Matthias went on.

'I thought we'd go back there once this was done. I thought there'd be enough of us left to build a proper community in one of the villages once the Nazis were defeated. That we could heal there together and plan our next steps.'

Noemi dressed in silence while Matthias stared out through the hollow that stood for a window, watching the crimson-and-ruby flames licking up through a carpet of smoke. The brickworks looked out across the Old Town. They should have been able to see St John's Archcathedral and the Prudential House on Napoleon Square, the highest building in the city. Instead, the skyline was empty. The cathedral had been shelled until it collapsed. There was nothing left of the Prudential except a twisted steel frame.

'But there won't be any healing now. There won't be enough of anything to rebuild. The Russians aren't coming, at least not yet and not this far. That's the other piece of news. There's going to be a ceasefire, or a surrender, call it what you like, but it'll be announced in the next couple of days. Whichever way you slice it, the Germans will have won and we'll be officially classed as prisoners of war.'

Noemi moved over to the window beside him and slipped her hand inside his. 'Which means nothing to the Nazis, and they'll shoot us as soon as the ink on the agreement is dry.' She stared down at the city they'd fought so hard to free as his hand tightened round hers. 'That can't be our ending. To be murdered and thrown away like rubbish into a pit. I refuse to believe that was always where our path led. And – after everything we've been through and fought for – I'm not going to make it that easy for them.'

'I never thought for a moment that you would.'

Matthias's laugh came out of nowhere, and the ice and the damp disappeared. Noemi turned her back on the darkness and the pain that would leach through the city for years, whoever laid claim to it, and pressed herself into his arms. She could feel his heart beating; she could feel the energy flowing back into his body. She closed her eyes and let the same strength flow through hers. They were fighters; they'd won victories. The Nazis had thrown all their weapons at them, but they hadn't been beaten yet.

Matthias leaned back a little so he could see her face. 'We're not going to die here then, you and me?'

Only a fool would answer *no* to that given the situation they were in. But Noemi had learned sometimes the only thing that mattered was being a fool. She let Matthias's smile wrap its warmth around her; she let the light in his eyes remind her they were young. She reached up and stroked his cheek; she pulled his face down to meet hers and tasted love in the touch of his lips. And she made him a promise filled with all the strength she'd brought out of the forest as they prepared to go back into the city, not to fight this time but to find their way out.

'We're not going to die at all.'

. . .

She lost him somewhere between Podchorążych Street and the river as the rain tipped thick curtains over the streets.

They'd been so careful; they'd come so close. Returning to the Kampinos was out of the question, which meant there was only one route they could take: across the Vistula River to Praga on the east bank. The Germans had finally been beaten out of that neighbourhood by the combined efforts of the Soviets and the Home Army, who were now fully in control there. If they could reach it, they could regroup – they could find a way out of the city if that was what they chose to do. The plan had seemed like a possibility when they built it, especially if the fighting really was almost at its end. They'd left the brickworks with a new sense of purpose. But there was no sense once they stepped outside into a newly brewing thunderstorm that a ceasefire was coming.

Bullets raced like maddened mosquitos round the two bombsites they needed to cross to find the river. They'd navigated their way safely through those, freezing their bodies flat on the ground until the worst of the gunfire was done. They'd found safety behind broken walls and deserted warehouses; they'd timed their dash from corner to corner without incident. But the third burst came from nowhere and caught them unprepared and out in the open. They'd had no choice except to fling themselves through it at full speed.

Noemi reached shelter. Matthias didn't. She could see that he was hit, that he was down. She could also see he was alive. But when she tried to run back towards him, he broke the silence that had followed the onslaught with a furious, 'Don't you dare.'

'I can't leave you.'

She didn't care how loud her voice was. She didn't care how many patrols came. But Matthias did and he wouldn't listen.

'I'm hurt. I can't follow you yet, but I will, and I'll find you. But I won't let you stay with me, so don't try.'

She could hear the pain in his voice – and the fear. But he was a fighter and so was she, and she also heard the order.

'I love you.'

She didn't know if he'd heard her over the sound of the machine gun which opened fire as she shouted. She chose to believe that he had and that the shadows would hide him until he could crawl to safety. She clung on to that belief as she weaved through the maze of streets that crowded the waterfront and searched in vain for an unbroken boat. There was nothing left on the shore beyond rotted splinters. There were no bridges intact or deserted enough to risk crossing. There was no other option if she wanted to reach Praga except to swim there.

I can't do it.

Her body ached; her heart was covered in bruises. There was no Matthias to spur her on. There was no certainty where she was going; there was no certainty she would reach it. There was nobody coming to the rescue. All she had was the river, and that felt like nothing worth having at all. If Matthias hadn't sworn to come and find her, she wouldn't have risked it. But he had, and ignoring that promise was impossible. It felt as if she was condemning him to death.

The water was so bitterly cold when Noemi slid into it, she almost went under with the shock. She struck out, her boots bobbing against her neck where she'd tied them, wondering if slipping away might not be the best thing. If the only freedom she could truly find was there beneath the black water. In the end, her body took over, pushing her on to carve out the next stroke, carrying her to the brief respite of a sandbank. She hauled herself onto that and stared back at the city. The view was almost beautiful. As long as she told herself that the red glow was the sunset and the rockets were fireworks, and the searchlights were the last dancing rays of the sun.

He might not be badly hurt. He might make it to Praga. We might find each other again.

So many *mights*, but she had to hold on to them. They were a reason to keep going in a world where reason had gone.

'I'll be waiting for you.'

The words danced away on the wind, in an echo of her last parting with Pascal. Noemi refused to be blindsided by that. This was about the future, not the past. This was about her and Matthias. They'd survived the ghetto and the worst days of the uprising; they could survive this.

She closed her eyes briefly and focused all her thoughts on Matthias, imagining his smile, imagining him healing. Then she turned her back on the city and slid down into the water again.

PART FOUR

CHAPTER TWENTY-ONE
FEBRUARY 1945

'Your secretary has informed me about your condition, Captain Lindiger, and I agree with her that you shouldn't be here. I appreciate that you want to continue with your work, but I won't allow it. You could make yourself worse. If it's typhus, which I strongly suspect it is, you could infect the rest of us. I'm going to arrange transport to the main hospital in Munich and send you for treatment right away.'

Pascal was still arguing as the commandant put the phone down and terminated the call. He closed his eyes and drew a breath that broke into a coughing fit. He suspected typhus too. His head was a scrambled mess; his shirt was plastered with sweat. His back felt as if a mule had kicked it. The livid red rash which had appeared on his chest that morning had drained the colour from his face. He was hardly surprised that his secretary had taken one look at him and fled. He also knew he urgently needed medical help, but there wasn't time to take it. He couldn't leave, not with the end so close and so much left to do.

He wiped his eyes and groped for a pen and paper, intending to make a list of the men he needed to speak to and save, until a thankfully lucid moment stopped him. The war might have entered its dying days, but that didn't mean the killing was done with at Dachau, of inmates or traitors. Any list he wrote would have sent them all to the shooting gallery. The irony of the situation – that he was now determined to stay alive and stay in the camp – wasn't lost on him, despite his severely weakened state.

He dropped the pen and held on to his desk as the room began quivering, running through the facts he was sure of in an attempt to hold himself together. The war was no longer Germany's to win and the path to defeat was accelerating – that was a certainty, even if Hitler wouldn't accept it. The Führer was obsessed, in public at least, with telling the story of his 'victories'. The brutal suppression of the Polish uprising in Warsaw. The panic caused by the deadly V2 rockets raining down on London. The offensive he'd launched against the Allies in Holland and Belgium which he swore would lead to the recapture of France. The Führer continued to make speeches claiming that Germany couldn't be beaten. That Germany could instead beat back the Russians, even though that army was less than eighty kilometres from Berlin and had never looked stronger. He continued to put the German people on an increasingly frenzied war footing. In public, Hitler acted as if victory was merely one more battle away. But the orders being sent to the camps hinted at a very different story behind the scenes.

Himmler has ordered the dismantling of the gas chambers at Auschwitz. Prepare for further orders to follow.

As soon as that memo had arrived on Pascal's desk at the end of October 1944, he'd seen it for what it was. The destruction of evidence; the concealing of guilt. The last panicked gasps of a monstrous regime. When the further orders came in, they confirmed it.

All bodies which have been buried at Dachau and in the

woods surrounding it are to be exhumed and burned without delay.

A shortage of coal had temporarily closed the crematorium which dealt with the rising death toll, but that was soon rectified. Now the ovens were churning day and night, and the forests had grown a carpet of ash. And February had brought a new influx of site-specific commands, which all began with *prepare.*

Prepare the camp for a new influx of prisoners. Prepare the guards for greatly increased numbers who must not be allowed to threaten discipline. Prepare evacuation plans in the form of a march that can be actioned at speed.

The Russians had discovered Auschwitz and its heart-stopping cargo of human misery at the end of January. They'd shared its horrors with the world. They'd fuelled the soldiers closing in on Germany from all sides with a new reason to hate the people they were about to conquer. And whatever Hitler had told those threatened people to believe, their enemies were unstoppable.

The Allies had crossed the Belgian border and taken Aachen; they had a foothold on German soil. They'd reached Strasbourg, which was less than three days' march away from Dachau. The Russians controlled most of Poland; they were advancing towards Austria as well as Berlin. The war was about to burst across Germany's borders and swallow it. More killing camps and more crimes against humanity were about be uncovered. But if Hitler had his way, more evidence – dead or alive – would be destroyed first. Which was exactly what Pascal, regardless of how ill he was or how many or how few inmates his efforts could save, had been determined to warn them about and stop.

. . .

'Germany is going to lose; it's inevitable, but Hitler won't accept it. He's demanding that last stands be made all across the country, so there's no guarantee the end will come quickly. In the meantime, more prisoners are going to be brought in here from the camps closest to the front lines. I don't have access to the exact date for those transfers yet, or to the numbers involved, but Dachau is already stretched to breaking point, and any new influx threatens chaos.'

Pascal paused. This could be the last clandestine meeting he was able to convene, and he needed the men hanging on his words to understand how even more fragile their existence was about to become, without stripping them of all hope that they'd survive. He wasn't sure if those two things were possible. And none of them had the time to waste on false promises.

'To put it bluntly, what's coming is worse than everything that's come before. The prisoners who arrive here will be starving and likely sick, and they'll have been marched beyond their endurance. There won't be enough rations to sustain them – or you. Or any way to prevent a mass epidemic breaking out if they bring typhus or dysentery with them, which we have to assume they will. And Dachau will only be a temporary stop; there'll be a clear-out here too. When the end does come, the Nazis' one concern will be their survival. Which your survival threatens.'

'You're a little ray of sunshine, aren't you?' Leon – who'd been one of the first inmates to decide Pascal was worth trusting, and could have been aged anywhere from twenty to sixty, his face was so devoid of fat – managed a smile which stretched his cracked lips. 'But you don't need to spell it out. We're evidence – we know that. They'll kill us here, or they'll march us out and kill us on the road, like they're doing with the rest. The question is, what can we do about it?'

'Get ahead of them.'

Pascal glanced round the small group of men who'd become

his lieutenants. So many more lives depended on their actions and their trust in him than the men he'd spoken directly to himself. And any one of the increasingly desperate inmates waiting in the wings could betray his plans and his accomplices for the promise of a freedom they'd never actually see.

Which has been the case since the first day I smuggled medicine in here and positioned myself as the 'good one'. No one betrayed me then; no one's betrayed us since. That's the best any of us can hope for.

His reply was greeted by a chorus of, 'What on earth do you mean?' that he could only partially answer.

'You need to do what the guards have been told to do and prepare yourself. Keep away from the new prisoners as much as you can. Find, or dig out, or build hiding places wherever they won't be found – underground, in the workshop stores or attics, in the barrack roofs if you can manage it. I'll help, I'll get you some tools, although you'll have to fashion most of what you need yourselves. If there's a chance to create a diversion to cover what you're doing, I'll take it. The main thing to do is to get started. Once the camp gets crowded, there'll be far fewer sweeps of it, which should help.'

He stopped again, waiting for the questions or concerns which would have been justified, but nobody spoke.

'It's a lot to take in, I know, and none of this will be easy to do. The only other advice I've got for you is to hold your nerve. Timing will be everything. You won't be able to disappear into hiding until the Allies are almost upon us, or roll calls have been abandoned, which might come first.'

'But if the roll calls continue, of the old sections at least, how will we know when the right time is? How do we avoid alerting the guards or getting swept up in a purge?'

The silence in the barracks hung so thick, Leon's whisper sounded twice as loud as it should have done, and everyone glanced nervously round. Leon wasn't trying to smile anymore.

The years had dropped from his eyes if not his face, and he looked young and afraid.

Pascal had only one answer for him. 'Because you can trust me – you know you can.'

Whatever else Pascal was worried about, it wasn't Leon's lack of faith in him. The box of Prontosil tablets Pascal had handed the dumbstruck inmate what felt like a lifetime ago had saved half a dozen lives. The bond that had created between them, and Leon's courage in persuading the other men – who'd watched guards like Rohmer torment the prisoners for pleasure and had no reason to trust anyone – that Pascal wasn't playing tricks, had never faltered. There was no reason for it to break now.

'And I'll be here until this ends; I'll send you a signal. I won't let you down.'

Leon didn't move for a moment, then he reached out his hand for Pascal's. The room breathed again as their handclasp turned into an embrace, and the men – who'd been shorn of everything that had made them feel like men on the day they were herded through the gates – were offered a new glimpse of life.

Which will crumble to dust if I'm not here like I promised. If there's no warning. So I can't leave, whatever the commandant says, not until I know they'll be safe.

Unfortunately, Pascal's body was no longer listening to his fever-soaked brain. The desk lost its solid edges. He tried to stand up and didn't know if he had made it to his feet. His last thought was a muddle of directions which involved him running to the barracks and saving someone, anyone, by swapping places with them.

I'm here. You can go. Put on my uniform and leave by the main gate.

A rumbling roared through his head, picking up speed like the train he could suddenly see racing towards him.

'We've made it this far – that's something to celebrate.'

There was a prisoner standing on the platform, waving at him and hurrying him on. No, not a prisoner, a pretty girl who he knew, who needed his help. Pascal held out his jacket towards her waiting hands, but her face kept shifting and melting, and he couldn't get close to her or remember her name – the letters it was made from kept dancing away from his tongue.

'N. There's an N in it, isn't there?'

Pascal thought the girl smiled as he spoke to her. He thought he saw an ice-capped mountain towering behind her and a snowflake falling onto her hair. She came closer. He could smell wildflowers on her skin; he could feel his lips tingling. But then his mind went blank and the typhoid fever which had him in its grip and was already sweeping its way through Leon's barracks and too many of the carefully concealed hiding places dropped him in an unconscious heap to the floor.

CHAPTER TWENTY-TWO
FEBRUARY 1945

I can't be near people until this is over. Nobody and nowhere is safe.

She'd had that thought before, in the ghetto and in the ruins of Warsaw. She'd had that same longing for silence and peace. Now the evidence that the war might be ending, although not before the horror had turned yet another dreadful page, stretched out in front of her and she couldn't go on. Watching the world's death throes and getting caught in them would make a mockery of everything she'd survived.

Noemi had forced herself off the sandbank and back into the water in October 1944 as Warsaw burst into flames behind her. She'd held on to her courage. But she'd left her stomach for the fight lying in the ruins alongside Matthias.

There'd been so many moments since the war began – since the years before that if she was honest – when fear and loneliness had been her closest companions. But she'd never felt as alone or as afraid as she did when she finally pulled herself out of the Vistula.

She'd convinced herself there would be a patrol waiting to catch her. There wasn't. There was nobody around at all. No soldiers, no civilians; no running battles or bodies. She'd huddled on the riverbank wondering if this side of the city was already dead. In the end, she'd made her way towards a tree-shrouded park and hidden herself in the undergrowth until her clothes dried and her strength trickled back. Those hours were a blank. She'd forced herself not to think about Matthias and how badly injured he might be until she could find help for him. She forced herself to focus on the map she'd memorised of the streets leading away from the water, and the buildings which she could safely approach and ask for shelter. She'd refused to dwell on the fact that if Praga was in the same shattered state as the neighbourhoods she'd left behind, the places promising sanctuary would no longer exist. She couldn't hold on to so much fear at one time.

Luckily, Praga, although a far more poverty-stricken place than the main city, was very much alive and broadly intact. Noemi had wound her way through dark alleyways and past peeling, dilapidated tenements until she eventually found the telephone exchange in Ząbkowska Street, where the Polish Home Army had set up its headquarters, and the place of safety she'd hoped for. Once she'd given them her name and the details of her partisan unit, she was provided with food and clean clothes and a bed. But there was very little time to rest. As soon as the news of her escape reached the local Soviet commander, she was taken to their compound and subjected to a series of questions about the German plans and placements on the other side of the river which demanded a level of military knowledge only a Nazi general would possess.

'You're not a prisoner; you're free to leave at any time. Although we will call you back until we're satisfied you've told us everything.'

Her interrogators kept saying she was free to go. Noemi didn't believe them, and she didn't believe *everything* had an end. After the second battle-hardened man had combed through her history and professed himself reluctant to believe that any German would fight against their own as a partisan, even a Jew, Noemi knew she wasn't safe. Or in a position to trade. If they'd been able or willing to provide her with any information about Matthias's whereabouts and condition, she might have stayed and carried on co-operating, but that possibility was quickly closed down.

'We don't have contacts who can help discover the fate of injured partisans. We don't have spies whose lives we'd risk for that.'

It was the same answer every time she asked for their help. The response from the Home Army was hardly more hopeful, although they at least acknowledged him as a fallen comrade and promised to try. A week went by with no news. Matthias didn't come for her, but the Soviets did, and their questions grew ever more hostile. The third time she was asked, 'What are you really doing here?' Noemi knew that – whether Matthias was coming or not – she couldn't stay any longer in Praga. And the fighters she'd taken shelter with knew it too.

'The Soviets won't liberate Warsaw. They'll let it fall, and then they'll sweep in and take it when the Nazis finally give up and run. They want to control Poland someday themselves; they don't want us to be free any more than the Germans did. They won't work with us, and they certainly don't trust you; they can't place you. This isn't your fight anymore, Noemi, and Matthias isn't going to make it here any time soon, whatever he promised. If there's anywhere you can go that's safer, if you've got a home waiting for you, you should go. And if Matthias does turn up, we'll tell him that's what you were ordered to do.'

Noemi no longer knew what safe meant. So many years had passed, she no longer knew where or who might mean home. But it wasn't Warsaw, and – although it broke her heart to accept it – it wasn't going to be with Matthias. Everyone else, including her, even if she wasn't ready to admit it, had given him up for dead.

She'd let another week go past, pretending to be ill to avoid the Soviets' demands that she return for questioning as she clung on to false hope. Then, because she had no other real choices, she'd joined the parade of civilian refugees streaming out of the city before the Germans dismantled the last pieces of it.

The crowd she joined was as wide as the river. It moved in a jumble of people and possessions that had once mattered to them, and it was drawn from all walks of life. Carts rolled along, piled high with a motley collection of suitcases and mattresses, dolls' houses and birdcages; with strings of pots and pans cresting their edges and children perched on the tops like sailors peering out from a fleet of crows' nests. Women walked beside her wearing flowered dresses, silk scarves and fur coats, as if they were on their way to a society wedding. Or dressed in a mismatched selection of rags they clutched round their bodies like armour. No one spoke above a murmur. Everyone glanced constantly up at the sky for the German planes they were convinced were coming to finish them off. Nobody would answer her when Noemi described Matthias and asked if they'd seen him. At night, parents and grandparents huddled round their children, and stray men and women weren't welcome. And too many of those who sat round the meagre campfires each night died on the road the next day.

While everybody else kept walking, even their families, because what else could they do? There was no time to bury them; there was no place to do it. There's no certainty anyone would survive to remember them or mourn.

Noemi curled herself deeper into the nest of dry leaves she'd fashioned for herself as a shelter in the curve of a small hill on the outskirts of Dresden. She didn't judge her fellow refugees for that. She was no better than the other broken people she'd walked beside. She'd left Matthias behind her on a bullet-strewn street as if he was dead. She'd stopped weeping for him somewhere along the endless road. She'd become numb and thanked God for it.

Noemi had lost count of the bodies she'd seen on the long walk out of Warsaw. Abandoned by the roadside along with the discarded furniture. Lying scattered across open fields like tumbled scarecrows. The retreating German armies had left a burned-out, charred world in their wake. Even the rain smelled of petrol. She'd stopped counting and looking and detached herself from the pack very quickly – there were too many damaged and desperate souls clinging to its edges to be comfortable walking near, and too many empty-eyed children. She'd spent her nights lying half awake and half frozen curled under branches or in deserted houses the earth had already begun to reclaim. Where saplings reached through the holes which had once been windows lit by welcoming candles, and nettles had swallowed up the splintered front doors. She'd avoided people as much as she could, especially the German soldiers she'd occasionally spotted wandering alone, their insignia torn from their jackets, their guns tossed away. Deserters, or so she assumed. Too dangerous to tangle with, although she couldn't shake herself free of them. Matthias's face had started to melt into Pascal's in her dreams.

Too many ghosts have started to haunt me as if they're trying to pull me back.

She wrapped her coat tighter against the wind's bitter chill, glad the night was at least dry and the winter's snowfall was past. The further she'd walked, the more the people she'd lost had come back to her. The memories had started creeping up on her in Breslau, at the convent which had been her home and her hospital for most of December and January. By the time she'd reached that, her body was in a state of collapse and her mind had seemed determined to join it. She'd forgotten how to sleep for more than an hour or two. The strangers she'd passed by and avoided had begun to turn into Frieda and Hauke, into Pascal more often than Matthias. She'd stopped being sure what was real. Or caring.

The nuns had scooped her up off their doorstep where she'd fallen and taken her in. They'd returned her body to health and given her the strength to start facing her past and how that might one day fit into her life again, although they had no simple answers to help her. She would have stayed with them and waited out the war's end, but the Russian army – and the frightening rumours they trailed with them – drew too close for any woman to feel safe. The nuns had closed up the convent at the first sound of the guns approaching. Noemi had begun walking again. But this time – perhaps because she'd found herself living as part of a community and grown stronger in it – she'd stopped walking away from places with no sense of her final direction, and started walking towards the only definition of home that she knew.

Unterwald had begun to tug at her during her quiet days in the convent. Her parents had stopped appearing in strangers' faces when she'd returned to health, but they'd come back to life in her head. And perhaps in more than her head. She'd started to rewrite their story around *I'm alive, so why can't they be too?* And the more Noemi asked herself that question, the more plausible the possibility became, and the more she longed to believe it.

She lay in bed recovering her strength and spinning happy endings. She discounted the lessons she'd learned in the ghetto. She discounted the death and destruction which had been the backdrop to her life for four years. She turned Dachau, and whichever camp her mother had been sent to, into survivable places. She turned her parents into warriors who were strong enough to overcome whatever cruelties had been heaped on them. Into heroes who would be left standing when Nazi Germany fell. Who would be waiting for her in Unterwald.

That thought wrapped round her with far more warmth than her thin coat. It needed a lot of luck to come true – she was prepared to accept that. But she'd met with as much luck as she had misery almost everywhere she'd been since the day she'd fled on the goods train to Munich. She'd gambled with death time and again, and it hadn't caught her. She'd survived two ferocious battles where the odds were firmly stacked against her. She'd crept through cities where people had been torn out of any understanding of what a civilised life meant without coming to permanent harm – including Dresden, where bands of thugs had roamed the streets, trying to hold on to the last shreds of their power and she'd decided not to stay. She'd started to believe her luck might hold. She could almost see her parents running towards her with their arms open. Until she heard the first plane.

The sound of the engine brought her out of the leaves and onto her feet. But it wasn't one plane; it was dozens, maybe hundreds. Setting up a rolling drone which filled the night sky as if a platoon of tanks was about to burst in formation out of the clouds. A moment or two after that, the sirens began to scream in the city below her. And a moment or two after that...

Noemi knew that – like the fires which had burned through the ghetto and through Warsaw – the lights which began dancing as she stared spellbound towards Dresden would linger on for years through her dreams. A flash of white flares came first, swinging through the darkness as if the planes had unleashed a wave of tiny parachutes. And after that bright flurry – which she quickly realised had set up a pathway from the sky to the ground – came the bombs. Swollen black raindrops which exploded in sunbeam darts of orange and scarlet and turned the heavens into a fireball.

Noemi fell to her knees as the weapons rained down and

the fires flew up. As the city disappeared beneath a pall of thick smoke through which the flames danced like a circle of stars. She pressed her hands across her ears as the planes' rumbling gave way to a never-ending chain of loud bangs which shook the hill and rattled the trees and threw up a heatwave inside a wind which seared through the air.

She clapped her hands over her ears, but she couldn't block out the noise. She closed her eyes, but she couldn't block out the sight. The fires continued to flare on her eyelids. She sat on the hillside and watched the light show while Dresden and its people crumbled to dust. Then she crawled into her nest and cried for the death of another city full of lost souls.

The planes had gone the next morning, and the hill was a silent place. But the smoke hung in dark bruises over its wastelands, and the fires flickered on. Noemi tried to make herself get up and go in search of Dresden's survivors. She'd been in wartorn places – there was help she could give. She tried, but she couldn't do it. She couldn't manage one step down the hill. She no longer knew how to move through a world which kept doing its worst, which had lost every sense on all sides of what was decent and good. She'd lost the last scraps of her faith in humanity.

A forest.

Even the word had comfort in it.

She looked at the scattered leaves she'd covered herself with and imagined a thick canopy of them curling over her head, forming a shield between herself and the bombs and the fires and the brutalised and brutal people. She pulled herself slowly up, took a deep breath and tasted the charred wood in the wind. She hadn't had a clear plan when she'd left Breslau beyond finding her way back to Unterwald. She hadn't considered where that journey would take her, although she knew it would involve German cities and towns whose allegiances might not have shifted away from the Nazis as quickly as she'd hoped. She couldn't face any of those people or places now. The war might be dying, but it wasn't dead yet, and now it was Germany's turn to suffer – or to hide.

I'm no safer than I was four years ago. I'll be German to the Russians. I'll still be a Jew to the Germans. I'll have stories to tell that shame them. Wherever I go, I'll be evidence of their crimes – all of us who survive will carry that with us. The ones with blood on their hands will hunt us down as hard as they ever did.

Nowhere was safe. Everyone was a threat. That was a horrible, isolating thought. But it could also, Noemi realised, be a blessing. She wouldn't stumble into danger if she faced it. She couldn't be fooled into thinking she was safe. And she knew exactly what she had to do. Even better, she was trained for it.

A forest.

The word was more than comfort – it offered sanctuary in a way nowhere else could provide. It was what she needed most. A forest to disappear into. A place to wait out the rest of the war on her own – and survive.

CHAPTER TWENTY-THREE
APRIL 1945

When did I become this ancient? When did twenty-four years turn into a hundred?

Pascal hadn't returned to Dachau, despite the promise he'd made to himself that he would as he'd weaved in and out of consciousness in the Munich hospital. The illness had hollowed him out and left him bedridden in Unterwald – where he'd been sent to convalesce after the overstretched hospital ran out of room – for a month. By the time he stumbled out of that, he was barely able to recognise the sunken face staring back at him from the bathroom mirror. Or believe that it was the middle of April and the war had only weeks, perhaps days, left to run.

The Russians were almost at Berlin. The British had liberated another death camp at Bergen-Belsen, the Americans had uncovered another at Buchenwald and they were marching towards Dachau. The horror stories were multiplying faster than rats. Thousands of emaciated bodies stacked up like straw bales. Thousands of starved and disease-racked prisoners clinging desperately to life. Thousands more marched out of one hellhole to the next and the dead lying thick as fallen leaves by the roads. And countless numbers consigned to the flames.

Germany had become a country of corpses and shame. Its soldiers were the monsters of Europe; its flag was a symbol of hate. Its leader was the devil incarnate. Except to the men and women refusing to let go of the myth. Like Viktor.

'The Allies can't beat us. They might not understand that yet, but Goebbels and the Führer do. They know our best weapon isn't our tanks or our rockets; it's our people and their unbreakable determination. That's the real Germany, the one they've not conquered yet and won't, not the lies the Allies and the Russians keep spreading about us.'

Pascal had been forced to endure the same lecture night after night while he was bedridden at the farm. Nothing could stop Viktor when he was in full drunken flow, not even an audience who despised both him and his rhetoric.

'We're unbreakable – that's the key. We'll fight with our fists if we have to. We'll defend every town and village down to the last man and to the last drop of blood because that's what our Führer expects us to do. Once the enemy gets a taste of that determination, they'll withdraw their armies and admit defeat – you see if they don't.'

Viktor had always been a believer; war had turned him into a fanatic. And he was determined that Unterwald would continue to take its cues from him, that it would prepare itself for a glorious battle he had no intention of physically fighting in. Pascal wasn't the only one he insisted had to listen to his views. He issued proclamations through the town's loudspeakers. He called public meetings and covered the market square with posters carrying Goebbels' approved slogans. Nobody would be allowed to misunderstand the message.

'Germany is fighting a war it intends to win; everybody has a part to play in this. Everybody is to remain vigilant.'

'Deserters are traitors – they are fighting against us, trying to weaken our spirit. They – and anyone caught harbouring them – will be executed without trial.'

'We must stand together to prevail, whatever the challenge. Anyone displaying a white flag in the event of enemy armies arriving, or engaging in resistance activities to aid those enemies, will also be executed.'

Every speech Viktor gave and every slogan he proclaimed started with an appeal for unity and ended the same way: with the threat of a bullet or a noose and no right to a hearing.

And no one dares to dismiss Viktor's call to arms, not when he's got Goebbels' speeches behind him and his own private army to make sure his orders are followed, who will follow him like lemmings off a cliff.

Pascal sat on a stone bench on the edge of the market square, watching another patriotic Sunday morning march circle around him as if he was caught in an endless loop of past and present. The town had produced a new breed of soldiers since he'd been taken ill: the *Volkssturm*, a 'people's army' of the old and the young who the Führer and his mouthpieces had declared were coming together to fight a holy war. They were a sorry sight. They were a long way from a German army founded on high ideals.

They're the same as the orders to destroy evidence. The last desperate gasp of a dying regime.

Pascal kept his mouth shut as he watched the mismatched ranks trying to march in time together. Young boys and old men, kitted out in whatever remnants of Hitler Youth and Great War and dead sons' uniforms they could find. Carrying guns more suitable for shooting rabbits than defeating the well-armed and well-trained soldiers they were about to face. Most of the cohort he was looking at were going to Munich to thicken the city's defences. Some – the younger ones, who Viktor had hand-picked – would remain behind with their pistols and their fists to defend Unterwald from American machine guns and tanks. All of them were facing an almost certain death.

'I can't bear it. I can't lose another one; I can't go through the horror of this twice.'

Pascal hadn't noticed the woman who'd sat down beside him as the motley brigade marched on. He'd been focusing on keeping his face blank as the ranks saluted him – a courtesy offered to serving officers that he didn't know Viktor had arranged to be extended to him. When he turned towards her, the first thing he saw was her patchily dyed black dress and the fingers twisted into knots in her lap. Her eyes filled with tears as she realised she'd spoken her thoughts aloud. The tears fell when Pascal tried to comfort her.

'Nobody should go through it at all. My condolences on your loss, madam. Do you mind me asking if it was your husband or your son?'

The woman stared past him as the *Volkssturm* members took a final turn and began to disperse. She was clearly battling to sound proud of the men she loved, but all Pascal could hear was her pain.

'My husband fought in the first war and was wounded; he's not a well man but he survived. It was my eldest boy, Alfred, this one took. He was killed at Stalingrad. and his body was never returned to us. Losing him was harder than I thought I could bear, but at least I had my Pauli, and he was meant to be safe.' She stopped and glanced around her before she went on. Nobody was looking their way. 'But that's all gone now, and that's what I can't face. Everyone knows the war is almost over, even if we're not supposed to admit it in public, and yet they've called my boy up to fight, and they don't care he's only twelve years old.'

'What did you say?'

The square was noisy – Pascal thought he must have misheard. He stared at the boys pushing and shoving each other and laughing as they compared their weapons, trying – and failing – to work out their ages. 'Twelve? That can't be right;

that's years too young. Did he lie about his age because his friends are older and he wanted to stay with them? If he did, that can be sorted out.'

Desolation swept over her face and settled deep into its lines. 'No, he didn't and it can't. Don't you know they're taking children now as well as the old men? They're sending them to the front regardless of how young they are, although not my Pauli, thank God. Herr Lindiger has chosen him as one of the group who'll stay and defend the town, which is something to be grateful for I suppose.'

The toy soldiers burst into a rousing song. The woman wiped her face, jumped to her feet and began clapping as quickly as if Viktor had pulled on her strings. Pascal stayed where he was, not trusting his legs to hold him or his temper to stay in check. He knew why his father had chosen the children to lead the town's last stand, and she had no reason to be glad about it.

They'll be as blind and deaf to reality as I was at their age, which is exactly what he remembers and wants. They'll have had their heads filled with heroes and glory for years; they'll believe their destiny is to die for the Führer. They don't know anything about war, or massacres, or murder on an industrial scale.

Pascal stared around the market square as the sun broke through the clouds and the war unfolded its last sickening chapter. At his father standing on a swastika-draped platform, wearing a uniform which had never seen action and never would, beaming at the boys whose lives held no meaning for him. At another generation of dead-eyed women who would live out their years wearing black and weeping over photographs because they had no graves to lay flowers by. At the grey hair and the weather-beaten faces of men dressed in faded jackets they'd last put on thirty years ago, who thought they'd fought – and somehow survived – their last battle. And at the bright-eyed children who were about to be sacrificed in the name of a cause that wasn't only evil, it was lost.

They are cannon fodder. Their deaths have already been written.

He knew what those boys would do because he would have done it himself at their age. They'd obey orders and they wouldn't give up. They'd throw themselves at the American soldiers with their hands empty once the bullets ran out, acting as if they possessed some superhuman skill. They'd turn the town into a war zone rather than let it surrender. And if they weren't captured or killed doing that, they'd run into the mountains and keep fighting until they were picked off one by one.

It can't happen; I can't let it. This won't be a repeat of the last time the regime sucked me back into its web.

That certainty ran through his body as fast as the fever had swum through his blood. He could no more stand by and watch Viktor turn the town's streets red than he'd been able to stand by and do nothing at Dachau. But this time he had a chance to see it through. He got to his feet; forced himself into a soldier's rigid posture. And when one of the boys looked his way, he smiled and beckoned him over.

'Foraging skills will keep you alive when you're on the march miles from anywhere and your supplies have run out, which they always do. Who's got the mushroom identification kit?'

They'd been walking along the damp riverbank for two hours, and Pascal badly needed to stop and rest, but he didn't want the boys thinking he was weak in any way. They had to believe he was a brave officer committed to the cause and helping them to fight for and win it if his plan had any hope of success.

You are required to report back to Dachau at once to

assist with an immediate prisoner evacuation. Please contact SS Hauptsturmführer Weiter's office to confirm the time of your return.

The summons had arrived a week earlier, on the twenty-fourth of April, luckily while Viktor was out of the house, or he would have driven Pascal back to the camp himself. Pascal's first inclination would have been to let him – not because he had any intention of co-operating with a march that was intended to kill as many of the prisoners as possible, and which he couldn't stop, but to try and warn Leon and his men to stay hidden while it set out. It didn't take him long to realise how futile that was. He'd been away for over a month and no longer knew how the crowded camp functioned. As hard as it was to let go, he had to hope that at least some of the prisoners would have built their hiding places and learned the warning signs for themselves. He was far more use now in Unterwald, providing he managed not to get himself executed as a deserter.

'I am so sorry, but perhaps my last communication didn't get through to the correct channels – I know how busy you all must be. The typhus returned, you see, and I suffered a relapse. The doctor hopes I'll be out of bed more permanently soon, but if you could allow me a few more days' rest, I'll be much more use to you.'

Lina, the camp commandant's secretary, was a motherly sort who had been very taken with Pascal's good manners. She also hated to bother her boss with the administrative issues he preferred not to be involved in, and she thought she could manage on his behalf. She'd poured her sympathy down the telephone line when Pascal rang and spoke to her in a voice that barely made it as far as a whisper. Then – 'in the strictest of confidence of course' – she'd given him the details of the march's route so he could meet up with it as soon as he was able. And given him a way to deal with Viktor's boy soldiers.

The prisoners were being transferred to a holding camp at Tegernsee and then on to the Ötz valley in the Alps, to build a new network of tunnels there according to Lina, although she had no idea what for. Pascal did. He'd heard the proposed scheme mentioned a number of times while he was at Dachau – and with increased urgency when the orders to draw up evacuation plans came in. The mountain facility being built in the Alps was intended to be a test area for rockets and aeroplanes which could fly at supersonic speeds. That anyone in the German High Command thought that capability was still needed at this stage in the war struck Pascal as the definition of insanity. But whether the testing area was ever used or not, he doubted many of the inmates would be able to complete the arduous walk there. And it was the evidence of that which – although he dreaded what they'd find – he needed the boys to see.

Viktor had been stunned, and initially suspicious, when Pascal had offered to take the youngest members of the *Volkssturm* on a riverbed walk to teach them survival skills. But the boys – whose hero worship Pascal had encouraged no matter how distasteful he found it – quickly won their mayor round, especially as Viktor was arrogant enough to believe he'd won Pascal's loyalty back. Which was why Pascal was now two hours into a carefully planned walk he hoped would uncover more than mushrooms and edible berries.

'What's that – over there? It looks like a body.'

That was everything Pascal had hoped and feared they would find. But he didn't hurry over to where the boys had started to gather. He wanted them to make the whole of the discovery for themselves.

'Why are they here where there wasn't any fighting? And why aren't they wearing uniforms?'

The bodies the boys were staring at were lying where they had fallen along the edge of the road leading to Bad Tölz, half in and half out of the daisies and clover sprouting up from the long grass. Some were face down, with bullet wounds visible in the backs of their necks. Some were gazing lifelessly at the sky, broken by hunger and exhaustion. One of the boys started to count them, but the line of corpses stretched out endlessly down the long road and he soon gave up. Then the wind changed direction and they all sprang back, their hands clamped across their mouths as the sweet scent of the flowers became something far darker.

'Who are they?'

The boy asking the questions was Pauli. He was no longer smiling proudly and standing tall the way he had in the market square while his mother wept and applauded. He looked much younger than twelve.

Pascal had only glanced for the briefest second at the bodies; he hadn't wanted his eyes to fill with tears and betray him. He was terrified he'd see a familiar face and crumple. He also needed the emotional response to come from the boys, not from him. He kept his gaze on Pauli as he answered.

'They're prisoners, most probably from the camp at Dachau. Russians, Poles, some Jews. It's likely they were being marched to a new location.'

He waited for them to flinch and harden as he listed the names they'd been taught to loathe, but they were too shocked at the spectacle to remember how callously they were supposed to react.

'Why are they all so thin? They don't look real; they look like skeletons with clothes on.'

The second boy – Niko – rubbed at his own well-padded arm as he asked, as if he was trying to make a connection between his fledgling muscles and the stick figures piled up along the roadside. Pascal took a deep breath. He wanted the boys to do that. He wanted to provoke empathy, not hostility or a disgust born out of long-ingrained lessons. He wanted the boys to feel that the bodies – who looked like anything but – had once been people just like them.

'No, you're right – they don't look real. But they're as real as you are, I promise. They look like skeletons because they've been deliberately starved in the prison camp and deliberately worked far too hard for their weakened bodies to manage. And probably because a lot of them were already very ill when they were forced onto this march, too ill to be walking anywhere in fact.'

He waited for one of them to dismiss the treatment as being all the dead men had deserved. His spirits rose a little when that didn't happen.

'But that's not honourable. That's not how we're meant to treat prisoners.'

Honourable. A word he'd finally learned was both a blessing and a curse. It didn't surprise Pascal that it was Pauli who had taken refuge in it. He'd been brought up in a military household – he imagined Pauli had heard the same heroic stories from his father growing up that he had. And now it was time to rip the scales from the boy's eyes and worry about the consequences later.

'No, you're right with that too – it's not. But it's what we do; it's what we've done throughout the entire war. To people who don't have the "pure" blood you've been taught about but that doesn't actually exist. To people who we've decided are different from us and therefore have no rights and no value.'

He paused, but none of them started arguing with his choice of words, so he decided to hammer the lesson home while he had their attention. He gestured to the road and told them to look at the corpses again, even though they protested. And he ran everything Noemi had said to him and he'd ignored because he'd thought he knew better through his carefully chosen words.

'There's too many bodies to count here. There's too many to

count everywhere. And what you need to understand is that this is where National Socialism – the system of beliefs we've all been following for the last twelve years – really leads.'

The boys stayed silent; they turned their backs on the bodies and stared at his face. He couldn't read their mood, but he couldn't stop talking.

'This is where everything you've been taught in school and in your Hitler Youth meetings about "pure blood" and "bad blood" and "vermin" ends. This is what happens when we follow leaders who teach hatred against Jews and Russians and anybody who's not what they call "Aryan". Who say that there are people who can't exist in their version of the world. This is what Hitler and the Nazis wanted all along. Innocent people lying dead on the road like pieces of scrap. Camps like Dachau where the brutality is terrifying and total.' He paused, took another breath, slowed down so they wouldn't miss or misunderstand a word. 'And this hatred is what you'll be fighting to preserve if you do what my father tells you to do and carry this cruel war on.'

No one spoke for a moment, but Pascal knew he hadn't instantly won them, that victory didn't come so easily. He had, after all, been through the same educational factory that they had.

'You sound like a traitor. You said *Nazis* as if they're bad people. You sound like you hate the Führer and you want Germany to lose the war.'

He wasn't surprised when Niko turned on him. Or when the others began squaring themselves up as if for a fight. He knew the next few moments could as easily end up in a rope round his neck as a breakthrough. But he was prepared for that too.

'Perhaps that's what I am. Perhaps all the word "traitor" means is somebody who's woken up and is willing to tell the truth. Well, let me tell you the rest of that. Whatever lies you've been fed about miracle weapons and the Germans' unbreakable spirit, and no matter how much you want it to be different, the war is lost.' He kept talking over their shock. 'The Allies will be in Unterwald within days, and here, and all over the country, desperate men are trying to hide their crimes or running away from the evidence of them, which is what these bodies are. And those men – those soldiers and officers and those people like my father who like to tell you what to do – won't stand alongside you in some crazed and pointless last battle. They'll let you die in their places while they cower at home and get their white flags ready.'

The boys stared from the bodies back to him, their faces a confused tapestry of anger-born red patches and fear-induced white, their fists clenching as their knees shook.

'How can you say such terrible things? You fought cowards like the Russians in battle and you beat them. You conquered Mount Elbrus. You're supposed to be a hero.'

The boy who shouted that was one of the youngest in the troop, and his voice hadn't yet settled on a register. He was still old enough in Hitler's eyes to die. And to try to blink back his tears as his dreams started to crumble. Pascal wished he could soften the blow, but that wasn't what he was there for.

'But I'm not a hero – that's the point. I wanted to be one when I was your age; I thought joining the Party and following the Führer would make me one. And yes, I fought in battles and I went up a mountain. But the Russians weren't cowards; they were as brave as we were, and as for Elbrus... It was a lie too. That photograph you've seen?' He shook his head as the memory flooded back. 'It wasn't taken on the day of the actual climb – the weather was too bad for that. We had to go up again because the Führer wanted his moment of glory recorded for the whole world to see. Except there wasn't any glory to be had. By the time we went back the next day, the Russians had already taken the summit again, and we had to dodge their snipers the entire way up and down. I imagine our flag was torn from the pole again in seconds. And we weren't heroes in that photograph, trust me: we were exhausted men afraid we were going to die a very pointless death. The real story then was how ferocious and fearless and unbeatable the Russians were. And that's the real story now.'

He stopped his tirade as one of the boys started to cry. Pauli and Niko wouldn't look at him. None of them would look at the bodies anymore. Pascal couldn't tell if he'd won them round or not. He dropped his voice and forced himself to remember they were children.

'I am so sorry I've had to put you through this, but it was the only way I could get you to listen to me. I know more about the way you feel than you think. I thought war was a glorious thing too and that soldiers were giants among men. I couldn't wait to follow the Führer and fight for my country and become a giant too.'

He had their full attention again now, and they deserved all his honesty, whether he had their trust and understanding or not.

'But there's not been anything glorious about this war or the part I've played in it. I've let down people I loved because I was blind, and I've put them in danger. I've let terrible things happen because I chose not to see that it was hatred not honour that fuelled the Party. I'm twenty-four years old and I'll carry shame and guilt with me for the rest of my life. And I don't want that for you. I want you to go home and take off your uniforms and wait out the last days of this terrible conflict safely with your families. I want you to live and rebuild something better. But I can't force you to make that choice. Any more than I can stop you from handing me over as a traitor. All I can ask you to do is stop for a moment, forget all the lessons you've been taught and think for yourselves.'

He had nothing more to say. He left them then and began

walking back towards Unterwald. He let the boys decide by themselves what to do. Whatever that would be was out of his hands, but he'd spoken up and made a stand, and there was some comfort to be had in doing that, for him if not for them. Not enough to erase the guilt that was lodged at his core – he couldn't imagine ever unseating that, no matter how many ways he atoned. But if his words had kept one boy out of the reach of a bullet or a tank, the noose Viktor would wrap round his neck if he knew what Pascal had done would be worth it.

He re-entered the town with the boys a little way behind him and no idea what any of their fates would be. But the world had moved on while they'd been out walking. People were standing aimlessly in the streets, staring blankly at each other, looking around as if they were waiting for someone to give them directions. And the same words were on everyone's lips.

'The Führer is gone – he is dead.'

CHAPTER TWENTY-FOUR
JULY 1945

I thought justice was meant to be the watchword now. I thought the country was going to be cleansed. So why hasn't that notion reached Unterwald?

Noemi dropped to her knees in the long grass, oblivious to the summer flowers spreading out like a carpet around her. Automatically reaching for the gun she'd thrown away when she'd thought her battles were done. If she'd had it to hand now, she'd be firing.

She'd been conjuring up images of the town for months, ever since she'd retreated into the forest. She'd walked up and down its streets and round the market square on dozens of long, lonely nights spent revisiting her old haunts, and she'd kept every inch of its landscape the same as it was when she'd been happy there. She'd promised herself the buildings would be intact and unscarred, that they wouldn't have seen bombs or fire. She'd kept the framework of her hometown safe in her head. But not the people who'd hurt her and her family, and especially not Viktor. He hadn't been in any of the pictures she'd conjured up once the way Germany was going to be governed had been explained to her, and she'd pictured him finished.

'You shouldn't encounter too many problems heading south, other than the obvious food and transport challenges. Munich and Nuremberg are wrecks of course, but the Americans are in charge in Bavaria, and that's a far better prospect than the Soviets. I imagine most people are hoping they'll be under their rule, or the British, once the country's fully occupied and carved up.'

Noemi couldn't find any pity for Munich or Nuremberg – they would only ever be places filled with bad memories for her. But she didn't want to see the evidence of their dying days, and she couldn't bring herself to trust any of the Allied troops while the war was still raging, not after the vengeance she'd witnessed from the hillside above Dresden. That was why she'd stepped back then and let the world carry on moving towards whatever peace might mean without her.

She'd fled into the depths of the Tharandt Forest the day after the city's destruction and made a home for herself there close to the banks of a well-stocked pond. She'd kept herself to herself as much as she could, moving round the scattered hamlets that edged the trees only at night, never speaking or showing herself to anyone. Nobody had noticed her pressed into the shadows outside their windows once night fell, listening to their radio broadcasts. Nobody knew who'd left a freshly caught carp or trout wrapped in leaves on their doorstep at the same time a shirt disappeared from a washing line or a tree mysteriously lost its fruit. Noemi didn't steal for stealing's sake. She only took what she needed; she always left some form of payment. Nobody came hunting for her, but she never felt safe. And it hadn't been easy to re-emerge from her isolation, even when the news about Hitler's death and Germany's surrender was all over the airwaves.

Her first steps back had been tentative ones, an exercise in rebuilding her trust. She'd spent a night in a barn here in return for a day's apple-picking, a few more in a town there in exchange for helping to clear up its bombed buildings. Her re-entry had become easier as she met more people like herself, alone and a long way in every sense from home. Wary but wanting to believe there might be kindness again in the world, or at least not wanting to add to the harm it already carried. Happy to cross paths and provide a little companionship for an hour or two and move on. Eventually, she'd begun to drift in and out of the Displaced Persons' camps, where there was hot food and clean clothes and volunteers offering advice. None of them had heard of Unterwald, but they'd all told her Bavaria was a sensible choice. That anything was preferable to stumbling into the Russians who controlled Berlin and the north-east of the country.

'The Americans hate Germans the same as everyone else does. But their soldiers are better disciplined, and they don't seem to have any problems with Jews, which is never a given with the Russians. They've also sworn to flush out Nazis from their sector and make them pay for their crimes, which would presumably make your hometown safer for you to go back to.'

That was welcome advice. It had allowed Unterwald to properly become the idyllic place of her childhood again. Noemi had forced Dresden out of her head; she'd grabbed on to her old dreams. She'd put her parents back into the town and into their businesses the way she'd imagined them when she was in the convent – as happy as they'd been before Hitler came to power – and rewritten her birthplace as if the war hadn't happened. That had been a comfort. But remembering them had also brought back memories of Pascal, and those weren't a comfort at all; they were cinders burning her skin. There wasn't a space for men like him, and especially not men like his father, in any version of the town where her parents could be safe. So she'd pushed Pascal away as hard as she'd pushed away Dresden's fires. She'd papered over him instead with a picture of Matthias – recovered from his injuries and alive and reunited with her – standing at her side in the café, with Hauke and Frieda smiling behind them. That had been a far safer image.

Noemi began the last stage of her journey home convinced her happy ending had to be waiting for her. It took her a long time to accept that she was fooling herself, that nothing about her future – and very little about her present – was in her control. Or that, for all their good intentions, the Americans – who rarely spoke the language and were struggling to force a silent and sullen population into categories they didn't want to fit into – couldn't control it either.

The conquering troops were overstretched and exhausted and deeply shocked by the scale and the horror of the crimes they'd uncovered. The conquered population was reeling from its defeat, afraid of discovery or guilt-ridden. To add to their disorientation, the Führer had done what he'd always sworn he would never do: he'd abandoned his people. Mouths clammed up in town after town. Memories failed. No one had seen anything; no one knew anything. No one had willingly joined the Nazi party; no one shared its beliefs. The Nazis were *they* and *them*, but never *we* or *us*. 'They ordered it... That was their doing... They said it had to be done.' On and on, the dance went in those early days, following a pattern that was too tightly woven for the Americans, or the rest of the Allies, to unpick. But Noemi didn't know that. Or at least not until she returned to the meadows above the town and watched the truth strutting round large as life in the market square below.

At least I didn't walk straight into a trap.

She'd nearly done exactly that. But the closer she came to the town, the harder it had been to throw off the survival instincts which had become as natural to her as breathing. No partisan approached a new place in the open – and after four years away and almost six years of war, everywhere in Germany was to some degree a new place, including Unterwald. They stayed invisible until they'd carefully surveyed every aspect of it. Noemi didn't want to do that – what she wanted was the joyful reunion playing out in her head – but she was a creature of caution these days, so that's how she moved. She'd left the main road before she reached the first houses and taken the mountain track which led her to a familiar perch in a meadow with a clear view down onto the square. A view that had led straight to Viktor.

She'd blinked and blinked and wished the sight of him was no more than a trick of the sunlight or her memories. But Viktor was there, as on show as he'd always been, swaggering around the town as he'd always done. Accompanied by the Chief of Police who'd arrested her father, and the hotelier who'd stolen his business. Shaking hands, patting small children on their heads, heading to the bar he had no rightful claim to, to hold court with his morning coffee.

He's not wearing a uniform anymore, or not on the outside, but Unterwald is still his.

Noemi sat back on her heels, rage roaring through her. Struggling not to scream as the dreams which had never been anything but dust in her eyes disappeared. Every aspect of the map she'd drawn in her head was wrong, starting with Viktor. He wasn't supposed to be there. He was supposed to be in prison, facing justice, or already tried and convicted and dead. Because if Viktor was in charge, there was no place for her parents. And if he'd carried on ruling the roost untouched, despite his long allegiance to the Nazis...

What about Pascal? What if he's back too? What if he's become some kind of war hero like he always wanted to be and has escaped punishment like his father?

She couldn't push him away this time. Images of Pascal – as she'd known him, as she feared he was now – and the truth of her last years in the town burst out with the speed of water pouring through a cracked dam. All at once, her head was filled with a reel whose twists she couldn't control.

The vanilla-scented bakery and her father grinning in his shirtsleeves as he tidied the bar. Moonlight and the flash of Pascal's eyes as he looked into hers; snow-capped peaks and the delicious warmth of his mouth. Brown shirts and swastikas and a hand pulling hard at her hair as uglier mouths shouted ugly names. Her father bruised and broken in a dingy prison waiting room. Viktor sat in a chair like a grinning toad and stealing their lives away. For every good memory, there was a cruel one waiting to swallow it. For every moment of happiness, there was twice the pain. Every time she'd imagined the homecoming she'd wanted, she'd been telling herself fairy stories.

What am I doing here? What good can it do to come back?

They were the two most obvious questions in the world, and she hadn't considered them. She'd let herself be led by hopes and dreams she'd always known in her heart were false.

Maybe the word isn't 'good'. Maybe that's not what I'm here for.

Noemi had been fighting and hiding and pushing down her fury for so long, she'd stopped feeling. That numbness had evaporated in her first sight of Viktor. Now all the years of anger and fear and betrayal were screaming as loud as the bombs and bullets that had filled her ears for too long. Unterwald had taken everything from her, but now the war was over and there was a reckoning coming.

She took a deep breath. She took a swig of water from the leather bottle in her rucksack. She climbed a little higher towards the comfort of the mountains, curled herself into the rocks and let the sun's rays find her. She could wait. She was very good at waiting. She would let Viktor and his town have one last undisturbed day. And then she was going to go down the hill to the streets she'd once loved and take back every last thing that he'd stolen.

CHAPTER TWENTY-FIVE
JULY 1945

Noemi came home to Unterwald as twilight settled over the streets and the town closed its shutters against the coming dark. She weaved her way round its corners like a ghost, noting what was old, what was new, what was gone.

There were no more swastikas – or at least none on show. The town was decorated instead in its traditional style for a summer wedding. Bunches of white campion and columbine hung from silver ribbons tied to the church's door handles. Garlands studded with deep blue and pale pink gentians decorated the colonnade which ran along the exterior of the ancient market hall. Long tables had been set out behind its thin columns, laid with an assortment of crystal and china vases ready to receive the fresher flowers which would come in the morning. Everything had been done in the way weddings were always done.

Except they won't have made my mother's special cake, and no wedding here is complete without that.

The instant Noemi pictured a laughing bride cutting into the almond and cherry layers, she had her plan. She made her way round the square by hugging its edges and headed towards the long row which housed the buildings which had once belonged to the Drachmanns.

The doors to the café, and to the bar and shop, were locked, as Noemi had expected. There was one lamp burning softly behind the curtains in the flat above them where she'd once lived. But there was no light at all at the back of the building; there wasn't even a cat to notice her coming as she circled round the side of the bakery.

The smells creeping from that were intoxicating. Vanilla, cinnamon, ground spices and fruit steeped in brandy. They promised a stockroom the war hadn't decimated – or a town with good contacts on the black market. And they led her to a window which, as she'd hoped, had been left slightly open to let the wedding feast cool down in time for the last flurry of decorating in the morning.

It took Noemi less than a minute to slide the window fully open and wiggle through. It took her a few minutes more to recover from the tide of memories which immediately hit her. Frieda in a flowered apron, teaching her how to balance the spice mix which gave *Pfeffernüsse* their distinctive bite, and how to shape delicate sugar pretzels. Scraping out mixing bowls with Pascal, both of them sticky with butter icing and crumbly *streusel* topping. The bakery had been both a school and a playground, and every inch of it belonged – whatever Viktor had done to remove her – to her mother. Noemi was an expert at reining in her feelings – the life she'd been living had demanded that. But when she spied Frieda's faded apron still hanging from the hook where she'd always kept it, the tears finally came. Noemi ran to it and gathered the soft material into her arms, convinced Frieda's violet perfume would be caught in its folds. The tears fell heavier when she couldn't find a trace of the sweet smell.

Time to get started now, Noemi; time to focus. Collect your ingredients up first – make sure you've got everything you need to hand.

It didn't matter that the perfume was long gone. Frieda's voice was in her head; her hand was on Noemi's shoulder, its touch as light as a dusting of flour on a rolling pin. *Ground almonds, cherry compote, raspberry syrup to colour the icing.* Her mother's voice danced on, listing the cake's ingredients and the steps needed to make it. Noemi mopped her eyes with her sleeve and followed Frieda's instructions into a pantry which was every bit as well stocked as the baking scents had promised. She deliberately searched at the back of the shelves, looking for – and finding – bottles and jars which bore the old Drachmann label and would bring their own brand of magic.

Frieda's voice guided her while Noemi gathered everything up. And stayed in her head while Noemi put on her mother's apron, assembled her tins and started to mix up her cake.

Noemi knew Unterwald's rhythms as well as she knew the seasons, so she was ready to greet the town long before it woke.

She'd worked through the night to finish and decorate the wedding cake, and to tidy herself. She'd used the bakery sink to wash the road's dust out of her hair. She'd taken off the apron – which was now safely stored in her rucksack – and changed out of her hiking clothes into her only dress. That was a leaf-green and white sprigged cotton shirtwaister which she'd liberated from a farmyard washing pile, leaving a woven straw basket full of mushrooms in exchange. It was a little large on the hips and a little too floaty for her taste and somewhat at odds with her heavy walking boots, but it was more appropriate for a party than her baggy twill trousers. According to the mirror in the bakery's bathroom, she looked as much like the Noemi she'd once been as the years and the life she'd lived would let her. She would be recognised instantly, there was no doubting that. Now it was time to set the stage.

She put the cake – which she'd covered in pink icing as soft as a dawn cloud – in the centre of the top table and sat down at its head. The only other change needed was to move the embroidered runner – which she'd last seen in her family's dining room and was waiting now to delight the bride and groom – to lie in place in front of her. Resting her hands on the strawberry motif which Frieda had stitched for her own wedding day made it seem as if her parents were there with her. That final piece in place, she waited.

The women came in twos and threes as the sun began to smile. Balancing piles of crockery and trays filled with cutlery. Laden with armfuls of freshly cut flowers. Laughing and chatting and looking forward to a happy day. Until they were hit with a shock none of them expected, exactly as Noemi had planned. First one woman dropped her jaw and her bundle of linen, then the next. It took no time at all for the ripples to spread.

'Good God. Is that Noemi Drachmann? What's she doing here? How on earth did she stay alive?'

The startled squawk ran down the line and stopped the rest of the women as abruptly in their tracks. A plate fell and smashed. Cutlery clattered over the cobbles. Noemi heard all that, but what she heard loudest was the shock and disbelief.

I wasn't meant to come back. I was meant to die with the others nobody cared about.

She'd grown more convinced of that the longer she'd lain in the meadow. She'd still hoped it wouldn't be true.

'And that's Frieda's cake. Surely she can't be back too?'

The women stopped being a blur of half-remembered faces and snapped into sharp focus. A hand flew to the speaker's throat, where it landed on Frieda's amber necklace.

Another woman – another one-time friend – gripped tighter to Frieda's beloved rose-patterned shawl. It appeared not every trace of her family was lost. Noemi's tired heart stopped hoping someone would smile in delight at her safe return and hardened.

'What if she is? Which outcome would you prefer? That we'd all survived or just me?'

She didn't add *or none of us*, but the words were there in the question all the same. She paused, searching the white faces for a kind answer, knowing the silence would last a beat too long. The swarm of, 'Of course we hoped all of you would make it,' and, 'It's a shock – that's all,' was too thin and too late when it finally came and brought her no pleasure. Pain pinched its sharp fingers through her body, but Noemi carried on poking at her audience anyway.

'So tell me, did you know? About Auschwitz and Dachau and Treblinka, and all the other places they sent my people to die? Did you know about the gas chambers and the ovens, and the execution pits?'

White faces turned crimson; heads turned away. Noemi's newly vulnerable eyes started to fill, but she would rather have died than spill a single tear.

'I know that you did – your silence is full of it. Like I know you kept supporting the regime and sending your men to fight for your beloved Führer even when you knew him for the monster he was. That's done with, I suppose, and can't be changed. But what happens now?' She gazed at the flowers and the wedding linen. 'Do you all simply move on with your lives and forget, hoping that the Jews and the Gypsies and the sick, and the millions of others whose blood you didn't like will be forgotten too?'

Nobody met her eyes. Nobody answered.

Noemi got to her feet and pulled the knife she'd taken from the bakery out of her rucksack. The instant intake of breath would have been amusing if the scene had been a play, not her life. One of the women had dumped a stack of plates on the end of the table. Noemi spread them out and began cutting the cake into thin slices.

'Well maybe that's a question for another day; this is a wedding after all. Although I'm sure whoever the bride is, she's made her own arrangements and won't actually need this. So why don't we use it to celebrate my homecoming instead?'

She began handing the plates round. None of the women refused to take one, but none of them took a bite either when she invited them to eat.

They think it's poisoned. They're afraid of me. They've no idea what I want.

But Noemi did.

She watched the women staring at the pink icing as nervously as if she'd coloured the fondant with deadly nightshade, not pressed raspberries.

'I need somewhere to stay obviously. A room will do... For now.'

For now was another deliberate stone, another ripple she intended to watch play out. Noemi looked from the necklace to the shawl: if no one offered her help out of kindness, she'd make them do it from shame.

'You can come to me. I've taken over Distel's farm now he's dead; I could do with some help with the animals.'

The woman making the offer looked vaguely familiar. She had Distel's square jaw and lean frame, but clearly not his twisted personality. Whoever she was, she would do. Noemi nodded and noted the sigh of relief from the rest.

'Does Herr Niehbur still work out of his old office on Goethestraβe?'

This time she enjoyed the gasp at the notary's name and the panicked look when she suggested that she might take a piece of cake with her as a gift.

They think I'm going to poison the whole town. Maybe I should have done that in the first place.

It wasn't a serious thought. Noemi was done with killing. But she wasn't done with revenge, and she certainly wasn't finished with the town. She'd barely even begun.

CHAPTER TWENTY-SIX
JULY 1945

He knows I'm here – word's spread.

Hauke had always referred to the notary as a punctual man who liked to get a good start on the day, but – although it was almost nine o' clock – there was no sign of him when Noemi arrived at his office. And when he finally did appear, he wasn't as dapper as she remembered. He was panting, he had a reddened patch of stubble on his chin. He looked as if he'd been hurried into his suit faster than he'd planned, which suggested she wasn't his first meeting.

'Fräulein Drachmann, so it's true and you're home. Do come in.'

He didn't waste time feigning surprise, and he didn't insult her by pretending to be pleased to see her. They both knew how much he'd profited from the forced transfer of the Drachmann properties. He was brisk and business-like instead as he ushered her inside and offered her a chair. He selected a folder from one of the filing cabinets lining the walls as quickly as if her return was a possibility he'd planned for. Because – as he was careful to point out as he sat down on the other side of his gleaming mahogany desk and polished his spectacles – he had.

'I am sorry to be the bearer of bad news, but it is highly doubtful that your parents survived.' He extracted a number of sheets of paper from the folder and placed them where Noemi could see their closely typed rows. His tone didn't alter despite the bleak news.

'These are copies of the deportation lists which the Red Cross have been collating since the end of the war. This one is from Dachau to Auschwitz in November 1943, and includes your father's name. The other is from the women's camp at Ravensbrück, also to Auschwitz in October 1942, and includes your mother's. They are both noted on these other papers as arriving at the camp, but as to what came next...' He spread his hands as if to distance himself from their fate. 'Unfortunately, a great deal of the later records were destroyed either before or after that particular site was liberated, so I don't have definitive proof of what happened. But at that time they went in, and given their ages, it's highly unlikely they survived there for long.'

Noemi knew. She'd always known. But she'd managed to keep them alive until the words were said. She wanted to close her eyes; she wanted to curl up and weep. But the darkness that lay that way was too deep, and it was safer to fuel her anger than to give way to grief. She swallowed hard and told him to put the lists away.

'Why do you have them?' She ignored Herr Niehbur's frown. 'Why do you have copies of my parents' deportation records? I don't imagine you really hoped I'd come back, so why would their fate matter to you?'

She should have known that answer too.

Niehbur carried on frowning at her as if she was a troublesome child asking questions she had no business to ask. She imagined that was exactly how he saw her.

'Your return was always a possibility, if perhaps a slight one. Herr Lindiger asked me to obtain these when such details started to become available, which was the right and proper thing to do. He is the mayor. It is his duty to ensure that everything in Unterwald runs smoothly.'

So Viktor had remained as mayor, despite his unswerving loyalty to Hitler's regime and the Americans' promises. Noemi could see Niehbur waiting for her to rail against the unfairness of that or give up whatever quest she was on. She wasn't about to do either.

'*Runs smoothly* is an interesting choice of words – it rather masks the facts, doesn't it? I assume what you actually mean is that he wanted to ensure the town's stolen property stayed with the thieves, in case any of us had the bad manners to survive and come back to claim it.'

She shook her head as Niehbur reared up to mount a defence, with his mouth full of, 'That's a preposterous choice of words.'

'Please don't waste your time or your breath – that cheapens us both. I assume you have a barrage of legal arguments ready to prove that my parents' home and their business dealings were lawfully acquired. Except, of course, they weren't. Everyone here knows that. And once I go to Munich and explain to the Americans exactly what happened – which I doubt anyone has done because why would they care – I think they'll take my part, don't you?'

She stood up and wasn't at all surprised when the notary immediately reached for the telephone.

'Go on – call Viktor. I presume he already knows I'm here, that whoever ran to warn you ran to warn him too. Good. The sooner he learns that it's the Jews holding the power now, not the Nazis, the better.'

She slammed out of the office and stamped down the stairs, hoping Niehbur would report the noise she made – and what that inferred about her willingness to fight – to Viktor along with her parting message. That he would describe her as fearless and not to be easily cowed. But when she reached the bottom of the dark stairwell where nobody could see or hear her? She stopped feeling as if she had any power at all. She sank onto the bottom step and hid her face in her hands.

They were gone. Her beautiful, loving, so alive parents had been swallowed up inside one of Hitler's death factories. They'd been dead the whole time she'd been imagining them taking up their old lives. The thought of what they must have suffered, coupled with the pain of their separation before their last journeys, was unbearable. The horror of it clawed at her insides; it paralysed her. She lost track of how long she sat in the darkness. When she finally pulled herself back onto her feet, she was a shell. She needed to hide from the world and lick her wounds. But the day wasn't finished with her.

'So it's true then. You're alive.'

Viktor was waiting for her outside the notary's front door. It was clear from his twisted lip and square stance that he wasn't about to offer her a welcome or tiptoe around the reasons for her return.

'Why are you here, Noemi? What do you want? And don't say the property or the businesses. They went legally out of your family's hands years ago.'

They can look at you and see a bully and a fool because that's what you are.

Hauke's words from the town meeting which had sown the seeds of the Drachmanns' destruction were suddenly in her head, as clear as Frieda's had been in the bakery. Relief ran through her. Her parents weren't gone. They were with her; they always would be. And the life they'd built together was worth fighting for and honouring. Noemi glared back at Viktor's drink-coarsened face and held tight to that.

'*Legally?* Don't take me for a fool. There was nothing legal about it. You can repeat a lie as often as you like, but that doesn't make it the truth. I don't know how things work now the war is over, or why you're still in charge. I do know that's not going to last. Whatever shield you've wrapped round yourself won't work against me. Once I tell the Americans the secrets you've been hiding, you'll be finished. You'll be staring at a noose. And everything you stole will be mine again.'

She watched his face darken; she watched him wish her dead. But he didn't have a weapon he could use against her. Or so Noemi thought until he began talking.

'Okay. If that's how you want to play it, let's see exactly how little you know about our lives. You're not the only returner; Pascal is back here too. Did you know that? And did you know he was quite the hero in the war? Perhaps you've already seen the photograph of him planting a flag for the Führer on the top of Mount Elbrus – I'm sure Niehbur has a copy in his office. No?' Viktor shrugged. 'Perhaps he did what I did and put it away for safe-keeping when the Americans arrived. I can get mine out for you though, if you'd like to take a look? It's not as if they'll be coming back.'

He'd turned the conversation too fast for her to grasp everything he was saying. She didn't want to hear Pascal's name paired with the word *hero*. She didn't know how to react to the news that he was in the town too. But she had to leave that alone for the moment. The rest of what Viktor was smiling about was more worrying.

'What do you mean, the Americans won't be coming back?'

Viktor settled his weight more comfortably before he answered. 'I've already heard your threats from Niehbur – they didn't need repeating. But you're a little late. The Americans have already been here. They raced through the town in the first days after we were forced to surrender, looking for stray soldiers to arrest. They didn't find any of course. Nobody was in a uniform by then; no one was flying a swastika. I made sure of that. Nobody stepped out of line and told tales, even if Pascal...' He stopped boasting, as if he'd suddenly remembered who he was speaking to. 'Anyway, they were very glad to see how well run everything was and that nobody was starving. That there were no "war criminals" they needed to deal with, as if we were about to hand dozens of our own people over. And they were more than happy to leave matters in my capable hands, given how many disasters they were already trying to manage.' His smile widened as he relived the memory. 'There's nothing you can do, so stop being a silly girl. Stop trying to threaten me. You of all people should know how dangerous I am when I'm crossed.'

He was leaning in so close, Noemi could smell the schnapps that tainted his breath, even though the morning had barely begun. She had to force herself not to take a step away from him.

'It was you, wasn't it? Who arranged the round-up and sent my parents to their deaths? Who would have sent me to mine if you'd caught me?'

His smile slid into a leer. Noemi had to twist her hands behind her back to stop herself from clawing his eyes out. One move like that and he'd surely arrest her and put her beyond help.

'Of course it was. It was my duty after all, as well as my pleasure. Even if I hadn't already been sick of the sight of my son mooning after you, threatening to defile my family because of a childish crush on a worthless little Jew, your father had it coming. He never knew when to shut up. And I would have caught you too if my fool of a wife hadn't interfered.'

Noemi's stomach rose at the realisation that he'd discovered Carina's involvement in her escape, but she swallowed it down as the earlier part of his speech came back to her. Something about that had been niggling at her – now it reared up and demanded her attention first.

'What did you mean before by *even if Pascal*? Did he try to do something when the Allies came?'

His laugh would have roused the whole of the street if anyone had dared to venture outside.

'Isn't it sweet that that's the bit you chose to hear. Why does it matter? What are you trying to do? Recast him and find yourself a happy ending? Didn't you hear what I said? He was a war hero. Oh, and I forgot the best bit.' Viktor paused long enough for Noemi to understand that nothing he was about to say fitted with *best*. 'After he was wounded – in the shoulder, nasty but not life-threatening – he was transferred to the SS and redeployed as a camp guard in Dachau. Isn't that a turn-up for the books? He's probably got some excellent stories from there that'll flesh out your father's last days. Shall I arrange a little tête-à-tête for you both? A candlelit dinner perhaps? Or another romantic night away in a hut on the mountain?'

This time Noemi couldn't hold herself or her churning stomach back. She was violently sick all over Viktor's highly polished shoes. The curses he rained down on her were filthy and frightening, full of the hatred that was as much a part of him as his precious pure blood. Noemi hardly heard them. All she could hear was Pascal's name next to Dachau, which was a far worse place for it to be than *hero*. All she could think as she stumbled away was, *Why in God's name did I ever come back?*

CHAPTER TWENTY-SEVEN
JULY 1945

'She's back. Your little Jewish pet's dodged the death camps and come home.'

Pascal normally ignored whatever his father said to him, not that Viktor said much to him nowadays. The fight the two men had finally had in the days after the Americans arrived had been a long time coming and brutal enough to end in blows. Pascal had won that one; he hadn't wanted another. Now the two men kept their distance from each other and were rarely in the farmhouse at the same time. But this was different. He forced himself to ignore the cruelty of *dodged the death camps*, but he couldn't ignore *she's back*. It sent too much hope surging through him. His mistake was in letting Viktor see that.

'Dear God, you're as pathetic as she is. Still holding on to feelings I should have crushed out of you both long ago. Well, at least that's done with now on her part.'

'What do you mean? What's done with?'

Pascal clenched his fists as his father's contempt spilled through the shabby kitchen.

Viktor saw him square up and grinned. 'It means I've put paid to that nonsense on her side this time, and you need to stay clear. She was meant to be gone for good, so let's hope she disappears again. The last thing I need's a Jew sniffing round causing me trouble.'

Viktor flung himself into a chair and reached for the bottle of schnapps he lapped at like water from morning to night. Pascal watched him, weighing up how to respond, wondering what revelation was coming next. Trying to hold his brain and body together. Noemi was back. Noemi was alive. His heart didn't know whether to soar or to crash. How could he face her? How could he not? In every dream he'd had about her returning, he'd never moved past the first sight of her face. He'd always stopped there, in that moment of perfection before the ugliness he carried could touch her. But now the impossible had happened and she was here, and Viktor had got to her first.

But I can't blame him for poisoning the well. I did that myself years ago.

He took a deep breath and forced himself to stay calm until he knew exactly how much extra damage he was dealing with.

'What have you told her about me?'

Viktor took another swig from the bottle; he'd given up on glasses long ago. 'I told her the truth about your heroic war. And I suggested you might be able to tell her some stories about Dachau, to fill in the blanks about what became of her dear departed parents.'

Viktor wasn't drunk enough. Pascal wasn't quick enough. By the time he grabbed the bread knife from the kitchen table, his father had pulled a gun from behind the cushion on his chair and pointed it at his son.

'Don't think I won't shoot you. I'm not getting caught out by you again. And don't think I'd get into trouble for it either if I did. The town will easily believe it was self-defence – most of them already think you're mad. Throwing yourself at the Americans, begging them to take you away. I should have let them do it, but I couldn't trust you not to bring us all down with your ridiculous need to confess or atone, or whatever the hell it was you wanted. I should have shot you then – or on the day you first raised your fists at me.'

Pascal gripped the knife harder as Viktor ranted, wondering how much damage he could do before a bullet hit him.

'Not enough.' Viktor's laugh grated across Pascal's ears. 'I know what you're thinking. I know you don't care if you live or die. Well that makes two of us. You've been a thorn in my side ever since you refused to give up on that girl and...' He stopped. 'Well, let's leave that for now,; let's just say it's been a long time since I had reason to trust your loyalty. And I was proved right, wasn't I? You're the reason why Unterwald surrendered. If those boys had done what I told them to do and kept the American tanks at bay, we might have beaten the enemy back. But oh no, not you. You couldn't leave well alone. You waded in with your lies and turned us all into cowards.'

Pascal stared at his father, at the drunken apology for a man he'd become, and couldn't fathom how he'd ever seen a single drop of goodness in him or why he'd been so desperate to follow in Viktor's footsteps. He didn't say that. He wasn't going to lay all the blame for the man he'd become and the path he'd chosen to walk on his father. That was too easy a way out.

He sowed the seeds, but I watered them. I drank in every promise Hitler made. I thought he was going to cover Germany – and me – in glory. That we'd win the war with honour under his guidance. And I hung on to that dream long after it rotted.

Honour. How much of his soul had he sold for a word he'd never truly understood? He put the knife down and felt stronger without it. He no longer cared about Viktor's gun.

'That's where you're wrong. I never turned you into anything: you were always a coward, but I pretended you weren't. I pretended that everything you did was for the greater good. None of that was true, and I doubt you ever loved my mother the way she deserved. You've always been a bully and a fool – Hauke got that much right.'

Viktor wasn't listening. The gun slipped from his hand as he took another swig of schnapps and carried on muttering about all the ways Pascal had let him and the Party down. But his interest rallied when Pascal swallowed his pride and his fury and asked him where Noemi was now.

'She's at Distel's farm, which is a nice touch given that's where she ran from in the first place. Why? You're not going to see her, are you?' Viktor tried to clap his hands in a mock salute when Pascal failed to answer, and spilled schnapps all over the chair. 'Dear God, you are. Have you no sense left in you? You were a Nazi. In her eyes, you're still a Nazi – I made sure of that. Unless you're hoping she'll be the one to put you out of your misery, is that it? What's she going to use, Pascal? Her body – or a bullet? Are you going to let her choose her weapon?'

He burst out laughing as Pascal headed for the door.

Pascal refused to ask his father how he knew the details of Noemi's escape. He kept walking and refused to react at all. Noemi had come back, which must have taken a great deal of courage; everything else could wait. He guessed she'd done it in the hope of finding her parents. He guessed from *causing trouble* that she wanted her family's property back. And he didn't know if she'd want to see or speak to him, but he had to speak to her. He owed her... An apology wasn't a big-enough word to cover all the wrongs that he'd done, but an apology had to be the start. And he owed her his loyalty in whatever new struggles she was facing.

If she'll only give me the chance I've never deserved.

* * *

'Pascal Lindiger is here. I doubt he's come to see me. I'll be out in the barn if you need me.'

Frau Hammerl – who had inherited the farm from her father but not a scrap of his mean spirit – slipped out of the back door seconds before Pascal knocked at the front. Noemi's first instinct was to run after her, as fast as she'd run away from Viktor. She'd only known the woman a few hours, but it was already clear that her watchword was kindness. She hadn't asked questions when Noemi had appeared with a tear-stained face and her clothes covered in the dust she'd kicked up from the road. She'd made her a cup of rosehip tea instead, and fetched hot water and clean towels and sent her for a long, calming bath. The only thing she'd said was, *When, or if, you need to talk, I'm a good listener.*

The knock on the door came again.

He won't leave easily if I ignore him. If he does, he'll only come back. I might not know him the way I did anymore, but I know that much.

Noemi got slowly up and walked what felt like a meadow's length to the door. She couldn't remember how to breathe when she opened it. Four years. It was a lifetime – and nothing. Pascal had grown taller, his shoulders were wider than she remembered, his frame had filled out with new muscles. He looked like the boy she'd loved and a man she didn't know. And he didn't look well. There was a milky tinge to his skin that suggested he no longer lived the outdoors life they'd both loved. There were deep purple shadows pressed under his eyes. He looked as if he understood what suffering meant.

But he doesn't know it from the same side as me. He wore their uniform. He carried out their work at Dachau. He's nothing to me now but the enemy.

She couldn't imagine there was anything he could say or do to change her mind about that; she wouldn't allow him to try. So she let him in, but she turned her face away from his and refused to listen to her treacherous heart's dancing beat.

'Why are you here?'

She sat down as she spoke, determined not to ask him how he was or give him an inch of herself. She tried to throw a sting through her words. But Pascal couldn't – or wouldn't – hear it.

'Because I wanted to be the one who told you what happened to your parents. I owe you that much.'

Noemi shook her head. 'I already know what happened to them, and you owe me far more than the telling.'

She thought that might stop him. It didn't.

'I know. And I don't know where to start, or if there's even a starting place. But the truth is I'm here because you are. And I've waited so long for that.'

It was an answer which rested in ties he no longer had any right to, and Noemi – whose head was spinning at the sound of his voice in a way it wasn't meant to – refused to indulge it.

'I'm not leaving. If your father's sent you here to tell me to go away, don't bother. I'm here to take back what's mine, no matter how hard he tries to stop me.'

'Good. It's what he deserves.'

It was the last response she expected. It forced her to look at him. She wished she hadn't – the longing in his face belonged to the boy she'd loved, not the stranger he needed to be, and it burned her to see it.

These are old flames, that's all, rekindled from shock. You can't trust them; you can't act on them. You betray everyone who died if you do.

It was Hauke's voice in her head; it was Frieda's. There was a lilt that could have come from Matthias. But it wasn't Noemi's, although she badly wanted it to be. Which meant she had to stay on the attack.

'Viktor denounced my family – did you know that? He as good as killed my parents himself, and he wanted to kill me too. You said you thought it wasn't him, but he admitted it. He enjoyed telling me what he'd done.'

Pascal swallowed hard before he answered; Noemi refused to let her face soften.

'I said a lot of things once with a certainty I shouldn't have. I'm sorry. I'm sorry I defended him and for everything he did. I'm sorry I ever saw any decency in him. I don't expect you to forgive me for that – or for anything. But I had to say it.'

It was clear from his reddened eyes that he was telling the truth, that he was no longer under Viktor's spell.

But he should have broken free from that years before this.

She clung to her anger and carried on pushing him away.

'I loathe your father and I always will, but it's Carina I feel sorry for, not him and not you. Please God she saw sense and got away before he completely destroyed her life too.'

The pause stretched longer this time. Pascal's voice fell to a whisper. 'My mother is dead. She died not long after she helped you escape. I don't know if the two things are connected – my father has always refused to discuss what happened to her, and I wasn't there when it happened.' He paused as if he was replaying a different conversation in his head and the last drops of colour leached from his face. 'But given something he stopped himself saying earlier today, I'm starting to wonder.'

If my fool of a wife hadn't interfered.

Noemi managed to stop herself blurting Viktor's words out. Only the hardest heart could have heard the pain in Pascal's reply and not grieved for him, especially given that his suspicions might well be true. And Noemi's heart was frightened, not made of stone.

'I'm very sorry for that.' She managed to meet his eyes briefly, but she couldn't linger there. 'She was a kind, generous woman, and I owe my life to her.'

She didn't add, *And to you.* She rubbed her eyes. She'd cared for Carina very deeply, but she couldn't bear to cry anymore, and she couldn't cry near him. The thought of Pascal reaching out and offering her comfort – which she instinctively knew he would do, whatever the circumstances – was impossible. So she struck at him again.

'Viktor said you were a war hero. He said you worked at Dachau. You have no right to be here if that's true. You have no right to speak to me at all if you worked where my father was sent to his death.'

That whip of the lash worked. His face froze.

'I wasn't a hero – that part's not true. I was a soldier, yes. I did terrible things on the battlefield, and then I... I wouldn't do what was asked of me next and Dachau was my punishment. And I tried to do the right thing there too; I tried to help, but...' He stopped and shook his head. 'No. I'm not going to do this. I'm not going to try and paint myself to you as a better man, any more than I'm going to blame my father for the choices I made. Never mind what else I did or didn't do, Dachau was a living hell for every poor soul who was forced through its gates. And yes, I was there, I was part of the machinery, although not when Hauke was, I can promise you that at least.'

He swallowed hard again and stumbled far less confidently on. 'You asked me once where all the hatred would end... I was a fool then with no idea what you meant, but I know the answer to that now. It ended in Dachau. And in a pit in a village no one's heard of, where mothers and children and old men were slaughtered for... for not being us. That was the end. I was there at that, and I was there at the start. I walked down that road and did nothing to change where it was going until it was far too late. That's the truth, and I won't hide from it.'

His words were filled with anguish. It was clear that his war had carried more layers than Viktor, or she, had allowed. Noemi didn't know what to say or think, or how to react. When he suddenly caught hold of her hand and the shock of his touch exploded through her skin, she didn't know which version of herself – the old one who'd loved him or the new one who didn't want to – to be. And he sensed it.

'I'm not him anymore, Noemi – I swear it. I'm not that arrogant, stupid and blind boy who thought I could pick and choose which bits of Hitler's masterplan to believe in and shape it my own way. I hate that boy – and that man. I want to atone for everything he did. Because I can't find a way to live with him if I don't. And I can't live with how much you – quite rightly – must hate me.'

His honesty was as raw as his words. It flooded his face and the hand gripping too tightly to hers. She wanted to believe him so badly it hurt. But Hauke and Frieda were there in the room with her. And Matthias. And the partisans she'd fought alongside, and all the broken souls she'd passed on the roads and the ones who'd never made it that far. The room was so crowded with the weight of their ruined lives, she couldn't breathe. Pascal was sorry – she recognised that. He'd clearly tried to balance his life in some way she didn't yet understand. She didn't know if that was enough. They had fought on opposite sides of the war. She was Jewish. After what had been done to her people, she would always be Jewish. And Pascal was...

The love of my life.

'I can't do this. You have to go.'

She pulled her hand away from his. She refused to look up until the door closed. She sat without moving until Frau Hammerl returned, trying – and failing – to make sense of their meeting.

'He was telling the truth, for what's it worth.'

Frau Hammerl – or Ute as she told Noemi to call her – listened to Noemi's explanation of their history and Pascal's visit without comment until she finished. Then she made more tea – chamomile this time, for its calming properties – and began talking.

'He tried to atone, or get punished, when the Americans came. I'm not entirely sure anyone, including him, knows which. He told them he'd been in the Nazi Party and had served with the SS at Dachau and deserved to be in prison – or dead. But some of the mothers whose sons he'd saved pleaded his case and they wouldn't let the army take him.'

'What mothers? What sons?'

Noemi forgot about her cooling tea as Ute told her the story about the four boys who Pascal had talked out of blowing up American tanks in the last frantic days of the war.

'And I think there's more to his time in Dachau than he's telling, which is another reason why the Americans never came back for him. According to a woman I know in Munich, who works for them and has begun to collect testimony about war crimes, some of the survivors from the camp had help from a German officer. Apparently, he encouraged them to carve out hiding places so they would escape the death march, or selections, and he also smuggled medicines in. And according to her, the officer was Pascal. If that's true and he risked his own life to save theirs, isn't he the last person who needs punishing?'

Noemi didn't have an answer. She closed her eyes. Who Pascal had been and who he'd become kept shifting, and she couldn't settle on a shape. But when she opened them again – to find Ute openly studying her – she wasn't ready to accept the better one.

'Maybe the survivor testimony is true and it was him. But what about the women here? What if they only helped Pascal because they had things to hide too? There were plenty in the town who supported Hitler and went unpunished, including Pascal's father. Did the mothers plead his case as well?'

Ute shook her head. 'No, they didn't. But nobody denounced Viktor either, so you've a right to be suspicious. I don't know why – maybe because times were harder here than they might appear on the surface, and Viktor...' She shrugged. 'He had connections; he kept people fed. Sometimes that's enough to keep people silent.'

'Despite the death camps and the ovens and the massacres?'

Noemi pushed her teacup away so hard it toppled. 'How lovely that a full stomach is all it takes to settle a conscience.'

Ute collected the cups and mopped up the spill without comment. When she sat back down again, she sighed.

'You're Jewish, so perhaps that allows you to be quick to judge, but I'm not as sure about the rest of us.' She shook her head as Noemi flared. 'Don't misunderstand me please or make me your enemy. I'm not trying to defend what's been done; I'm sickened by it. I've also examined my conscience, and it's not clean. I closed my eyes and ears with the rest, I'm as guilty of looking away as anyone and we've all got to take our share of the blame. But I can't condemn every person in the town, and I certainly can't condemn Pascal, whatever you choose to do.'

She paused. Noemi could feel her weighing her words carefully.

'And what about your war, Noemi? I'm not judging you either, but are you the same person now that you were before?'

Noemi replied without taking the moment to reflect she sensed Ute wanted her to take. 'No, I'm not. Never mind what happened to my parents and what that did to me, I was a partisan, and I killed people. But I was a soldier fighting other soldiers in a war. I didn't target innocent civilians, I didn't kill based on twisted notions of good or bad blood. I've got nothing to be ashamed of.'

Ute's smile was a gentle one, but there was a hint of sadness in it that spoke of losses she hadn't yet shared.

'I didn't ask if you were ashamed. I believe there's a difference between a battlefront and a gas chamber the same as you do. And I don't believe for a moment that killing came easily to you, especially not at first. I imagine you saw the parents and the wives standing behind the first soldiers you shot at and regretted the suffering that was coming for them. But what I asked was if you were changed, and I know the answer is yes. And I worry that the need for revenge that you're harbouring now won't help you rebuild your life, that it will destroy you instead.'

'So am I.'

It wasn't the first time Noemi had faced that fear, but it was the first time she'd trusted anybody enough to voice it.

'I'm afraid I'll never be able to get past it. I'm afraid revenge is all I am. And I don't know what will become of me if that's true.'

Ute reached out for her hand. 'I know. I hope you'll find a way to forgiveness, if that's what you want. I don't know if you can. I don't think you're close to it yet. Not many of us can look at our neighbours – or ourselves – and say that we are either, however carefully we go through the motions. But we have to find it one day, don't you think? If we don't, we'll be trapped by this war forever.'

They didn't talk anymore. The hour was late and the light was gone and Noemi was exhausted. She crawled into bed with her heart aching. *Forgiveness.* It was an easy word to say and an impossible state of mind to imagine. But *trapped* was surely worse.

And trapped is where I am.

It took a long time for sleep to come. When it did, her dreams were filled with barred doors and dead ends. With Pascal always out of reach. And Viktor watching her from the sidelines and laughing.

CHAPTER TWENTY-EIGHT
AUGUST 1945

'I'm sorry, ma'am, but from what you've told me – and I'm not saying I think this is right or fair – I expect we'll find that the paperwork approving the sale of your family's property, and the records of the payments that were made in connection with it, will be in order. Our people will do their best to check the details when they're back in the town, but I don't want you to get your hopes up. I'm afraid that – given the problems with food supplies and the lack of housing for starters – the issue of reparations is nowhere near the top of our list. You're going to have to be a little patient with us.'

However conflicted Noemi's feelings about Pascal might have become since their meeting, she'd hadn't shifted an inch when it came to Viktor. And whether her head decided to call her fight against him justice or revenge, the need to fight him hadn't altered. Not that the process was proving to be an easy one. It had taken Noemi almost two weeks to track down the right person to speak to in the American headquarters in Munich, and the hurried appointment that had led to had been very frustrating. The clerk had also refused to give her a second one. 'Speak to one of the investigation team who'll be stationed in with you and get your case logged there,' was the best he could offer. And *stationed* suggested a far more permanent presence than the two days the Americans were actually planning to stay in the town while they attempted to denazify it. Her heart sank when she realised how restricted their timetable was in comparison to the promised scale of their ambition.

Registration Order:
All males over the age of eighteen must report to the Unterwald town hall between the hours of 9 a.m. and 5 p.m. on 14th August. All those registering will be required to complete a form detailing their association with any and all National Socialist organisations which they were a member of between 1933 and the present date. These forms are to be completed and returned by 15th August. New ration cards will only be issued to those who correctly complete the form.

'This was apparently sent to every household.' Ute handed Noemi the flyer which had arrived at the farmhouse with the morning post. 'It's a bit fanciful, don't you think? Asking people to tell tales on themselves. I don't see how they'll be able to check the entries, not in the brief time they'll have before they need to sort out rationing. I don't imagine much good will come from it.'

Neither did Noemi. She'd seen for herself how the town closed ranks. Once it became clear why she had returned – and whether it was because they didn't believe she was entitled to restitution, or because of guilt over the way her family and the other Jewish residents had been treated – no one spoke to her longer than they were required to; no one made eye contact. If she went into a shop, she was dealt with efficiently, but there was never a moment of warmth.

'You're an irritant and a reminder of a time they'd rather forget. You being here is making them look in the mirror, and at each other, and dredge up old sins.'

Noemi had no doubt that Ute was right, but the suggestion Ute followed that observation with sat far less easily.

'If the Americans can't help you – and the town won't – do you think it's perhaps time to consider moving on? That it might be better to start afresh somewhere else?'

She'd probably been right in that too, but Noemi wasn't ready to hear it. She'd been chased out of Unterwald once; she wasn't going to be chased out again. If and when she left, it would be on her own terms. And whether anyone else could help her wasn't the issue: Noemi had plenty of fight of her own.

'What are you doing? And where on earth did you get these?'

Noemi whirled round, splattering paste off her brush in a messy arc over the pavement. She thought she'd checked the square thoroughly when she'd started – there'd been no sign of anybody around then. The presence of the American investigation team in the Unterwald Hotel had sent the town's residents scurrying home early. And the last person she'd expected to see – or to have to explain herself to – was Pascal. She hadn't been intending to see him at all. She'd been avoiding him since their meeting at the farm, although he'd been taking up far too much space in her thoughts. Which wasn't anything he needed to know. She glanced at the poster dripping with paste on the wall, and decided to answer at least part of his question. It wasn't as if he was going to call the police.

'The printing shop has a cylinder press and very weak window locks, and I've run this kind of stuff off before. It wasn't difficult to do.'

Pascal didn't ask where she'd learned any of the skills she'd just admitted to. Instead – in an uncomfortable echo of the

Karwendelhaus which she instantly dismissed – he picked up one of the posters from the bundles at her feet. She waited while he read it, to see how he would react, before she volunteered any further information.

'These are really good. "Who will bring him to justice?" That's a brave question.'

The respect on his face took her by surprise. The posters weren't actually very good at all – they were a crudely printed list of Viktor's crimes under the heading *Nazi in Hiding* and his name, but Noemi was proud of them. She'd included his treatment of all the town's Jews, his property thefts and the dealings she suspected he'd had with the black market, and his plan to send young boys out to their deaths in a last-stand attack on the enemy. It was the kind of smear campaign the partisans were good at, and – following the patterns she'd learned in her days as one of them – she hadn't picked only one target. She hesitated for a moment and then reached for a sheet from a separate bundle.

'There's this one too. I'm not as certain of the details, but I'm sure I'm right with the allegation.'

The second poster she handed him was a mirror of the first. The Nazi she'd accused on it of being in hiding was the town's doctor; the crime she'd referenced was participation in the euthanasia of the physically and mentally ill at the Hartheim hospital. And the question she'd finished with this time was, 'Do you know what happened to your children?'

'This goes back to the day we met in the hotel, doesn't it? Before I went to Sonthofen?'

Noemi nodded, but she hurried over Pascal's question. She was surprised he'd remembered their exchange, but she had no intention of straying into awkward personal territory.

'I told you then I'd overheard things while I was waitressing, and that one of those discussions concerned the "special arrangements" Doctor Brodmann had made for a child born with a twisted leg. Hartheim's come up more than once in the papers as a killing centre for the sick, and I think that's what he meant – I think he had the child sent there. And based on other gossip that I've heard since I came back – about the type of people who disappeared while they were under his care – I doubt that child was the only one he despatched.'

Pascal's hand shook as he returned the poster to the pile. She knew his, 'You're right about the practice; it was commonplace, and I think you're right about him,' hid a darker story of his own behind it. Whatever that was, she wasn't ready to ask, and he clearly wasn't ready to offer it.

I should tell him to go away again. I should make it clear this has nothing to do with him.

She dipped her brush back into the paste again, hoping he would take the hint if she said nothing else. She didn't want an argument or raised voices that could lead to her discovery before the task was complete. But Pascal had other ideas.

'I assume these are for the Americans' benefit?'

She carried on sticking up the next poster, wondering at which point he would leave. She certainly wasn't about to edge round the truth.

'Yes, they are. I want a proper spotlight shone on your father, and the doctor, to start with. But they're for the town too. Hopefully once people read these, they'll remember the ones who were sent away and never came home, or were punished because someone held a grudge against them. And then, who knows, perhaps – if another wave of denunciations follow – these registration forms will start to gather real weight.'

'Because nobody deserves to escape justice, including my father. And nobody should stand by and let that possibility happen.'

He'd completed her thought process in the way they'd done for each other since they were tiny.

Before the world drove the worst kind of wedge between us.

She didn't respond. When Pascal picked up her spare brush and began pasting the posters about Viktor onto the market square's buildings, Noemi didn't stop him either. But the crack she felt run through her heart as she watched him help her spread the evidence against his father around Viktor's town felt like an opening, not a break.

By the time dawn began to creep in pink ribbons across the mountaintops, the town was awash with posters, and Pascal and Noemi's arms were stiff with stretching. The empty bucket seemed to have tripled in weight as they hauled it, and themselves, back along the path out of town.

'You didn't print a poster about me.'

Noemi had been waiting for him to mention that omission since he'd read the allegations against his father and the doctor. He wore his guilt too heavily to pretend it wasn't there. She stopped walking. They needed to get the evidence of their sticky bucket and brushes away quickly, but she knew he'd keep asking unless she told him why.

'No, I didn't. I would have done when I first came back, when Viktor told me where you'd served and what you'd done. Hearing that fired the anger I'd been carrying with me about your choices for years. But then I talked to you, and other people talked about you to me. And now...'

She paused. It was one thing to have admitted to herself that she loved him. It would be an entirely different thing to admit it to him. And it wasn't a step she was sure she would ever be able – or would ever want – to take. She chose to acknowledge her confusion instead.

'You once divided people into good and bad when those divisions didn't exist. Perhaps I've done a similar thing with you, without acknowledging that the truth may be a little more complicated. You've walked both sides of that line. I know now that I don't hate you—'

'But you can't forgive me, and you don't know if you want to try.' Pascal didn't smile, but his face suddenly looked less weary. 'You don't hate me, and that's better than I hoped for. That feels like more than I deserve, and I'm grateful you said it, so thank you.'

There was barely a hand's breadth between them on the path. She could smell the hay on his shirt from the previous day's harvest. She could hear the love lying thick as a winter snowfall in his voice.

I'll never really come home until I find some way back to him.

The realisation came from nowhere and hit hard. She didn't know what that pathway looked like. She knew it couldn't involve reaching for his hand, which would have been the simplest way once upon a time. But she was certain this time that she didn't want to completely ignore the shift in her heart. So she offered him something of her life since they'd lost each other instead.

'I fought, in battles too. I was a partisan. I fought in the ghetto in Warsaw when it rose up against the Nazis, not because I was in there as a prisoner but because that was what I chose to go and do. And I fought in the battle against them for the city the following year. I've seen things and done things my mind wants to run away from. And – if I'm honest – I don't yet know what all the killing and suffering I've seen, and caused, has turned me into. I don't know how much of the girl who once roamed the mountains and meadows here is left.'

She couldn't remember the last time she'd spoken so honestly about her feelings. Not since her mother had vanished, and perhaps not then – their last conversations had been too clouded by fear of the future for Noemi to speak freely. Certainly not with Matthias – most of their driving force had been rooted in survival, not in worrying about what kind of people they might become if the fighting was ever done. And for all she'd hoped their bond would deepen, they'd never reached the level of understanding she'd forged with Pascal. Too many pieces of their hearts had stayed closed to each other.

Which was my doing as much as his. We met in a world where trust had gone, and that coloured who we could be.

She glanced up. Pascal was looking away from her, out towards the mountain ridges where their bond had once been unbreakable, where their minds and bodies had worked as one. His face was so clouded she knew exactly what he was seeing. She could picture the scene he was watching: the two of them scrambling together across the ice and the snow, linked by a rope and by trust.

Perhaps nobody will ever know me like he did. Perhaps that's another part of me that will always be lost.

The thought of walking on through the world without ever again finding such a deep-rooted tie to another human being was terrifying. She didn't want to face it.

Because, despite everything, I want him.

The urge to tell him that, for good and for ill, was suddenly overwhelming. She began to say, 'Pascal, I…' with no idea where *I* was heading. She didn't get a chance to find out.

'The town's up, look. Maybe the game is up too.'

Some noise she'd missed had jerked Pascal out of the memories he'd tumbled into. He pointed down the slope to the market square. It was filling up, people running in all directions. Every person who arrived was gesticulating to the next. And then Viktor was suddenly there, his entourage running in his wake. The posters rapidly turned into confetti.

'Get back to the farmhouse, Noemi. Pretend you never left your bed and get Frau Hammerl to lie for you if necessary. He's no fool; he'll know who's behind this, and – if your plan fails and the Americans don't haul him in quickly for questioning –

he'll make you pay. Whatever else comes out of this, I can't stand by and let him hurt you again.'

She didn't need to be told twice. She didn't want to put Pascal at risk of taking any kind of action that would rebound on him. She ran down the pathway without looking back. But she wasn't afraid. Someone would run to the Americans with a poster before they were all torn up and ruined – there was always somebody desperate to be arm in arm with the winning side. And the Americans would come for Viktor before he came for her – she could feel the certainty of that as strongly as she could feel the rising sun's warmth kissing her skin.

Viktor's going to be made to pay for what he did, not me. He's finally going to be forced to face who he is.

She felt lighter than she'd felt for years as she flew through the empty kitchen to her bed.

CHAPTER TWENTY-NINE
AUGUST 1945

The posters worked. The Americans took Viktor and the doctor away for questioning at once and nobody came to the farm to search for Noemi. Nobody knew for certain what had happened to the arrested men either, but the rumours flew as thick as crows after harvesting as the town's busybodies competed to fill in the blanks.

'They've been taken to Munich, to the old Gestapo prison. They're going to be charged with making false statements in order to hide their pasts.'

'No, it's worse than that. They're going to be charged with actual war crimes, to do with the Jews who were rounded up, like the posters said, and the sick kids who disappeared.'

'You're out of date. It's moving very fast. Both of them have confessed to everything that's been said about them. They're going to be made into examples; they're going to be executed.'

Every time Ute went to the marketplace, she brought back a new version of the story. The town was also busy speculating about who had put up the posters. Noemi was, of course, the main suspect, but nobody seemed to be in a hurry to confront her. Peace didn't always mean peace, and everybody knew it. The end of the war had papered over the cracks the conflict had caused but not fixed them. The summer was hot, and tempers were short. There were past grudges – and new ones – to be settled, and old patterns of taking revenge that could very easily do that job. Which put a new candidate in the frame every day.

'So don't go down there, okay? Or at least not until we've got a proper sense of what's happening. Plenty are worried that if Viktor goes down, they'll be pulled into trouble along with him, and they're looking for scapegoats to denounce in their place. Don't offer yourself up on a platter.'

Noemi did as Ute asked and stayed out of sight while the town boiled. And, also on Ute's advice, she made no attempt to contact Pascal. The days when Unterwald's gossips had joined their names together in one breath were long gone, but even the smallest risk that someone might think to do that again and implicate Pascal in the poster campaign was too great – Noemi didn't want to give Viktor any more ammunition against her if he was to return.

She stayed put, but she couldn't stay still. Instead, she threw herself into the kind of work she'd loved doing in more innocent days. She stripped the farm's orchards and made use of every scrap of fruit she could find, until the kitchen was so crammed with jellies and jams and bottles of cherries in syrup which all required tasting, Ute had to plead for her waistline and beg her to stop. Noemi put away the copper pans, but then her idle hands turned to baking, and the kitchen became filled instead with apple cakes and *streusel*-topped sheet bakes and trays packed with vanilla-scented sweet pretzels which Ute was equally as powerless to resist.

It was a relief for them both when a note finally arrived from Pascal and put an end to the waiting.

The allegations are being taken seriously and the Americans intend to keep Father in detention. I've spoken to Niehbur, and he thinks it might be worth revisiting your property claim – he doesn't want to be accused of complicity if the legality of the transfers is open to question. He's made some suggestions we need to go over. Come to the farm tonight, but meet me in the far barn – you know the one – not the house. It's not clear yet what's happening with Brodmann as there's less evidence against him, and I don't want to risk the two of us being spotted in case he's allowed to come back. Let's put our heads together and see what we can do to at least make the legal process move quicker.

Everything about the message was good news and exactly what Noemi wanted to hear. And far too much about it was wrong.

'I've never had a letter from Pascal before – we were rarely apart when we were young, and he was hardly one for putting his thoughts, or anything else, down on paper then – so I've nothing to compare this with. But the writing is far neater than his scrawl used to be and the style doesn't feel like him either.'

She was even more certain of that when she read the message aloud to Ute; the cadences and the content didn't fit with its supposed author.

'Pascal's always had a very direct turn of phrase. He'd say charges, not allegations, and prison, not detention, and *worth revisiting* isn't him at all. The style is too formal. And even if that's a product of officer school, there's too many other oddities. Why would he go to the notary without checking with me first, when the transactions were none of his business? And why would he suggest meeting in the far barn in such an oddly coy way? *You know the one.* That's just peculiar when he knows what bad memories it would be sure to bring back. And why would anyone notice me going to the house? Pascal knows I'd take the back road if I went there.'

Ute didn't waste time trying to respond to questions she couldn't answer. She went straight to the heart of the matter instead.

'Do you think Viktor wrote this then, not Pascal? Do you think he could have sneaked back without anyone knowing, and this is a trap?'

Noemi let out a breath and nodded. That had been her instant assessment, but she'd wondered if her imagination was spinning out of control. It was a relief to hear Ute – who was built from common sense – suspecting the same thing.

'It could well be. The writer knows enough to almost hit the right marks, but he's done it the wrong way. And if Viktor has been released, it's me he'll come after.'

'And are you going to share these suspicions with Pascal?'

I can't stand by and let him hurt you again.

He'd meant it – Noemi had no doubt about that. In the same way that she had no doubt Viktor wouldn't care what he did to his son if he found himself cornered. Or if he cornered her, and Pascal leapt to her defence.

'No. This could be a trap for us both, and I've no way of getting a message to Pascal in time anyway. We don't have a working phone, and I can hardly make a call like this from the post office with the customers, never mind the switchboard operator, listening in.' She paused as the years began rolling back and made her mind up. 'This is a confrontation that's been a long time coming. Whatever Viktor's planning, I have to deal with him by myself.'

'Then you'll need to take this.'

Ute went over to the old dresser which took up most of the kitchen and returned with a metal strongbox. She unlocked and opened it carefully, gently putting aside the medals and photographs it contained, until the only thing left inside was a gun.

'This was my son's. He died at Stalingrad. There was no body, no burial. One of his friends returned this to me so that I'd at least have something Stefan touched.' She blinked and stared at the gun. 'It was an odd thing to do, given how my boy's life ended, but there was a kindness in the act that helped me at the time. Now I'm glad of it. I presume you know how to use it?'

Noemi took the pistol from the box and nodded. It was a Walther P38, standard German army issue. She'd taken more of them from dead bodies for reuse in the ghetto and on Warsaw's streets than Ute ever needed to know.

'I'll take it for protection, but I won't use it. This isn't about more killing.'

She said that for comfort's sake, but she didn't fool herself or Ute. Both women knew that if it really was Viktor who'd sent the note, he'd have a gun of his own. And he would be more than ready to turn it on Noemi.

She circled the Lindiger farm using the high path she'd walked along with Carina on the day she'd fled from the round-up, all too aware of the route she retraced and the consequences of that meeting. The path brought her down through a copse of heat-crisped trees which ended a few hundred metres from the barn. She'd assumed *tonight* meant after dark, but she was in place long before sunset. Crouched down, covered by the treeline; invisible but with a clear view of anyone entering or leaving. In the best position to ensure that Viktor went into the barn first and she would be the one closest to the door. Because it would be Viktor who came. She'd stopped telling herself she was wrong and the writer could be Pascal the moment she'd accepted the gun.

Viktor arrived as the sky's edges blurred from indigo to black and the shadows stretched out to swallow the barn. Unlike her, he hadn't made any effort to conceal his approach – he was carrying a lantern before him whose light bobbed around his bulk in a hazy yellow arc. There was an arrogance to that which released Noemi's tight shoulders. His overconfidence made him more vulnerable than he knew. She still stayed where she was for another ten minutes, and let him wait and wonder.

The mistakes she'd been counting on to wrong-foot him continued to pile up. He had his back to the door when she finally slipped silently through it. He was standing near the rear of the barn, his gun visible in his holster. That would have looked more threatening if he hadn't been partly crouched over with his hands on his knees, if she hadn't been able to hear the wheeze as he sucked in his breath. From the dishevelled state of his clothes, it was clear that he'd come straight to the barn after being released rather than taking time to rest. Noemi doubted the Americans would have used Gestapo-style techniques on him, but Viktor was overweight and wasn't in good health, and a few days in prison – and away from the bottle – would have taken its toll.

She took another silent step forward, making sure the barn door remained open behind her. Viktor had placed the lantern on a patch of ground next to the barn's timber frame, she was well outside its circle of light. He hadn't heard her come in; he hadn't sensed her presence. His broad back was a perfect target.

Noemi eased the gun out of her pocket. The feel of it was safe and familiar. She ran her fingers round the barrel, found the trigger, looked at the bulky shape of him that she could have hit without taking aim. She imagined him falling. And stopped. She had never shot a man in the back before and she wasn't about to start doing it now. She stowed the gun away again instead and stepped forward to a point where he would be able to see her, crunching her heel into a clump of dry straw as she did so. Let him think she'd only that moment come in; let him think he'd caught her out with his letter. He'd grow more careless if she played the fool.

Viktor instantly whirled round at the sound, and his bent body straightened. But it was Noemi who deliberately widened her eyes and gasped as if in surprise.

'What are you doing here? I thought from the note I was meeting Pascal.'

His hand came away from his holster, and he grinned. 'I'm sorry to spoil your night.'

His eyes were bloodshot; he had to narrow them as he peered through the gloom at her. He was drunk, slurring his words, unsteady on his feet. Noemi doubted he'd be able to fire a bullet in a straight line, but she didn't doubt that he'd try.

Let him talk. Let him swagger. Do what you're good at: watch and wait.

'I don't understand what's happening. I thought you were in prison.'

She shrank into her coat and made herself smaller as she spoke. She let him hear fear in her voice. His grin disappeared in a flash of contempt Noemi was glad to see. It was a better reminder than his smile that he was a dangerous man, that this was a balancing act, and she could lose her footing just as easily as him.

'I bet you did. That's where you wanted me, wasn't it? That's what your nasty little posters were intended to do.'

His hand strayed back to his holster. Noemi forced herself not to react. She was younger, she was sober; time and speed were on her side. She was certain she could shoot through her coat pocket faster than he could draw his gun. She let him have the floor and didn't interrupt him.

'That was all a very dramatic little game, but it didn't work. It was never going to. I've dealt with the Americans before, remember. They don't have the time to sort out *petty local grievances*, as they put it, especially as nobody came forward to support your allegations. Apparently, they're getting denunciations like this in every town they visit. They questioned me for a couple of days, but it got them nowhere – my accent got stronger with each answer; their German was barely good enough to order coffee with. I don't think they were sorry to see me go.' He swayed a little; recovered himself and his grin. 'So I thought I'd come back and have a little fun myself – before I get a proper welcome home tomorrow.'

A show-off in a sad uniform.

Hauke had added that to *fool* and *bully*. The uniform was gone, but the rest remained true. Whatever else he had planned for her, Viktor wanted her to know what he'd done: she was there as his audience. Now all she had to do was play up to the part while she worked out what to do with him.

'By fun, do you mean tormenting me?'

He shrugged as if to say, *What else?*

Noemi took a step back as if she was afraid and noted how he enjoyed that too. 'I was right though, wasn't I? You did all the things I accused you of, whether the Americans care or not. You got rid of everyone in this town who didn't fit with your vision of Germany. None of us stood a chance from the start.'

Viktor stopped swaying and stood straighter, striking the same kind of thumb-in-belt pose he used to adopt when he stood on the stage below his beloved swastika. The moment he did that, Noemi's body responded. Hatred surged back through her on a wave of humiliation and pain-filled memories.

He can think he's in charge all he likes, but he's not leaving here alive. This is the last time we go through this.

She was going to shoot him. That decision had been taken the moment she'd picked up the gun, whatever she'd promised Ute. She didn't let any trace of that appear on her face. Instead, she let Viktor carry on having his moment.

'I did a good job of it too, didn't I? I got rid of everyone who was unworthy, everyone who crossed me, everyone who was a stain. Although perhaps I should give you some of the credit for that. Your carelessness did me quite the favour.'

Noemi didn't understand what he meant and she said so.

Viktor glanced across to where he'd placed the lantern and waved rather theatrically in its direction. 'Don't you remember what you left under there?'

She didn't at first. All she could see was a mouldering heap of sacks. Until realisation crashed in and she was suddenly the one fighting to stay steady.

'Oh dear God, it wasn't Carina or Pascal who found them; it was you.'

Shock ripped through her, but – unlike Victor, who was too busy enjoying her reaction to take any notice of anything but his own pleasure – one wave of emotion, no matter how strong, wasn't enough to switch off her senses. She'd registered the slight shuffle behind her and the thickening in the shadows. She knew they weren't alone. She moved slightly, to block the doorway Viktor hadn't bothered checking, as he answered.

'The clothes and the papers you left kicked underneath the sacking? Of course it was me – didn't you work out that Carina wouldn't have had the wit to check, and as for Pascal... Who knows or cares why he left them. He must have forgotten. What a gift it was. You might as well have stuck up a sign in the corner saying, *Ask your treacherous wife or your son where I am.*'

Noemi couldn't risk dwelling on her mistake, although she knew she'd need to grieve over it and the consequences for Carina once her business with Viktor was done. It was more important now that she take control of the situation she was currently in. She assumed Pascal must have seen the light from the lantern and followed it from the house to the barn. She willed him not to move, not to shout out. She gestured with her hand behind her back for him to stay where he was and prayed he could see it. She had an awful feeling he already knew where her mistake had led.

But Viktor has to say what he did so there's no mistaking it. Pascal has to hear exactly what happened, from his father, not from me, so there's never any doubt.

'So what did you do next?' She left a deliberate pause; gave a deliberate gasp. 'Surely you didn't denounce your own wife?'

Noemi had pitched her shock at exactly the right level. Viktor couldn't help himself – his smile oozed with satisfaction. It was hard to watch it spread and not be sick.

'Of course I did. She was a traitor. Admittedly, it took a little time to get the truth out of her, and a little... let's call it persuasion. And she didn't want to give up Pascal's part in your escape, but she spilled that too eventually.'

Noemi could feel Pascal behind her. He hadn't moved, he hadn't given himself away, but the air around him quivered with horror. And there was nothing Noemi could do to spare him from more misery: it would have been a lie not to expose the truth. She took a deep breath. The only thing she didn't have to pretend was how disgusted she was.

'But why on earth would you do that? She would have been arrested, like everyone else who was called out publicly. That surely can't have been what you wanted?'

Viktor's amused, 'Of course it was,' confirmed it.

This time Noemi let a little of her outrage show. 'But that didn't need to happen. She wasn't a danger to anyone. You could have kept quiet and protected her.'

Viktor's face lost its smile and its doughy softness. The lantern's light glinted in his eyes and set up a fire there that burned with hatred. Noemi had to force herself not to look away from him. She'd been so focused on her refusal to be afraid, she'd lost sight of his malevolence. There was no mistaking it when he answered.

'Not a danger maybe, but a disgrace. Old, barren, timid as a mouse. "She's no kind of a wife for a man with ambition." Himmler himself said that to me, and he was right. You did me a favour; you gave me the grounds to get rid of her.' Viktor's hand strayed back to his gun. 'At the moment, that's the one reason you're alive.'

Noemi shuffled her feet to mask the sound of Pascal moving forward. One more step and he would be visible even to Viktor's blurred eyes. And she had no idea how much longer he would be able to hold himself together. But she was sure Viktor hadn't yet told the whole story, and she needed him to finish that.

'Whether that's true or not, there's still one thing I don't understand. Weren't you worried that her downfall would instantly lead to yours? A timid wife is one thing, but a wife who helps Jews escape? Surely you took a risk in turning her in?'

Viktor read an admiration that wasn't there into her question. He struck his conqueror's pose again.

'It wasn't a risk because I didn't let it be. Carina took all the blame for smuggling you out; I beat that promise into her. And I played the horrified husband perfectly, which was easier to do given that I wasn't here. I even offered to throw myself on my sword. Nobody wanted to see that scandal play out – a loyal Nazi's wife helping a Jew escape justice? It broke every rule and was best hushed up, and besides – luckily for everyone – Carina very conveniently died and the problem disappeared.'

It was the little smile on *conveniently* that gave him away. That carried prison guards on his payroll inside it, and the hint of an empty staircase or one too many interrogations or freezing-cold nights. That spoke far more clearly about the depths of his cruelty than words ever could. This time Noemi didn't try to mask anything. She stepped aside and let Pascal come, with all his fury roaring.

'You ruined her life and you killed her. And there's not one speck of remorse in you. How did I never see you for the brute you really are? How did I let her go on living with you?'

The boy who'd worshipped his father was gone. The man roaring past her, screaming out his pain, was haunted and broken, and fuelled by rage. Noemi had to force herself not to throw herself after him, but – as much as she would mourn Carina herself – this agony was his, and the confrontation was no longer hers to control. And it wasn't Viktor's either. Pascal's sudden appearance caught him off guard. He stepped back, slipped, caught himself before he fell, but the gun he'd instinctively grabbed fell from his hand as he stumbled. Pascal caught it as it clattered to the ground and waved it in Viktor's face.

'What was the plan tonight? You tricked Noemi into coming here – that much is obvious. Were you going to kill her too and complete the family set?'

Viktor had curled into a boxer's crouch, but his fists loosened a little despite the gun pointed at him, as if he'd found a better way out than a fight.

'I hadn't decided that.' He blustered on as Pascal called him a liar. 'I tricked her here, yes, but I'd have let her go as long as she promised never to come back.' He glanced over at Noemi as if that lie might make her grateful to him. 'There's nothing left for her – she knows that. The Americans aren't interested in her allegations, and nobody wants her in the town raking up the past. I wanted to make her realise that, with her gone, life could get back to normal for the rest of us, which is what we all need. She's not a fool; I thought she'd see sense and clear off.'

'*Normal?*' Pascal threw the word out like a punch and couldn't stop swinging. 'Let's leave to one side for a moment the fact that I don't believe you. That I believe you would have shot her without a second thought once you'd finished showing off just how evil you are. Why don't you explain to me instead how in God's name you think life will ever be *normal* again? Don't you get what we've done? We pledged ourselves to a madman.

We helped him tear through Europe spitting out hate. We turned our backs on anyone without his godforsaken idea of "pure blood" and pursued them to their deaths. What part of that leads any of us back to *normal*? And what part of you confessing to killing my mother, your wife, leads me and you back there?'

Viktor's body had coiled again, but Noemi wasn't sure Pascal had noticed. He raised his gun towards his father and didn't flicker when Noemi – who could see the murderous rage flashing in Viktor's eyes and was convinced it would take at least two bullets to stop him – reached for hers too. But although they'd moved physically in the same way and at the same time, they'd never fought together before, and she hadn't read his mind. Pascal didn't press the trigger, and he told Viktor too much.

'You won't be dictating what happens in Unterwald after this. You've lost that right, and there won't be any more killing. I'm taking you back to the Americans, and this time when they arrest you, I'll make sure the charges stick.'

Noemi understood there was strength in Pascal's decision. Viktor saw only weakness.

He lunged forward faster than either of them realised he could move. He spun Pascal's gun into the air with one punch and knocked Noemi flying with another. He was maddened, bellowing. A bull filling the air with his rage. Noemi scrambled to her feet, raking through the straw for her dropped weapon as Pascal hurled himself at his father. She found the gun, but there was no clear line of sight – the men were locked together, rolling and snarling, fists colliding with bone. They moved in and out of the light, their shapes blurring and resetting as Noemi tried to fling herself into a better position and fire.

She was moving as fast as they were. Which meant she missed the moment when Pascal somehow broke free and launched the blow which connected like a sledgehammer with

Viktor's chin. But she heard the crunch. She saw Viktor fly backwards, she saw his boot kick the lantern. She saw the straw around it catch alight in seconds and the flames leap like dancers across the wooden wall. And the fire which had eaten the ghetto and destroyed Warsaw and Dresden roared its hungry way out of her dreams and back to life.

CHAPTER THIRTY
SEPTEMBER 1945

'Move!'

The fire had raced in two directions at once, running faster than Noemi could shout. Up the timber wall in a sheet of bright orange and in a zigzag line across the dry clumps of straw which were scattered haphazardly from one side of the barn to the other. It spread in seconds as the flames fattened, sending up clouds of acrid black smoke in its wake.

'We've got to leave him. We've got to get out of here now.'

'I can't reach him, but I can't leave him to die like this. Whatever he's done, he's still my father.'

Their words collided as the flames flew up and crackled into the hay bales stored in the roof space, turning the beams that supported the loft into torches. Viktor was lying behind the fire's barrier, his head bleeding, his eyes closed.

As Pascal lunged towards him, a breeze blew through the open doorway and caught hold of the burning straw. The strands whipped up from the floor and cascaded down from above. There was a strange beauty in the sight of the straw dancing through the singed air like tiny falling stars. For a brief moment, Pascal and Noemi were hypnotised. Until the first cinder bit into bare skin and the first beam began to crack.

'There's nothing you can do, Pascal. There's no way to reach him without being killed yourself.'

He didn't want to listen. The good son who couldn't betray his father was still lodged somewhere inside him. It took all of Noemi's strength to pull his shaking body out of the burning barn. Her hair was singed by the time she forced him through the door; her hands were pocked with blisters. Pascal was coughing so hard it was as if he was entirely made out of smoke.

They ran doubled over and fell into the rough safety of a stubble-filled field as the barn collapsed in on itself and the sparks and the flames flew away into the sky. Pascal's head sank into his hands; tears tracked through the dirt on his cheeks. Noemi wrapped her arms round him as he sobbed out his shock. She didn't know what to feel. Viktor, the man who had destroyed her family, was finally gone, but there was no satisfaction in that, no sense of relief or justice served. Instead, there was another burning building and another dead body and – in whatever form it took for Pascal, whether it was based purely on hatred or on some last vestiges of love, or more for his mother than for his father – there was another loss to mourn.

It wasn't supposed to be like this. Viktor will never pay for anything now. His crimes will be forgotten. There'll be a day when memories fade and somebody talks about him as a good man.

Noemi had watched the flames shrink as the barn disappeared inside a column of black smoke that smudged dirty fingers across the night sky. Viktor would be rewritten in time; so would the doctor and all the rest who'd judged and condemned and murdered by inaction if not by their own hands and would never be caught. The town would heal and move on, with all its secrets buried.

And I can't stay here and bear witness to that. I have to find a place where I'm wanted.

'Noemi, are you all right?'

She jumped as Pascal spoke, unable for a moment to tell if he was speaking to her from the past or the present. Three weeks had gone by since the fire, but the memory was still vivid and it wouldn't let go of her, any more than she knew it would let go of him. She couldn't stop herself drifting back to it no matter where she was.

'Herr Niehbur was saying that there's no more documents after this to sign. This is the last one.'

She gave herself a mental shake and forced herself to focus on the sheet of paper waiting for her signature, while the notary forced a smile and passed her a pen. She glanced at Pascal. His eyes were pouched, the shadows under them as grey as if the smoke from the barn had permanently marked him.

He needs a new life too. He needs to be somewhere he can remake himself.

She dropped her gaze to the document and quickly added her name. What Pascal did or didn't need – and how important that was to her – was a minefield she hadn't worked out how to navigate, especially now Viktor was dead. Everything he had stolen from the Drachmanns – the shop and the bar, the bakery and the bottling and distilling workshops – had reverted to Pascal with his death. And Pascal had refused to accept them. He'd had the papers drawn up for their transfer to Noemi before his father was buried; he'd insisted their return would set her free. She hadn't been able to ask him, *From what?* She'd barely seen him outside the notary's office since Viktor's funeral and the truth of his mother's death had shut him away from the world.

'Well there we are, that's everything, Fräulein Drachmann. I hope this goes some way to help resolve your... situation.'

Niehbur whisked them out of the door before Noemi could find him an answer. It was hardly *everything*. She had the businesses back, but not the people who'd spent their lives building them. The café and her home, which had been the centre of her lost life, remained out of her reach, as the notary well knew. Getting those returned would involve a fight nobody would thank her for starting. And as for staying and stepping into her parents' shoes?

'Can you do it? Can you stay in Unterwald? Do you even want to?'

Noemi stumbled as Pascal read her mind and tried to blame a loose cobblestone. She didn't know how to answer as he took her arm and helped her to steady herself; she wasn't ready for him to start seeing her thoughts again.

'Sit down with me, Noemi. We can do that much, can't we? We don't have to be strangers.'

The weather was mild, a gentle September day. There was a table tucked into the corner outside one of the town's inns where the late season's hikers wouldn't take any notice of them. She let him guide her there and order them both a glass of wine. The last thing she'd ever wanted to be was strangers.

'Perhaps I shouldn't have asked you that, especially given that I've tied you here now. But this has hardly been a happy homecoming for you, and leaving's been on my mind a lot lately.' He paused and looked at his wine glass. 'Do you remember all those years ago when you asked me to go away with you? When you asked me to leave Germany and go somewhere where nobody cared what our beliefs were?'

'Yes, I remember.'

She could have said a lot more. She could have reminded him that the second part of what she'd said was *somewhere we can be together and be in love without fear.* She could have told him the truth – that she'd never forgotten asking him to choose her, or how much his refusal to do so had hurt. She didn't know if that was a line she wanted to cross. They'd discussed what they'd done in the war since she returned but only within closely held boundaries. They'd discussed Viktor's death and the heartbreak that was Carina's, but only in the broadest terms. They'd discussed the restitution of Noemi's property and its practicalities. But they'd avoided discussing their shared past. They'd never once reached back for the people they'd been, or not in a way that said, *We were far more to each other than this.* Now she didn't know how to start, but it was all Pascal seemed to want to do.

'I wish to God I'd been braver. I wish I'd said yes. Our lives could have been—'

'Someone else's.'

Noemi finished his sentence without thinking. She wasn't sure as she said them whether her words were filled with regret or intended to stop him raking over old memories. But they filled her eyes – and his – with tears either way.

'I'd like to have met them, the Noemi and Pascal who left Unterwald that day. I think they would have been happy.'

Pascal's hand was suddenly over hers as he spoke. His touch should have felt wrong, but it felt like safety. It made her look up and properly at him. His face was so familiar, despite the changes that war had written across it. She couldn't stay in the town; she knew that, but she couldn't imagine never seeing him again either. His hand tightened round hers as if he sensed the shift.

'Do you think they would forgive us for what we threw away? Do you think they'd forgive me for what I became?'

'I don't know.'

She answered again without thinking, but she told him the

truth. She saw his eyes cloud. She knew what he was really asking, but it wasn't a simple answer.

'The words might come if they wanted to make each other happy, but it would take time and care and a lot of patience before that forgiveness felt real. For her anyway.'

She stopped. It was too big a conversation for *they* and *her* and pretend. She had to have her whole self in it or nothing of herself at all.

'None of this is easy; there's no clear answer. I won't pretend I've no love for you anymore, Pascal, even if that might be simpler. I haven't wanted that or looked for it. I've tried to lose it often enough, but nothing works. Loving you was what I did for so long, it's buried deep in my bones. And I doubt I could ever love anyone else in the same way I loved you.'

She paused for a moment, wondering if she should say more, knowing this wasn't the right time to tell him that she'd tried. 'But forgiveness?' She drew a long breath in. Nodded as she looked back at him. 'That's a different thing. I hope it's there too; I want it to be. I hope it can wipe away the boy who talked about "good" and "bad", who let his heart so horribly rule his head. Who sided with people who wanted my people wiped away from the world. I'll try to find it, truly I will, because the alternative is too bleak if I don't, whatever happens or doesn't happen with us. But – despite all you've done to balance the scales – I can't promise that I'll always be able to hold on to it. I can't promise my memories of that boy, and that man, won't reappear and make me question you all over again.'

'I know that.'

Pascal slipped his hand out of hers as if he was giving her the chance to get up and leave him. He didn't drop his gaze from her face. He breathed a little steadier when she stayed.

'You're right – nothing is easy or clear. I live with your version of me, and I struggle with him every day. That's how it should be, but it brings a darkness with it too that I don't want you burdened with. I hope there won't always be days when I don't feel fit for the world, but – like you – I can't make promises I don't know I can keep. But maybe that's the best we can do: be honest with each other, no matter how hard that might be.' He took a deep breath of his own and finally found the smile Noemi recognised. 'That there's love on both sides feels like a miracle – you have my heart like you've always done, and I think, I pray, I have yours. The younger me, who only saw what he wanted to see, would have said that was enough. The older me knows better. But he's young enough to have hope.'

Hope.

Noemi let the word settle into her heart and find a safe place there. Maybe in the end that was all forgiveness was: the hope something new could arise from the ashes of the old. The willingness to listen to the love the flames hadn't destroyed and try to keep choosing it. The decision not to be trapped.

'I still have this.' Pascal reached into his pocket and pulled out a small velvet box. 'I gave it to you when I was a boy with no real understanding of what love is. I'd like it to be yours again, if you want it.'

The box lay open on the table between them, waiting for Noemi to open it. When she did, the locket shone up at her from the silk lining, its blue a mirror of the sky, its enamelled flowers as fresh as if they'd just been plucked from a spring meadow. Noemi picked it up and let the stone catch the light; felt Carina and all her hopes for the two of them flickering inside its shining heart. And found the right words for Pascal.

'She would be happy with this, with us, wouldn't she? She wouldn't care how many cracks our hearts carried as long as we could find room in them for each other.'

Pascal's eyes were as bright as the jewel, his smile as sweet as the flowers. Noemi reached for him then – words would no longer do.

Their kiss was a tentative one. An exchange between two people who were both sure and unsure of each other. Who carried scars that might never fully heal and the weight of loss and guilt heavy around them. Who knew the possibility of hurt ran as deeply as the possibility of love. It was a tentative kiss, but it was heartfelt and wanted. It held the possibility of home.

CHAPTER THIRTY-ONE
SEPTEMBER 1950

'That's the last arrivals for the week checked in. They're a lively group – they've already demolished the apple cakes you put out. If they actually do all the climbs they're planning to complete, they'll keep the kitchens busy.'

Noemi wriggled her toes in the soft grass as Pascal bent down to scoop Karoline off her knee. The one-year-old's impromptu nap had sent her mother's legs to sleep too.

'That's fine; we can get extra help in from the village if it's needed. What about Debora? Is she comfortable in the cottage? Does she know she can have her meals there, if she doesn't want to deal with a crowd?'

Pascal nodded and waved to three-year-old Robin, who was busily collecting leaves to make a forest for his toy fort. 'She's all settled in, and she knows where you are if she wants to talk.'

Noemi blew her husband a kiss as he lifted Karoline onto his shoulder and stretched out under a sun that still held the last rays of summer, grateful for a few moments where nobody needed her. The lodge they'd opened four years earlier overlooking the pretty Swiss town of Appenzell – with the proceeds of the sale of both the Drachmann and Lindiger estates – was rarely quiet. It catered for the hikers and skiers who came all year round to explore the surrounding mountain ranges and the town's prettily painted wooden houses. Noemi's first thought when she'd seen it was, *It's not Unterwald, but it's as close to a replica of the lives we had there as we'll ever build for ourselves.*

That first impulse hadn't changed. The future could never have been their home town, it could never have been Germany, but they needed something of the familiar to hold on to. Now they lived in a place where the seasons mattered, and life was tied to nature's rituals. They lived close to mountains where they could wander – together and alone – if the world slipped off-kilter. And they lived in a country which hadn't been torn apart by the war. Where people accepted incomers of all sorts and didn't ask what had brought them there.

What had started for the two of them as a skiing holiday in the early months of 1946 had become a home the moment they saw the 'For Sale' sign outside the flower-decked lodge. They'd bought it at once and got married at once, hearts racing with the possibility of the fresh start they were desperate to find. And in the years that followed that decision, the lodge had become a place of sanctuary for far more lives than just theirs.

'It's a perfect tourist spot, but we could provide a refuge here too. Somewhere for people to come when the outside world is too much. And a place perhaps where we could put the things we've learned since the war to good use.'

Neither Pascal nor Noemi could remember whose idea it was first, not that it mattered. The idea had borne fruit and seeded itself through the connections Noemi worked hard to forge and Pascal worked as hard to sustain. Including Rabbi Mendel, who'd returned to Munich and his own synagogue and wept with delight when Noemi's refusal to let anyone important go from her life found him. With his advice and guidance to steer them – and with the help of the men from the town who gave their time freely to refurbish an old cottage beside the main lodge – they built a hideaway for the wanderers whose lives had been snapped in two by the war and hadn't yet healed.

The building those visitors used was completely self-contained; stays in it had no time limits. Some sought it out for a day or two; some came for a month – or more. Most of the lost souls who found their way to it were Jewish but not all. A lot of them wanted to talk, a lot of them didn't; each visitor set their own rules. And some needed practical help with visas or tracing services, or with the ongoing fight for reparations. Whatever was required by them was found.

And they've brought so much hope with them, which has helped us too. Even the ones who've suffered terribly don't want to give up their faith in the world.

Noemi got reluctantly to her feet as the sun started to dip. It was still warm in the meadow – she could have happily followed Karoline's lead and taken a nap. But the food at the Drachmann Lodge – which was the only name they'd ever considered for it – was one of its biggest draws outside the area's breathtaking scenery. Noemi not only had to oversee the dinner preparations, she also had a celebration cake waiting to be iced in her trademark blush and cherry pinks.

'This came for you. Give him my regards when you write back.'

Pascal passed her the envelope addressed in Matthias's looping hand as she stretched up to kiss Karoline's head. She checked his expression while she took it – checking his expression and assessing his mood was a habit she doubted she'd ever break – but there were no questions lurking in his eyes, and there was certainly no doubt, which was a relief. It had been a different story the first time a letter came.

I hope this has found you and that you are happy and well. I couldn't think of anywhere else you would have gone except Unterwald after you left Warsaw, or after I hope you left. I don't even know if you survived the city's downfall – I never could find anyone who'd known you, although I tried.

I didn't think I'd make it through if I'm honest. My leg was in pretty bad shape by the time rescue came, and you know how rough the hospitals were by the end. I hope you were spared from witnessing that. The Nazis took the city apart with dynamite and flamethrowers after the surrender, and the Soviets let them do it. They captured me with the rest of the partisans, but they put me in a prisoner of war camp in Woldenberg, not one of their terrifying death camps – they never guessed I was a Jew. Once that was liberated, I went to Poznań, but the family I came looking for here are all gone too. I can't face returning to Warsaw – there's nobody there but the dead. I don't know if I'll stay in Poland. I suppose I don't know where my place in the world is anymore. Should I wonder if it's with you?

Matthias's first letter had appeared in Unterwald in December 1945, although it was dated some months earlier. It arrived after the inquest into Viktor's death – which was deemed to be an accident, despite Noemi's presence in the barn when the fire happened, and the rumours that it might not be. It arrived before either Pascal or Noemi had decided what to do with their respective inheritances, or each other. And in the middle of one of the black moods which continued – although with far less frequency – to descend over Pascal.

Noemi followed her kiss for Karoline with one for her husband. Neither of them liked to dwell on those days, but the truth was that for every step they'd taken towards each other as they tried to reconnect, they'd both found a reason to step back. The circling – the constant fretting over whether they could ever really love each other enough to live with the past – had become exhausting. Noemi had started to fear she might become as trapped by that as she nearly had by her thirst for revenge. Matthias's letter, and the choices that came with it, had shaken them both. Pascal had been terrified that Noemi would return to the man who'd fought beside her, not against her. Noemi had compared the man she loved and the man she thought she should, and wavered more than Pascal knew. The fight they'd had in the wake of *Should I wonder if it's you* – when the Hitler-following boy and the scared Jewish girl resurfaced – had torn layers of skin off them both.

'I'm going to leave you.'

'You should.'

They'd flung the possibility forward and back, trailing, *it's what you deserve*, on both sides behind it. They'd dug their claws into the softest skin in the way only people with a long history and deep feelings could.

But we didn't give up on each other, and I'm glad of it. Because he's my past and my present and my future and – for all the wounds we could, and do, pick at when the shadows come – nobody else could ever be all those things.

Noemi smoothed the envelope and put it unopened into her pocket; there was no need to read it straight away. Matthias had his own family now, a wife and a son he doted on. He'd gone to America in the end, and found a community of Polish refugees he could share his memories and his hopes with. Matthias was happy, and so was she.

She gazed out across the flower-studded meadow. Her husband and children were making daisy chains that they would no doubt soon insist she wore alongside the silver locket she never took off. She could have been watching an echo of herself and Pascal weaving the bracelets and crowns they'd once draped over their own mothers.

There's no breaking from the past because the past never finishes. Its legacy lives on, good and bad.

That had been the hardest lesson she and Pascal had had to learn. That as much as they loved each other, they couldn't move on and never look back, that their past selves would continue to rise up and get in the way. They'd acknowledged that possibility five years earlier outside a tavern in Unterwald, but now they'd lived it, and that life had brought them both happiness and pain.

But both sides are worth it, because we've learned to pick up the past and carry it in a way that won't break us, and one day our children will do the same.

Pascal turned and saw she was watching them. He waved and burst out laughing as Karoline – who was Frieda in miniature – threw the pile of daisy chains up into the air and they landed on her brother. His laugh was everything to her. Their children were everything to them both.

We've rewritten the landscape. We've filled it with kindness and forgiveness and promise.

She smiled and waved back, her heart bursting with the new family they'd created out of the best bits of themselves and the good people who'd loved them. Then she went to the kitchens to finish her mother's cake, ready to be presented to the next happy couple taking a leap into the future and a chance on the hope baked into love.

A LETTER FROM CATHERINE

Dear Reader,

Thank you so much for choosing to read *The Secret Locket*. If you enjoyed it, and want to keep up to date with what's coming next, just sign up at the following link. Your email address will never be shared, you can unsubscribe at any time and you'll get a free short story download, *The Last Casualty*, as a thank you!

www.bookouture.com/catherine-hokin

I often cite multiple inspirations when I'm writing a book, and this one is very tied to place, which I'll come back to in a moment. The main trigger for this one, however, was a stunning 2017 Hungarian film called *1945*. As the name suggests, this is set at the end of the war and it's about two Jewish men returning to a village they've clearly been uprooted from, presumably maliciously. The film doesn't reveal what happened then or what's happened to them since; it's about the consequences of their silent return for the villagers, but I couldn't stop thinking about the untold parts, and that's what eventually led to this novel. I'd urge you to watch it if you can.

This is also a book about place. I come from the Lake District in the North of England. I was brought up among mountains, and the landscape has shaped me more than I think – I've never liked flat places, and I love forests, the deeper the better. But despite that, I'm a city girl at heart, and cities are very important to this story. I read a quote while I was researching it, which I'm paraphrasing here, to the effect that cathedrals were the legacy of the medieval period and bombed-out ruins were the legacy of the modern. It's a sobering thought. Terrible things were done in cities, and both sides did terrible things to them. And we don't seem to have improved in many ways.

Anyway, I'd love your thoughts on this story and anything that's gone into its building. There are lots of ways that you can get in touch, through my social media pages, Goodreads or my website. The details are all given below.

Thank you again.

Best wishes,

Catherine

https://www.catherinehokin.com/

ACKNOWLEDGEMENTS

As always, so many books went into the writing of this one, but there are some specific sources I would like to acknowledge and recommend if you want to know more about the subjects that I've covered in *The Secret Letter*.

For the background to the village and life in the Third Reich: *Travellers in the Third Reich* by Julia Boyd; *Backing Hitler* by Robert Gellately; *Darkness Over Germany* by E. Amy Buller; *A Social History of the Third Reich* by Richard Grunberger; *The Lost Café Schindler* by Meriel Schindler. For stories of the resistance and Warsaw: *The Hitler Kiss* by Radomir Luza; *The Avengers* by Rich Cohen; *A Square of Sky* by Janina David; *The Bravest Battle* by Dan Kurzman; *Fugitives of the Forest* by Allan Levine; *Warsaw 1944* by Alexandra Richie. And finally for the Alpine Brigade, *Alpine Elite* by James Lucas.

And now to the thanks which are always heartfelt. To my editor Harriet Wade for doing such a wonderfully collaborative job in editing my novels and for her excellent direction when I've got lost in the weeds. To the Bookouture team who are rightly detailed in the following pages, and all deserve my thanks, especially Sally and Sarah. To my friends and family who haven't jumped ship yet and sometimes, maybe, even read the books. To Robert, who still manages to brim with enthusiasm for everything I do, despite having to watch my eyes spin as I describe three plots at the same time. And to Claire and Daniel for all their love and cheerleading. Much love to you all.

PUBLISHING TEAM

Turning a manuscript into a book requires the efforts of many people. The publishing team at Bookouture would like to acknowledge everyone who contributed to this publication.

Audio
Alba Proko
Sinead O'Connor
Melissa Tran

Commercial
Lauren Morrissette
Hannah Richmond
Imogen Allport

Cover design
Eileen Carey

Data and analysis
Mark Alder
Mohamed Bussuri

Editorial
Harriet Wade
Sinead O'Connor

Copyeditor
Sally Partington

Proofreader
Laura Kincaid

Marketing
Alex Crow
Melanie Price
Occy Carr
Cíara Rosney
Martyna Młynarska

Operations and distribution
Marina Valles
Stephanie Straub
Joe Morris

Production
Hannah Snetsinger
Mandy Kullar
Nadia Michael
Ria Clare

Publicity
Kim Nash
Noelle Holten
Jess Readett
Sarah Hardy

Rights and contracts
Peta Nightingale
Richard King
Saidah Graham

RAISING READERS
Books Build Bright Futures

Dear Reader,

We'd love your attention for one more page to tell you about the crisis in children's reading, and what we can all do.

Studies have shown that reading for fun is the **single biggest predictor of a child's future success** – more than family circumstance, parents' educational background or income. It improves academic results, mental health, wealth, communication skills, and ambition.

The number of children reading for fun is in rapid decline. Young people have a lot of competition for their time, and a worryingly high number do not have a single book at home.

Our business works extensively with schools, libraries and literacy charities, but here are some ways we can all raise more readers:

- Reading to children for just 10 minutes a day makes a difference
- Don't give up if children aren't regular readers – there will be books for them!

- Visit bookshops and libraries to get recommendations
- Encourage them to listen to audiobooks
- Support school libraries
- Give books as gifts

Thank you for reading: there's a lot more information about how to encourage children to read on our website.

www.JoinRaisingReaders.com

www.ingramcontent.com/pod-product-compliance
Ingram Content Group UK Ltd.
Pitfield, Milton Keynes, MK11 3LW, UK
UKHW040030160725
6910UKWH00003B/175